Dear Reader,

At this festive time of year, we'd like to send you our very best wishes for the holiday season and the New Year. Between the parties and the presents, I hope you can steal away some time for yourself and enjoy some special treats from Harlequin Duets.

In Harlequin Duets #15 we have two delightful Christmas tales; from award-winning Lori Copeland comes *Fruitcakes and Other Leftovers,* and from the equally talented Kimberly Raye comes *Christmas, Texas Style.* The true meaning of family—its responsibilities and joys—is the theme of both stories. Pour yourself a glass of eggnog, nibble on a ginger cookie and dive into these wonderful romances.

Duets #16 celebrates the New Year with a bachelor and baby in *Bringing Up Baby New Year* by Vicki Lewis Thompson. Vicki's books are always treasured by readers, and this sparkling comedy will entertain you and warm your heart. Then Tracy South mixes business with pleasure in *Frisky Business,* a hilarious office romance. You'll never look at your co-workers in the same manner!

Happy holidays. I hope you find a lot of romance novels in your Christmas stocking!

Malle Vallik

Malle Vallik
Senior Editor

Darcie had good taste coming out her ears.

And she definitely wanted him badly. Why else would she leave him a rose on his pillow one week and chocolate the next?

Joe had her phone number, but he needed an excuse to call her. Maybe his housekeeper flirted this way with all her clients. He'd know the lay of the land if he talked to her on the phone. Scratching his head, he thought for a moment. Then he knew—he could ask that she bring a different type of flower. A sexy flower.

Moments later, he stood in the study thumbing through a botanical guide. Roses, nah. Been there, done that. Daisies were too virginal looking, and carnations reminded him of his senior prom. There it was—tulips. They even looked sort of European. Well, Dutch, but heck, at least they grew on the other side of the ocean. Two-lips. Perfect.

What better way to let Darcie know *whose* lips he was really interested in?

For more, turn to page 9

Frisky Business

Kyle kissed her.

And although he had decided the kiss this morning had been a fluke, Kyle had hoped it wasn't the last time he'd taste Laura's lips. She responded with a sigh that sent him reeling.

Laura broke off the kiss. When she looked at him, her hazel eyes completely serious, he felt an ache of responsibility for how open and honest and vulnerable she was.

"Let's not talk about it," she said.

"Not talk about what?"

"Why we've been kissing." She lifted her arms from him. "You know how I overanalyze things, but since our boss is counting on us to solve this crisis, I need to concentrate on work and not use my brain trying to figure out why we suddenly can't keep our hands off each other."

"Because we're attracted to each other?" Kyle ventured.

She frowned at him. "You're talking about it."

"Sorry." And then because he couldn't help himself, he smiled. "If you'd like to kiss again without talking about it, let me know."

For more, turn to page 197

HARLEQUIN DUETS

ISBN 0-373-44082-0

BRINGING UP BABY NEW YEAR
Copyright © 1999 by Vicki Lewis Thompson

FRISKY BUSINESS
Copyright © 1999 by Tracy Jones

VICKI
LEWIS
THOMPSON

Bringing Up
Baby New Year

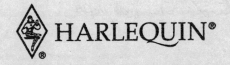

HARLEQUIN®

TORONTO • NEW YORK • LONDON
AMSTERDAM • PARIS • SYDNEY • HAMBURG
STOCKHOLM • ATHENS • TOKYO • MILAN • MADRID
PRAGUE • WARSAW • BUDAPEST • AUCKLAND

Dear Reader,

I love doing Christmas and I love doing it big. My idol is Clark Griswold from *National Lampoon's Christmas Vacation,* so when it comes to lights, I subscribe to the Clark Griswold school of thought. You can never have too many.

However, the rumor that I've caused blackouts by turning on the Thompson Yuletide Extravaganza each year is completely false. The rumor that my husband routinely needs to be resuscitated after opening the December electric bill is, unfortunately, true.

My neighbors can always tell when the holiday is upon us because I'll be balanced high in the branches of one of our front-yard trees stringing so many lights that we've been mistaken for a casino. So if you happen to fly over Arizona this season and notice a glow radiating from the southern half of the state, that would be coming from my house.

My hero and heroine in *Bringing Up Baby New Year* go to similar extremes. I hope you enjoy reading about their adventures in decorating!

Happy holidays,

Vicki Lewis Thompson

A millennium New Year's toast to every woman
who's ever taken on the duties of a mother,
whether you gave birth to the little darlings
or simply did what needed to be done
in the absence of the biological mother.
The world would not turn without you.

1

THE FRENCH MAID could sure hoover a room.

Joe Northwood entered the Scottsdale home he was house-sitting for the winter and gawked at the wonders of a cleaning service. He'd never had one before and wouldn't have one now, except that the owner, Edgar DeWitt, was paying for it.

And he must be paying a bundle. The place had been cleaned within an inch of its life. Every surface gleamed, and there were three, count 'em, *three* vases of flowers that he could see—two in the living room and one on the dining room table. The house smelled of lemon and pine and pretty flowers. When Joe had answered DeWitt's ad for a house sitter, he'd never imagined a perk this fabulous would come with the deal. He felt like rolling on the carpet.

But he was curious enough to head upstairs to check out his bedroom first. More flowers! Damn, but he could learn to like this. His bed was made and the sheets *turned back.* Talk about your five-star treatment. He almost expected a mint on the pillow, but instead there was a little note with flowers decorating the border of the paper. When he picked it up, even the paper smelled good.

Dear Mr. Northwood,
As part of my services, I've laundered your linens with products designed for sensitive skin. Should

you experience any irritation, however, please don't hesitate to let me know. Also, if there are certain flowers you prefer, I would be delighted to provide them. Your satisfaction is my goal.

Au revoir
Darcie, the French Maid

"Mmm, Darcie baby. Satisfaction is what *I'm* talking about." Joe held the notepaper to his nose and took a deep sniff. Then he held it next to his temple as if he could get a telepathic image of the person who wrote it.

"I see dark eyes," he droned, "eyes the color of…a melted Hershey's bar. Lashes thick as the fringe on a Persian carpet. Hair in ringlets to her shoulders, and a body to make a Dallas Cowboys cheerleader weep with envy."

He sighed with longing and took another whiff of the notepaper for inspiration. "She wears…cashmere and silk, and when she bothers with underwear, it's a scrap of black lace. She speaks with a French accent and says *oui* a lot, but I can understand her perfectly, especially when she says with her lips kind of pursed, 'I want you, *chéri,* you big, beautiful man you.'"

Grinning to himself, he decided to write a note back to her for the hell of it. Nothing ventured, nothing gained. After searching out a pen, he turned her stationery over and was about to start writing when he had a better idea.

One of the guys at work loved making stationery for people on his home computer. Joe pictured a sheet of nice paper with only his initials at the top, maybe in navy blue. A classy woman like Darcie would probably go for that.

"GUS, YOU LITTLE LEPRECHAUN! You've peed in your eye!" Darcie threw a clean diaper over the stream arcing

from Gus's stubby equipment and grabbed a damp washcloth. "Must you always demonstrate what a little man
you are? We're already running late."

Gus wailed pitifully as she wiped his face.

"Well, I'm sorry, but I'll be glad when you've learned
to control that little bobber of yours." She leaned down
and kissed his cheek and gave him a nuzzle, tickling him
gently until he began to chuckle. "Are you making me
late on purpose?"

Gus cooed and blew bubbles at her. *I do everything
on purpose, lass. Sometimes my aim 'tis a wee bit off is
all. Meant to get it in my hair, I did, so I could have
another bath.*

"Maybe you know what day it is. We're cleaning for
Joe Northwood again today, and you're jealous—green
as a shamrock in a wheelbarrow full of manure, as your
Grandpa Angus was so fond of saying. He would have
been fond of you, too." She poked Gus's round tummy
gently and he giggled. "I have one of his baby pictures,
and you're the spitting image of him. Sometimes I swear
I see his spirit shining out of your green eyes."

Gus crowed and kicked his legs. *Could be, lass. Could
be.*

"Hold still. You're squirmy as a wee elf this morning.
I swear you're all O'Banyon, not a drop of Butterworth
in you, which is good thing, considering your father
closely resembles the backside of a mule." Darcie
winced. "There I go again, speaking ill of your da, which
the baby experts say is very bad." She smiled down at
her red-haired son. "But I am *so* glad you look like me
and your dear departed grandfather, and not that spawn
of Satan who ran out on us. Now let's change the subject."

Gus grinned at her, displaying his first two teeth, both bottom ones, gained with much fretting and fussing, but in at long last.

She picked up a T-shirt from a pile of clean clothes. "So, Gus, do you suppose Joe Northwood could be Black Irish? I found a couple of black hairs in his comb. Wavy, too. His name sounds more Brit than Irish, but maybe he's Irish on his mother's side. I like that dark mysterious look in a man, don't you?"

Gus sucked his fist and gazed at her. *Faith, I'd rather have them rich and slow on the uptake.*

"Present company excepted, of course. On you, red hair is the perfect color." She pulled the T-shirt over Gus's head. "I checked his shirt and pants size, and I think he's close to six feet tall. His clothes aren't starched and fussy, a choice I happen to like. I suspect he has a *very* nice body. I'll reveal a deep, dark secret, Gus, but you mustn't tell because he's a client and this is confidential information. He sleeps naked. Told me so himself in a note. 'The soap doesn't irritate my skin,' he said. 'And that's good for someone who doesn't believe in pajamas.'"

Darcie paused and fanned herself with her hand. "Jesus, Mary and Joseph, as your grandpa would say, that sure sets the kettle to boiling."

Or the baby to puking. This bounder could be trouble.

Darcie picked up a pair of overalls and started putting them on Gus. "Now, in my opinion, a man who sleeps naked is by definition a sensuous person and confident about his body, as I'm sure he has a right to be. I wouldn't be surprised to learn that he's very intelligent. His handwriting surely looks intelligent."

She tied some little moccasins on Gus's feet and picked him up. "He works at that big home improvement store in north Scottsdale—Home World—and he must be some executive there because his stationery is very elegant. A man who sleeps naked and has stationery with only his initials at the top—I'll bet he runs the place, Gus.''

"NORTHWOOD!''

Joe tried to control his irritation as he excused himself from the customer he'd been advising about having an oak chair rail installed in her dining room. "Yes, Mr. Rucker?'' The guy had a name you could do *so* much with in private. He was the sort of little twirp who gave short people a bad rep.

Rucker thrust out his belly, like a frog puffing himself up to look bigger and more intimidating. "We need someone over in the gardening department right away. Some idiot ran a forklift into the bags of manure, and the place is covered with sh—'' Rucker glanced at the customer. "Uh, covered with manure. Get on over there and clean it up.''

Joe had perfected a technique to keep his blood pressure under control when he was around Rucker. He imagined Rucker's belt snapping under the strain of his protruding gut. His pants would fall down around his skinny ankles, right in the middle of the store, preferably in front of a customer. A female customer. "I wonder if you'd be able to help this lady?'' he asked, keeping his tone even. "She has some questions about oak molding.'' Joe knew that Rucker didn't know shinola about oak molding, but the little dweeb wouldn't ever admit such a thing.

"Uh, of course.'' Rucker strutted over to the customer. "Now, oak, there's a wood for you,'' he said. "Look at that grain.''

Look at that brain, Joe thought as he walked away. Totally empty, ear to ear.

Shoveling spilled manure gave him some time to think, and mostly he thought about his cousin Derek's phone call the night before. Derek was finally ready for the two of them to open their own cabinet shop in Denver after the first of the year. Joe had set some money aside for this contingency, but not enough.

If he could come up with about three grand more to add to his share of the start-up cost, he could ditch this job and head for Denver. God, how he'd love that moment of handing his notice to Rucker, knowing there was a good chance he'd never have to work for anyone else again.

Of course, he'd have to give Edgar DeWitt plenty of warning so he could find another house sitter. And he'd have to give up the French Maid.

He smiled. She was definitely flirting with him. Her last note had mentioned that she'd evaluated all the sheets and determined which were the softest so that she could put those on his bed, considering that he didn't wear pajamas.

Apparently, the stationery and the information that he slept naked had captured her attention. Last Wednesday instead of the usual bouquet of flowers on the nightstand, she'd left a bud vase with a single red rose in it. Today before he'd gone to work he'd taken the wilted rose and scattered the petals over the unmade bed.

In his fantasy, he imagined her reaction, considering that she was French and all. The French were very sensuous people, according to what he'd heard. Uninhibited, too. He visualized her taking off her clothes to roll around on the bed for a while, just to enjoy the feel of those rose petals against her skin.

He pictured her with very pale skin to contrast with her dark hair. But as she rolled around among the rose petals, her skin might become flushed with excitement. In fact, she might get so turned on that she'd—

"Northwood!"

If Rucker hadn't startled him in the middle of an outstanding daydream, he never would have lost control of the contents of his shovel like that. And if Rucker hadn't hollered so loud and leaped unexpectedly to one side, the stuff would have gone into the wheelbarrow where Joe had intended to throw it, instead of all over the irritating little store manager. It really wasn't Joe's fault at all. Or at least that's what he tried to tell himself.

And he certainly should have been given more credit for not laughing. It had taken all his self-control, but he'd kept a straight face, knowing with absolute certainty that if he so much as cracked a smile, he'd be fired.

ROSE PETALS IN THE BED. How lovely and romantic. Darcie wondered if he'd actually slept with the rose petals, but they weren't wrinkled and smashed, so he must have tossed them on the sheets for her to see. If she didn't have Gus hollering from his playpen downstairs, she'd have taken off her jeans and T-shirt and stretched out on those rose petals, just for a minute.

Was he inviting her to do that? The thought gave her goose bumps. This flirtation couldn't go anywhere, of course, but it was harmless fun. Goodness, she needed a romantic distraction in her life. She had no time for the real thing, so this charade was perfect. Scooping up the rose petals, she hurried downstairs to take care of Gus.

Cleaning the large house claimed all her attention for the next hour, but before she left she hurried back upstairs with a note written on her scented paper.

Dear Mr. Northwood,

Tending to your bed was especially pleasurable today. If you don't mind, I'm taking the rose petals home with me. They're wonderful floating in a warm bath.

Au revoir
Darcie, the French Maid

On top of the note she laid a single piece of expensive chocolate.

She tucked the plastic bag full of the rose petals in with her cleaning supplies to lift her spirits as she packed Gus into the car and drove to a much less pleasant task—her weekly cleaning appointment for Mr. and Mrs. Bart Butterworth.

That was how she'd first met Bart Junior, the original hit-and-run-man. Now Mrs. Bart—her name was Trudy, but Darcie had never been able to call her that—used Darcie's cleaning day as a time to play with her grandson, Gus. Darcie could hardly deny her the privilege, but Trudy with Gus made her nervous. The woman was entirely too possessive of Darcie's baby.

As Darcie waxed the dining-room table and thought about Joe and his rose petals, Trudy walked in carrying Gus. Tall, blond and tailored, she didn't look entirely comfortable with the baby, which gave Darcie some satisfaction.

"I can understand why you wanted to name him after your father," Trudy said, "but you really should let him go by his middle name. Gus is a ridiculous name to hang on a little baby, don't you think?"

Gus chortled away. *May you have warts on your bum for saying that, Granny.*

"I rather like it myself," Darcie said as pleasantly as

she could while her teeth were clenched. "My da used to say it falls on the ear like April rain on a thatched roof."

"Well, that's charming and so very Irish, but the Irish are so blessed poor, Darcie. Gus sounds like, well, like a peasant."

Gus patted Mrs. Bart's cheek. *I was thinking how you'd look with a layer of paste wax on your face, Granny.*

"Nothing wrong with peasants." Darcie polished harder and worked to hide the temper she'd inherited from her ancestors, peasants all. Not a CEO in the lot. But she couldn't lose her temper with Mrs. Bart. The woman had been her first client and had mentioned Darcie to her friends in the upscale Scottsdale subdivision of Tannenbaum. Soon Darcie had signed up all the business she could handle in this one subdivision, which centralized her operation nicely.

But Darcie figured that what Mrs. Bart had created she could take away again. A carefully dropped hint at a Tannenbaum social event that things had gone missing in the Butterworth home after Darcie had been there, and her thriving business would collapse.

That would be bad enough, but Mrs. Bart had an even bigger hammer to hold over Darcie. If she became really angry, she might find the means to take Gus away. She and Mr. Bart could give Gus all sorts of advantages, while Darcie was struggling to keep pennies in the sugar bowl.

The court would probably side with Darcie unless Mr. and Mrs. Bart hired a fast-talking lawyer. Darcie wouldn't put it past them if they had enough provocation, so she tried not to give them any trouble. Her sainted father had taught her the Golden Rule—those that have the gold make the rules. She'd temporarily forgotten it when dealing with Bart Junior, but now it was burned into her memory for all time.

"I suppose peasants have their place," Mrs. Bart said. "But I'd rather not have any in our family. In fact, I was thinking the other day it would be nice if you really *were* French, the way you market yourself. It has a certain cachet."

"I'm afraid I can't speak the language."

"Well, that could be remedied. Our whole family speaks French. Which reminds me, I heard from Bart Junior last night," Mrs. Bart said. "He—ouch! That hurts, Gus!"

Only wanted to see if the hair was attached is all.

"Watch how you do that, Gus," Darcie said, holding back a smile. In the reflection of the polished table, she saw Gus give another yank on Mrs. Bart's sleek hair before she was able to untangle his chubby fingers.

"Bart Junior is not a bad boy," Mrs. Bart said.

"Of course not," Darcie said. More like a bad man, she thought.

"He's just a dreamer and he had to follow his dream."

"Yes, he always did have his head up his...in the clouds," Darcie quickly amended. "I'm so delighted he's in the Amazon jungle." She thought of him battling man-eating crocodiles there.

"You have a generous heart, Darcie. I'm glad you understand that Bart Junior's one of those free spirits who can't be expected to abide by conventional standards."

Darcie smiled at her. "No. He's set a whole new standard."

"I'm so glad you bear him no ill will. Because I feel

sure when he's ready he'll return and assume his fatherly duties.''

That thought scared the hell out of Darcie. She'd heard of fathers swaggering in years later and trying to lay claim to their children. If that nightmare should ever come true, she wanted to be ready.

First of all, she wanted to be more stable financially, which was why she needed to go back to school. Second of all, if Bart Junior showed up again, she'd like to be married. Finding the right man would be tricky and couldn't be rushed, but she'd like Gus to have a father, especially if Bart Junior suddenly decided to claim that right.

''I wish you'd let us pay your tuition so you can finish up your studies in interior design,'' Mrs. Bart continued. ''It's a shame you had to quit with only one semester to go.''

Darcie knew she couldn't accept. Once Mr. and Mrs. Bart paid for her tuition, they'd start winding ropes of dependency around her that she'd never be able to loosen, and in the end Gus would become theirs as surely as if she'd handed him over. But she had to be gracious in her refusal.

''You're very kind to offer, Mrs. Butterworth.''

''Call me Trudy, dear. I've asked you to do that many times, but you persist with this Mrs. Butterworth nonsense.''

''I worry about doing that because you're also a client, and if I start calling you by your first name, I might slip and do it with the others. It's a professional point with me that I don't get too familiar with my clients.'' She thought briefly of Joe Northwood, but those were only harmless notes. ''I'm sure you understand.''

''Well, I suppose I do, Darcie. Your clients wouldn't

want to think you'd forgotten your position with them, I suppose."

Gus poked her in the eye.

"Ooo! Gus, you are aggressive today!" Mrs. Bart wiped carefully at her eye so as not to disturb her makeup.

Darcie leaned down to pick up the paste wax so that Mrs. Bart wouldn't catch her grin. Gus was really on his game this afternoon.

"So, how about the tuition?" Mrs. Bart asked. "I seem to remember you needed about two thousand or so. You might even be able to slip in a French class. I'll be happy to write out a check today so you can start back in January."

Darcie thought fast. "I'll tell you what, Mrs. Butterworth. I'm expecting word on an inheritance from my father's estate. With a bit of luck, that should come through in time. If not, I'll let you know. I'd like to keep your kind offer in reserve in case I need it, but I think I can manage on my own." Her father hadn't left her one thin dime, but he must have passed on the gift of blarney for her to make up such an outrageous story.

"Well, if you're expecting some money...."

"Oh, it's practically a sure thing." Darcie wondered if she'd have to tackle a leprechaun and force him to lead her to his pot of gold. She couldn't continue her present program much longer. As long as Gus wasn't walking yet, she could continue to haul him around with her while she cleaned houses, but once he could climb out of his playpen, her cleaning days would become much more difficult. She needed to change horses and she was already way behind in her plan to do so.

"Well, we'd all be relieved if you'd finish your degree

and get into a profession," Mrs. Bart said. "It's somewhat of an embarrassment, you know."

Darcie tried to keep the sarcasm out of her voice. "You could mention to your good friends that I'm a domestic supervisor."

"Oh, I do! But…" She paused and wrinkled her nose. "Perhaps you'd better take Gus. I think he's done something disgusting in his pants."

"Ah, well. As sure as swallows fly and lambs bleat, babes poop."

Mrs. Bart gave her a weak smile as she handed Gus over. "I suppose that's another of your father's quaint sayings."

"No. I made that up myself." Darcie took Gus.

Mrs. Bart turned her gold bangle watchband so she could read the time. "I have to be going anyway. Madge Elderhorn is expecting me for coffee in ten minutes."

"Give Mrs. Elderhorn my best."

"I'll do that. Don't forget to lock up after yourself." Mrs. Bart made a quick exit.

Darcie hugged her baby close and planted a big kiss on his rosy cheek. "Well done, Gus."

Sure and I believe in the timely poop.

JOE HELD DARCIE'S NOTE in one hand as he paced the kitchen, trying to decide what to do. He took a bite out of the chocolate. Mmm. Good chocolate. The woman had taste coming out of her ears.

And she wanted him, which was sure good for the ego, considering what a classy woman she was. She wanted him bad. Why else would she leave him a rose one week and chocolate the next? He already had her phone number. DeWitt had given it to him along with the number for the yard service, the plumber, the electrician and the exterminator.

He needed an excuse to call her, though. Maybe she flirted this way with all her customers, although he didn't want to think so. He'd know the lay of the land if he talked to her on the phone. But what would he say he was calling about? Flowers. That's it. He could come up with a flower request the way she'd suggested. A sexy flower. DeWitt had about every reference book in the world, so he'd look one up.

Moments later he stood in DeWitt's study thumbing through a botanical guide. Roses, nah. Been there, done that. Daisies were too virginal-looking and carnations reminded him of the senior prom. There it was—tulips. They even looked sort of European. Well, Dutch, but hell, at least they grew on the other side of the ocean. Two-lips. Perfect. She was French. She'd get it.

At this very second she was probably up to her long, graceful neck in a bubble bath, sipping a glass of French wine, with the roses from his bed floating in her perfumed bathwater. Frenchwomen knew how to take a bath like nobody else in the world. Maybe she was sudsing herself right now, her eyes closed....

He snapped the book shut and hurried toward the kitchen, where Darcie's number was posted above the telephone. Hot damn, he was about to make a French connection.

2

TRUDY BUTTERWORTH SAT on Madge Elderhorn's burgundy flowered sofa, an empty cup and saucer on the coffee table in front of her. Through the large picture window she could see Edgar DeWitt's house perfectly. Her dawdling until she'd nearly encroached on the cocktail hour had paid off. The house sitter had just come out to retrieve his evening paper.

"He's good-looking enough," Trudy said once he'd gone back inside. "No wonder Darcie had that sparkle in her eye today." She turned to Madge, a large-boned woman sitting at right angles to her on a matching love seat. "But you've never actually seen them together, right?"

"Not actually, but you know something has to be going on, with him looking like he does and her looking like she does. It's pheromones. They can smell each other."

"I wouldn't doubt it, but I want proof," Trudy said. "If Bart Junior knows she's involved with someone else, he might come home."

"If it's proof you want, I can handle that."

Trudy smiled at her neighbor, who gave the term "Neighborhood Watch" a whole new meaning. Madge also had community leadership aspirations. "I knew I could count on you, Madge." Trudy stood and smoothed her skirt. "You're exactly the sort of person who knows how to keep an eye on things. That's why your name has been mentioned as the possible chair of the Tannenbaum Christmas Festival and Good Cheer Committee.''

Madge stood also, and her eyes gleamed. "Really?"

"That's what I hear. I'll let you know if there's more news on that. And in the meantime, I'd really appreciate it if you'd keep me posted on what goes on across the street."

"Consider it done."

DARCIE HAD DECIDED to experiment with having Gus feed himself. To that end, she'd steamed some sliced carrots until they were soft and put them in a plastic bowl. "There now, Gus." She put the bowl on the tray of his high chair. "Try one."

Gus calmly reached in the bowl and picked up a piece of carrot. *Hmm. Orange. Squashy. 'Tis a likely decorating item.*

"Good boy! I knew you were advanced for a wee sprout!" Darcie congratulated herself on knowing the exact moment to introduce this new activity to her son. She was indeed Supermom.

She watched expectantly as Gus raised the piece of carrot to his mouth…and flung it on the floor. "Oh, Gus! We can't waste food." As she crouched down to pick up the carrot, he knocked the entire bowl on top of her head.

Score one for the wee sprout!

"Oh, *Gus*." His aim was so good that she wore the bowl like a beanie, with squashed carrots and orange juice oozing down over her hair and onto her shirt.

Gus crowed and banged on his high-chair tray. *Fetching. Goes with your green eyes, it does.*

As she glared at him, the phone rang. "Murphy's

Law," she muttered. In an attempt to contain the mess, she clamped the bowl more firmly onto her head as she got up to answer the phone. "You'd better hope that's not somebody calling to ask for a donation, Gus, because at this minute I'm thinking I might donate you." Wiping her free hand on her jeans, she picked up the receiver. "Hello?"

"I'd like to speak to Darcie, please, if she's available." The voice was male and very pleasant. A telemarketer.

Considering she had no money to spare, she'd developed a strategy to deal with sales calls. "May I tell her who's calling?"

"It's Joe. Joe Northwood."

Darcie almost dropped the phone. "Just…just a minute." She brought the receiver down and held it against her chest, then moved it immediately to her stomach when she was afraid her pounding heart would boom right into Joe's ear. *Joe Northwood.* His voice sounded so…masculine. She didn't know how a man could let you know he had good pecs just by the way he said his name over the phone, but she was getting that message loud and clear from Joe Northwood.

She thought quickly of the image she'd been trying to portray in the past few weeks. Sexy. And French.

He would hardly expect her to be the Irish mother of a baby, let alone one with a blessed bowl of carrots clamped on her head.

She took a deep breath and brought the phone back to her ear. *"Allô?"*

"Darcie? This is Joe. Joe Northwood. I guess that was your roommate who answered the phone."

The man had a damned sexy voice. She felt all warm and fluttery listening to it. "My roommate. *Oui.*"

"I hope I'm not disturbing you."

Darcie did her best imitation of a French accent, which wasn't particularly great. French-Irish, in a manner of speaking. "Not at all. I was, how you say it? Giving myself the facial." Carrot juice ran down the side of her face and dripped onto the floor.

"Ga-ba-ba!" Gus yelled.

"What was that?" Joe asked.

"Just zee teevee. I keep it on to improve my Eenglesh."

"Your English is fine with me, Darcie. Listen, you asked me to let you know if I had a certain type of flower I'd like you to put in the arrangements you leave every week."

She heard the song of the sea in his voice—deep and powerful. She was certain he had a position of authority at that store. And outstanding pecs, too. "But of course! Whatever you would like, Monsieur North*wood*." A drop of carrot juice dangled off the end of her nose. She caught it with the tip of her tongue.

"Ga!" Gus said, and started banging on the tray of his high chair.

"That TV show must have a baby in it," Joe said.

"*Oui.*" Darcie searched her memory, trying to recall some of her high school French. "A *bambino.*" She had a worrisome feeling that was Italian, not French. "As they say in my neighboring country," she added. "What flower would you prefer, *monsieur?*"

"I thought maybe tulips."

"Tulips?" Faith, but they cost the world this time of year. But if the man wanted tulips, the French Maid would provide them. She'd make it up by giving the Butterworths mostly carnations next week. "*Oui.* I shall provide the tulips, *monsieur.*"

His voice deepened. "Red tulips, Darcie. Deep red. There's something sexy about deep red tulips...the petals are soft, and the way the flower opens is so...inviting."

Darcie forgot to breathe.

"Do you like tulips, Darcie?"

She sighed into the phone. "Oh, yes. I mean, *oui*. When zey open up, zee—how you say that middle part?—zee pistils, they are so...erect."

His voice sounded a bit strangled. "I know what you mean. I've always been interested in the mechanics of...pollination."

She lost her grip on the carrot bowl and it clattered to the floor.

"Darcie? Are you okay?"

"*Si!* I mean, *oui!*" *Be still my heart. I'm cleaning house for a solid gold, dyed-in-the-wool love god.* "I dropped my...*bidet*."

"Your *what?*"

Dammit. It was the first French word she'd been able to come up with. What did he want from a woman who only managed to earn a C in the class...and was presently having a sexual encounter with him on the phone? "*Pardonnez-moi.* My *bouquet.* I was—how you say?—arranging flowers when you rang me up."

"I thought you were giving yourself a facial."

"*Oui.* A facial with flowers. We crush the flowers, yes? And pat them over the tender skin. Eet eez very...stimulating." The carrots, freed from the bowl, were starting to ooze down over her forehead. She tilted her head back.

He sucked in a breath and his voice deepened again. "Did you like the rose petals?"

She lowered her voice to a throaty purr. "*Oui, mon-*

sieur.'' A piece of carrot plopped onto the front of her T-shirt.

"Good. Maybe, when the tulips wilt, we can…work something out."

Her heart hammered at the image he conjured up. If only…but it couldn't happen. He believed in a fantasy, not the real thing. "I would like that, *monsieur*. Eef my shed-jule permits."

"I could work around—"

Gus started banging again, louder.

"I must go," she murmured. "Zee jungle drums, zey beckon."

His voice grew hoarse. "Jungle drums? What are you doing with jungle drums?"

"Never mind, *chéri. Ciao.*" She hung up and squeezed her eyes shut when she remembered that *ciao* was Italian. Oh, well. Maybe he'd think she was multilingual. Or multipersonality, more like it.

She felt fragmented, having just given the world's worst impersonation of a French temptress while covered with mashed carrots. She wondered if he'd believed any of it. And if he was as hot and bothered as she was.

MADGE WHIPPED OFF her earphones. The listening device she'd ordered from a catalog hadn't worked perfectly, but well enough. She opened the door to her sewing room a crack to see if Herman happened to be roaming around upstairs.

The family-room TV blared as usual, so he was probably still down there. Good. He barely approved of binoculars, let alone listening devices. If he happened to notice the suction cups on the window, she planned to tell him they were for hanging sun-catchers.

She closed the door again, picked up the phone and

punched in Trudy Butterworth's number. Trudy answered.

"Can you talk?" Madge pitched her voice low in case Herman happened to walk by in the hall outside. He was too curious for his own good.

"Madge? Are you sick?"

"No. I have *news*."

"You saw them together?"

"No, but I have a tape of a *very* interesting phone conversation."

There was silence on the other end. "I'm switching phones," Trudy said. After a couple of clicks, she was back. "Okay, I'm in the bedroom. Bart Senior was right there next to me in the kitchen. Madge, what do you mean, a tape? Have you broken in and bugged the phone?"

"Do you want me to?"

"Good heavens, no! But how did you get a tape?"

Madge couldn't keep the smugness out of her voice. "Oh, with this nifty little device that attaches to my sewing-room window and picks up what's going on in the house across the street."

"You're kidding."

"Nope. I don't have all the bugs out of it yet. I got the economy version and maybe I should have ordered the deluxe. But I picked up enough to prove that a connection was made."

"This feels...unethical."

Madge was crushed. "Then—"

"Deliciously unethical. Tell me everything."

Madge's spirits lifted like one of her prized soufflés. "Well, the thing didn't pick up everything he said, but I gathered he'd like her to do a certain something every week. Just use your imagination."

Trudy made an impatient noise. "That could be something like cleaning out the refrigerator."

"I don't think so. He mentioned tulips. I heard the words *sexy* and *inviting*. Does that sound like cleaning out the refrigerator to you?"

"No, it does not." Trudy's voice rang with excitement. "It definitely does not. We're onto something Madge."

"And how about this? He talked about *pollination*."

"Oh, my God. That's blatant."

Madge felt as if she was tossing down trump card after trump card. "He also mentioned jungle drums."

Trudy gasped. "Jungle drums? Darcie is not the jungle-drum type!"

"Maybe the house sitter is, and she's learning."

"Oh, Madge, you simply have to order the deluxe version. We need every word, every syllable, every... thing."

"I'm on it."

"And Madge, you'll be getting a visit from the Tannenbaum Board of Directors tomorrow. They want you for the chair of the festival committee."

Madge's chest expanded with pride. Hard work and effort were rewarded after all. "That's good to hear, Trudy. Very good to hear."

JOE TOSSED AROUND most of that night, afraid that he'd started something he wouldn't have the sexual sophistication to finish. The French Maid was obviously very hot, but she might be out of his league.

There had definitely been jungle drums in the background when she hung up, but they didn't sound like something on television. They sounded as if they were right there in the room with her, and he'd heard some

strange grunts and squeals, too. Maybe she'd made up
the part about the baby show on TV and she'd invited
some primitive jungle type over for an evening of fun
and games.

Joe's experience didn't stretch to tribal rituals. And
that's what he suspected was going on at her place with
the crushed flowers and the drums. Maybe she cleaned
house for someone from Africa or South America.
Maybe she had all kinds of international connections.
She'd had a tough time sticking with one language when
they talked. Joe's good old American lovemaking would
probably seem pretty tame to a woman who'd been exposed to all kinds of exotic techniques.

Still, he was fascinated, and curious as hell. Not to
mention very, very turned on. All that talk about pistils.
He'd looked it up and the pistil was technically the female part of the flower. But so what? He'd known exactly what she meant, and he'd reacted. Oh, how he'd
reacted. He'd used up a lot of cold water getting over
that reaction.

She might be too much woman for him, but he was
tempted to find out. At any rate, he didn't have to do
anything until the tulips, complete with their erect pistils,
arrived on Wednesday. Then it would be his move, and
he could decide whether to pursue this or back out before
he showed himself up.

EVERYBODY SHE CLEANED FOR would get carnations this
week, Darcie decided as she plunked down an unholy
amount of money for red tulips the following Wednesday
morning. But she had to get the tulips to find out what
Joe would do next. So long as she never had to meet
him, she could continue this harmless but very exciting
flirtation. It took her mind off her financial difficulties.

Once at Joe's house, she set up Gus's folding playpen and put him in it with some soft toys and his teething ring. Then she headed upstairs to strip the bed and gather up the towels, her heart pounding in anticipation of another note on the pillow.

Sure enough, a piece of paper lay in the indentation left by Joe's head. She picked it up and put off reading the note while she leaned down to sniff the fragrance of his aftershave on the pillow. The spicy scent was fast becoming her favorite brand. She ran a hand over the bottom sheet and imagined him lying there in all his glory, a Chippendale calendar boy, for sure.

She finally allowed herself the pleasure of reading the note.

Dear Darcie,

I can't stop thinking of you. I want to meet you. How about Saturday night? I would be glad to cook dinner for you here, although maybe, being French, you'd rather cook for me. Just tell me what ingredients you'd like and I will provide anything you want. Anything.

Au revoir,
Joe

Darcie pressed the piece of paper to her chest and tried to get her racing pulse under control. Now that she'd heard his voice she could imagine him talking to her as she read the note. Talking and promising that he would provide anything she wanted. *Anything.*

And he wanted to see her Saturday night. Not her, though—and there was the weasel in the potato bin, as her da would say. He wanted to see the French Maid. Even if she decided to hire a sitter for Gus, she couldn't manage the French Maid disguise in person. Not with red hair, green eyes, freckles and a tendency to slip into Irish speech patterns she'd never quite got rid of even though she hadn't set foot on Irish sod for sixteen years.

But what was she thinking? Even if she looked very French, even if she happened to *be* very French, she couldn't get romantically involved with a man unless he knew all about Gus. Unless he came to love Gus as passionately as she did. Her fun little frolic with Joe Northwood would have to come to an end. Somehow. Before she left the house today, she'd come up with a plan to free herself from this sticky problem.

In the meantime, she had a house to clean. She pulled the sheets from the bed and tried not to think about the lovely and available man who had slept on them. While taking the towels from the racks, she worked to ignore the image of a tall, dark-haired man rubbing that towel all over his magnificent, Black Irish body. Her arms full of laundry, she went downstairs and out to the garage to start the washer.

An hour later, she returned to the garage and gasped in horror. Her preoccupation with Joe must have caused her to dump too much detergent in the washing machine. The washer was foaming at the mouth, and a stream of water and suds had soaked a cardboard box sitting nearby.

She raced over to wrestle the large box out of the way and the soggy cardboard came apart in her hands. With a groan she stared at the ruined contents. She'd just drowned Santa, his elves, his reindeer and Rudolph. As if she didn't have enough financial worries, now she'd have to replace Edgar DeWitt's entire Christmas yard display.

THE STORE INTERCOM BEEPED. "Joe Northwood, line two."

Joe left the pile of two-by-tens he'd been stacking in a bin and walked over to the lumber department's wall phone. He took off his gloves, picked up the receiver and punched the second button. "Northwood."

There was a muffled groan on the other end of the line.

"Hello? Listen, do you need 9-1-1? I could—"

"Not 9-1-1, but if you happen to have a miracle around, I could use that."

"Excuse me?"

Whoever was on the line heaved a large sigh. "Joe, it's…Darcie."

"*Darcie?* The French Maid? You don't sound French."

"I'm too upset to sound French right now. To begin with, Santa Claus is a wee bit…oh, Joe, Santa Claus looks like he's…he's been on a…three-day toot!" With that, the French Maid sniffed and then sniffed again, as if she could hardly keep from crying.

It was way too much for Joe. This woman he'd hoped to have a hot date with on Saturday night had been either inhaling the paste wax or liberally sampling DeWitt's brandy. In any case, she'd switched nationalities and now had a decidedly Irish accent. And unless he was mistaken, she had somehow participated in some kind of binge with Santa Claus.

At least she had a conscience and had called to notify him, but apparently she was much wilder than he'd thought. With any luck, this alleged Santa Claus hadn't done any damage to the house, and Darcie only needed help getting the boozed-up guy out of the place.

Joe kept forgetting it was December because the daytime temperature was still in the eighties in Scottsdale. But the calendar said it was the Christmas season, and guys in red suits were everywhere. Maybe the French Maid had decided to invite one of them in for a drink. Or twenty.

He had to do something. As the house sitter for DeWitt's expensive home, it was his duty to check out the situation.

"Calm down, Darcie," he said. "I'm due for a lunch break. I'll be there in ten minutes. We'll get rid of Santa Claus."

"No! You needn't come home! I'll dispose of Santa Claus if that's what you want."

He didn't like the sound of that at all. "He might be difficult."

"No problem. I'll throw him into the Dumpster. You'll never have to lay eyes on him."

This woman was crazed. "Darcie, I'm coming home."

"You don't have to. I can manage." She sniffed. "I only wanted to warn you about Santa Claus. And the elves. They're out on the lawn drying out."

Great. More drunk people hanging around DeWitt's house. She must have thrown a hell of a party. Maybe it started at her place and spilled over to DeWitt's this morning. "Darcie, don't do—"

"I'll pay for everything." She sniffed again. "Don't worry about that. But I didn't want you to drive up, see the elves and wonder if a tidal wave had hit."

"A tidal wave? You're scaring me, Darcie."

"Oh, dear. I was afraid you'd be upset about Santa and the elves. You may as well know about Rudolph, too."

"Are we talking about a *reindeer?*"

"Well, he was a reindeer. But now you can't really tell what he was."

Oh, God. They'd slaughtered an animal as part of the revelry. "I'm coming home."

"No! I'll throw Rudolph in the Dumpster, too! Really, I can manage. You don't have to—"

"Oh, I most definitely do need to, Darcie babe." Joe slammed down the phone, visions of lawsuits swirling in his head as he punched out on the time clock. He headed out the service door and leaped into the cab of his truck. Checking for cops, he gunned the engine as he screeched out of the parking lot.

3

JOE COULDN'T HELP BLAMING himself a little for this disaster. He'd encouraged the French Maid to think of him as somebody besides a client, and now she thought she could hold orgies in the house he was responsible for. Well, he'd put a stop to that kind of thinking once and for all, but if she'd caused any damage to the house, Joe figured he'd be the one who should pay for it instead of filing an insurance claim.

He didn't really want an orgy with Santa Claus and the French Maid to be on the record where DeWitt could read it. That could start a whole line of questioning he didn't relish. If DeWitt confronted the French Maid, she might tell him that Joe had come on to her, which he had, no question. And there would go Joe's references if he ever wanted to house-sit again.

If only the damage could be minimal. He winced at the idea of dipping into his savings account and putting the cabinet shop even further out of reach.

But the *reindeer*. That was the topper. He didn't know anyone twisted enough to take a reindeer into the suburbs and barbecue it. Good thing this had happened before their date Saturday night. He'd have been in way over his head.

As he whipped into the driveway, he noticed that some neighbors were already gathered there. No wonder, considering what Darcie and her friends had been up to inside. They couldn't have been particularly quiet about it. Fortunately, she must have shuttled all the drunks inside because nobody was passed out in the front yard anymore.

The garage door was open, and a dilapidated heap of a car was parked in the garage—probably belonging to that right jolly old elf with a taste for the juice of the grape. In the driveway stood the middle-aged couple from across the street—the Eiderdowns or something like that. DeWitt had warned him they were a pain in the butt, so he'd taken care to avoid them.

They were talking with a short redhead with generous breasts and a baby on her hip. All of them were probably wondering whether to call the police. He hoped they'd held off.

He got out of his truck and approached the group carefully, not wanting them to think he was especially worried. The middle-aged couple—maybe their name was Evenrude—looked grim, and on them grim didn't look so hot. Mr. Evenrude/Eiderdown was on the short and scrawny side, while the missus was at least a head taller than he was and looked like she could take her husband two out of three falls. And had, judging from his hangdog expression.

The mother with the baby looked…quite nice, to be honest. Her curly hair wouldn't stay in the clip she'd used to hold it and it formed a red-gold frame around her freckled face. Joe felt a zing of sexual awareness, which was weird because this baby-toting earth mother wasn't his type at all. He liked tall, slender women. Women without babies.

He'd had his fill of babies. The year he turned fourteen his mother had produced triplets, and Joe had changed enough diapers in the next couple of years to last him the rest of his life.

The redhead looked nervous, probably wondering if this neighborhood was wholesome enough for her baby. The kid was the spitting image of her—same reddish-gold hair and uptilted little nose. And although Joe wasn't drawn to babies, he recognized that modeling studios would lick their chops over this little leprechaun. Cute as hell.

"Good morning, folks," he said evenly. "I heard there was a little problem here, so I came by to check things out. I'm Joe Northwood, the house sitter."

"So we finally meet the elusive house sitter." Mrs. Eiderdown eyed him with a gleam in her eye.

Mr. Eiderdown stuck out his hand. "Joe, I'm Herman Elderhorn, and this is my wife, Madge. We came about the elves."

Elderhorn. That was it. Joe shook the little man's hand and hoped maybe the damage could be contained. "Yes, I'm here to handle the elf situation." Although the neighbors had seen drunks wearing tights and pointy shoes passed out on the lawn, maybe they didn't know anything about a blitzed Santa and a barbecued Rudolph.

Madge Elderhorn drew herself up until she looked twice the size of her husband. "As chair of the Tannenbaum Christmas Festival and Good Cheer Committee this year, I must object to those elves."

"I understand," Joe said. It didn't sound as if anybody had called the police yet, which was a relief. "I'll take care of it."

"I took them inside," the baby's mother said.

"You?" Joe gazed at her with respect. She looked soft and even voluptuous, but she had nerves of steel if she'd faced a bunch of drunk guys by herself. And she had

amazing green eyes. Looking into them made him think
of spring and budding leaves and tender new grass. She'd
be great to lie in the grass with.

"I thought you'd appreciate it."

"I do." There was something familiar about that
voice, he thought. As he continued to study her eyes, he
noticed they were a little red-rimmed, as if she had al-
lergies or had been crying recently. *Crying.* A niggling
thought started working on him.

He glanced away from her to allow himself to concentrate on that niggling thought and discovered Madge
studying him closely. Too closely. With something re-
sembling a smirk. Something was definitely up. He
hoped he wasn't the star of some *Candid Camera* episode.

Finally, Madge spoke. "Considering that the elves are
done for, I wondered what you had planned."

"I think we can handle this discreetly, Mrs. Eiderdown."

"Elderhorn."

"Right. Sorry. Mrs. Elderhorn. I can have the elves
out of here before you know it."

"That's all well and good," Madge said. "But the
question is, are you planning to replace them?"

Joe stared at her in shock. "I wasn't planning to *hurt*
them, just remove them from the neighborhood."

"Well, somebody might make use of them, sweet
cheeks, once they've dried out," Herman said.

"Don't be ridiculous, Herman. You saw what shape
they were in. Someone would have to be desperate to
want to use those elves. They're warped. I say get rid of
them." She looked at Joe. "Want me to do it?"

"No! I'll take care of everything, Mrs. Elderberry."

"Elderhorn."

"Right. Elderhorn. Maybe I can find a rehab facility that will take them." Joe wasn't sure exactly what Marge meant to do with those elves, but he wasn't willing to find out. Even warped drunks deserved a second chance.

"So what are you going to put in their place?" Madge asked. "You have to come up with something."

Joe had completely lost his place in this conversation. He shook his head in bewilderment. "I have no idea what you mean. I wasn't aware the elves were serving any function."

The redhead spoke up. "Mrs. Elderhorn, I don't believe Mr. Northwood knows about Tannenbaum's Christmas display."

He whipped around to face her. *That voice. That Irish lilt. He knew where he'd last heard it.*

Her green gaze pleaded with him, as if she feared he would make a scene in front of the neighbors. "You see, Mr. Northwood, each home is required to put up a yard decoration every year. I guess Mr. DeWitt—"

"Didn't mention it?" He gave her a piercing look, then studied the baby. "No, he didn't." *The baby. Maybe there really had been a baby in the background, and not jungle drums. Maybe he'd been totally, completely had.*

She looked deeply distressed, as well she should be. Her freckles stood out against the paleness of her cheeks like cinnamon sprinkled over a vat of cream. "So, when the washer overflowed and…soaked Santa and the elves, Mr. DeWitt's yard decorations were ruined. They were made of cardboard."

He finally got it. No orgy. No barbecued Rudolph. An overflowing washer had soaked some cardboard Christmas decorations. For that he'd driven two miles of cop-infested streets like a madman, thinking his future was about to go down the drain in a deluge of lawsuits.

He drilled the French Maid with a look that should have burned a hole right through her. Some French Maid. Instead of tall, willowy and exotic, she was short, curvy and wholesome. He could forgive the short and curvy part, but for her to be disgustingly wholesome was a cruel blow. And to top it all off, she had a baby!

He cringed as he thought of the notes he'd written to her, the daydreams he'd concocted, the fantasies he'd indulged in, all encouraged by her sexy paper, her flowers, her *chocolate,* dammit. How dare she toy with him like that?

Her voice faltered. "You...look a bit like a thundercloud."

He realized he needed to cool it, or the Elderhomes would soon know what a fool he'd made of himself.

He forced a smile as he gazed at her. "Really? *Pardonnez-moi.*" He paused for emphasis. *"Darcie."*

To his satisfaction, she turned very pink and seemed to be at a loss for words.

But the little guy she was carrying wasn't. He waved his arms and grinned at Joe. "Da-da!" he cried.

Darcie might have felt more humiliated at some time in her life, but if so, she couldn't recall it. As her da would have said, Joe looked as if he'd discovered rabbit droppings in his bowl of porridge.

To make matters worse, he was all she'd dreamed of and more in the looks department. His Home World T-shirt and jeans and battered truck confused her a little, considering the initialed stationery he used, but maybe he liked to fit in with his employees and enjoyed restoring old trucks.

The jeans and T-shirt went a long way toward showing him off to good advantage, though. And to top off the picture, he had a square jaw with the faintest dimple and dark wavy hair that she longed to bury her fingers in. She couldn't see the color of his eyes because of his aviator sunglasses, but maybe that was a good thing. From the frown wedged between his eyebrows, she didn't think she'd want to see his eyes.

Madge Elderhorn seemed not to mind Joe's frown. "It would appear, Mr. Northwood, that you'll need to come up with an alternate decoration," she said.

"I will help him," Darcie said.

"Color me surprised," Madge said.

Ignoring Madge, Darcie hoisted Gus more firmly onto her hip. "It's the least I can do."

Joe glanced at her. "The very least."

"Uh-huh," Madge said.

"But listen, I have an idea," Joe continued. "How about recycling what I have and calling it *A Christmas Nightmare?* We'll use the whacked-out Santa and his elves after all. Then I can round up some old tires, spray 'em green so they look sort of like rubber wreaths, and I'm sure somebody has a dead pine tree I could borrow. A few broken toys, a rusty sleigh—"

"Ha-ha!" The laughter coming out of Herman Elderhorn seemed to astonish everyone, including Herman.

Gus, always happy to join in when there was laughter going on, added his little baby giggle. *'Twould be grand to get a pint or two in that one and watch the show.*

Madge glared at her husband. "Her*man?*"

"I thought it was funny, honey lamb."

Madge gave him a dark look before turning back toward Joe. "Well, *I* fail to see the humor in it, Mr. Northwood."

"I wasn't being funny," Joe said.

Joe's voice had the strangest effect on Gus, who turned his little head immediately toward Joe and took on Joe's serious expression. *Faith, we can't have you looking dark and mysterious. Don't know why she fancies that, but she does.*

Darcie had never seen her son identify so quickly with anyone. She wondered if it was a Sign.

In any case, she decided that she'd be wise to support Joe's idea and try to get back in his good graces. Besides, she enjoyed the idea of tweaking the noses of the stuffy Tannenbaum residents. "What a creative plan!" she said.

Madge's chin went up at least an inch. "It's a terrible idea, and we can't have it, especially in this cul-de-sac, which is known for its outstanding displays. After all, people pay five dollars apiece to tour the community, and—"

"*Five bucks?*" Joe gaped at her.

"Jesus, Mary and Joseph," Darcie muttered. The tollbooths hadn't ever been up when she came through in the daytime to clean.

"I think it's a little steep myself," Herman ventured. "I think maybe three for adults, two for children, and maybe four dollars for a family *with* children, and of course you shouldn't charge for a baby who's not even walking, and if some old lady has to be pushed in a wheelchair, then—"

"Herman!" Madge quelled him with a look.

Joe shook his head in wonder. "You really find people willing to pay that much to see yard decorations?"

Darcie couldn't believe it, either. She'd never shell out good money to wander around staring at other people's lights and decorations, but then she didn't have any spare cash for such goings-on in the first place.

"You don't understand," Madge said. "These aren't a few colored bulbs strung along the eaves. These are scenes that move, lights that blink, steam that billows, even authentic noises.''

"All except the belching snowman last year, lotus blossom. The Landernoths finally admitted that was not a real belch, but a taped sound of pulling a plunger out of a toilet. That's why they were disqualified, you remember.''

"I'd sure demand a real belch for my five bucks," Joe said. "So, what do you do with all that cash?''

"We donate it to the homeless," Madge said, "except for five thousand we give as the grand prize.''

Darcie gasped. "You give the winner five thousand dollars?" Tuition, new tires, a sandbox. And money left over.

Joe cleared his throat. "Well, now, that puts a whole new slant on things. Suppose I put together a display that won the grand prize? Would it belong to me or DeWitt?''

"You wouldn't win," Madge said.

"By St. Paddy's beard, he most certainly might!" Darcie blurted out before she could stop herself.

Madge and Herman stared at her. So did Joe, for that matter.

"I only mean, it's a free country. We all get a chance." She sneaked a peek at Joe and imagined a smile trying to break through. Madge Elderhorn didn't look the least bit pleased, however. Darcie had to be careful. She cleaned house for Madge and couldn't afford to get the woman's knickers in a twist. But the idea of that sheepfaced Madge Elderhorn telling Joe, who practically ran a home improvement store, that he couldn't win!

"Humor me," Joe said. "Assume I create the winning display. Who would get the money?''

"Well, I don't know," Madge said. "What do you think, Herman?''

As if basking in the temporary limelight, Herman stroked his chin and cleared his throat.

Madge thumped him on the arm. "I asked for a quick opinion, Herman, not a Supreme Court decision!"

"Had to think on it," Herman said. "The way I see it, technically it would belong to Mr. DeWitt."

Madge opened her mouth. "Well, I—"

"On the other hand," Herman continued as if making a speech, "I don't see how he could take it in good conscience, considering that Mr. Northwood would do all the work."

Madge opened her mouth again. "Yes, but—"

"Still, it *is* Mr. DeWitt's property."

"Fine," Madge said. "However—"

"Yet Mr. DeWitt has never cared about our festival before."

Darcie could see the debate going on forever and Gus was getting squirmy. "I think Mr. Northwood should just call Mr. DeWitt and ask whether he could keep the prize money or not," she said.

"Great idea," Joe said. "Edgar's a fair guy. I'm sure he'll say that if my goodies win the prize, I should keep it."

Darcie was encouraged enough by his tone of voice to risk addressing him directly again. "Furthermore, I would be honored to help you display your goodies."

Watch your tongue, lass! For the love of St. Paddy, don't be offering to help the bounder display his goodies.

Joe gazed at Darcie, and his expression was definitely gentler than it had been a few moments ago. "Thanks for the support, but I think I can handle it myself."

I don't like the looks passing between these two. But methinks Mr. Dark and Mysterious is not overfond of babies. Gus held out his arms toward Joe. "Da-da!" he crowed.

Darcie's cheeks heated. "Now, Gus, you must stop saying that to perfect strangers."

"He seems to know Mr. Northwood," Madge said.

"Gus?" Joe's mouth definitely tilted up at the corners this time. "Did you call him Gus?"

"It's his name." She was a bit touchy on the subject.

"That's cute as hell."

Cute? 'Tis a name of high distinction, blarney breath!
Darcie lifted her chin. "He's named after my dear departed father, Angus Sean O'Banyon."

Joe gazed at her. "Strange, but there doesn't seem to be anything French about that name."

"Oh, Darcie's not French," Madge said. "She's as Irish as St. Patrick himself. The French Maid thing is just a clever marketing tactic of hers. I must say it's paid dividends, hasn't it, Darcie?"

"It has at that, Mrs. Elderhorn."

"And kept the wolf from the door," Madge added. "But don't despair. I imagine Bart Junior will be coming home again and will give this baby a name."

Gus wiggled in Darcie's arms. *Let me at her, lass. Could take her, I could.*

"He has a name." Darcie flushed as she struggled to hold on to Gus and her temper at the same time. Perhaps Madge meant well, but she considered Darcie below the salt, which was why she made so free to air Darcie's dirty linen in public. Madge couldn't imagine that someone who cleaned houses for a living had any pride. If Darcie had hoped to maintain a scrap of dignity in front of Joe, that hope was dashed now.

Joe noticed the color rise in Darcie's cheeks, and despite his anger over the way she'd fooled him, his heart went out to her. Getting shafted by some jerk was bad enough. Having people gossip about it in front of others was even worse. "And his name fits him perfectly," he said. "I've never seen a more authentic little Irishman in my life."

Don't be trying to get on my good side, you bounder. I know what to expect from the likes of you.

Darcie's whole face lit up with gratitude as she smiled at Joe. "He is quite a kid, isn't he?"

Her smile hit him like a ton of bricks. When Darcie smiled, she smiled all over. Her green eyes sparkled and her cheeks dimpled. Even her curvy little body seemed to levitate with happiness. Warmth flooded through him, and that zing of sexual feeling sailed right along for the ride.

And in the midst of all that good feeling, he became inspired. He knew how he was going to win the grand prize, and he also knew that he would split it with Darcie. From the looks of her car, she could use it as much as he could. He only needed half of the five grand anyway, and he'd be Denver-bound to join up with his cousin.

He turned toward Madge and Herman. "I'll come up with a decoration for the front yard. I'll contact DeWitt and see if he'll let me keep the prize. If he won't, I'll put up something basic. If he will, I'll go for the gold. When does the festival start?"

"December fifteenth," Madge said smugly.

"Ouch. That doesn't give me much time."

"I'd advise you to stick with a basic design," Madge said, "and save yourself the heartache of losing. We've won three out of five years and came in second place the other two years, which is not a cash prize but does involve a rather nice plaque. We intend to win again this year, right, Herman?"

"That's what you keep telling me, sugar lump."

"Who are the judges by the way?" Joe asked. He needed to know if this was a loaded contest where the winners just happened to be best friends with the judges.

"Scottsdale business owners for the most part," Madge said. "Three of them. We never know who it's going to be, but in the past they've shown excellent taste."

If she kept up her superior attitude, Joe might be goaded into competing for the prize even if he couldn't keep it, just to prove it could be done. "We'll see what DeWitt says." He checked his watch. "If I call now, I might catch him before he goes to bed. Thanks for dropping by, Mr. and Mrs. Flugelhorn."

"*Elder*horn." Madge's smile was icy. "Come along, Herman."

"Nice meeting you," Herman said as he trailed after his wife.

Halfway down the drive, Madge turned back. "See you on Friday, Darcie," she said. "You'll need to pay particular attention to the front windows this time. They're very smudged for some reason."

"They'll sparkle like dew on a rose petal," Darcie said. After Herman and Madge crossed the street, she muttered, "And they'd stay that way if your dogs wouldn't plaster their wet noses all over them five seconds after I wash them."

Joe understood perfectly the note of frustration in her voice. He'd had his share of being treated like a servant, which was why he wanted to win this contest and open a cabinet shop. Then he planned to become so successful that he didn't have to take anybody's business unless they treated him with respect.

He turned to Darcie. "Let's go inside. I have a proposition for you."

4

DARCIE BACKED AWAY from Joe, Gus clutched protectively against her. "Now wait a minute, mister. I may have played a silly game with the rose and the chocolate. And I may have a baby with no father in sight, but that doesn't mean I'm some flibbertigibbet who can be had for the price of a sweet word and a smile!"

Joe shook his head quickly. "No, I'm talking about the contest. I've changed my mind about needing your help."

"Oh." Her cheeks warmed. She felt like an idiot. And a little disappointed that he wasn't offering her a different sort of proposition. She wouldn't accept, of course, but it would be exciting to be asked. She hadn't been propositioned in a very long time.

He took off his sunglasses and tucked them in his T-shirt pocket. Then he gazed at her with dark eyes the color of seduction. "And whatever a flibbertigibbet is, I can't believe it comes close to describing a woman who runs her own business and takes care of a baby at the same time."

"Th-thank you." She'd fantasized what his eyes might look like. As she became lost in their deep brown color and lush fringe of lashes, she realized her imagination hadn't done him justice.

"Will you help me?"

"Of course. After all, I'm the one who soaked Santa and the elves."

"And scared the living daylights out of me. I thought Santa and his elves were real people and you'd had a drunken orgy in DeWitt's house. I even thought you'd barbecued Rudolph."

She stared at him in astonishment. Once the picture he'd painted registered, she clapped her free hand over her mouth, but her laughter seeped out anyway.

Joe's incredible eyes warmed and his mouth curved in a smile.

Gus picked up on Darcie's delight and started in with his cute little baby giggles, drooling and showing off his shiny new teeth. *See these teeth, you with the gleam in your eye? Sharp, they are. Very sharp.*

Joe turned toward the garage. "I'm going in to call DeWitt. No use talking about this until we find out what he has to say." He started through the garage toward the door leading into the kitchen.

She followed him into the kitchen. "I'm sorry to have caused you all that worry. You must have been beside yourself."

He glanced back at her. "If we can win this contest, all the worry will be worth it, Darcie. Let's see if DeWitt's home."

"I'll just feed Gus a bit of lunch, then." She placed the baby efficiently in the high chair sitting on a drop cloth in the corner of the kitchen. Then she tied a bib around his chubby neck. The bib said, "Kiss me, I'm Irish."

As Joe waited for the international connection to go through, he had nothing to do but watch Darcie move around, preparing to feed Gus. He liked the way she moved.

The hotel's front desk finally answered.

"Edgar DeWitt, please." He prepared to wait some more.

Darcie took the lid off a plastic bowl and laid cut-up veggies directly on Gus's tray.

"You don't put those in a bowl?" Joe asked.

"I tried that once. Didn't work very well."

Watching Gus mangle his food was like a rerun from the past for Joe, with two exceptions. Only one baby sat in the kitchen instead of three, and that one baby was not Joe's responsibility, thank God. But like the triplets, Gus was a human Veg-O-Matic, mashing, grinding and spewing food everywhere. Joe was glad to be across the room out of the line of fire.

"Edgar DeWitt here," said a voice on the other end.

"Edgar, it's Joe." Remembering his own recent panic at Darcie's phone call, he spoke quickly. "First of all, nothing's wrong."

"That's a relief. When I heard your voice, I had visions of the place in ashes."

"Nope." He'd had those visions himself not long ago. But he couldn't seem to stay angry with the woman responsible for taking five years off his life. Instead, he found himself admiring the swell of her breasts under the T-shirt. And he shouldn't be doing that, either. "Listen, I just found out about the Christmas decorating contest."

"Sorry. I forgot to tell you. There's some cardboard stuff in the garage. Shouldn't take you long to set it up."

Joe glanced over at Darcie, busy coaxing some of the orange and green veggies into Gus, who seemed just as determined to finger paint himself with them instead. Joe couldn't bring himself to squeal on her. Anyone struggling with a kid less than a year old deserved a break.

"I'm afraid I dropped a bucket of water and the stuff got wasted," he said.

Darcie stiffened and slowly swung around to face him, her eyebrows lifted. Joe smiled at her. Looking bewildered, she returned her attention to Gus.

"Oh," DeWitt said, "well, then—"

"I'll work out a new display," Joe said. "I have some ideas. But I was wondering…if I happened to put up something that wins that five grand they're offering, would the money be mine or yours?"

DeWitt laughed. "Yours. And you'll have earned it. I got a great deal on that house because the previous owners couldn't take the Tannenbaum Christmas Festival another year. They said the neighbors in our little cul-de-sac acted as if they were going for the Nobel Prize or something."

"That would mainly be the Elderhorns, I'll bet."

DeWitt laughed. "So you've met them. They'll be tough to beat."

"Yeah, well, I'd like that five grand." Joe decided not to tell DeWitt about the cabinet shop yet because there was always a chance he wouldn't win the money. But he certainly planned to do everything in his power to win and finally get his life going the way he wanted it.

"Good luck," DeWitt said. "How're you managing with everything else?"

"Just fine."

"And the French Maid's working out for you?"

"She's a hell of a cleaner." Joe watched Darcie lean over to pick up a piece of carrot that had escaped the drop cloth. Nice tush. Now that he'd adjusted to the fact that she wasn't French, he'd gone back to thinking about the notes they'd exchanged and that wild conversation about tulips and erect pistils.

Darcie might not be French, but she sure seemed hot-blooded. The Irish were known for that, now that he thought about it. Earlier, he'd had an image of lying with her in the grass. It could as easily be shamrocks. Or on the sheets she washed in nonirritating soap to pamper his naked body.

She was a woman who thought about such things, a woman who liked chocolate and rose petals. If he didn't have this Denver thing on the horizon...but no, she had a baby.

No way would he think of getting involved with a woman who had a baby. That was a total turnoff. Or it should be. He couldn't imagine why he was able to watch her feed that kid and still have fantasies of rolling with her on soft sheets. The notes she'd written must be to blame. He'd get over it.

As for Darcie, she'd already been dumped on once. This time she'd be going for the white lace and promises for sure. He wasn't into that right now. He had too many other things to do first.

"Let me know if you win that contest," DeWitt said. "And Merry Christmas."

"Same to you." Joe hung up the phone.

Immediately, Darcie turned to him. She might have looked engrossed in her baby, but she'd obviously been hanging on his every word. She twisted a damp rag in her hands. "Sounds as if you fibbed for me."

He shrugged. "A little." He hadn't seen many fair-skinned women who looked good without a speck of makeup. Darcie did. Her lips were naturally pink, and her eyelashes might be pale, but they were long and thick and looked just right with her green eyes.

"I'm obliged to you for that."

"Yeah, you'll have to give me your firstborn."

Terror filled her eyes. Behind her, Gus began making an outlandish racket banging on his high-chair tray.

"Just kidding! Sorry. Bad joke." He felt like a jerk. Darcie obviously didn't have much of a sense of humor about this baby of hers.

"Don't mind me. I'm sure I overreact on that subject." She turned a loving gaze on Gus, who'd smeared yellow and green vegetables all over his face and into his hair. He looked like a crazed fan painted up to cheer on the Green Bay Packers in the Super Bowl.

"I imagine everyone wants him," Darcie said.

Behind Darcie's back, Joe rolled his eyes. "Yeah, I can see that," he managed to say with an amazing amount of sincerity. He didn't want to insult her or the kid right now. He needed them both.

Joe figured Darcie was curious as to whether the deal with DeWitt was on, but instead of questioning him about the conversation, she started cleaning Gus's face with a damp cloth. He admired her restraint. No doubt about it, the French Maid had class even though she wasn't French.

He watched Gus squirm and scrunch up his face trying to avoid the swipe of the rag. Peggy, Ryan and Marty had done the same thing every time he'd tried to clean them up. All he'd wanted was to finish the job quickly so he could play ball or work on his car, and he'd been impatient. Darcie wasn't impatient. He felt a moment of regret for not treating his sister and brothers with a little more tenderness. They'd been so little.

"DeWitt said I could have the money," he said.

"That's what I would have expected." She folded the cloth and rubbed it through Gus's coppery curls.

"How would you like to have half?"

She whirled and stared at him. "Half of the prize money?" Her voice squeaked with excitement.

"Yep." He was gratified by her response. She obviously needed a break like this as much as he did.

She looked really happy at the prospect, but slowly the joy faded from her expression and she narrowed her eyes. "Why would you give me half?"

"Because I want you to help me."

"I already said I'd help you for free. It's unusual for a man to pay for what he can get for free."

He heard the hurt behind her statement. Damn Gus's father for taking a bright spirit like Darcie and making her so suspicious. "But you didn't know what I had in mind. You may feel differently when you hear my plan."

She folded and refolded the cloth in her hand. "Would this be having anything to do with tulips and pistils?"

He noticed that her hands were small, and cinnamon freckles dotted her skin there, too. He'd bet those small freckled hands would feel perfect stroking his.... Nope. Couldn't go there. Remember the baby, he reminded himself. He should make it a slogan, like Remember the Alamo. Remember the Baby. "I promise it has nothing to do with tulips and pistils." Unfortunately.

Gus started pounding on the tray of his high chair.

"Or jungle drums, for that matter," he added because he was human and he wanted to see if she'd blush. She did, and it made her eyes sparkle even more.

She rolled the cloth into a cylinder. Surely it was an accident, he thought, the way she clutched it. The way she squeezed...oh, God.

"Then you'd keep your pistil to yourself?"

"Yes." His answer came out a croak. "Put the damned cloth down, Darcie."

She glanced down at the cloth as if she hadn't realized

it was there. She gasped and flung it to the table. "I
wasn't—"

"I didn't think so." He took a deep breath. He'd almost wished she had been teasing him. It fitted the image
of her he'd carried for weeks. "Look, I might as well
tell you straight out that if I'd known you had a baby, I
never would have called you last week or asked you to
come over Saturday night. Nothing against you. Even
though you're not French, you're a very pretty woman,
one any guy would be lucky to have a chance with,
but—"

"You don't date women who happen to have babies."

"That's it," he said gently. "Right now I'm in tran-
sition, a rolling stone. I travel light."

She nodded. "That way, if the headhunters come for
you, you're ready to move."

"Headhunters?" Maybe he still didn't have the whole
story on Darcie. Maybe she'd had some jungle types in
her apartment the other night after all, and she was telling
him in her own subtle way that if he stepped out of line,
she had connections with people who would handle the
situation. "Darcie, you don't have to threaten me with
your jungle friends. I wouldn't lay a hand on you. Honest."

"Jungle friends?" She looked confused. "I don't—
oh!" She laughed nervously, which caused Gus to join
in and bang on his tray some more.

Joe glanced into the little gremlin's face and almost
imagined Gus had understood all that had been going on.
But, of course, that was impossible. He wasn't even a
year old yet.

"I meant the sort of headhunters who go around hiring
people away from their jobs," Darcie said. "Not the kind

who lop off your noggin and shrink it down to the size of a coconut.''

"Oh." Heat climbed up from the neck of his T-shirt. "Well, I don't have those kind of headhunters looking for me. I only work in the lumber department at Home World.''

"And here I thought you were in charge of the whole shebang!"

"I'm not even in charge of a small part of the shebang.''

"So what was all that with the fancy stationery?"

Ah, he had her there. "What was all that with yours?"

"Business!"

"Uh-huh." He crossed his arms and gazed at her. "And the single red rose by the bedside? Was that business, too?''

She glanced away, her color high. "So I flirted with you. You flirted with me, too, telling me you slept naked. Strewing those rose petals around. Making me think of...things I shouldn't be thinking of.''

Remember the Baby. Remember the Baby. "Like what?" he asked softly.

She turned to him, the look in her eyes giving her away. He'd imagined that look in the French Maid's eyes. He took a step closer.

Back up that hay wagon, blarney breath! Gus started rocking violently in his high chair. *The things I'm called upon to do to save you, lass. Sure and I hate this part.* He banged his head against the back of the high chair and started to wail.

Darcie snapped out of her trance and raced to the high chair. "Gus! Oh, Gus, what did you go and do that for?"

Sacrificed myself to preserve your good name. He continued to cry as she cuddled him.

"Is he okay?" Joe asked.

"He'll be fine in a minute. Just a little bump. I don't know what got into him."

Joe couldn't shake the eerie feeling that the baby had intended to interrupt the moment. He supposed a little kid like that could experience jealousy if he sensed his mother wasn't paying enough attention to him. Well, at least the moment *had* been interrupted, whether Gus had meant to do it or not. Joe ran a hand over his face. What had he been thinking?

Gradually, the baby's sobs subsided.

Joe cleared his throat. "I guess we'd better get back to the issue of the contest. Are you ready to win it with me?"

"I admire your spirit, but I don't think it will be that easy." She rocked back and forth with Gus, who was staring right at Joe. "The Elderhorns—"

"We can beat them," Joe said.

"How?"

"By giving the judges something the others in this subdivision don't have. Tannenbaum is short on kids, I've noticed."

"True. Hardly any."

"So who else could present a live Nativity scene but you, me and Chief Carrot Juice here?"

Darcie stared at him, obviously dumbfounded. "Jesus, Mary and Joseph."

He grinned at the epithet. "That was pretty much my concept."

MADGE HAD PROMISED HERMAN she'd help him shop for one of those flat televisions that hang on the wall, which about killed her because she couldn't stay home to monitor her listening device while those two across the street were actually in the house together doing Lord knows what. But Madge could imagine what. Babies took naps after all.

The expedition took forever because Herman wanted to debate the issue as if world peace depended on it. Finally, Madge insisted they buy the silly thing so she could get home and find a private moment to call Trudy.

While Herman was busy hooking it up, she hurried to her sewing room, closed the door and made her call.

She didn't even identify herself anymore. She and Trudy had become that close. "Was she any different today when she cleaned for you?" She was out of breath from climbing the stairs and the excitement of her news.

"A little distracted maybe. Very fast. Why?"

"We have contact confirmed," she said, shivering with delight.

"Confirmed? What did you do, install a security camera in the house?"

"I keep telling you I don't break and enter. Unless you think—"

"No, no. What do you mean, confirmed?"

"He came home for *lunch.*"

"Oh, *lunch.*"

"Exactly. Fortunately, Herman and I were there."

"You went over there for lunch, too?"

"No, I had to go over in my official capacity because Darcie was drying elves on the front lawn."

"Elves? What—"

"Never mind about that. The important thing is that *he* showed up. And let me tell you—fireworks."

"You mean fireworks as in lust?"

"Triple strength, baby. Looks passed between them that would singe the hair on your arms." Madge paused for dramatic emphasis before she added the final stroke to her picture. "He spoke French to her."

"Oh, my God. French."

"And they've come up with a cover story to disguise what's going on. Supposedly they're going to work together to put up a Christmas display in Edgar's yard, ha-ha. This Joe Northwood pretends like he's after the prize, as if any of us would believe that."

"No one ever would," Trudy agreed.

"I think you're safe to tell Bart Junior he'd better get on home if he wants to protect what's his."

"I think you're right, but I never know when he's going to call. So keep gathering information. I might as well have plenty of ammunition when the time comes."

"Will do. Over and out."

5

BECAUSE THEY BOTH had to leave—Joe heading back to Home World and Darcie driving to the Butterworths'—they had no more time to discuss the plan. They agreed to meet at DeWitt's house that night after dinner and figure out the details.

But Darcie was already figuring out details. She tried not to become too excited about the prospect of twenty-five-hundred dollars, but she couldn't help herself. After whipping through the Butterworth house in record time, she hurried home and started digging in her closet in search of costumes.

She took time to fix a quick sandwich for herself and shovel more food into Gus before she decked herself out in what she'd found in order to demonstrate the outfit to Joe. Her chenille bathrobe formed the central part of her Virgin Mary costume, and she tied a towel around her head with a piece of rope. Tucking Gus into his car seat, she started out.

The car seemed to cough and sputter more than usual during the trip.

"You sound as if you need a mustard plaster," Darcie lectured the car. "I don't have the time or the money to tend to you, and even if I should get some money, I don't want to spend it on your cranky innards, so stop your shenanigans this minute."

Less than a mile from DeWitt's house, the car did stop...completely.

"Traitorous vehicle! See if I buy you new tires if I win the lottery this week!" Darcie glanced at the elegant homes around her. "Well, it's not a total disaster. You've plunked me down in an upscale neighborhood at least."

Taking Gus from the car seat, she walked to the nearest house and rang the bell. Icicle lights hung from the eaves, flashing on and off as Darcie waited.

Gus burbled and pointed at the lights. *Bet those run up the bill faster than an alderman in a tavern.*

"I know. They are lovely." Darcie felt guilty that she hadn't put up any lights yet for Gus to enjoy, but she hated to spend the money when she was guarding every penny. And now her car had given up the ghost.

She heard someone coming to the door and reminded herself that people were nervous about letting strangers enter their houses, which was sensible these days. She wouldn't ask to go in and use the telephone. She'd ask them to call Joe for her and she'd stay out on the porch.

The weather was so nice she didn't mind. After living in Ireland until the age of thirteen, and then in New York City until her father's health forced a change, she still couldn't believe the mild temperatures of an Arizona winter night. And this season seemed even warmer than usual, which was why she'd even consider Joe's plan to park them all on the front lawn every evening.

The door opened and a woman with a long mane of golden hair and absolutely no eyebrows peered out. She looked startled, Darcie thought, but a person with no eyebrows might always look startled, so Darcie couldn't tell for certain.

"Excuse me for disturbing you," Darcie said. "My

baby and I need a little help. If you would be so kind as to—"

"Heavens!" The woman reached out, grabbed Darcie by the arm and pulled her through the doorway. "Get in here. Did he follow you?"

"Who?" Darcie blinked in the light of the living room and clutched Gus a little closer. She hoped she hadn't stumbled upon the house of a madwoman.

"Your tyrannical fanatic of a husband, of course. Don't worry. I saw *Not Without My Daughter.* You'll be safe with me. What a darling baby. Must not take after his loathsome father."

The woman might be missing an oar on her dinghy, but she had that last part right. "No, he doesn't, as a matter of fact."

"That's lucky. You can sleep in the spare room if you like. Now that the ratfink has decided to leave me, I'm here alone, and I'd be delighted to offer you and your baby safe haven for as long as you like. In fact, I insist on helping. Women who are victims of men's cruelty should stick together."

Darcie tended to agree, but she'd been too busy to find another woman to bond with on that issue. And she was too busy now. "Thank you but I only need a telephone, Mrs...."

The woman laughed. "It's Jefferson. And in case you're wondering, the ratfink is my philandering husband."

"Oh." Darcie smiled in understanding. She had a few choice names for Bart Junior, too. "Well, Mrs. Jefferson, my car is dead, and I really do need a telephone."

"Of course. Is there an underground for women in your situation?"

"Underground?" The room smelled of nail polish, and

Darcie realized the woman must have been in the middle of giving herself a manicure from the look of the tools arranged on the coffee table. Maybe she had been enjoying the occasional beverage while she was painting her nails. "I don't think so. I think women's cars get towed to the wrecking yard the same as men's. I've never heard of storing them underground, although it's not a bad idea. Broken cars are unsightly, aren't they?"

The woman stared at her for a moment. "Then you really are having car trouble?"

"Not just car trouble. Car disaster. I've prayed over that bucket of bolts until I'm blue in the face, but I think what it needs is a good mechanic. And good mechanics cost a lot of money."

"If you're not running away from some tyrannical husband from the Middle East, then why are you dressed like that?"

For the first time, the woman's comments made sense. Darcie had totally forgotten that she was wearing a bathrobe and turban. Perhaps her costume was a success. "Would you take me for the Virgin Mary?"

The woman cocked her head to one side. "Not with that beautiful red hair sticking out, which makes you the mother of that darling baby and no virgin, at least not in this century. And then there's your freckles. Is that what you're supposed to be? The Virgin Mary?"

"Yes." She adjusted the towel to try to hide more of her hair, but that drew Gus's attention to it and he began trying to grab it. "Stop that, Gus."

"*Gus?* Baby Jesus's name is *Gus?*"

Here we go again. Going all sheep-faced over my blessed name.

Darcie lifted her chin and aimed a challenging look at this eyebrowless woman. "Yes. Gus. G-U-S."

"I love it! Come here, Gus." She held out her arms.

To Darcie's amazement, Gus went right to her. Then he reached up and pulled at her hair. The whole thing came off in his hand, revealing a mop of gray curls underneath. *Just wanted to see if it was attached. Wasn't.*

"Oh, I'm so sorry!" Darcie snatched the wig away from a startled Gus and ran around to put it back on the woman's head.

"Oh, leave it," the woman said, grabbing it with her free hand as she jiggled Gus expertly on her hip. "And tell me why you want to be the Virgin Mary."

"Because..." Darcie started to tell her, but then she remembered that the plan for the yard should be kept secret. Tannenbaum designs were always kept secret. She'd been given strict orders not to peer under the tarp covering something very large in the Elderhorns' garage. She was only a mile or so from Tannenbaum, and this woman might know some of the residents. "I'm afraid I can't tell you," she finished.

"Doesn't matter." The woman waved the wig in the air. "I'll help you look like her if you want. You didn't contradict me when I called this baby's father loathsome, so I assume you're a victim of some man's cruelty, in any case."

"I suppose I am, but what I need most desperately at the moment is a telephone."

"Right in there." She gestured through a doorway. "The light switch is on the wall to your left as you go in. That used to be the ratfink's office. Don't mind the mess. I think the phone still works."

"I'll take Gus if you—"

"Gus and I will be fine, won't we, peaches?"

That all depends, bright eyes. Seems risky to trust a

lass whose hair comes off in your hand like a dead mongoose.

"Grandma might have a graham cracker in the kitchen for you."

Then again, I like living on the edge, I do.

Graham crackers were one of the few treats Darcie gave her son. From the way he grinned, she decided he'd understood what "Grandma" had just said, and she'd have a very upset baby on her hands if she said no. "One, then. And thank you." With some misgivings, she hurried into the office, switched on a light and gasped. "Mrs. Jefferson!" she called. "You've been vandalized!"

"No, I haven't. And you can call me Geraldine." The woman came to stand in the doorway to survey the files spilling out of open drawers, the jumble of papers on the desk and fax paper unrolled all over the floor. "After twenty years of being his wife and secretary, handling every detail of his life with no thought to a career of my own, I had to listen to his sickening confession that he'd found someone else. Found her awhile ago, in fact."

Understanding exactly how she might feel, Darcie looked around the room again. "Used restraint, didn't you?"

"I did. I think the phone's under that pile of blue folders. Gus and I will be in the kitchen looking for a graham cracker."

Darcie watched them go, still amazed at how quickly Gus had taken to Geraldine. Darcie felt quite at home with her, too. It would have been nice, Darcie thought wistfully, to have a mother like Geraldine who really was Gus's grandmother. But she was letting herself get carried away over a chance meeting by thinking such thoughts.

She found the telephone right where Geraldine had told her it was and she dialed Joe's number.

He answered on the second ring, sounding worried. "Hello?"

"It's Darcie."

He sighed with relief. "Thank God. I called your apartment and got no answer. I was ready to check with the police."

"My car broke down."

"Where are you?"

"At a house owned by a nice woman with no eyebrows named Geraldine Jefferson. She's in the kitchen giving Gus a graham cracker."

"Uh, okay. How far away from here?"

"Not far."

"That's good. Why doesn't she have eyebrows?"

Darcie lowered her voice. "Some women shave their eyebrows and put them on with pencil later. I caught her by surprise without her eyebrows. If you come here, don't stare."

"I wouldn't dream of staring. What's wrong with the car?"

"It won't go."

He chuckled. "No kidding."

Something about the way he laughed low and sexy reminded her of the time he'd called her apartment to talk about tulips. Maybe it was the influence of standing in Mr. Jefferson's office and thinking about how women got run around the mulberry bush by men. Some were obvious about it, like Bart Junior and Mr. Jefferson. Others sounded sexy like Joe, making a woman yearn, but wouldn't deliver the happily-ever-after.

Still, she'd had Joe on the ropes once and she couldn't resist trying to get him there again. "Zee car, she is—

how you say?—zee ley-mon. Zee pistons, zey will not pump up and down."

He cleared his throat. "Uh, Darcie, maybe it would be a good idea if you didn't talk like the French Maid anymore."

Another French word came back to her. *"Pourquoi?"*

"Because something about it really gets to me, especially talking about pistons and things like that, and we've agreed it wouldn't be a good idea if we got involved."

"Ah. *Monsieur* doesn't date zee woman with zee *bambino*. I—how you say eet?—forgot."

"Uh-huh. Give me the address and I'll come over and see what I can do about your car."

She liked the fact she'd rattled him. She'd cooperate with him to win this money, but maybe she shouldn't make the whole thing too easy for him. "Okeydokey." She gave him the address. "And remember not to stare at Mrs. Jefferson even if she looks strange."

STRANGE DIDN'T EVEN COVER the sight that greeted Joe when he was ushered into Mrs. Jefferson's living room. And the lack of eyebrows on Mrs. Jefferson wasn't the worst of it.

"Ta-da!" Darcie said, holding out her arms. She wore a bathrobe and some sort of turban affair that hung down to her shoulders, but that wasn't the most startling part. She seemed to have dyed her hair black and her face had been darkened with some sort of makeup.

Before he could react to that, he noticed the strangest little blond dog waddling along the floor toward him. The dog had paws that looked like...like hands. Then the dog looked up at him. It was Gus, practically covered in a Dolly Parton wig.

"What do you think?" Darcie asked.

He hardly knew how to start navigating this land mine. "About what?" he asked cautiously.

"Do I look like the Blessed Virgin or not?"

Not. "Did you...dye your hair?"

"No. It's a wig Geraldine loaned me."

He let out his breath, not even aware he'd been holding it. He shouldn't care if she dyed her hair purple, but the thought of her changing the color of that soft, curly, wonderful mass of red hair made his stomach ache.

Darcie turned to Geraldine. "This is Joe Northwood."

Geraldine nodded, but her gaze was assessing. "Nice to meet you. I understand you don't date women with children."

Joe's jaw dropped as he swung back to Darcie. "What next? A public service announcement on TV?"

"You never said it was a secret."

"Well, no, but—"

"Geraldine and I are soul mates," Darcie said. "We tell each other everything."

"You just met each other!"

"When it's right, it's right," Geraldine said. "Fate sent Darcie to my door. I even helped her look like the Virgin Mary, though she wouldn't tell me why."

"I see." Joe was beginning to wonder if he really understood what he'd gotten himself into. Darcie wasn't quite as sweet and uncomplicated as he'd thought.

Gus reached out a fist and took hold of the leg of Joe's jeans. Slowly, with great purpose, he pulled himself upright and wrapped both arms around Joe's leg. "Da-da," he said softly, peering out from under the bangs of the blond wig.

"WELL, THERE GOES the neighborhood, Herman." Madge Elderhorn had perfected a technique whereby she could poke her binoculars out through a slight gap in the front drapes so that someone outside would have to really look to notice what she was doing.

Santa Claus had brought her the binoculars last Christmas, and they were just what she'd wanted—the kind with an infrared feature so a person could see what was going on at night. Well, Santa hadn't *really* brought them. She couldn't trust Herman to pick out the right kind, either, so she'd bought them for herself, put Santa's name on them, then put them under the tree.

"Did you hear me, Herman? Riffraff is as riffraff does."

Herman kept his gaze focused on the latest episode of *The X-Files* displayed on his new flat TV. "How so, sugarplum?"

"It's not bad enough that we have to put up with that old clunker of a truck the house sitter drives, but he just pulled into the driveway *towing* the maid's car. Uh-oh. She's getting out of the car, which we have to assume is not running."

"That's usually when cars get towed, luscious lips."

"Oh, my God, Herman. She's wearing a bathrobe! You can see exactly where this is leading."

"Maybe her plumbing went out, babycakes, and she's come to borrow DeWitt's shower."

"Oh, I think her plumbing is in fine shape. I think Mr. Joe Northwood is quite interested in her fine plumbing, if you ask me."

"No, sugar lump. Mr. Northwood is a carpenter, not a plumber."

Madge blew out a breath in exasperation. How Herman managed to find his shoes in the morning was beyond her. "Will you look at that? He's carrying the baby's playpen into the house for her, so it's obvious she plans to stay awhile. And they're leaving both of those disreputable vehicles right in the driveway. Next thing you know, one of them will be up on blocks, mark my word. I told Edgar DeWitt he should hire a professional house-sitting service, but he wouldn't listen to me.''

"No doubt it'll be his downfall, snookum-wookums.''

"Two old rattletraps like that, and they think they can win Tannenbaum's Christmas Festival and Good Cheer Contest! What a laugh!'' When the man, woman and baby had finally gone inside, she scanned the neighborhood one last time. "Well, Herman, I really need to get back to my sewing project.''

"You've spent a lot of time on that, love bundle. Is it a Christmas surprise?''

"You might say that,'' Madge replied as she headed for the stairs. Trudy had wanted ammunition. Madge was about to provide an entire munitions dump.

6

JOE SET DOWN THE PLAYPEN and unlocked the front door. "I can probably get it running long enough to get you home, but there's more oil pouring out of that engine than one of J. R. Ewing's wells. You need either a major overhaul or a new car." He gestured her into the dimly lit living room.

"By the shine on a leprechaun's britches, I just knew it." Darcie tried to keep her voice low so she wouldn't wake Gus, who was sleeping in her arms. "The very minute I have a chance of getting ahead, up pops another blessed expense!"

"Where do you want the playpen?"

"Right here will be fine, thanks." Once he'd set up the playpen, she laid a sleeping Gus inside. He should be home in his own bed, she thought, but sacrifices would have to be made on all sides in order to win the festival prize, which she and Gus now needed more than ever. The baby stirred, and she leaned over the edge of the playpen to rub his back.

"Want something to drink?" Joe asked softly from the doorway leading into the kitchen.

She glanced over at Joe and was hit by the reality of being here alone with him, this man she'd flirted with, the one she'd imagined sleeping naked on the sheets she changed every week.

"Wine, maybe?" he asked. "And I think there's some

flavored coffee in the freezer I could grind, or...would you like some plain old hot chocolate?''

Wine might affect her good judgment and coffee would make her more wired than she already felt. "Hot chocolate sounds nice.''

She imagined he'd make instant and it would taste like chalk, but at least they'd each have something to hold on to while they discussed this display, which might prevent her from dreaming of holding on to him. Besides, hot chocolate sounded homey, not seductive, and she needed to concentrate on this contest, not Joe Northwood's beautiful body.

She followed Joe into the kitchen. No light was on in the kitchen except the fluorescent one over the stove. The lighting was way too intimate, but Darcie couldn't figure a graceful way to suggest flipping on the overhead. "Do you need some help?''

"No, thanks.'' To her surprise, he took down sugar and a can of cocoa powder from the cupboard. Apparently, he planned to make real hot chocolate, the kind that made you think you were swallowing a cupful of heaven. He measured sugar and cocoa into the pan and stirred in a little water. "I take it you don't have a lot of spare cash for car repairs.''

She watched him put together the hot chocolate with an efficiency that showed he was used to doing it that way. "Not if I had any hope of paying for tuition in January. And that's saying we'll win the contest, which isn't a foregone conclusion.'' She pulled off her turban and the wig Geraldine had loaned her and draped both of them over the back of a chair.

"We'll win.'' Joe poured milk into the saucepan. "What's the tuition for?''

"For the past several years I've been paying my way

through school, slow but sure, so I could become an interior decorator.'' She thought he had the sexiest behind she'd seen in ages and she liked the way he moved, like a man comfortable with his body.

"And then Gus came along."

She rested her chin in her hands, unable to take her eyes off him. "That's right. I had one semester to go. And don't tell me I was dumb to get pregnant,'' she added. "I already know that. Bart Butterworth Jr. made all sorts of promises, but in the end he slipped out of every one slick as a whistle.''

Joe stirred the cocoa. "And where is this slimy Butterworth character?''

She appreciated his gallantry. Too bad she hadn't met Joe earlier in her life, but then she wouldn't have her son, and everything she'd been through was worth it because the end result had been Gus.

Sighing, she leaned back in her chair. "When I told Bart Junior we'd be expecting a baby in seven months, he suddenly remembered an important appointment in the Amazon jungle. Called it—let me get this straight now—'a spiritual quest for a true connection with the oneness of the universe.'''

Joe snorted. "Sounds like he'd made one too many connections before he left.''

"He certainly did.''

Joe turned off the burner. "What did you say your last name was?''

"O'Banyon.''

"That's pretty damn Irish,'' he said over his shoulder as he walked to the refrigerator and took out a metal can. "Were you born over there?''

"I was. Came here with my da when I was thirteen. In high school I tried so very hard to change my speech so I'd sound like I'd been born in the United States. But Irish expressions still slip out now and then.''

"The brogue sounds good, Darcie. Don't try to change it.''

"Apparently, I can't.''

He had his back to her, but she could hear two distinct whooshing sounds, and when he turned around with the mugs of hot chocolate, each one wore a cap of whipped cream.

Darcie clapped her hands together. "How perfect!''

Joe's grin was boyish. "I'm glad to have an excuse to do it. Most women I know are too sophisticated to enjoy....'' He paused in confusion. "That didn't come out right. What I mean is, I—''

"Never mind,'' Darcie said. "I'm not sophisticated and I know it. I'm the daughter of a janitor and I clean other people's houses for a living. It's my dream to become an interior decorator, but I won't be putting on airs then, either.''

"I hope not.'' He set the mugs on the table and pulled out a chair for himself. "But if you're so down-to-earth, why did you name your business The French Maid?''

Darcie would have liked to reach for his strong, capable hand and bring it to her lips, kissing the tips of each of those blunt fingers. Instead, she picked up her mug and flicked her tongue over the whipped cream— an acceptable substitute. "Because other people like putting on airs. They would sooner hire The French Maid than Darcie's Dirtbusters.''

Joe watched Darcie lick the whipped cream off the top of the hot chocolate and regretted his impulse to serve it that way. Sitting there in his kitchen in a bathrobe, with her hair tousled from being under the wig, she looked as if she'd gotten up from a lover's bed to revive herself with a cup of hot chocolate so she could go another round. Once again, she was turning him on, and he didn't think she even meant to this time. Obviously, she could manage it by being herself.

He scrambled to remember what they'd been talking about. "How do you know they wouldn't hire Darcie's Dirtbusters?"

"I tried that first. Not a single call. But they called The French Maid." She took a sip of her hot chocolate and gave herself a whipped-cream mustache, which she disposed of with one swipe of her pink tongue. "This makeup Geraldine put on my face itches."

"I don't think you'll need that stuff." He had the urge to scrub it off himself. Or maybe that was just an excuse to touch her. He'd fantasized the French Maid in a bathtub of perfumed water and rose petals, and himself with a soft washcloth. He wouldn't mind giving Darcie a bath even if she wasn't French.

"The Virgin Mary was not a freckle-faced redhead, now was she?"

That's what he missed. Looking at her cinnamon freckles. He longed to get that makeup off her. "No, but Baby Jesus wasn't a carrottop, either."

"We'll wrap him in swaddling clothes." She swirled her tongue in the whipped cream again.

Damn, he was getting an erection. He'd promised this wouldn't be about tulips and pistils. "Exactly what are swaddling clothes?"

She shrugged. "I haven't the slightest idea, but Baby Jesus is always wrapped up tight, so we'll make sure you can't see his hair." She took another drink of her hot chocolate and her lashes fluttered down in obvious enjoyment.

He imagined her eyes closing right before he kissed

her. But, of course, he wouldn't kiss her. That would be asking for trouble.

Putting her mug down, she focused her green eyes on him. "I've been meaning to say this—I don't want him out there in that manger for very long. It's still fairly warm out at night, but I still don't want him getting chilled."

Joe loved the way her red-gold hair curled around her face. He wanted to bury his fingers in that mass of color. "You can decide how long we should have him in there. It's really only important when the judges come by."

"I'm glad to hear that. I brought you a costume," she said. "An old bathrobe of my da's that I never had the heart to give away to charity." A flicker of some potent emotion brightened her eyes. "Considering that you sleep in the nude, I wouldn't expect you to have a proper bathrobe, either."

And there they were, talking about bedroom habits again, and it was all perfectly legitimate, so he couldn't ask her to stop. But that sparkle in her eyes made him think she might be enjoying the topic. She was attracted to him. And he didn't want that. Yes, he did. God, was he confused.

He took a breath. "I don't have a bathrobe, but I would hate to use something that has so much sentimental value for you."

She waved her hand. "It's a ratty old thing. Don't know why I've kept it so long. Besides, we're partners in this. I'm counting on you to build the stable and the manger, so it's up to me to be in charge of costumes."

"That sounds fair. I should be able to get enough lumber from the scrap bin to make most of what we need." If he concentrated on the construction angle of this project, he might be able to forget about running his hands all over her creamy little body.

She eyed him. "From the looks of that five o'clock shadow, you can grow a beard quick-like. I'd advise you to grow one rather than glue one on or dangle it from your ears. Some do that, but it looks like they have a dead rat hanging from their face, in my opinion."

Dead rats. That should cool his fevered libido. But he kept watching her mouth as she talked and wondering how that mouth would feel against his.

"And besides, a stiff wind could come through and blow it into the next county, and there you'd be, chasing your beard."

He choked on his hot chocolate. She probably didn't know what that word meant in crude slang terms. "Can't have that." To cover his amusement, Joe ran a hand over his stubble.

"Right."

He'd never worn a beard, but he didn't relish gluing something to his chin, and Darcie had made the hook-on beard idea sound so stupid he wouldn't be caught dead wearing one. Maybe he'd look good with a beard. Dashing, even.

"So what are you planning to have on under the bathrobe, then?"

"Does it matter?"

"I would say so!" The gleam in her eye became more pronounced. "Bathrobes can come undone, and we wouldn't want you standing there flashing the carolers, now would we?"

He was getting more agitated with every minute they talked about clothes or the lack of them. "I may not wear pajamas to bed, but I won't parade around in the front yard naked under my Joseph costume. I'll wear jeans and a T-shirt."

"No good. Jeans would show at the bottom. It's inconvenient that you sleep buck naked because a nightshirt with a rope around the waist would do nicely, if you had one." She tapped her finger against her lower lip.

He wished to hell she wouldn't do that. Her lower lip was one of the most seductive things about her. Full and pink, with a little crease in the middle that he couldn't stop looking at, especially with all this talk about being naked. "Well, what *are* you wearing under *that* bathrobe?" The minute the words were out of his mouth, he knew he shouldn't have asked.

She stood immediately, whipped open the robe and showed him. "It's a nightgown."

He could see that. He also could see how the delicate white fabric draped across her breasts and tucked in at her waist before falling in soft folds to her feet. Furthermore, he could see how the style dipped just enough to reveal her generous cleavage, full and inviting. And finally, he could see how this nightgown she'd be wearing under her bathrobe would drive him insane if he thought about it much more.

So he thought about the dark makeup she had caked on her face, which he definitely hated.

"You don't like it?"

He took another deep breath. "It'll do, I guess."

"It's a little flimsy."

Flimsy might be his favorite type of nightgown now that he'd seen this one on her. "Yeah, it is."

"I don't expect anyone to see it. But in case a strong wind comes through, I'll—"

"That would be the beard-blowing kind of wind."

"Exactly." She retied her robe to his great relief.

Now he'd just have to forget that she had it on under there, he thought. "Then instead of jeans, I'll wear shorts and a T-shirt."

"No, you can't do that, either. The T-shirt neck will show above the bathrobe and you'll look like some fellow in the old folks' home sitting around in the common room in his underwear and robe." She snapped her fingers. "I have a sleep shirt that's *very* big on me. You could wear that."

"No, Darcie, I could not wear that. Your father's bathrobe is one thing. A woman's sleep shirt is something else."

"Don't be stubborn. It would be perfect. It has a scoop neck and will come almost to your knees. We'll turn it around backward so the writing doesn't show."

"What writing?"

"Um, does it really matter? It will be backward."

He was losing patience. Or maybe sexual frustration was making him cranky. "Darcie, what writing?"

"'God created Adam to see if Eve could take a joke.'"

Joe crossed his arms. "I'm not wearing it. I refuse to be a traitor to my own gender."

"I bought it right after Bart Junior left for the Amazon, and my opinion of men was not the best. I found it in the large women's section, which is why it's so big. I bought it for the saying, but I don't wear it anymore." Her green gaze pleaded with him. "It would really be perfect for your Joseph costume and it goes with one of the stripes in the bathrobe. The color's bad for me but perfect for you."

He had to ask. "What color is that?"

"Peach."

"*Peach?* You want me to wear a woman's nightshirt with a women's-lib slogan on it, in *peach?* Just how far do you expect me to go?"

She lifted her round, little chin. "Far enough to win."

"I don't see why what I wear under my bathrobe will make such a big difference."

She leaned forward, her expression earnest. "You never know about those details, Joe. One thing I've learned in my classes is that small things make or break a decorating scheme. One wrong note, and the whole shebang falls apart. I'm worried about Gus's teeth. Baby Jesus shouldn't have four shiny new teeth."

He leaned forward, also for emphasis, of course. He had a feeling she was capable of taking this project to extremes. Besides, she smelled like wildflowers. "You're not going to blacken little Gus's teeth?"

Her eyes widened. "Goodness no! I wouldn't do that to my baby. But I'm thinking that everything else must be perfect to take attention away from those four teeth."

This close, he could see the blend of colors that made up the interesting shade of her eyes. He loved looking into them. "I'll hang a big lighted star over the stable." Her eyes looked like stars. The closer he got, the more they glowed. "That'll take attention away from his teeth."

"It's a good idea." She leaned a little closer herself. "And an angel. Could you make an angel with a trumpet and hang it over the stable, too? Then they really won't notice Gus's teeth."

"An angel. Sure. A revolving angel." He had no idea how he'd make an angel, let alone a revolving one, but he'd figure it out. Right now, with her looking at him like that, he had the feeling he could do anything. "We'll hang all kinds of things over the stable. They'll all re-volve.''

Her voice grew softer, her breathing shallow. ''And you'll wear the nightshirt?''

For one kiss from those rosy lips, he'd wear sequins and feathers. ''Sure.'' He leaned close enough to feel her warm breath on his face. ''Nobody will notice Gus's teeth, I promise.''

She sighed. ''I hope not.''

A kiss would be harmless, his fevered brain whispered. A friendly kiss to seal the bargain. Gripping the edge of the table so he'd remember to keep his hands to himself, he slowly leaned close enough to brush his lips against hers. She didn't pull back. Yeah, he could handle this.

Closing his eyes, he made contact again, keeping the pressure light. So sweet. Her lips were plump and moist, drawing him back a third time, and a fourth. But he was still in control. Maybe his pulse rate was up a little, but he was okay. He was cool. And she tasted so good.

Daring more, he ran the tip of his tongue along the delicate crease in her lower lip, the spot that had been driving him crazy ever since he first noticed it. That felt so wonderful that he outlined the entire curve of her lips, top and bottom. Surely it wouldn't be too dangerous to explore the sweetness inside. He dipped his tongue in slowly. At the gentle penetration, she moaned.

And he lost it.

Suddenly, his fingers were buried in her soft hair and his tongue was deep in her mouth.

''Ma-ma!''

Gus's wail severed the connection as they leaped apart.

Joe gazed at her, his breath coming in gasps. Her eyes were downcast, her color high. ''Darcie, I'm sorry. God, I didn't mean—''

"It's my fault, too." She stood, not looking at him, and her voice quivered as her brogue became more pronounced. "But you have a lovely mouth on you, Joe Northwood, and you tempted me."

"Ma-ma!" Gus called again.

"I'll be right with you, my wee elf!" She put her hand to her chest and took a deep breath.

Joe gazed at her, all flushed and ready for more kissing. "You have a lovely mouth on you, too, Darcie O'Banyon."

"But we shouldn't be pressing those lovely mouths together anymore, all things considered," she said.

"No, probably not."

She glanced up at him, her eyes still sparkling in the afterglow of his kiss. "It's obvious that we're attracted to each other, but I have to be practical about such things, now that I have a baby."

"I understand. And I apologize for kissing you."

"We were both involved in it, so don't heap ashes on your head. But from this moment on, I'll keep my mouth to myself if you'll promise to do the same."

He'd never had to make a promise that felt so wrong. He wanted to have another meeting of their mouths right this minute. He wanted more than that. But that was selfish of him. She needed to save her mouth, and the rest of her tempting body, for a guy who would agree to walk her down the aisle. "It's a deal," he said.

7

GUS SEEMED WIDE AWAKE, and considering that he'd saved her from total disaster, Darcie decided she'd be wise to keep him on her lap until Joe worked his magic on her car's innards. With her arms full of her baby she wouldn't have room for an armful of Joe.

She flipped on a light in the living room and settled into an easy chair with Gus on her lap. From her experience, taking a car from dead as a doornail to alive and kicking took some time. Which was a good thing because she needed time to compose herself after that whale of a kiss. The man certainly packed a wallop.

Curiosity had tripped her up, as it had many times in the past. Curiosity and a weakness, only recently discovered, for the charms of the opposite sex. Once she'd known that he meant to kiss her, she'd had to find out what that lovely mouth would feel like. Now she knew. It felt delicious.

Geraldine had warned her about this very thing, had told her to take charge of matters and not allow Joe to get the bit between his teeth. Darcie was very much afraid that at the end of that kiss Joe had taken the bit firmly between his teeth. And she'd been more than ready to go for a gallop.

"I'm glad you woke up," she murmured to her baby. *From the looks of this, I'll be so busy keeping an eye on the pair of you I won't have time to bless myself.*

Nestled in her arms, Gus stared up at her, fighting sleep. But even if he went back to sleep, she was determined not to lay him back in the playpen. She'd hold on to him like a shield until she could put him in the car seat and drive them both to the safety of their apartment.

Now that she and Joe each had their assignments straight, they wouldn't need these late-night meetings. Being in this house at night with Joe was entirely too cozy, and neither of them could be blamed for what had happened. It wouldn't happen again.

Much calmed by that thought, she started singing Gus an Irish lullaby, one her da had sung to her when she was a little girl. He'd been mother and father to her for as long as she could remember, and she missed him terribly. But whenever she used one of his favorite expressions or sang one of the songs he'd been so fond of, then he seemed, for a moment, to be close at hand.

She leaned over Gus as she sang softly about her homeland, of green fields and frolicking lambs, a tiny cottage and a warm fire. Then something made her glance up, and she saw Joe leaning in the living-room doorway, gazing at her. The tender look on his face made her heart pound like the heart of a rabbit caught in a snare.

He didn't want a woman with a baby, she reminded herself. No matter that he was looking at her like that. Probably hormones put that expression in his eyes.

"Is my engine running?" she asked.

He smiled and started to say something. Then he stopped himself and looked away, and when he glanced back at her, the smile was gone. "It's so damn easy to flirt with you, Darcie."

Watch yourself, blarney breath. I'm on the job.

Darcie wondered if curiosity would be her undoing. "You were planning to flirt with me just now?"

"I started to, but I stopped myself. Flirting leads to kissing, and kissing leads to—"

"I know exactly where kissing leads." Her cheeks warmed. "To Gus."

"Not necessarily." He paused. "Or maybe it does, in your case. Maybe you don't believe in birth control."

"I most certainly do! Someone else didn't want to wear an overcoat on his bobber. He said we were getting married, and like a fool, I believed him."

Joe muttered something that sounded like a very strong curse word.

"But I'm not sorry for how things turned out," she said. "Not for one minute. My biological clock was ticking, which is why I allowed myself to believe Bart Junior meant for us to get married. I didn't want to miss the boat and suddenly be too old to have children."

"And how ancient would that make you now? Twenty-five?"

She was pleased that he'd underestimated her age. "Thirty my next birthday."

Joe shook his head. "Not possible. They must have fouled up your birth certificate back in Ireland. You're so young-looking, so fresh-skinned, so..." His voice trailed off as he gazed at her.

The intensity in his eyes made her squirm a little, and the longer he looked at her the more she remembered the imprint of his mouth on hers. She laughed to cut the tension. "Don't feel obligated to stop. I'm enjoying this."

Stop or I start spitting up graham crackers.

"I think I'd better watch myself. In fact, we'd both

better watch ourselves very carefully from now on, with
what we say, what we do, what we wear.''

"Why?"

"I've gone over and over this problem, and I only
have one solution. I can't get your car to run. It'll take
lots of money to do that. You won't have that kind of
money until we win the contest, so for the next three
weeks we're down to one vehicle.''

She smiled nervously. "You sound as if we're old
married people with that kind of talk.''

"Worse than that. We're going to have to live together.''

Gus threw up all over Darcie's lap.

"THAT MAN IS UP to something," Geraldine said.

"I've turned it over in my mind a million times and I
can't think of a different solution, either," Darcie said.
She'd stopped at Geraldine's after finishing her cleaning.
"I can't afford to rent a car, and there's no way I can
haul Gus and my cleaning supplies around on a bus.''

Fresh from a nap, Gus cruised around Geraldine's coffee table, which she'd cleared off in preparation for the
baby's visit. Geraldine had given him a short, curly
brown wig to wear the minute he came in the door, so
he looked like one of the Three Stooges. Geraldine got
such a kick out of dressing him in her wigs that Darcie
didn't have the heart to stop her. Besides, Gus was turning into a regular little ham, seeming to love the limelight.

"I could advance you the money to rent a car," Geraldine said. "Or just give you the money. I intend to get
lots of it when the divorce is final, and I can spare some
now.''

"Thank you, but no." Darcie laid a hand over Geraldine's and squeezed. "You're very kind to offer, but I couldn't take it. At least Joe has a stake in my transportation needs."

"So do I. That runaround I married also cheated me out of having kids, which I didn't realize I craved so desperately until you walked in the door last night with Gus. I've decided to watch over you like, well…like your mother would have done if she could be here."

Darcie's eyes filled unexpectedly. "You…you will?"

"Unless the idea fills you with horror."

"Absolutely not!" Darcie threw her arms around Geraldine and gave her a big hug. Geraldine's blond wig nearly smothered her, but she didn't care.

Geraldine hugged her back. "So, will you take the money for the car?"

"No." Darcie drew back with a watery smile. "Just having you in my corner is more than enough."

Geraldine shook her head. "Okay, but I don't like the looks of this arrangement. It's trouble—you in such close proximity to a man who looks like Joe and has announced he'll have nothing to do with a ready-made family."

"But it makes sense for the contest since Gus and I will need to be over there a lot anyway. And he can easily loan me his truck because we're really not that far from Home World. He can walk it in no time."

"Just don't go feeling obligated for the loan of that truck." Geraldine had on eyebrows today, carefully drawn above her gray eyes. She also wore the blond wig Gus had pulled off her the night before, and a bright red jumpsuit to match her fingernails. "He needs you in order to create this live Nativity scene. I just wish I could be sure he's not setting you up for a live bedroom scene at the same time."

"After what happened last night, we each promised to keep our mouths to ourselves."

Geraldine's penciled brows shot up. "What did that weasel do to you last night?"

"It wasn't all him. We kissed each other." The memory still made her weak in the knees and moist in other significant parts of her body.

"Darcie O'Banyon, wipe that gaga look off your face this instant! Please don't tell me you looked at *him* that way after it happened."

"It's possible." She was pretty sure she had, come to think of it.

Geraldine groaned. Then she turned to Gus, who had worked his way around to her knee. "Gus, look at me."

Gus stared up at her through the brown bangs of the wig. *Here's lookin' at you, kid.*

"Okay, Gus, this is a critical situation. Do you understand what I'm saying?"

Gus crowed and flexed his knees. *Critical as they come, and I'm not just spitting shamrocks.*

"It's up to you to chaperon these two, Gus," Geraldine said, her tone completely serious. "And you don't have a lot of strategies open to you. But you have one that's sure to work with the likes of Joe Northwood."

I'm way ahead of you, lass.

Darcie smiled. "Gus called out to me last night, almost as if he wanted to break us up. And it worked."

"Excellent. But, Gus, you may need to pull out all the stops to protect your mommy from the big bad wolf. If Joe Northwood steps out of line, I want you to let him have it with both barrels. Poop in your diaper. And I'm not talking one of your average, ordinary loads, Gus. I want you to give it all you've got. I've yet to see the man who can face that and maintain his…enthusiasm. Do you understand, Gus?"

Gus held on to the table with one hand and babbled his nonsense syllables while he patted Geraldine's knee with his free hand. *'Tis the Duke of Doo-doo you're addressing. I can handle this.*

Darcie couldn't help laughing. "You needn't worry so, Geraldine. Joe is as frightened of me and Gus as I am of him."

"Uh-huh. He's petrified. That's why he's moved you in within twenty-four hours of laying eyes on you."

"It's all connected with the contest."

"I wish I could believe that, but I think there's more than this ridiculous contest on that man's mind. He'll make a move on you." She took a swig of her drink, which was definitely *not* ginger ale. "And I'll be there when he does."

EVENTUALLY, DARCIE PRIED Gus loose from the brown wig and continued on her way over to Joe's house with a sense of anticipation. Ever since Joe had suggested that she move in until the contest was over, she'd had a bubble of excitement growing inside her that had nothing to do with the money they might win.

She'd never admit such a thing to Geraldine because Geraldine would lecture her about maintaining her defenses so that she wouldn't end up with a broken heart. Darcie didn't want a broken heart any more than the next woman, but she'd spent the past eighteen months living like a blessed nun. Besides that, cleaning for others and taking care of a baby the rest of the time left her feeling like a sexless drone. There were days she wondered if she'd ever be interesting to any man again.

But from the evidence of that French kiss Joe had

given her, she wouldn't be overstating the case to say that he was in lust. Basking for three solid weeks in his presence while holding him off, of course, would put the bloom back in her cheeks. Already she felt her sexual self-confidence returning.

As she operated the garage-door opener and parked the truck inside, she spoke to Gus, who was belted into his car seat next to her. "I've decided how we should look at this turn of events, Gus. We're going to pretend we're on vacation."

Gus chortled as he waved his hands and wiggled, ready to be out of his seat. *You may be on vacation, lass, but I'm on a mission.*

Darcie got out of the truck and went around to fetch Gus. "You've never had a vacation, have you? Come to think of it, I've had few to none myself." She lifted him into her arms. "Don't misunderstand me. We'll have to work like always, but we'll be living like the lord and lady of a castle. Wait until you see the tub. Not a chip in sight. And the towels! You'll think you've died and gone to heaven when I wrap you in one of those thick towels. Like a lamb's pelt. I can hardly wait to try out the tub myself."

"Ma-ma." Gus grabbed her around the neck, got a fistful of hair and pulled. *You'll not be taking tub baths on my watch. Not with that bounder roaming the halls.*

"You're going to pluck me bald, you little leprechaun." She disentangled his fingers from her hair and carried him toward the door leading into the kitchen. She'd left her hair loose instead of pulling it back in a clip, and the reason, the one she blushed to admit, was Joe. When he'd buried his fingers in her hair as he'd kissed her, she'd suspected he liked doing that. So she'd washed and brushed her hair with special attention this morning.

"Are you ready, Gus? As your grandpa used to say, we'll be knee-deep in shamrocks and ass-high in daffodils for the next three weeks." She opened the door and almost dropped Gus.

Staring at her through the kitchen window was…she blinked and looked again…a cow.

Gus bounced in her arms and pointed, drooling and spitting bubbles in his excitement. *Reinforcements! Cow chips!*

"I must be imagining things," Darcie muttered. But the cow was there after she blinked several more times.

Gus became more excited by the minute. "Da-da!" he crowed.

"No, sweetheart. Your da was a pig, not a cow." Darcie stared at the cow, a handsome golden beast with a white blaze down its nose. It stared right back, its jaws working.

"We need to do something about this cow, Gus." Darcie aimed a stern look at the animal. "Do not slobber on my clean window, Bossy." With one last glance at the cow, she carried a wiggling Gus into the living room and put him in the playpen she and Joe had left set up from the night before.

Gus didn't like that one bit. He hung on the side and fretted. *Bossy and I have business to discuss, we do.*

"Sorry, baby boy." She handed him one of his squeaky toys, which he stuck in his mouth. "You stay there while I call someone about this cow. Maybe Joe left a gate open and it wandered in, though I can't imagine where it came from. Dairy cows are against the deed restrictions in Tannenbaum, I expect. I'd better call 9-1-1. And report a stray cow."

She walked into the kitchen, then reached for the phone just as it rang. Although she'd never answered the phone in this house, she decided to answer it now. She'd notified her clients that she could be reached at this number for the next three weeks. She was living here now after all.

She plucked the cordless receiver from its cradle. "Hello?"

"Darcie!" Joe said. "I'm so glad you're there."

"I'm very glad, too. You see, there's a—"

"I know. A calf in the backyard. I wonder if you—"

"It's not a calf. It's a full-grown cow!"

"Now, Darcie, it might look big to you, but it's just a calf. I figured we could smuggle it in, get it used to us and then make it part of the manger scene the night the judges come by. You know, to take attention away from Gus's teeth. I'm considering a burro, too, if I can locate a small one."

Darcie walked over to the window and gazed out at the cow. "It's the first calf I've seen with an udder. Looks like she's ready to be milked."

"An udder?" Joe laughed indulgently. "Darcie, are you sure you're not confusing an udder with some other dangling parts? Maybe this is a well-hung little boy calf."

Darcie rolled her eyes. As if she hadn't milked cows many a time as a girl in County Kerry. As if she hadn't helped castrate her share of rams from her uncle's flock of sheep. As if she couldn't tell the difference between an udder and those other parts, the ones male animals were so all-fired proud of. "Let me describe the dangling part to you, Joe. About the size of a basketball, with four little knobs hanging from it. Does that sound like your average testicle?"

"Oh, my God, it is a cow."

The cow chose that moment to make herself heard. She stuck her nose right up to the window and bellowed.

"Oh, my God," Joe said again. "I'll try to get hold of Bill. There's been a mistake."

The cow let out another loud moo.

"Damn," Joe said. "Darcie, can you keep her quiet until I can get home? If I can get somebody to cover the last hour of my shift, I can be there in ten minutes if I jog. We have to take care of this."

"I'll do what I can, but—"

"I'll be there as quick as I can. Don't let the neighbors see her. Or hear her."

The doorbell chimed.

"That would be the neighbors, I expect," Darcie said, "asking about the cow we seem to have in the backyard. What would you have me tell them, Joe?"

"I don't know, but we don't want them to get wind of our Nativity scene idea. Aren't the Irish supposed to be good storytellers? Maybe you could make something up." The line clicked.

"Make something up, the man says," Darcie muttered. "As if it would be duck soup to explain a cow in the backyard." She scooped up Gus on her way through the living room. After peering through the peephole in the door, she opened it. "Hello, Mrs. Elderhorn, Mr. Elderhorn. I suppose you've come about the cow in the backyard."

8

JOE DIDN'T JOG. HE RAN. He had no luck getting in touch with Bill, the Home World customer who had a small farm on the outskirts of town and had offered to rent Joe a calf for a few weeks. At least that's what Joe had thought he was renting. Bill was getting on in years and he might need his hearing aid adjusted.

Sprinting up the sidewalk to the front door, Joe stopped to catch his breath before he walked in. A block patio wall kept the cow invisible from the street, and she wasn't making cow sounds at the moment. He wondered if Darcie still had one of the neighbors inside and if she'd been able to pacify them without giving away his idea of a live manger scene.

Good thing Darcie had been there. In the back of his mind, he registered a tingle of excitement knowing that, beginning now, she would be there every night when he came home.

Running his fingers through his sweat-dampened hair, he walked in the front door. No one was in the living room—even Gus's playpen was empty. Joe heard voices coming from the kitchen and headed there.

Darcie sat at the kitchen table with Madge and Herman Elderhorn, and in what Joe considered a stroke of genius, she'd served everyone a foaming mug of beer. Or maybe two. There were enough dead soldiers on the drain board that somebody was on his or her third round. She'd even found the mugs he kept chilled in the freezer. Gus sat in his high chair holding a cup with a spout on it. Joe assumed Gus was drinking juice and not swilling beer like the rest of the crowd.

Darcie glanced up and smiled as he came in. Just like that, she could make him feel like a king. Then he realized that she'd had more than one story to make up for Madge and Herman. Not only did she need to explain the cow that was sure enough staring in the kitchen window at all of them, but she'd had to come up with a reason why she was moving in.

He figured he'd better let her lead. He tipped his head in greeting. "Afternoon, folks. That beer looks good."

"We helped ourselves to your Guinness," Darcie said, "while I explained to Mr. and Mrs. Elderhorn about your Save the Animals Millennium Project."

Joe blinked. "Uh, right. Animals are people, too."

Madge Elderhorn looked at him with such mellowness that it was a safe bet that she'd been the one who polished off two beers and was on her third. "I had no idea you were so highly placed in the SPCA, Mr. Northwood," she said. "I'm a friend to animals myself."

"Call me Joe." He poured himself a beer, pulled up a chair and glanced at Darcie. "All my animal friends do."

Mrs. Elderhorn simpered. "Only if you'll call me Madge."

"It'd be a pleasure, Madge." He'd never been much for simpering, and on Madge, who bore a strong resemblance to the animal peering in the kitchen window, it was enough to make a guy's stomach queasy, but he managed a smile. If Darcie could sling it around, so could he.

"I've been telling Mr. and Mrs. Elderhorn about the Hollywood celebrities supporting your cause."

This promised to be a humdinger. Joe wondered if he should have given Darcie her head. But he hadn't had much choice. "Well, yeah. Mel and Cher gave me the old thumbs-up. And Oprah, of course."

Madge gasped. "You've spoken personally with Oprah Winfrey?"

"His people have spoken with her people," Darcie said quickly. "That's how these things work."

"Oh, why yes, that makes sense." Madge nodded wisely and took another long swig of her beer.

"Quite a practical joke one of them pulled," Herman said, "delivering a cow to your door."

Joe gazed at Darcie in admiration. "You know these Hollywood people. Can't resist doing something outrageous."

"We can't figure out if it was Robin Williams or Eddie Murphy," Darcie said, "but the cow came with a sign around her neck that said Milk Cows Are Udderly Oppressed. Robin and Eddie are both huge supporters of Joe's campaign. Huge. But naturally, they like to make their point with comedy."

Madge's gaze was worshipful. "Imagine having a Hollywood insider right here in the neighborhood. Do you...think any of your friends will...drop by?"

Joe took a sip of his beer. "Hard to say. Shooting schedules are tight. These are big stars, and they're in demand."

Herman leaned forward. "How come we haven't seen anything about this on TV? You'd think *20/20* would have done something."

"All the media is set to break on New Year's Day,"

Darcie said. "More impact. A big event's in production during halftime of the Super Bowl."

Joe managed an indulgent laugh. "You mean the *Rose Bowl*, Darcie. That's the one played on New Year's Day. The Super Bowl comes later in January." He turned to Madge and Herman. "Her heart's in the right place, but she doesn't know a tight end from a tightrope."

Darcie sent him a challenging look. "Seems to me they all have tight ends nowadays, so who could tell? And they're proud to show them off, too, in those shiny pants that look painted on."

Madge rolled her eyes. "Oh, I know what you *mean*, Darcie. I never used to care about football, but lately, with the way those satin knickers fit, when they get into that three-point stance…oo-la-la. I started taking my binoculars to the Cardinals' games."

Herman stared at his wife in total amazement. "That's why you take your binoculars, sugar lump? To ogle their fannies?"

Madge drained the last of her beer and set the mug down with the exaggerated care of a person who is slightly in the bag and doesn't want anyone to know it. "I take notice, Herman. That's all I'm saying. I mean, they're right *there*."

"But, sugar cakes, you said you wanted to take your binoculars to the game so you could see the plays. I had no idea you were interested in fannies."

"There are many things you have no idea about, Herman." She rose ponderously to her feet. "We have to be going now."

"But love button, if I'd known all along that you were interested in—"

"Time to go now," Madge said, raising her voice a notch. "I left something on the stove." She gripped her husband purposefully by the shoulder, stopping short of hauling him to his feet, but her grip was firm enough that it could easily be her next tactic.

Herman sighed in resignation and stood. "Yes, honey lamb."

Joe made sure he didn't look at Darcie for fear they might both start laughing and lose all the ground they'd gained. "Thanks for dropping by," he said. "And I'll do something about the cow. A joke's a joke, but I realize we can't have a full-grown cow in Tannenbaum."

"If any of your friends come to town, I'd be happy to have them over for a glass of eggnog and some fruitcake," Madge said as she shoved her husband toward the living room.

"That's hospitable of you, Madge." Joe followed the Elderhorns to the door, and Darcie picked Gus out of the high chair and came along, too, probably to protect any places that might come unraveled in her outrageous story.

Before Madge went out the door, she turned back, her gaze shrewd. "I can't imagine how you'll have time to put together an animal rights campaign and still build a holiday display, though."

"That's where I come in," Darcie said. "Joe plans to win the prize so he can donate that to the campaign, as well, and I've agreed to help out by being his hostess and providing assistance in any way I can."

Madge lifted her eyebrows. "I hope he's paying you well for that assistance. See you both later."

Joe closed the door after the Elderhorns and turned to Darcie with a grin. "Incredible. I have no idea how you're planning to keep that story alive, but I'm blown away by your imagination."

"I'm counting on Geraldine to help me," Darcie said.

"She offered to do anything I needed done. And I already know she loves to play dress-up. We can make it look like all sorts of people are coming and going from this house."

"Sounds like an *I Love Lucy* episode." He wasn't sure he liked the idea of Geraldine coming and going all the time. The woman didn't seem to care for him and apparently considered him a threat to Darcie's happiness, which he wouldn't be. In fact, he was trying to help her win twenty-five hundred bucks. That shouldn't make him the villain.

"I think Geraldine will enjoy it," Darcie said.

"A Save the Animals Millennium Project. How did you come up with that?"

Gus bounced in Darcie's arms. *Do you even have to ask?*

"Maybe it's being around this leprechaun all day."

Gets all her best material from me, she does. Gus began to wiggle impatiently in Darcie's arms. *And don't be making cow eyes at her, laddie, unless you fancy having me pinch your shamrocks next time I'm in the neighborhood.*

Darcie glanced at Joe. "He needs a change and some dinner. I'd best get his diaper bag from the truck and take care of him before I unload our belongings."

Joe heard the tired note in her voice and realized she must be exhausted after cleaning houses all day, loading up her stuff and then having to deal with a cow and the crazy Elderhorns.

"I'll bring in the diaper bag," he said. "Then you can take care of Gus while I try to get Bill on the phone again. Then I'll unload everything from the truck and start some dinner for us."

She blinked. In the whole long list of activities he'd

listed, the last one truly captured her attention. She hadn't
considered how they were going to manage the food
question. "You cook?"

He smiled. "I do." He winked at her and headed out
toward the garage.

Darcie gulped and fanned herself with her hand. "Oh,
Gus, that's quite a smile and wink the man has!"

*Oh, he's a darlin', he is. Wouldn't trust that lad fur-
ther than I could toss a keg of Guinness.*

"And did you see how he looked when he first came
in, sort of tousled and sweaty-like? My heart almost
stopped beating."

*Never did take kindly to a winking man. Now let me
get the lay of the land here.* Gus wiggled to get down.

"Not yet, Gus." She glanced around the living room
and noticed all the hazards there—lamp cords, decorative
glass, potted plants, even the stairs leading to the second
floor. She wondered if Joe realized how different the
house would have to look in order to childproof it and
if that would bother him. "We have to work out some
things before I can put you down to roam, baby boy."

"Here's the diaper bag," Joe said, bringing it in.
"Want me to take it upstairs for you?"

"That would be great. Which bedroom did you want
us to use?"

He hesitated a fraction of a second.

In that short space of time, Darcie suddenly realized
how very close they were going to be to each other and
how deliciously tempting it would be for both of them.
From the look in Joe's eyes, so did he.

He cleared his throat. "Since there are three bedrooms,
would you like to set Gus up in the smallest and you
take the other guest room?"

Darcie's first thought had been to share with Gus so

as not to take up too much room, but in her apartment she'd given Gus the bedroom and she'd set up her bed in the living area. Gus had taken to rocking himself to sleep if he awoke in the middle of the night, and he rattled his crib something fierce. In desperate need of rest, she'd given up the bedroom to Gus. Still, having the baby in her room here would be some protection from temptation.

Ah, but to have her very own room again for a change, that would be heaven. And she'd decided to consider herself on vacation. "That sounds fine to me," she said.

Should have stashed us in the same room, lass. Here comes a peck of trouble, sure as my name's Angus Sean O'Banyon.

"Good." Joe gestured toward the stairs. "After you."

Hoisting Gus to her shoulder, Darcie climbed to the second floor ahead of Joe. She'd never been more aware of a man following her. Perhaps he wasn't looking at her bottom, but she suspected he was.

Quite the gentleman, aren't we? After you, he says. Got my eye on you, though. Don't trip over your tongue going up the stairs now.

Darcie reached the top of the stairs out of breath, although she climbed stairs so many times in the course of a day that she could hardly be winded. It was the idea of having Joe follow her up that was stealing her breath.

She turned into the small bedroom to her left. Her bedroom would be one door down, straight across from the master bedroom. Fortunately, it was a very wide hallway.

"Here you go." Joe set the diaper bag on the floor next to the first twin bed. "Did you bring his crib?"

"I did." She put Gus on the bed and he promptly started crawling toward the edge of it. She grabbed him with one arm around his middle and reached for the diaper bag.

All the while she was aware of Joe standing there in the small bedroom, watching her. The light outside the window was fading and soon it would be dark. She and Joe would sleep under the same roof tonight with only a small baby as chaperon. "I had to take the crib apart, so it has to be reassembled."

"You look like you could use some help." Joe approached the bed. "What can I do for you?"

Stop drooling over her and set up the crib, Romeo.

Keeping a firm grip on Gus, Darcie glanced at Joe.

He met her gaze and his eyes grew warm and dark. His eyes had taken on that look the night before, just as he'd kissed her.

She swallowed. "Don't ask me what you can do for me. You might not like the answer."

His voice was husky. "Or maybe I'd like it too much."

Faith, I'd like to cut my next tooth on you, Joseph Northwood.

"Either way, we'd both be heading for trouble, Joe," Darcie said gently. "You'd better go downstairs. I'll handle Gus."

"Right." With one last glance at her, he left the room.

Not long afterward, he was back, moving a small dresser to make room for Gus's crib in a corner. "I decided to do this before I called Bill so that you could feel sort of moved in and settled."

"Thank you." Darcie had decided to change Gus on the floor, and she glanced up from her work for a moment to see if Joe had the idea of what to do. Apparently, he did. "You look as if you've done that a time or two," she said.

"A time or two. And I've always been handy when it comes to how things fit together."

By St. Paddy's beard, this one never lets up.

Darcie figured she was demented. Joe's statement was a simple explanation of his skills, not a boast about his ability in bed. He was talking about assembly of furniture, not the meshing of body parts.

And yet from this angle, as she admired the fit of his jeans, that was all she could think about. Apparently, she'd been too long without sex—that would explain her preoccupation.

"There we go." Joe gave the crib an experimental shake. "Now I'll go get his mattress and your suitcases." And he was off, bounding down the stairs like a mountain goat.

Such energy, Darcie thought as she snapped Gus into his overalls. Even Gus seemed interested in Joe's burst of activity. A fine specimen, that Joe. If he put that much energy into making love, the result could be electrifying. And there she was again, focusing on the very thing she needed to put out of her mind.

By the time she'd dressed Gus, Joe had carried all their belongings up to the second floor and had contacted Bill to arrange for him to come over and pick up the cow. Then he headed downstairs to start dinner.

Darcie decided now was the best time to make up Gus's bed so that she could pop him into it when he grew sleepy. Scooping him up in her arms, she walked into her room to unpack his crib sheet and blanket from one of her suitcases.

In the doorway she paused with a little gasp of surprise. On the bedside table sat a vase of red tulips.

JOE BROWNED THE CHICKEN and worried about the tulips. He'd been a half hour late punching in this morning because he'd jogged over to the florist, bought the tulips and put them in her room before leaving for work.

There was also a bottle of wine chilling in the refrigerator, to sip with dinner. The wine was okay, he thought. Lots of people drank wine with dinner.

At the time he'd bought them, the flowers had seemed like a great idea, too, sort of an inside joke and a cute way to welcome her to the project. But now he wasn't so sure he should have done it.

When she came into the kitchen with Gus on one hip, her color was high. "You bought tulips and put them in my room. Why?"

"I thought…" He paused and glanced at her while the chicken spit and crackled in the pan. "I thought you'd laugh, I guess. That you'd like having someone bring you flowers and put them in your room for a change. Hell, it was probably a mistake."

Her green eyes grew misty. "No, it wasn't a mistake. They're beautiful, and I love the thought that you took the trouble to put them there, but I have to know your intentions, Joe. Geraldine said you were up to something, moving me in like this. Are you?"

He gazed at her standing there holding Gus, who was eyeing him very suspiciously. Because of that baby, she deserved the most honest response he could give her. "This situation has messed with my head, Darcie. We started our whole relationship with fantasies about making love to each other."

She gulped. "I guess we did."

"I've tried, but I haven't been able to erase those fantasies even though you're not French, not anything the way I pictured you, in fact. But you're still very…desirable." Even now he found himself enjoying the sweet rise and fall of her breasts, wanting to touch her, wanting to kiss her again.

"Thank you."

"I'm not trying to flatter you. I'd be better off if you were a dog, to be honest. Then there'd be no distractions. We could work on this contest, win the damn thing, and I'd have the money to go partners with my cousin Derek in a cabinet shop in Denver. I really want to do that, Darcie."

"I understand. But then why did you bring me tulips, Joe?"

"Because...." He hadn't brought them to lure her into bed. Once they were in bed together, he'd be caught, and he didn't want that. So what was his lamebrained excuse for those damned tulips? "I guess I wanted to make you smile," he said at last.

Bless me, the man came up with the right answer.

Tears gathered in Darcie's eyes. "My da used to say that when he'd bring me a little present."

Joe's heart ached for what he couldn't offer this woman. Someone needed to love and cherish her. Someone needed to give her all the warmth and security she deserved. But he wasn't that someone. All he could provide were tulips and some spare cash, and that didn't seem like very much right now. "You're not smiling, though. You look like you're ready to cry."

"No, I'm not." She sniffed and wiped at her eyes with her free hand. "Thank you for the tulips, Joe."

"You're welcome."

"Now you'd better tend your chicken. It's burning."

JOE MANAGED TO SALVAGE most of the chicken, but between the cow mooing at the kitchen window and Gus demanding attention, the meal was so frantic it didn't much matter what they ate. Joe didn't even bother to take the bottle of wine out of the refrigerator. He couldn't imagine what he'd been thinking. Didn't matter if you had one baby or three—people with babies didn't have time to sip wine during a meal.

After dinner, Darcie took Gus upstairs for his bath and Joe drove to Home World to scrounge up some scrap lumber. The errand made him feel like a typical husband, and he resented that feeling. Or so he tried to tell himself. As long as he was in the store he decided to buy baby gates for the top and bottom of the stairs. Fooling with the damned gates was going to be a pain in the rear and he hated having to bother. Or so he tried to tell himself.

But as he pulled into the driveway and saw lights on in the upstairs bedroom where Darcie was putting Gus to bed, something warm and sweet stirred in his heart. She was doing her part for the little guy, and by installing gates to protect him from falling down the stairs, Joe was doing his part.

He blamed this sudden softheadedness on the sentimentality of the season. Everywhere he went he was confronted with pictures and songs about babies in mangers and idealistic scenes of little kids dancing around a

Christmas tree. In reality, he knew what a disaster you could create with kids dancing around a Christmas tree. The triplets had demolished at least two trees he could think of, maybe more.

The upstairs light winked out. Gus must be going to sleep, which was a good thing. He was glad the baby was out of his hair for a while. Sure he was. That little stab of disappointment, as if he'd missed something by not seeing him before he went to bed, was another example of the effects of Christmas.

After unloading the wood in the garage, he hauled the gates into the kitchen. On the way in, he reminded himself to leave Darcie strictly alone. He shouldn't tempt her to do something that wasn't in either of their best interests. She wouldn't even be here now if she didn't need the money. He wouldn't have invited her to stay if he didn't need the money. They both needed to concentrate on the money.

He carried the baby gates into the living room and found her there laying out a faded bathrobe and a peach nightshirt on the sofa. The nightshirt was facedown, as if she hoped by displaying it that way he'd forget about the obnoxious saying on the front.

She glanced up and smiled when he came in. He wished she'd quit doing that. If she'd glance up and scowl at him, he'd be a heck of a lot better off.

Her gaze fell on the baby gates. Then she looked back up at him, a question in her eyes.

"I'll set them up first thing in the morning." He leaned them against the wall next to the stairs. "We can't have Gus getting hurt."

Her expression grew soft. "What a thoughtful gesture, Joe. I'm touched."

Damn, but he liked making her look happy.

"And let me tell you, those gates are even better than tulips. I've been wondering if I could safely put Gus down to crawl in this house, especially with the stairs. Thank you." Her eyes got that glow in them that he found so hard to resist.

"You're welcome." It was a moment that should have ended with a kiss, as they said in some song he vaguely remembered. But kissing was on the list of forbidden activities.

She crossed her arms almost as if reminding both of them that barriers needed to be erected. But the invitation was still in her eyes. She cleared her throat. "How is that you know so much about taking care of babies—things like setting up cribs and baby gates?"

"When I was fourteen, my mother had triplets."

"Triplets?" Darcie put both hands to her cheeks. "I can't imagine. Gus is enough of a handful. If I had three like him, they'd have to come after me with a butterfly net." She studied him. "Any other brothers or sisters?"

"Nope. Just me and the triplets."

"I'll bet you spent a good part of your high school years helping take care of those babies, didn't you?"

"Pretty much."

"I'm beginning to understand why you're not ready to sign on for another tour of duty in the near future." She shook her head in wonder. "Triplets. Think of the diapers."

"I try not to."

"I don't blame you. Don't worry, I won't ask you to change Gus while we're here."

"That's good." And it was good, he thought. He had no interest in taking over any part of the care of that rugrat. None at all. Changing diapers was no picnic, although he remembered how Marty used to lie there kicking his chubby little legs and laughing to beat the band because he'd loved being naked. Ryan had been pretty cute about that, too, and Peggy used to smile at him as if she had some secret she was keeping. Ryan used to love having his tummy tickled. Marty didn't. His specialty was peeing all over you.

"Joe?"

"What?" He blinked.

"You were staring off into space and grinning. I just wondered what was so funny."

"Uh, nothing." Great. Staring into space and grinning like an imbecile. Nice picture. But now that he thought about it, he wondered when was the last time he'd talked, really talked, to his two brothers and his little sister. They were almost grown up now, and yet it seemed only yesterday they were toddlers. He decided it was time to change the subject. He pointed to the costume on the couch. "I take it that's mine?"

"Yes." She picked it up. "I need you to put it on so I can see how you look."

He wasn't eager to put on the dorky outfit, so he stalled. "Has Bill been by to pick up the cow?"

"Not yet."

"Good. I really need to talk to him. I..." He paused as a steady thumping noise began overhead. He glanced up at the ceiling in alarm. "Is that Gus?"

"He's rocking himself to sleep. Pay no attention. Listen, about that cow—"

"Pay no attention? It sounds like a pile driver's operating up there!" Or a passionate couple was really going at it, he thought. He sure didn't need that kind of suggestive noise right now.

"He'll stop in a little bit. Now about that cow—I found some rope and tied her to the back gate, but she's eaten a fair amount of the greenery, and there are cow-patties all over the pool deck.''

"Yeah, I figured there'd be a mess out there.'' Joe raked his fingers through his hair. "I'll clean it up once Bill takes the cow. I'm sure if we had something smaller, a cute little calf or maybe a woolly lamb, then—''

"You're not seriously planning to get another animal for the display?''

"Sure.'' Her know-it-all tone got his back up, but maybe that was better than getting a rise out of other parts of him. "A smaller animal. Like maybe a burro. Burros are small.''

She pursed her luscious lips and shook her head.

"What? A little burro would be perfect. Big eyes, long ears. Burros are very Biblical.''

"You've never lived on a farm, have you?''

"Not exactly.'' He saw his vision of the manger scene becoming compromised, and he didn't like it. "But I've been to the petting zoo. I think we could handle an animal or two.''

"Joe, trust me on this. When I was a girl in County Kerry, we had all sorts of livestock, and you don't want creatures like that eating and pooping on DeWitt's patio. You'll never repair the damage. You have some heavy-duty scrubbing ahead of you as it is.''

He wished he could sit next to her on the couch and put his arm around her while they talked about this. She was the kind of woman who made a guy long for physical contact even when she was being a know-it-all. To occupy his arm, he rubbed the back of his neck. "Here's the thing. I've been talking to some of the guys at Home World about last year's displays. I didn't realize they were so...fantastic. Almost like Disneyland, they said.''

"I guess so. I've never been here at night, so I can't

say.'' She twirled a lock of her red-gold hair around her finger.

He knew how that silky strand must feel, and his throat ached from wanting to bury his fingers in her hair again the way he had the night before. He didn't want to talk about Christmas displays. He didn't want to talk at all. But talk was all he had.

"These guys have taken their families through Tannenbaum over the past few years," he said. "And from what they described, I'm not so sure having a live Jesus, Mary and Joseph in the manger scene will have enough of an impact. I think in order to win, we need live animals, too." He needed her, is what he needed. Right now, on the rug, on the couch, up against the wall.

"I think you're inviting chaos if you bring live animals in here."

He gazed at her, his sexual frustration fueling his frustration at not being able to create the display he was sure would win the damned prize. At this moment, it seemed to him everything was out of reach—Darcie, the prize, his cabinet shop. "Then I think we need to come up with another idea."

"How can we possibly do that? We have no time!"

"I know we have no time, dammit! But do you want to win or not?"

"Of course I do! According to Bart Junior's mother, that bastard could show up at any minute, demanding his fatherly rights. So I desperately need the money—for my car, for school, and to fight Bart Junior in court if necessary."

Joe's emotions swung from frustration to anger. "Don't tell me that sorry excuse for a man would have a chance at getting Gus." He wanted to believe she was exaggerating the danger rather than think such a horrible possibility actually existed.

"Of course he stands a chance! He's the biological father and he'll have all the financial backing he needs from his parents." Her voice quivered. "There's even a chance they'd use this against me."

"This?"

"Living here with you."

"That's a business arrangement!" Joe could hardly stand the thought that instead of making life better for Darcie, he might have helped screw it up.

She laid the robe and sleep shirt on the couch. "Then I hope you can come up with another idea for the display so we can support that position. Right now, I can't think of a single thing. I'm tired, and I'm going to take a bath."

"A…a bubble bath?"

"Yes. I've been looking forward to it all day." She stalked up the stairs.

Oh, God. She was going to take a bath. Just like in his fantasy. He listened to the water running in the guest bathtub and fought the desire churning through him. Muttering an oath, he stomped over to the TV and turned it on, flicking through the channels until he found an old movie starring Arnold Schwarzenegger.

He sat in front of the violent movie not seeing it at all. Instead, his head was filled with images of Darcie, her cinnamon-freckled body sinking into a tub filled with thousands of shimmering, glistening bubbles. Terrific. He had no prizewinning concept, which meant they wouldn't win. Darcie would be sitting with no funds and a questionable reputation, and he wouldn't get his cabinet shop. And on top of that, he was sharing this house with a very sexy woman he didn't dare touch. Life just didn't get any better than that.

DARCIE STEPPED INTO the just-right water with a sigh of relief. As she sank down to her neck in bubbles, she took a deep breath and vowed not to worry about anything for the next fifteen minutes.

Her vow lasted for exactly fifteen seconds. What if she and Joe didn't win the contest? Although she hadn't wanted to admit it to Joe, she'd asked Trudy a few questions about the displays from previous years, and Darcie was no longer sure a live Nativity scene, even with the incomparable Gus center stage, was enough to win. Live animals might help, but she knew Joe would never get away with keeping them in the backyard all day without major damage to DeWitt's property. Besides, the neighbors would probably file a protest because of the noise and the smell.

Worse yet, Trudy had begun dropping large hints that Bart Junior would soon return from the Amazon and assume his place as Gus's father. Darcie would rather have an aardvark assume that place. A picture of Joe in that role flashed through her mind, but she pushed it away. Triplets. He'd been burned out on babies by the time he was seventeen. No help there.

A knock sounded on the bathroom door. "Darcie, are you in there?"

She sank farther down in the tub, suddenly aware of her naked state and the slim piece of wood separating her from Joe. "No, indeedy, I'm not in here. I've slid right down the drain like a water sprite. Only my voice remains, calling up through the pipes."

"Listen, don't be discouraged about the display."

His voice brought a ripple of reaction from her body. "Who says I'm discouraged?"

"I saw the look on your face. And I know you're worried about the money situation." He paused. "Look, if we don't win, I won't be able to go in with my cousin anyway, so I won't need my savings. I'd be glad to loan you—"

"Stop right there." The gesture made her want to cry. And after she cried, she would get out of the tub, open the door and invite him in. She couldn't do any of those things. "I could never take your hard-earned savings, Joe."

"Why not? It'll only sit there moldering. And even if we don't win, I want you to go back to school, or take Bart Junior to court, or whatever you need the money for. I want you to have the security of knowing you can count on that much at least."

She swallowed the lump in her throat. She couldn't take his money, but she was incredibly moved that he'd offered. Such an offer from Joe, who had scrimped to put together a nest egg, was a hundred times different from that same offer coming from Trudy, who had tons of money and was filled with ulterior motives.

"We're going to win that money," she said.

"Do you have an idea?" His voice rose hopefully.

"Sort of." Her mind was a blank except for the hot need for Joe's arms around her, but maybe she'd think of something. She had to think of something. She didn't want to suffer through all this frustration for nothing. "I'll sleep on it and we can talk in the morning. And thanks again for the offer, Joe. You're a sweetheart."

"Oh, maybe not."

"Why?"

"I could have made that offer in the morning instead

of using it as an excuse to come up here and talk to you while I pictured you lying naked in that bubble bath. Good night, Darcie.''

TRUDY BUTTERWORTH WASN'T in the habit of calling to get information. Madge was supposed to report in to her, but Madge wasn't living up to her responsibilities. Finally, Trudy picked up the phone and dialed Madge's number.

When Madge answered, Trudy didn't waste any time on superficial small talk. ''What the devil's going on? Why haven't I heard from you?''

''Technical problems,'' Madge said in a low voice. ''I can't be real specific because I'm on the kitchen phone and you-know-who is right in the next room. But it seems the deluxe version got held up in transit and the cheaper version went belly-up yesterday. I have squat.''

''You mean to tell me that they've been in that house together for several hours, and you have nothing?''

''I gave you something.'' Madge sounded out of sorts. ''I've confirmed that they're now living together, didn't I? And I'm keeping a constant watch for celebrities. Until the deluxe version arrives, it's the best I can do.''

Trudy sighed. ''I guess so. It's just that I so want something dramatic to let Bart Junior know he's being replaced. Something to awaken his territorial instincts. I told him that Darcie's involved with someone else the last time he called, and he didn't react the way I expected he would. I thought he'd be consumed with jealousy, but he doesn't seem to be.'' His behavior was a trifle embarrassing. He needed to come home and take his place as the father of Trudy's grandchild, but he didn't seem to realize that. Much more of this dillydallying on his part and she might be forced to cut off his allowance.

"You want a tape of them doing it, don't you?" Madge said.

Trudy made a face. Madge sounded entirely too excited about that concept. And yet, such a tape might turn Bart Junior around. "It's a thought."

"Leave it to me. Once that deluxe version arrives, I can provide you with all the groans and moans you want."

JOE WOKE THE NEXT MORNING to the sound of a fiddle and a banjo plucking merrily away downstairs. The music wasn't loud, but it sounded live. He wouldn't have been surprised to find that Darcie had invited a couple of Irish musicians for breakfast and a jam session, so he pulled on briefs and jeans before venturing to the first floor.

Halfway down the stairs, he paused and eased himself to a sitting position on the carpeted steps, unwilling to interrupt the scene unfolding below.

The music came from DeWitt's expensive sound system in the living room, not a live band. But the entertainment was real. Darcie and Gus were dancing a jig.

They looked as if they'd come straight out of a Disney movie—a cherub and a wood sprite kicking up their heels for the sheer joy of it. Gus wore only his diaper and Darcie had on stretchy exercise wear in kelly-green, the perfect color contrast to her red-orange mop of hair. The tight fabric also emphasized every curve that he was supposed to ignore, and those curves were moving. Sunlight streaming in the large windows created a natural spotlight for the performance.

As Joe watched in total fascination and more than a little lust, Darcie whirled Gus up in her arms and bounced him on her hip as she kicked in time to the music. Then she set him back on his feet, linking her hands with his and holding him upright.

While she sang the cheerful words to a song Joe didn't recognize, she swayed rhythmically. All parts of her swayed rhythmically. Wow. Joe quietly drew in a deep breath and decided to watch Gus so he could cool off some.

Stomping his bare feet and bobbing his rear end in perfect time, Gus grinned up at her in the purest expression of delight Joe had ever seen. He really was cute, with his fiery cap of hair, his round little tummy and his chubby arms and legs. That's how babies sucked you in, Joe thought. They looked so adorable that you forgot how much work they were. But he knew. He knew.

The tempo increased, and Darcie picked the baby up again. Balancing him on her hip, she executed some amazing footwork while Gus bounced and crowed his approval. The music ended in a flurry of banjo chords. Giggling and breathless, Darcie collapsed with Gus on the cream-colored carpet.

Without realizing he meant to do it, Joe started applauding.

Darcie looked up and blushed. "The music woke you."

"I needed to get up anyway." And boy, was he up.

"I tried to keep it low, but Gus loves our little dance in the mornings, and I hated to disappoint him."

"No problem." More in control now, he stood and came the rest of the way down the stairs. The sunlight did fantastic things to her hair, making it flash and sparkle. And the exercise had made her cheeks pink—brought a bloom to them, he figured the Irish would say. She'd filled his dreams all night, but the real Darcie was much more potent than a dream lover.

"I hope you don't mind, but I've moved all Mr. DeWitt's breakable objects up out of Gus's reach for the time being."

"That's fine." When she looked so flushed and desirable, she could have said she'd thrown them all in the trash and he wouldn't have cared.

"And I've shoved the furniture up against the lamp cords so he can't reach them in case I let him crawl around in here."

"Good idea."

Gus gazed up at Joe with a solemn expression. *We've taken over the place, blarney breath. Deal with it.*

Joe hooked his thumbs in his belt loops. "You're quite a dancer, Darcie."

Look at that he-man stance, will you now? Here it comes. More sheep-dip.

"My da taught me, so I'm teaching Gus. I think he inherited his grandfather's rhythm."

Also his way with the ladies. Watch and learn. Gus turned his face up to Darcie's and smiled, exposing his four teeth.

She leaned down and kissed both cheeks soundly.

"He seems to have good timing all right," Joe said. "And dancing babies are in right now. Maybe you should give him a top hat and a cane and put him on the circuit."

"Maybe I should. I'd better not tell Geraldine or she'll have him wearing a top hat in no time." She looked up at Joe.

Gus watched her face. *Uh-oh. When she gets that look in her eye, like butter's churning in her noggin, trouble's coming, sure as the Lord made little fishes.*

"Are you thinking what I'm thinking?" Joe asked.

"A black top hat," she said with a grin.

Joe nodded. "The year 2000 on a sash."

She hoisted Gus in the air like a fresh mug of beer. "Look," she said. "It's Baby New Year!"

10

DARCIE CAME HOME from her cleaning job late the next afternoon to discover that the cow was gone and Joe had finished putting the baby gates in place, one at the top of the stairs and one at the bottom. She was free to put Gus down to crawl in the living room.

With a sigh of relief, she did exactly that, watching him scuttle around the cream-colored carpet exploring every nook and cranny. About the time Gus had worked his way over to the entryway, she heard a key in the front door lock.

She made it to the door in time to snatch Gus from harm's way. Sure enough, the door swung wide, smacking against the stopper on the wall as Joe walked in, two bags of fast food in his hands.

"Your hair's practically standing on end," he said. "What's the matter?"

Darcie struggled for breath. "You nearly made a pancake of Gus when you flung open the door like that."

Gus babbled and waved both hands. *If I'm going to get smashed, I prefer to do it with a pint of Guinness.*

"Oh." Joe glanced back at the door and winced. "Sorry. I didn't even think. It's been a few years." He looked crestfallen.

Now that the adrenaline rush was over, Darcie regretted laying any of the blame on him. "Never mind. It's my responsibility to watch out for him, not yours."

In other words, she doesn't think you're the sharpest tool in the shed.

"He's not only your responsibility, Darcie. I invited both of you into this house, and damned if I want either of you hurt as a result."

She appreciated his protective instincts, but she wondered if he was including broken hearts in that sweeping statement.

"Now let's eat." He lifted the fast-food sacks. "I got burgers for us and some extra French fries for short stuff there."

I may be short, but I'm good.

"He's never had French fries before," Darcie said. "He'll probably love them."

"Then let's get to it." Joe headed for the kitchen. "We have a ton of planning to do for this Baby New Year display. We can't put him out there by himself obviously, so we have to find a way to work you and me into the theme, and time is getting tight."

As Darcie followed him into the kitchen, she thought of telling him she'd put Geraldine on the problem after swearing her to secrecy, but she sensed Joe wasn't crazy about Geraldine, so she kept quiet. Besides, she had another matter to clear up with her housemate.

"Joe, we have to talk about expenses. You've bought dinner and the gates. Then, too, I'm using electricity and water. I need to pay my share, but I'm on a limited budget, and some things may be beyond my means."

"First of all, we're going to win that contest." He scrubbed his hands at the sink and dried them with a paper towel.

"I'm glad to hear you say that, but—"

"And second of all, Gus is the reason we're going to win the contest."

Well, scratch my britches and call me Angus. Finally some credit.

"The gates are to protect our main asset," Joe continued, pointing at Gus. "The French fries are to keep him fueled up. I have as much of a stake in that as you do right now. You're bringing Gus to the project, so it seems perfectly fair to me that I pay your utilities, buy a couple of gates and a meal now and then."

"And what if we don't win the contest?"

Leave it to me, lass.

"We will," Joe said. "This concept has legs. Now let's eat. Fast food doesn't improve with age."

Darcie settled Gus in his high chair. She'd like to believe that providing Gus for the display was enough of a contribution to justify all sorts of extras Joe had thrown in, like a roof over her head, bubble baths and French fries for her baby. It's not like she expected it from him. In fact, she'd stopped by the grocery store on her way home and she could feed herself and Gus from the supplies she'd bought. She could even feed Joe.

But in the months when she'd been the sole wage earner and the mother of a new baby, she'd never come home to find that someone else had provided the dinner. Perhaps she was becoming indebted to Joe in ways she shouldn't allow. Still, she couldn't deny that she thoroughly enjoyed having another person share the burden of the daily chores and expenses for a change.

She snapped on Gus's bib and sat down in the nearest chair.

Joe reached in the sack for the bag of fries. "Can I give him one?"

"Are they very hot?"

He picked out one pudgy fry. "Not really."

"Okay, he can have one, but you'd better break it into small pieces first. He only has four teeth."

But I can gum with the best of them. Lay that French fry on me.

Joe took a plump fry out of the package and broke it into bite-size pieces. "See how that goes down, Gus."

Gus picked up a small chunk, put it in his mouth and gummed it experimentally. Then his green eyes lit up and he grinned. *Saints be praised, I hear the angels singing.*

"Look at him!" Darcie said. "He loves it!"

Don't bother me, lass. I'm having a spiritual experience.

"Like that, do you, Gus?" Joe grinned at him. "I knew you were all right."

Gus shifted the morsel around, drooling with delight. *Might have been mistaken about you, too, blarney breath. You might have one or two redeeming personality traits. Just keep those French fries coming, and we'll talk.*

When the doorbell rang, Joe pushed back his chair and stood. "That better not be the Elderhorns again. We've cleared out the livestock and I've even thrown away Santa and the elves, so they don't have a beef left as far as I'm concerned. And we're not serving them Happy Hour every night, either. Madge drinks like a fish. Did you notice?"

Darcie smiled at Joe. "I think Madge enjoys the occasional beverage. She must have a drop of Irish blood in her."

Nothing wrong with a pint or two now and then. Steadies the mind. A pint and fries. Now there's a meal fit for a king.

The doorbell chimed again and Joe left to answer it.

From his unenthusiastic greeting, Darcie assumed it was the Elderhorns after all, but soon he walked back into the kitchen with an incredibly well-endowed blonde wearing sunglasses. If Darcie hadn't seen the wig before, she never would have recognized Geraldine, whose chest seemed to have expanded to a size forty-eight triple E.

"Howdy, y'all!" Geraldine said, and giggled.

Joe gave Darcie a deadpan stare. "It's Dolly Parton come to support the Save the Animals Millennium Project."

Darcie burst out laughing. "I love it!"

Geraldine spread her arms and twirled around. "Awesome, wouldn't you say?"

Joe rolled his eyes. "I'd say you've watched way too much *Grand Ol' Opry.*"

"From a distance, I'll bet you look just like her," Darcie said. "But how did you get the…?" She paused and held her cupped hands in front of her chest.

"Balloons, honey. Good thing you don't have a kitty cat around here or I'd have a dramatic reduction thing going."

Joe glanced at Darcie. "I take it you mentioned to Geraldine that I was supposed to be involved in the Save the Animals Millennium Project?"

"I did." Darcie hadn't dreamed that her friend could whip up a costume this fast, however.

"Well, does Dolly want a hamburger and fries?"

Watch how you give away my fries, laddie, or this new relationship may take a nosedive right into the duck pond.

"Y'all are too kind to this poor country girl. I could also manage a dry martini."

Darcie glanced at Joe, then back at Geraldine. "Are you driving home?"

"She hired a stretch limo," Joe said. "It's parked out front."

"Geraldine, you didn't!"

"Darling, I have *always* wanted to arrive somewhere in one of those things, and this was the perfect opportunity. I had so much fun I'm planning to do it again. I'll be somebody else next time."

"Elvis?" Joe asked blandly.

Geraldine sent him a scathing look over the top of her sunglasses. "Don't you have some bartending duties, young man?"

"Sure thing." He started out of the room. "Oh, and, Geraldine, I can see your...balloons."

"Voyeur." Geraldine stuffed the balloons, one red and one yellow, more firmly into the bodice of her dress. Then she pulled a chair over near Gus and sat down. "How's my darling Baby New Year? You've been on the job, I hope, protecting your mother from the advances of Mr. Happy Hormones."

I've been consorting with the enemy, lass. Greased my palm with fries, he did. How's a fellow to resist nectar of the gods?

"Geraldine, I haven't told Joe that you know about the New Year plan."

"Well, you'd better tell him because I have the perfect solution to working both of you into the display."

Joe came back into the kitchen, a stemmed glass in his hand. "One martini, very dry."

"Thank you, Joe. Over the teeth and over the gums, look out, liver, here it comes."

Gus banged on his tray. *Some of us are out of fries here.*

Joe broke up another French fry to put in front of him. "There you go, Gus."

Obliged. Beginning to rethink my opinion of you, lad. You might be a fine fellow after all.

Darcie cleared her throat. "Uh, Joe, I should mention to you that I let Geraldine in on our plan to use Gus as Baby New Year in the yard decoration."

"Oh, you did?"

"Don't worry, Joe." Geraldine plucked the olive from her drink and popped it into her mouth. "I am the soul of discretion."

"Uh-huh." Joe sat down and unwrapped his hamburger.

"I also have the most marvelous idea for the display," Geraldine said. "Gus is Baby New Year, so you, Joe, are Father Time. First, you come out, stooped over, wrinkled, long white beard, white bathrobe. You hobble across the yard, propping yourself up on that curved thing Father Time carries."

"A scythe," Darcie said. "Oh, it's a wonderful idea, Geraldine."

"A scythe," Geraldine repeated, taking another swig of her martini. "So do you get the picture, Joe? You're old, very old. You can barely make it across the yard, you're so old. People can hardly wait to see you gone. You're decrepit, toothless, impotent—"

"I get the picture, Geraldine."

"Then Baby New Year comes out," Geraldine continued. "He's young, he's adorable, he's full of smiles and dimples."

I'll work for fries.

"I've been thinking about his costume," Darcie said. "Maybe I could dye a knit outfit flesh color so he won't get cold."

Just so I get fries.

"That would probably work," Geraldine said. "Anyway, with the top hat and the sash, people will get the idea. And they'll be crazy about Baby New Year. They'll cheer, they'll laugh, they'll throw confetti in the air. Gus will be the man of the hour."

I like it.

Geraldine glanced over at Joe. "Meanwhile, Father Time is history. Outta there. Eliminated. Phased out. G-O-N-E."

Faith, he's my man with the fries! Let's not go overboard, lass.

Joe gazed at Geraldine. "You're really enjoying this, aren't you?"

"It has a certain appeal."

"I need to point out that Baby New Year isn't walking yet," Joe said.

Geraldine drained her glass. "I've thought of that. Darcie will bring him in. Maybe you could get a remnant of red carpet from Home World, Joe. Darcie can set Gus down and he can crawl across the carpet toward Father Time."

"In all the pictures I've seen, Baby New Year isn't brought in by his mother," Darcie said. "Won't that seem awkward?"

"Not if you're wearing spangles and a crown and a sash across your chest proclaiming you as...Miss Millennium!"

"Wow," Darcie said. "That's certainly creative and timely. And it solves the problem about how to gracefully get Gus on the scene." She noticed Joe wasn't leaping on the suggestion. "What do you think, Joe?"

"She's wearing spangles, a crown, a sash, and what else?"

"Oh, I think something sexy, something brief," Geraldine said. "Don't you?"

"No, I don't. I—" He turned as Gus started making a lot of racket banging on his tray table. "Hungry for another French fry, short stuff?"

Do bears poop in the woods?

Joe fished out another fry, broke it up and laid it on Gus's tray.

"Think about this, Joe," Geraldine said. "You're the comedy routine, Gus is the cute and adorable element, then Darcie hits them with sex appeal. You've covered all the bases."

"It's the middle of winter. She'll catch cold," Joe muttered.

"The middle of winter in Arizona," Darcie added. "And I'll only be out there a little while. I can take it, and I think maybe Geraldine's right."

"You're a mother," Joe said, turning to her, his expression belligerent. "Mothers shouldn't be running around half-naked."

"Oh, really? And who made that rule?" Darcie was becoming irritated. Geraldine had a perfectly good idea, and Joe was using old stereotypes to squash it. "I never realized you were such a prude, Joe."

"I'm not a prude. I just..." He stopped talking and glanced at Gus. With an oath, he leaped from his chair, tipping it over as he lifted Gus out of his high chair.

Darcie jumped up, her heart hammering. "What—"

"Choking," Joe bit out. He turned Gus on his stomach over his forearm and hit him between the shoulder blades sharply with the heel of his hand. A piece of fry flew out and landed on the floor, and Gus began to cry. Joe turned him back over and gathered him against his chest. "You're okay, little guy," he murmured, rocking the baby gently. "You're okay now. Easy does it, little leprechaun."

Darcie stood gulping in air and watching Joe cradle her baby. He knew exactly what to do, exactly how to hold and comfort Gus, and Gus nestled against Joe as if he belonged there. But what really amazed her was the look of tenderness on Joe's face. Gus was more than a means to an end for Joe although he might insist otherwise. He was beginning to love her little leprechaun.

Joe glanced at Darcie, his dark eyes filled with remorse. "Sorry about that. Maybe the fries weren't such a good idea."

Darcie gazed at him, her heart full of gratitude, and something else, something she probably shouldn't allow herself to feel for this man. Lust was one thing. This other, deeper emotion would be harder to control. "It's not your fault. Babies choke on things. It happens. Next time we can soak them in milk to make them softer. I should have thought of that."

Gus stopped crying and Joe brushed his thumbs over Gus's damp cheeks with such gentleness that Darcie's heart squeezed.

He smiled down at Gus. "Okay now, sport?"

Saved my bacon, you did.

"He looks fine," Darcie said. "Thank you, Joe. Thank you for noticing, for knowing what to do. I was so wrapped up in this new plan that I wasn't watching him as closely as I should."

"Me, either," Geraldine said. "Nice job, Joe," she added with new respect in her voice.

You know, blarney breath, never thought I'd say it, but I'm beginning to think we need you in the family. Maybe I'll see what I can do about that.

ALL THROUGH TANNENBAUM, vehicles sat in driveways, and garage doors stayed firmly closed, hiding the secret projects being feverishly constructed inside. The DeWitt house was no exception. Joe pushed Darcie's car out and kept the truck parked in the driveway while he labored on the set design in the garage until late into the night.

Once the basic plywood structure was finished, Darcie had offered to help him paint, but in the meantime she stayed inside sewing their costumes. He was afraid to ask what Darcie's would look like. He was even more afraid to examine the reasons why he didn't want her out there for every Tom, Dick and Harry to ogle, so he'd decided to ignore the subject of her costume.

Geraldine had the limo bring her over on several different occasions as she impersonated other celebrities, but she seemed to favor her Dolly Parton outfit the most. And each night Darcie always managed to pop into bed before Joe came in from the garage, which reduced temptation for both of them.

That was definitely a good thing, Joe told himself. The more time he spent in Darcie's vicinity, the more he wanted to be there. He was becoming way too attached to the lilting Irish songs she sang in the morning, the sight of her dancing with little Gus, the scent of her flowery cologne when they happened to pass in the hallway.

Darcie fascinated him, and he'd begun noticing every little thing about her. He knew she drank tea, not coffee, and preferred it with a splash of half-and-half and no sugar. He knew that watching *The Quiet Man* made her homesick for Ireland, but she loved sniffling through it anyway. He knew her favorite color was green and she didn't much like the freckles sprinkled all over her creamy skin. He liked her freckles. Way too much.

He told himself that she was making this deep impression on him because they weren't having sex. Probably if they had been having sex, he'd have gotten past this obsession with her and would have stopped doing idiotic things like counting the freckles on her nose. But they couldn't have sex because she wouldn't want it to be casual and he wouldn't want it to be serious.

So every night he hammered and sawed, which should have taken his mind off Darcie, but didn't. He had nicks and a purple thumbnail to prove his lack of concentration.

They'd decided on a Times Square backdrop, and he'd propped a travel brochure up on the workbench. Thanks to the invention of chasing lights, he'd figured out how to duplicate the Happy New Year message running across the top of the triangular Allied Tower Building.

A combination of plywood forms and pegboard inserts with lights strung through the holes would give the impression of skyscrapers at night. Everything would be painted black for simplicity. Joe also wanted to design a lighted ball that actually dropped when Miss Millennium brought in Baby New Year, but he hadn't quite worked out the engineering on that yet.

Around midnight two nights before the opening of the display, he finished the plywood structure and was close to a solution on how to drop the lighted ball. He and Darcie would have to paint like crazy to finish in time, but he thought they could make it. Stretching, he switched off the lights in the garage and went into the kitchen where, as usual, Darcie had left a light burning over the stove to welcome him back inside.

The house was quiet, and he knew instinctively that she had gone to sleep, a step ahead of him as usual. If she were still awake, he couldn't imagine that he wouldn't sense some kind of electricity in the air. Now the tension belonged to him alone, and although it was

late, he didn't feel sleepy. Sex would fix the edginess
that was always with him lately. Damn.

He took a beer out of the refrigerator, popped the tab
and carried the can with him into the dark living room.
Across the street he could see light coming from under
a crack at the bottom of the Elderhorns' garage door.
Herman was probably in there painting and needed the
ventilation.

Good idea, Joe decided. He'd be sure and do the same
when he and Darcie were painting tomorrow night so he
wouldn't asphyxiate both of them. Besides, he was loopy
enough with sexual frustration without getting even
higher on paint fumes.

Joe would love to know what sort of competition
Madge and Herman planned to throw at him day after
tomorrow. He thoroughly expected to win, but he was
still interested in knowing what was going on behind the
Elderhorns' garage door. Then he'd have an idea whether
he needed to add any of the embellishments he'd been
considering, like a giant bottle of fizzing champagne and
a wind machine blowing confetti around. If he crept over
there and lay down in front of that crack under the garage
door, he could probably see everything.

Laughing at himself, he took another swig of his beer.
The Tannenbaum mentality must be getting to him if
he'd started thinking of stunts like that. He and Darcie
would win fair and square.

Above his head, he heard the steady thumping of Gus
rocking his crib. It had become a nightly routine. About
the time Joe came in from the garage, Gus woke up and
started banging the crib around. Darcie was apparently
used to it because she didn't wake up.

The first night it had happened, Joe had gone into
Gus's room and picked him up. They'd had a nice little

chat, not that he needed that contact with Gus or even wanted it. Babies were a lot of work.

After he walked Gus around the darkened room a while and they discussed a few things, like whether the Diamondbacks had a chance this year and how Gus liked their pitching staff, Joe put him back in his crib, located his pacifier and patted his back.

Eventually, between the pacifier and the patting, Gus dozed off. Encouraged by his success, Joe had tried the same technique the following night, and it looked as if his services would be needed again. Not that he liked doing it or anything. But somebody needed to. Maybe tonight they'd evaluate the outfield and see if Gus thought the Diamondbacks needed to make any trades before the season started.

11

THE DELUXE VERSION of the listening device had taken forever to arrive, but it was finally in Madge's hands. Grateful that Herman was completely occupied in the garage putting the finishing touches on the yard display, Madge closeted herself in the sewing room. She told Herman that she had Christmas projects to finish and a yen to listen to her Barry Manilow tapes. Then she started setting up shop.

The device turned out to be much trickier to hook up than the cheaper version, but at last Madge had contact. The good news was that the catalog description had been accurate. She could pick up nearly everything going on across the street. The bad news was that nothing of interest was going on, and she was becoming very bored. Even her three miniature poodles were bored and snoozing on the furniture.

So far, Madge had recorded Darcie singing to that little red-haired baby, the whir of a sewing machine, the whine of a circular saw and the pounding of a hammer. Now the lights were out and everyone was probably in bed. She started to take off her earphones when a thump came through loud and clear. Then another thump, and another, until a steady rhythm had been established.

Gasping, she held the earphones away from her ears as if they were as hot as a stove burner. Then she clapped them back on again. Thump, thump, thump. There was no mistaking what *that* was to anyone with half a brain. Pay dirt.

Thump, thump, thump. Scandalous. Absolutely scandalous.

Then she heard a soft murmur and clutched the earphones closer to her ears, straining to hear.

"Aren't you tired of being up on your hands and knees all this time?" Joe said softly.

Madge felt faint. They were doing it doggy style and she had it on tape!

"Come on, baby. I know it helps you go to sleep, but you must be worn out from all that rocking back and forth."

Madge couldn't believe it. Joe seemed to be trying to talk Darcie out of having sex, as if they'd already spent far too much time engaged in the activity. Amazing.

The thumping stopped. For a second, Madge thought that would be the end of that. But no, Joe was talking again, this time about…*baseball?*

Madge's eyes crossed as she tried to imagine why a man would interrupt hot sex to discuss baseball. Unless it was some sort of code for sexual behavior she'd never heard of.

She heard the rustling of sheets. Uh-oh. They were about to get back to it.

"Here, suck on this," Joe said. "That should calm you down."

Madge pressed her hand against her heart. He sounded so matter-of-fact, so *patient!*

"That's good," Joe crooned.

Madge nearly passed out.

"Lie down, okay?" he said. "Now you can sleep. And I can sleep better, too. Good night."

In the silence that followed, Madge removed the earphones with trembling hands. Then she turned off the tape recorder. When she ejected the tape, she almost expected it to burn her fingers. Wait until Trudy Butterworth got a load of *this*.

TWENTY-FOUR HOURS until the judging, Darcie thought, trying not to panic as she thought of what they had left to do. After a quick dinner of Chinese takeout, she stood in the garage next to Joe, holding Gus, and surveyed Times Square rendered in plywood and pegboard. Now they had to cover the entire thing in black paint, which looked like a huge job to her.

But Joe had already worked miracles by getting the structure built. She found his competence with power tools very sexy and regretted not watching him put the backdrop together. Yet she hadn't dared, knowing how she constantly had to fight her impulses toward him.

Even now, as they stood with their shoulders almost but not quite touching, she could feel the energy vibrating between them. It was so tempting to move a fraction of an inch closer, to brush against him casually and feel the sparks run from the point of contact to the awakened nerves in every part of her body.

But she didn't. "You did a great job building that," she said.

"I did, didn't I?"

She laughed. "And so modest, too."

"Hey, when it comes to my carpentry skills, I'm not going to give you the foot shuffle and the aw-shucks routine. This is how I plan to make my living after we win the contest. I'd damned well better be good at it."

Darcie smiled despite the pain that squeezed her heart every time she remembered part of their goal was to help

Joe leave town. "You're very good at it," she said, glancing at him.

"Thanks." Joe's gaze warmed. "I'm glad you like it."

Gus crowed and reached over to grab a fistful of Joe's T-shirt. *Show her what else you're good at. Stop busting your buttons about this blessed display and plant one on her. Time's a-wasting, laddie.*

"Hey, Gus." Darcie disentangled the baby. "Don't be grabbing Joe now."

'Tis plain somebody has to.

"No problem," Joe said. "I probably gave you the idea I hate babies, but the truth is, Gus reminds me that I had some good times with those triplets, too."

And more good times are ahead if you'll get off the bloody dime.

Darcie allowed herself to sink into Joe's warm gaze for a moment, to imagine what would happen if he took her in his arms. He wouldn't, of course, especially while she was holding Gus, but she could have a private little fantasy all the same.

A wee lip lock. 'Tis all I ask. Don't mind me. You can take it from there.

Joe cleared his throat and broke eye contact. "I guess we'd better start painting."

"Guess so. Time for you to go into your playpen, little boy."

Help! Trapped! Jesus, Mary and Joseph. How am I supposed to arrange things if I'm locked into this cage?

"Here's your stacking toy, Gus." Darcie crouched down and plopped the first bright ring over the base. "Now you put on the next one. Here."

I'd like to put this ring around your neck, lass.

Couldn't you have worn something a little more inviting to this painting party? That T-shirt has seen better days.

"Now I have to go help paint. Be a good boy and amuse yourself."

I'll amuse myself all right. Gus threw down the ring and pulled himself up on the side of the playpen. *You two are as dense as a hedgerow when it comes to the fair art of courting. Let me out of this thing.* He rattled the top bar.

Joe stopped stirring the paint and turned toward Gus. "What's all the racket about, buddy?"

"Oh, he doesn't want to stay in there with all the fascinating stuff around. Once we start painting, he'll probably settle down and play with his toys."

"I don't blame him," Joe said. "The smell of the sawdust, all those shiny tools lying around. Maybe he's a budding carpenter."

And maybe you're a blooming idiot. But I'll take the cards dealt me. Pick me up, then. Gus held out his arms to Joe and babbled.

Darcie went over to the playpen and crouched down. "Sorry, Gus. Joe's busy, and so am I." She picked up a soft ball and handed it to the baby. "Play with your ball, okay?"

Hey, blarney breath. Think fast. Gus threw the ball at Joe.

Joe's eyes widened as he caught the ball. "Did you see that?"

"Pure accident," Darcie said. "He doesn't have the coordination to throw a ball at you yet."

"Maybe he's advanced." Joe came over and crouched down next to Darcie. "Nice pitch, short stuff. Want me to notify the D'Backs that you're available? We talked about their needing another relief pitcher."

Darcie's body went on red alert as Joe's hip and shoulder brushed hers. "What do you mean, you talked about it?" Her words came out suspiciously breathy.

"Oh, at night when he'd go into his rocking routine, I'd stop by his room and pick him up for a while. We talked baseball, didn't we, sport?"

You talked baseball. I was working my plan to lure the pair of you into my darkened room and let nature take its course. Night after blessed night I tried. Came up empty, I did. Dumb as posts, both of you.

Darcie felt a tug of emotion so wrenching she couldn't speak. Joe probably had no idea that his nightly attention to her son was such potent medicine.

"Maybe you don't approve of my doing that," Joe said. "I know you said he'd stop on his own, but I thought—"

"No, it's fine." She turned to him as she reined in the impulse to put her arms around him and kiss him until neither of them could think. "I appreciate it. I'm sure the contact was good for him. You can't hold babies too much."

A little contact wouldn't hurt the likes of you, either. Gus grabbed one of Joe's hands and one of Darcie's. *Seems I'll have to draw you a picture. Now, isn't this lovely? Just the three of us, joined like the three leaflets of a shamrock.*

Darcie noticed the way Gus was holding their hands and swallowed the longing that tightened her throat. Not five minutes ago, Joe had referred to his dream of opening that cabinet shop in Denver. "We really have to go paint," she said, and pushed away from the playpen.

Jesus, Mary and Joseph. I'll have to resort to extreme measures. Gus leaned over and bit Joe on the hand.

"Ouch! Hey!"

Darcie whirled back to the playpen. "What happened?"

"Gus bit me!"

"Oh, no. Did he break the skin?" Darcie grabbed his hand and examined the spot.

"It's not bad. Surprised me, though."

"I'm really sorry." Darcie could only see two small red spots where Gus's teeth had been. No blood. But Joe's hand was so warm, so firm and strong, so filled with promise that she pretended to examine the spot longer than she needed to.

"I'm not sorry." His voice was husky.

Excellent. Pucker up.

Still holding Joe's hand, Darcie glanced up at him. The light in his eyes made her pulse frolic like a lamb in springtime.

"Darcie." Her name came out as a sigh. Then his lips found hers. The pressure was light, but the effect nearly brought her to her knees.

When she trembled, he wrapped an arm around her waist to steady her. Then he went deeper, molding his mouth to hers with a sureness that told her he'd been thinking of this for a long time.

And God help her, so had she. Unwise though she knew it to be, she kissed him back, pouring all her days and nights of frustration into her welcome.

He shuddered. Then, with a groan, he released her. "I can't do this, Darcie. We can't do this."

Looks like you were doing a fine job of it to me.

Breathing hard, she gazed up at him. "I know." She swallowed. "You're right." How she yearned for him to take her back in his arms and block out the voice of reason. But he was strong, stronger than she was. Dammit.

Surely being so near to Joe and not making love to him would be impossible, but with her heart breaking, she knew she had to try. He might be attracted to her, might like kissing her, but he wasn't in this for the long haul. And she needed a staying-around man, for Gus's sake as well as her own.

She was trembling so badly she wouldn't be able to paint now if her life depended on it. "I'll...take Gus upstairs and give him a quick bath. It's probably not too soon to put him to bed. Then I'll be back to help you."

Bed? No! You'll never clinch the deal without me around!

"Darcie, let me do the painting. I can probably finish it."

"I'm not so sure." She avoided looking at him. "And I will be back to help, but I need...a little while. I hope you understand."

"I understand. And if you come back down here, I'll control myself."

"It's not just you." Figuring the longer she stayed, the worse things would get, Darcie scooped up her baby and hurried through the kitchen door into the house.

BY THE TIME DARCIE returned to the garage, she was in better control of herself. Leaving the kitchen door open so she could hear Gus if he woke up, she walked over to pick up a paintbrush. Joe glanced up from where he was brushing paint on the plywood, but he didn't smile, which was a blessing. His smiles could melt the Blarney Stone itself, as her da used to say.

"The paint that was on sale was oil-based, not water-based," he said. "So we'll have to use paint thinner to clean up."

"That's fine." The mere sound of his voice made her

long to kiss him again. She'd have to keep conversation to a minimum. And stay busy painting. Maybe then she'd forget about the glory of his mouth moving against hers.

Her hopes of that died five minutes after she picked up a paintbrush. She happened to glance over to where he was working—well, to be honest she glanced over there constantly because his backside made such a tempting picture, especially when he leaned over like that.

He'd raised the garage door a couple of inches for ventilation, but the night breeze coming through didn't cool her down any. She was growing warmer by the minute watching the denim stretch across his behind. And in the process of watching him paint, she noticed a flaw in his work.

"Oh, there's a spot you kissed," she sang out, plain as the black nose on a woolly lamb. "I mean *missed.* A spot you *missed.*"

He glanced back at her, his dark gaze unreadable. Maybe he hadn't heard what she'd said. "Where?"

She was sure her cheeks were red. They felt hot enough to melt butter. "On the left side of the Chrysler Building. I can see the plywood showing through the black."

He turned to where she was pointing. "Got it." He swiped the paintbrush across the bare spot. Then he kept working, his shoulder and back muscles putting on a nice show for her as he stroked the brush back and forth.

"Yes, you got it."

She fell to painting furiously, spattering black paint on herself and the drop cloth Joe had laid down to protect the garage floor. Joe, she noticed, was taking slow, measured swipes with his brush as if he had all night. They needed to get this job finished and retreat to their separate rooms.

But he was slow. Too slow. "You'd better shake your tail feathers or we'll never get to bed," she said. Even before he groaned, she realized that wasn't a good thing to say. "Sorry," she muttered.

"Maybe we'd better not talk to each other," he said.

"You're right." Slap, slap, slap went her paintbrush. The sharp smell of fresh paint always perked her up like a nip of brandy. She dipped her brush deep into the paint can. Her painting philosophy was to get as much paint on the brush as possible each time she went back to the can. She considered it the most efficient method.

"On the other hand, silence is its own special torture."

She dipped her brush deep into the can and lifted it up. "Have you been...tortured these past few days?" It would help some to know that he'd been as frustrated as she had.

"You have no idea," he said with feeling.

His fervent tone made her pause and stare at him working away with his back to her. He'd always seemed so cheerful, so busy with the project. She'd assumed that he'd been focusing on the money they were out to win and had put her to the back of his mind. Apparently not.

As she stood there contemplating Joe's frustration level, paint oozed down the brush handle and spread over her hand like tar. "Leaping leprechauns," she grumbled, tipping the brush back down over the can to let the paint run back the other way.

Joe turned to her. "Did you just say *leaping leprechauns?*"

"Well, what would you say after you'd dripped paint all over your hand?"

He laid his brush across the top of the can with a sigh and picked up a couple of rags as he started toward her.

"I'd probably say something a little stronger than leaping leprechauns."

"I mostly say those things because they're what my da would have said."

"Yeah, and dammit, that's part of what makes you so blasted endearing." He sounded upset.

"Sorry."

"You can't help it. Here, let me take the brush while you clean up." He used one of the rags to pluck the paint-smeared handle from her grasp and gave her the other one.

She wiped the paint from her hand. "Ugh. I'll be weeks getting this out from under my fingernails. It will look like I've been playing in the coal cellar."

"A coal cellar. I've never even seen one."

"Believe me, I've seen plenty. Peat bogs, too."

Joe wiped the handle clean and leaned down to scrape the excess paint off on the edge of the can. "I was wondering...oh, never mind."

"What, Joe?"

"Probably none of my business."

"Why don't you let me decide that?"

"Okay. I was just wondering. What happened with your dad?"

To her surprise, Darcie discovered that she wanted to tell him about it. She seldom had the chance to reveal the sad story to anyone because few people in this part of the country, except for the hospital personnel, had known her father.

She concentrated on cleaning as much of the paint off as she could, which made the moment easier. She wanted to tell him, but she didn't want to get all choked up doing it. "He had asthma, probably made worse by the chemicals he used as a janitor. We moved out here from New

York to see if that would cure him, but he was too sick. He...died two and a half years ago.''

''That's rough.''

The lump in her throat was there no matter how much she tried to be matter-of-fact about those events. ''I really miss him,'' she admitted.

''That might help explain Bart Junior,'' he said gently.

''Maybe.'' She glanced up from working on her paint-stained hand to find that he'd laid down the brush and was watching her, that light in his eyes again.

''I don't know what to do,'' he said.

''About what?'' Her heart beat faster.

''About your hand.''

''Oh.'' She swallowed.

His gaze fell to where she clutched the paint rag. Slowly, he took it from her and dropped it to the floor. Then he took her hand in his and examined it. ''I'd really like to get this off, but I hate the idea of putting paint thinner on your skin.'' He rubbed his thumb over the back of her hand, which was no longer black, but a funny shade of gray, almost as if she'd just died.

She wondered if she might in fact die, her heart was beating so fast. She should take her hand away right this minute. Right now.

They drew closer, as if they'd been tumbled in a clothes dryer and filled with static electricity. She felt the tiny hairs on her arm lift the nearer he came.

The moment stretched between them like taffy until she thought she might go out of her mind. She had to say something, do something, or she would fly apart and blow away in the wind like the seeds of a dandelion. ''It was my own fault. The way I was tossing paint around, you'd think I was a countryman slopping his hogs.''

The glow in his eyes deepened. ''Forgive me, Darcie.''

And with no further preparation than that, he pulled her into his arms and brought his mouth down over hers.

It seemed as if she couldn't resist him, either. She fastened herself to him like a burr. With a moan of happiness, she opened her mouth, inviting him in. And in he came, making himself right at home as if he planned to stay for a good long while and drive her crazy with pleasure.

She believed that he might. That body of his felt as magnificent pressed close as she'd imagined it would when she had watched him from afar. Her hands wandered over his brawny shoulders and lower down until she was shamelessly clutching the backside she'd admired while he painted.

His hands did their share of wandering, too, until he was plastered against her tighter than a mussel to a jetty. His intentions were no mystery at that point. She feared that hers weren't, either, with the way she whimpered and tucked herself against that lovely promise he was silently making.

He lifted his mouth away from hers, and his breath came quick and fast as he kneaded her bottom with strong fingers. "Can you stop what's happening? Because I don't think I can. I should, but I can't."

Her brain wouldn't function properly, but the rest of her was tuned up just fine, running smooth and hot. "I...don't think I can, either."

His breathing roughened. "Here? In the garage?"

Fire leaped through her and settled at the spot where they were squeezed so desperately together. She opened her eyes and gazed at him. She'd never seen a finer sight in her life. "It's where we met."

"No, it isn't." He slid his hands up beneath her T-shirt and unhooked her bra while her heart beat in triple time. "We met in the driveway." His voice grew husky as he eased his hands around until he cradled her breasts. "And from that first moment I saw you, I've wanted to touch you like this."

She sighed with pleasure and leaned back to enjoy more fully his attentions. "Joe, that's so lovely," she whispered.

"You are what's lovely," he murmured. "You feel like velvet." He gently released her breasts and cupped her face in his hands to feather her mouth with a kiss. "And we're not going to do this in the garage. I'm taking you upstairs to bed."

"No." Something told her that between the garage and his bedroom she'd lose her nerve or come to her senses, and she didn't want to do either. She wanted to be swept away and deal with the consequences later. "Here."

"Darcie, you deserve—"

"A garage adventure. I've never had one before." Grasping the waistband of his jeans, she sank to her knees, guiding him down with her.

"Darcie—"

"Kiss me, Joe. Your last kiss is wearing off."

With a groan, he delved into her mouth again, which made her delirious, but she tried to keep her wits about her enough to unfasten his jeans.

He lifted his mouth from hers. "What are you doing?"

"Trying to get rid of your jeans." She slid the zipper down and reached inside the denim to stroke his erection through his cotton briefs.

He closed his eyes and sighed. "I guess it'll be the garage."

"Good." As she caressed him and felt him tremble, she felt herself moisten with growing anticipation.

"God, I've been going crazy. I'm still going crazy."

Raining kisses over her face, he unsnapped her jeans and worked them over her hips.

She continued to explore the impressive length of him, even slipping her hand beneath the elastic of his briefs, which made them both gasp. But although she was fairly engrossed in discovery, she began to realize that while she remained on her knees, he'd end up with an engineering problem as he tried to get her out of her jeans. He felt so silken and firm that she hated to lose hold of him, but she would have to help him with the clothing problem.

She released him reluctantly and eased away from his kisses. She was having trouble catching her breath, but she needed to explain the situation. "You need...to let me sit down...so I can take my shoes off and get these jeans off properly."

His breathing was ragged, too. "I knew...we should have gone upstairs."

"No. This will be fine. You'll see." Even with the drop cloth over the concrete and her panties still on, the floor was cold and hard on her bottom, but she didn't mention it as she stretched out her legs...and kicked over the paint can. "Watch out!"

He moved surprisingly fast for a man half-in and half-out of his pants. Moving crablike on his knees, he scrambled away from the spreading paint, but she was not so fortunate. It soaked right into her running shoe and the leg of her jeans before he could grab the can and set it upright again.

"Oh!" She glanced up at him. "What now?"

He gazed at her, his eyes still somewhat glazed, his breathing labored. Then slowly, after what seemed like an eternity, the dazed look cleared. He stood and gave her a rueful smile. "I guess I need to help you out of your shoe and your jeans."

"And then?" She knew the answer. She'd never heard of anybody making passionate love after spilling a can of black paint on their leg. Had it been something sexy, like chocolate fudge sauce, then maybe the moment could have been saved and some interesting variations included in the resulting activities. But black paint was a different matter altogether.

"And then nothing." His voice was heavy with regret and recrimination as he zipped up his jeans. He looked into her eyes. "I'm sorry, Darcie. More sorry than I can say. It was a bad idea from the beginning, but after you told me about your dad, and you were there, so close, so sweet..." He sighed. "It's your good luck that you kicked over the paint."

Because she was Irish, Darcie believed that good luck was a natural part of her heritage. She could vouch for having experienced good luck many times in her life. But this definitely did not feel like one of those times.

12

MADGE HAD FINALLY SHUFFLED Herman off to the garage to put the finishing touches on the yard display and was preparing to go upstairs to the sewing room. She had a pretty good idea when the thumping would start, and she didn't want to miss a single night of Joe's strange baseball murmurings following a bout of wild sex. Darcie, however, was the most silent bed partner Madge could imagine. Never let out a peep, not during the thumping and not during the baseball portion of the event, either.

Madge was halfway up the stairs when the doorbell rang. She returned to the first floor and opened the front door to find a distraught Trudy Butterworth on the other side. Her usually sleek hair was windblown, her mascara smudged, and she even had her Ralph Lauren wool jacket buttoned up wrong.

"He doesn't care," Trudy said. "I sent him the thumping tape and he just doesn't care!"

Madge drew Trudy inside and closed the door. Herman had the garage door cracked open and Trudy's wailing might carry in there. "You're sure he understands that the mother of his child is engaged in steady sex with another man?"

"I'm sure he understands, although it's not the sort of thing I like talking about to my son, especially on a transhemispheric phone call." Trudy's shoulders sagged.

"After I hung up, Bart Senior wanted to know what was wrong with me. I couldn't exactly tell him since he's already quite disgusted with Bart Junior. So I pretended it had to do with the festival committee. I walked over here so I could work off some of my frustration."

"I'm sorry, Trudy. Children can be a trial." Or so Madge had heard years ago, which was why she'd elected to forgo the experience.

"Bart Junior was always a joy until now. I really thought he'd come back when he heard that tape. I thought he'd sweep Darcie off her feet and marry her. Then she'd take French classes and become an interior decorator, and we'd change the baby's name to Bart Butterworth III, and I could hold up my head in this community again."

"There, there." Madge patted Trudy's shoulder. "The residents of Tannenbaum won't blame you because your son turned out to be a worthless piece of slime."

Trudy's head snapped up. "I did *not* say he was a worthless piece of slime. He's a free spirit! I should have known better than to try to chain him to conventional behavior."

"Well, I suppose that would be the wrong thing to chain him to," Madge said. Personally, she'd never liked the kid and thought Darcie was better off with Joe Northwood, even if the guy did have a baseball fetish going on. But if Madge's tape had been able to bring Bart Junior home, Madge might have become chair of the Tannenbaum Christmas Festival and Good Cheer Committee in perpetuity.

"Anyway, I came by to tell you to stop taping. It's no use."

"Stop taping?" Now that Madge had learned how to use the listening device, she couldn't imagine life without it. In fact, she needed to get up to the sewing room soon or she'd miss tonight's episode.

"Yes. I'll pay you for that machinery you bought, unless you think you can return it and get a refund."

Madge waved a hand vaguely. "Don't worry about that."

Trudy frowned at her. "You won't continue to use it, of course."

"Oh, of course not." Madge hoped she looked innocent. "What use would I have for something like that now that I know you don't want the information?"

"Exactly." Trudy sighed. "Well, I'd better toddle home and see if Bart Senior has our display finished. Tomorrow's the big day."

"It certainly is."

"I'm sure you have something wonderful, as usual."

"Oh, yes." But amazingly, Madge realized she didn't much care. In fact, she wasn't sure why she wanted the chair of the festival committee in perpetuity. The whole yard decoration business was pretty boring, come to think of it. At the moment, all she wanted was to get back to her sewing room.

"Well, see you later, Madge."

"See you later, Trudy." Madge did her best not to slam the door in the woman's face. Once she'd closed it, she nearly ran up the stairs.

In thirty-five years of marriage, Herman had provided better-than-average housing, enough money to eat out at Denny's whenever they wanted, a new Lincoln every three years and a big-screen TV. He had not provided bedroom experiences to curl her toes. She'd never imagined in a million years that she'd say this, but she envied Darcie O'Banyon.

Closed safely in her sewing room at last, she put on

her earphones. Then, as she fine-tuned the control knobs on her listening device, she heard a thump. And another thump, and another. They were at it again. Insatiable. Such naughty behavior. Deliciously naughty. She strained to hear voices.

At last she was rewarded.

"You've got it in too deep," Joe said clearly above the sound of the steady thumping. "That's what caused the problem the last time."

"That's how I like to do it," Darcie replied, bold as brass. "Besides, we don't have a lot of time to work on technique. Morning will be here before you know it."

Madge leaned forward, her heart going like gang-busters. At last, Darcie was going to say something about the experience. Goodness, but she was an impatient little thing. And Madge couldn't comprehend how putting it in too deep was a problem. She'd never have to deal with that problem in Herman's case, that was for certain.

"You'll make a bigger mess that way," Joe said, sounding patient and loving, but very, very sexy. Thump, thump, thump.

Herman never used that tone of voice in bed. He never used any tone of voice. During his performance of The Act, he was as dumb as a stone. Which actually made it easier to pretend he was someone else, so muteness had its advantages.

"You can't do this without making a mess," Darcie said as the rhythmic thumping continued.

Madge started to hyperventilate as she imagined the scene. Herman hated messes of any kind. Neat as a pin, that Herman. And hung like one, come to think of it.

"You can minimize the mess, though," Joe said.

"But the way I do it saves all that going back and forth," Darcie said.

Good gracious! Madge had always thought going back and forth was the whole point. Her sexual knowledge obviously was too limited. But Joe socialized with jet-setters and Hollywood insiders. He probably Knew Things.

"Here, let me show you what I mean," Joe said.

Heavens, he was instructing her in the art of love! Madge thanked her lucky stars she was getting this on tape. Maybe Herman could be reconditioned.

"Put it halfway in, like this," Joe said. "Then bring it back out and press it gently as you bring it up against the rim. See?"

"If you say so. But I think it'll take a lot longer that way."

"I predict you'll finish up about the same time as if you did it the other way." He spoke in such an easy voice, as if they weren't thumping away at the same time. Amazing.

"Oh, all right, then. But don't expect me to like it."

The little ingrate! Here she was getting expert love-making instruction from a man who was personal friends with people like Dolly Parton and Robin Williams, and she was giving him an argument about technique.

Joe's amused chuckle gave Madge goose bumps. What a man. Patient, understanding and well endowed. You couldn't get much closer to heaven than that.

"Try it for a while," Joe said. "I think eventually you'll see what I mean."

Madge knew *she* would, that was for sure. She turned up the volume knob, anticipating some moans of plea-sure. Then, her deluxe listening device, the one that "professionals swear by" according to the brochure, cut out on her, giving her only static.

Madge bellowed a word she'd never said in her entire

life. She turned knobs and adjusted wires, but only fizz and crackles came through the earphones. She yelled the swear word again. It was the only one that fitted the situation.

Herman pounded up the stairs and burst into her sewing room. "Sugar cakes, what's the matter? I heard you yelling an...an obscenity!"

"Perhaps I did, Herman. What of it?"

"Well, now you're all red in the face! I've never seen you red in the face from listening to Barry Manilow. Should I call 9-1-1?"

Madge put her hand to her chest and forced herself to take several deep breaths. "No, Herman, do not call 9-1-1."

"Is there anything I can do, cherry blossom? You look so upset."

She gazed at him. Well, any port in a storm. She'd heard enough to give her some ideas, and for the rest, she'd improvise. She stood and walked toward him. "Yes, Herman, there is. There most certainly is."

JOE'S ARMS ACHED from painting, but they were nearly finished with that part. He figured Darcie was in the same cramped condition. At least after agreeing to adopt his methods, she wasn't splattering as much paint on herself as she had in the beginning.

They'd worked ceaselessly, grabbing moments to gulp coffee and eat most of the package of chocolate chip cookies he'd found in the back of a cupboard. He'd hoped to get the lights in the pegboard before he went to bed, but he was dog-tired and might louse up the job.

He dropped his brush in a can of paint thinner. "I'm going to call in sick tomorrow so I can finish the lights and get everything put up in the yard before it gets dark.''

Darcie paused and wiped her arm over her forehead, leaving a smear of black paint there. ''I hate for you to miss work.''

He winced at the smear of paint on her skin. ''No problem,'' he said. ''I can do it easier than you. I have the sick days coming, but if you don't clean, you don't get paid.''

''True enough. And during the holidays, my clients plan their parties around my cleaning schedule so the house will look good.'' She glanced up at a clock mounted on the garage wall. ''We still have a couple of hours before sunrise. Why don't I help you put the lights in now?''

Joe shook his head. ''I know you must be exhausted. Go on up to bed.''

She walked over and nestled her brush beside his in the paint thinner. Cozy. Then she looked up at him and a wave of hot desire hit her like a tsunami. She fought the impulse to throw her arms around him.

As she gazed at him, she realized that they'd never be closer to making love than they had been tonight. The tension still crackled between them, but if they managed to stay away from each other until sunrise, they'd probably be able to hang on to their resolution for the rest of the holiday.

The thought was so deeply disappointing that she almost groaned aloud. She wanted him so desperately that she could taste his kisses, feel his hands caressing her, hear his murmurs of need. The picture taunted her like a desert mirage taunts a person dying of thirst.

In that moment, when deprivation cut like a knife, she made a decision. Maybe fatigue had weakened her and she wasn't thinking clearly, but she didn't care. Making love to him felt right, and if they couldn't have forever, she would settle for right now.

Joe, however, would take some convincing.

"Go on up," he said again.

"I'm not going unless you come with me."

He wished she meant that literally, but of course she didn't. Shouldn't. "I'll be up in a little while." He rolled his shoulders. "I want to fool around with the mechanism for dropping the lighted ball. The judges will come through at seven, right? Before they open it up to the general public?"

"That's what Madge Elderhorn told me."

"That should give me time enough. I want the ball to be a dramatic surprise, something unexpected, to wow the judges. My idea is to hide it behind the display until the perfect moment, when you and Gus are ready to come out. Then it'll rise up over the Allied Tower Building and slowly descend while you parade in with Gus."

"Sounds spectacular."

He gazed down into her green, green eyes. Even after staying up most of the night working, even after spattering and smearing black paint over most of her exposed skin, she looked wonderful. Kissable. Lovable.

"Come on to bed, Joe," she said.

His chest grew tight as he imagined how he'd feel if she were really inviting him to bed and not simply suggesting he get some rest. "You go ahead." He reached out and tucked a red-gold curl behind her ear. "And thanks for hanging in there with me. You're a trouper."

"I want this as much as you do."

Oh, but this conversation could have been so much more interesting if they were talking about something besides a yard display grand prize. "Well, you certainly deserve it."

"We both do."

His breath caught at the look in her eyes. But no, he was engaging in some extremely wishful thinking brought on by exhaustion. What he saw in her eyes was probably sheer determination to stay upright until the work was finished. "Go on upstairs," he said. "I'll be there soon."

"Don't be long."

"I won't."

She turned and walked toward the kitchen door.

He watched her the whole way. Maybe the paint fumes were getting to him. As she approached the doorway, her hips seemed to sway more seductively than he'd ever noticed them before.

She walked up the two steps to the kitchen level and glanced over her shoulder. Her voice grew sultry. "Promise me you won't be long."

His mouth went dry and his heart hammered. If he weren't so damned tired and high on paint fumes, he'd swear she was coming on to him. But they'd had that discussion and they'd both decided to stay away from that particular activity. Hadn't they?

He must be hallucinating. She wouldn't be coming on to him. Not after what they'd already been through with their aborted lovemaking attempt. Not after painting for seven hours straight. Not at four-thirty in the morning.

He cleared his throat. "I won't be long."

After she left, he tried to concentrate on the weighted pulley mechanism he had designed for the lighted ball, but he kept seeing the way she'd looked at him over her shoulder. If that wasn't a come-hither look, then he'd never seen one.

So what the hell was she doing, come-hithering like that? Now that he thought about her walk and her backward glance, he was sure it was a come-hither. Okay, so she'd painted by his side all night, and he admired her grit. But that didn't give her the right to tease him with a come-hither at the end of the night. Not by a long shot.

Throwing down the pulley apparatus, he stalked over to the garage-door button and jabbed it with his thumb, sending the door down with a solid whack. Then he flipped off the garage light and went into the kitchen, closing the door firmly behind him. Time to get a few things straightened out with Miss Come-Hither.

Adrenaline overruled exhaustion as he strode right up the stairs. No lights were on anywhere except for the little night-light in Gus's room. She'd obviously skipped right into bed, not even kept awake by a guilty conscience. Well, he'd give her conscience a working over for toying with him like that. A guy could only take so much before he cracked. And Joe had cracked.

He walked straight to her darkened bedroom where the door was partly ajar and gave a no-nonsense rap on the door frame. "Wake up, Darcie O'Banyon. We're going to have a talk."

No answer.

"I give you fair warning, Darcie. Playing possum isn't going to work with me."

Still no answer.

"Darcie, now stop pretending to be asleep and answer one simple question. Were you, or were you not, come-hithering when you walked out of that garage?"

"Sure I was."

"Aha! I thought so! I..." Then he hesitated, confused. Unless she was good at throwing her voice, it hadn't come from her bedroom. It had come from his.

As the implications of that information sank in, he felt as if somebody had just plugged him into an electrical outlet. Slowly, he turned toward his open bedroom door, but he couldn't see anything in the dark room. "Darcie?"

"Yes?" She snapped on the bedside table lamp. The light cast a glow over her lightly freckled shoulders and her red-gold hair spread across his pillow as she lay in his bed, the sheet pulled modestly over her breasts. She'd managed to get most of the paint off her face, and she looked scrubbed and soft and...incredible. She smiled, the perfect touch to an outstanding picture. "Taken your own sweet time, haven't you? Now come to bed, Joe Northwood."

He blinked and told himself he was dreaming. In his experience, reality had never looked this good.

Her heart jumping like a rabbit's, Darcie waited for his reaction. He looked frozen in place, as if she had him on film and had pushed the pause button.

Finally, he spoke. "This is a bad idea. A really bad idea."

"Do you have a better one? I don't know your habits in this area. Perhaps you'd rather do it in the shower, or some men like chairs, I'm told, and you have a great armchair over in the corner there. Or the floor is another popular spot for some. Or up against the wall, or—"

"Stop! First you come-hither me and now you're getting me even hotter by suggesting variations!"

"Are you too tired?" She braced herself for rejection. She'd left her robe within reach beside the bed in case he sent her out of the room. She'd found a box of condoms in the bathroom cabinet and put them in the bedside-table drawer in case he didn't send her out of the room.

"A half hour ago I was totally wasted, but at the moment every single part of me is awake. One particular part is *so* awake. But I don't get it. Why would you want to start something that can go nowhere?"

"Because I need you now, more than I can stand. We'll worry about the rest tomorrow." She drew back the sheet, revealing both herself and the tulip petals she'd scattered over the bed. "So are you coming to bed, or would you prefer to stand there debating the matter for what's left of the night?"

His gaze moved over her very, very slowly. He swallowed. "Tulips." His voice sounded raspy. "You would have to throw in tulips."

Darcie smiled. "Zee pistil ees so...how you say? Erect."

"No kidding." He took one step into the room and stopped. "I just don't want to be in the same category as Bart Junior, that's all."

"Other than the fact you're a man and he's a man, you're in totally different categories. Bart Junior lured me into his bed. I'm already lying buck naked in your bed, and I'm the one trying to lure *you*. I didn't think it would take this long."

He sighed and came into the room, stripping off his T-shirt on the way. "You have to make allowances for the fact that I'm an idiot."

A beautiful idiot, she thought, her pulse racing as she admired his bare chest.

"I need to get something from the bathroom," he said.

"Just a minute." She reached in the bedside table and took out the box she'd found. "Would this be what you're after?"

He gazed at her. "You really have thought this through, haven't you?" he said softly.

"I have. I won't repeat the mistakes I made with Bart Junior."

"You know what?" Joe hopped on one foot and took off a shoe and sock. "Let's not mention him anymore." He hopped on the other foot and repeated the process. "Is that okay with you? Because I think I could go my whole life and not hear his name again, and I would be very happy with that."

"We won't mention him again." She caught her breath as his hands went to unfasten his jeans. Ah, but he was well put together. "Black Irish," she whispered.

"What?"

"I've been wondering if you're Black Irish," she murmured as he shucked the jeans and briefs in one motion. Oh, my. "Definitely Black Irish."

He approached the bed, his gaze hot as he looked at her lying there in the midst of red tulip petals. "How can you tell if I'm Irish?"

"By the cut of your jib." She stared in frank admiration at his erection.

He put one knee on the mattress and propped a hand on either side of her head. "The cut of my jib has nothing to do with being Irish. That has to do with finding a naked Irish maid in my bed."

Her heartbeat thundered as she saw the desire raging in his dark eyes. Still, she needed a little more reassurance. She'd never presented herself naked to a man before. "I hope you're not terribly disappointed that I'm not a French maid."

"If you've noticed the condition of my jib, then you know for certain that I'm not disappointed."

"Your jib does look...interested." She reached over and curled her hand around it. "Very interested indeed."

He made a strangled sound deep in his throat. "Easy, Darcie. I'd like to make this last awhile."

"So would I." She stroked him gently, and in response her body seemed to flower like the tulips she'd shredded to decorate his bed.

"Enough," he whispered, taking her hand away. "My turn."

"Would you be kissing me soon?"

"Very soon." His dark eyes sparkled and his lips curved in a delicious smile, a smile full of anticipation. "And where would you like me to kiss you, Darcie?"

"Anywhere that takes your fancy."

"Then I guess I'll kiss you here." His lips brushed her forehead. "And here." He moved to her eyelids. "And here." He touched his mouth to her cheek. "Oh, and here." He kissed the corner of her mouth. Then he lifted his head to gaze down at her. "To tell you the truth, every sweet, creamy, freckled inch of you takes my fancy. I've dreamed of licking each of your freckles to see if they taste like cinnamon."

She thought her heart might pound right out of her chest with excitement. "I suppose you'd better get busy, then. We don't have all night."

"Don't remind me," he said as he kissed his way down her throat. "To think we could have been doing this instead of painting the town black."

She buried her fingers in his thick, silky hair. "We had...a reason."

"Wonder what it was? Mmm. I do believe you taste like cinnamon. And sugar. And honey. Damn all that time spent painting."

"We're trying to—" she gasped as he reached her nipple and pulled it into his mouth "—win money," she finished breathlessly.

He rolled her nipple against his tongue before kissing his way to her other breast. "But this is priceless," he murmured, and captured her other nipple against his tongue.

She sighed in agreement as he gradually turned her into melted butter. Then he proceeded to kiss and lick every freckle on her skin.

"I'm following the dots, trying to make a picture," he murmured against her skin. "If I make a good picture, I might win a prize."

"I...think you might at that," she said, gasping at his intimate investigation of her body.

"I've always loved to play connect the dots."

She was fast becoming partial to it herself. And the picture he was making was breathtaking. For the first time in her life, she longed for more freckles.

13

JOE KNEW HE'D LOST his mind, and he wasn't the least interested in looking for it. Right now, there was only Darcie—satin-smooth skin covered with cinnamon freckles, red-gold hair that curled around his fingers, pink mouth that tasted like exotic fruit, green eyes growing softer and dreamier by the second.

"An ache's building inside of me, Joe," she murmured, low and sexy and pitched to drive him wild. "And it needs filling."

He forced words past a tight throat. "That's the prize I've been going for." He decided then and there that nothing could be sexier than an Irish brogue spoken by a willing woman stretched out beneath him in his bed. Forget the naughty French accent or the sultry Southern drawl. Give him an Irish brogue any day. Give him Darcie.

Her kiss-reddened lips parted, and damned if her Irish eyes didn't smile. He'd thought it was only a catchy phrase in a song.

"Then claim your prize," she said.

He'd never rolled on a condom so fast in his life. Heart beating like a jackhammer, he eased between her warm thighs. He gazed down at this freckle-faced angel of a woman and wondered if she had any idea the value of the gift she was giving him at this moment.

"You should be pampered and spoiled," he said, his

voice husky. "Showered with jewels. Fed champagne and caviar. I can't do any of that for you."

Her eyes darkened and she grasped his hips, urging him forward. "Do what you can," she said in a throaty purr, "and, by all the saints, I'll try to make the best of what you can give me."

Pure, unadulterated Darcie talk. He was crazy about her. No point in denying it to himself. "I don't deserve this."

"Perhaps not. But I do."

"Ah, Darcie." He sank slowly into her, savoring every moment of the trip, watching her eyes widen and fill with passion. So lush, so ready. The pleasure enveloped him, wrenching a moan from deep in his chest.

"It's good for you?" she asked, sounding breathless.

He was ready to explode from the intensity of being buried within her heat. "Passable," he said. "And you?"

Her breath came in quick little gasps. "I've felt worse in my life."

If he hadn't been on the brink of an orgasm, he would have laughed. Instead, he gave her a tight smile. "Should we...go on with this, do you think?"

"We might...oh, goodness." A tremor passed through her. "We might give it a try."

He moved carefully. He'd always prided himself on his control, but then, he'd never made love to Darcie O'Banyon. Every time she lifted her hips, he wanted to shove deep and lose himself in her. Once he did that, his world would come apart. He wanted hers to come apart first. If he couldn't give her the world on a silver platter, at least he could give her this.

So he tried to distract himself from the warm, wonderful feel of her body surrounding him, tried to tell himself that being inside her wasn't driving him absolutely, totally, around the bend.

He leaned down to drop a kiss on her full lips. "Talk to me, Darcie. Tell me how I'm doing."

"You're doing fine."

"Good."

"However..."

He lifted his head to look down at her. No guy liked to hear the word *however* in connection with his lovemaking technique. "However?"

"You're holding back."

"But I need to hold back, Darcie. The way you're affecting me is too...powerful."

She held his face in both hands. Her eyes burned into his.

He felt his control slip a notch just from looking into her eyes. "Darcie—"

"It's that power I want, Joe."

With a groan of surrender, he drove into her, and drove into her again. She arched up against him, her nails digging into his back, her gasps becoming whimpers. And her eyes glowed like precious emeralds. He couldn't look away from the fire in her eyes.

"Like that?" he murmured, shoving forward, his body straining with the need for release. "Like that, Darcie?"

"Oh, yes. Like that. Like *that*. Oh, Joe! Yes! Now!"

Her convulsions came a split second before his, and he wrapped her tight in his arms. Rocked by tremors such as he'd never known, he felt himself spinning, hurtling, through space. But Darcie was there. Darcie would save him. Darcie was all he needed. Oh, no. No... He was falling...in love.

DARCIE WOKE UP to the same sound she'd been waking up to for months—her baby crying out for her. That much felt normal.

But the minute she opened her eyes, she knew nothing else was normal about this morning. She was in Joe's bed, and by her own choice, too. So she had no one else to blame for the fact that she'd turned her life inside out in the space of an hour.

Or perhaps a little longer than an hour. For they'd made love again, once the first time had worn off some. She'd given his jib a treat. And they'd rubbed each other with tulip petals and then he'd given her the same sort of treat she'd given him. Seems he was fascinated by more than her freckles.

Last night, she'd felt very sure that loving and losing was better than never having loved at all.

That was last night. This morning, as she looked over at Joe sleeping next to her and realized that soon this passionate man would be gone from her life, she didn't feel so very sure of herself. Time to pay the piper, and she was fresh out of gold coins. And not a leprechaun in sight.

Only one thing for it, she decided as she crept quietly out of his bed, slipped into the robe she'd left on the floor, and tiptoed out of the room. Sort of like closing the barn door after the horse had escaped, but better than leaving the barn door wide open for the chill wind to blow inside. She'd loved, and now she must prepare herself to lose. For that, she'd have to stay out of Joe's bed from now on.

He wouldn't like it. She wouldn't like it much, either, but she hadn't figured on how quickly she'd bond to this man. One brief interlude in his arms and she was ready to abandon every ounce of her pride and beg him to stay with her forever. The words had trembled on her lips several times while she and Joe had been locked in passion. She'd managed to suck them back inside her lips and swallow them, though it had nearly choked her.

However, if she allowed herself to be locked in passion with him a few more times, she might not be able to control those pleading words. Even now they hammered inside her heart, demanding to get out. Words of love and commitment. Words Joe didn't want to hear, and had no intention of saying, either.

By being very quiet, she managed to dress herself and Gus without waking Joe. She packed Gus's food in the little cooler she carried to her cleaning jobs and checked her wallet to make sure she had enough money to pick up a fast-food breakfast for herself. Then she took the keys to Joe's truck from the hook in the kitchen and slipped out the front door.

At five in the afternoon, when she dragged herself and Gus back to Joe's house, she felt raw, like a sheep that had been shorn in the dark of winter, as her da used to say. She wanted to crawl under a soft wool blanket and sleep forever.

But there was no time for that. Tannenbaum was bustling. Trucks equipped with cranes sat at each intersection. Men hoisted high in the buckets by the cranes were stringing lights around the sixty-foot Aleppo pines that grew on each corner and helped give Tannenbaum its Christmas-tree look.

That morning, the front yards had all been bare. It so happened that the two houses she'd cleaned today didn't care about the competition and had put up last year's decorations—a family of snow people in one case and a cowboy Christmas theme in the other, featuring a buckboard and a tumbleweed tree. Both were nice enough and would satisfy the deed restriction requiring a yard display.

But Darcie paid them little attention. As she drove through the subdivision at lunch, and again when she finished her second house, she evaluated the displays that weren't repeats from previous years, the ones that were obviously in contention for the grand prize.

By the time she pulled into the driveway of Joe's house, she was in a black mood from seeing all the elaborate decorations in the rest of the subdivision. Noticing that Joe was just now carrying the backdrop out of the garage didn't lift her spirits, either. She chanced a peek across the street to the Elderhorns, expecting a wondrous decoration to be rising from their perfectly groomed grass, as well.

To her total amazement, the Elderhorns' yard was a scene of mass confusion with the display only partly erected. Herman and Madge scurried around getting tangled in strings of lights and bumping into each other.

A sign announcing Christmas in Space was staked into the ground, but the lights Darcie assumed would outline the letters weren't working yet. A pile of red in one corner of the yard might eventually be Santa in a space suit, and other pieces lying around looked like aliens dressed as elves. A giant green nose cone was half-decorated with ornaments.

Darcie couldn't imagine what catastrophe had befallen the Elderhorns that their display wasn't up and running by now. Maybe Joe would know, although he looked far too preoccupied to chat. She climbed out of the truck and went around to get Gus from his car seat. With her son on her hip, she walked into the garage where Joe was wrestling another piece of Times Square out the door.

He looked a mess, sweaty and tired. He glanced at her.

"Maybe you meant to be nice, not waking me up this morning, but I would've liked you to tell me goodbye. I also would have liked you to make sure I got up in time to erect the display."

A wave of remorse washed over her. She'd wanted to postpone the awkward moment of telling him they wouldn't be having sex anymore and she'd taken the cowardly way out. She couldn't pretend she'd let him sleep because she'd thought he needed the rest. Escape had been the only thing on her mind.

He leaned the plywood section against the door frame. "Oh, hell, I'm sorry," he said. "Don't look so guilty. We'll get the damned thing up." He grinned at Gus. "Hey, you little leprechaun. How's it hanging, buddy?"

And why would the lass be waking you up this morning? And why would you be wanting to tell her goodbye all of a sudden, when you never did that any other blessed morning? Faith, maybe inspiration finally bit you in the backside, lad. Proud of you, I am.

"I'll put Gus in his playpen in the garage so I can help you," Darcie said.

Gus waved his arms. *Oh, sure. 'Tis the playpen for Gus. Better put me where I can keep an eye on you two. From the look of things, I wouldn't say the contract is signed, sealed and delivered.*

Joe stepped closer and lowered his voice. "Hold your nose, sweet lady. I'm all sweaty and smell like a goat, but I need to apologize for biting your head off just now. I know you meant well, leaving so quietly this morning. I got some sleep, but you must be dead on your feet. How are you?"

By St. Paddy's beard, something did *go on when I was getting my beauty sleep!*

"I'm fine. But, Joe, I *didn't* mean well, leaving while you were asleep. I meant—"

"Shh. We'll talk later." He held out his arms. "Let me take short stuff for a while so you can go inside and have a minute to rest, or freshen up, or whatever it is mommies do when they have some time off."

"I don't know if either of us should take any breaks. You should see some of the other displays, Joe. They're wonderful. I don't know why the Elderhorns' isn't wonderful yet, but it probably will be."

"I can't figure the Elderhorns, either. When I finally woke up at two this afternoon, I thought for sure they'd be done over there, but they were just getting started. I wonder if anything's wrong."

"Oh dear." Darcie glanced over at the pandemonium in the Elderhorns' front yard. "I hope nothing terrible has happened."

Herman was trying to blow up the inflatable Santa in a space suit while Madge ran around propping up alien elves and putting little green caps on their heads. On one of her trips, she passed behind Herman, reached out and gave him a soft swat on the behind.

Darcie gasped. "Did you see that?" she said in a stage whisper.

"What?" Joe peered across the street.

"Madge patted Herman's backside!"

"No. You must be seeing things. Madge isn't the backside-patting type."

"There! She did it again! And poor Herman is so distracted he can't blow up the inflatable Santa!"

Gus bounced in Darcie's arms and gurgled. *What's this, then? A hanky-panky epidemic? 'Tis spreading through the neighborhood! I think I like it.*

Joe narrowed his eyes as he gazed across the street.

"I'll be damned. She *is* patting his butt! You don't suppose they're late getting the display up because the two of them...nah. Not those two. They've been married a million years at least."

After the night she'd had and a day spent cleaning, Darcie's Irish temper was at flash point. "And what is that supposed to mean? Just because two people have been married for a million years, that they could never be as frisky as rabbits?"

"Not in my experience. The longer people are married, the easier it is to get in a rut. I've seen it happen all around me. Two people start out full of fun and adventure and then they get bogged down with diapers and orthodontists and leaky faucets and crabgrass. And before you know it, they're more worried about finding dust bunnies under the bed than acting like bunnies in bed."

Darcie glared at Joe. "I get the message. And I don't expect you to take care of Gus. I'll find him something to eat, change his diaper and put his costume on him. I'll be out to help when I'm finished."

Now don't be so hard on the lad. He's a wee bit confused, but he's coming around.

Joe frowned. "Look, I didn't mean that I wasn't willing to help out so that you—"

"I'll be back shortly." She carried Gus through the garage and into the house. She hurried through the kitchen and fumbled with the first baby gate. "Bloody gate," she muttered. "Bloody, damn gate!"

Now don't be forgetting who put in those gates. The lad has promise. Rough around the edges, but I'm not finished working on him.

Darcie finally got the gate open, stormed up the stairs and through the second gate, which she'd left open.

She'd left the first gate open, too, but Joe must have closed it when he came down.

"How dare he be so considerate, Gus!" She carried him into his bedroom and put him in his crib while she started banging around, collecting the changing supplies. "And so manly-looking and such a good lover and—" She burst into tears.

Aw, don't cry, lass! Or I'll start crying, too. I know the odds were against him in the beginning, but he's coming on. Don't lose faith.

Darcie sniffed and swiped at her tear-streaked face. "Sorry, Gus. Your mama is head over heels in love with a man who doesn't want her. And it's breaking my heart."

By all the saints, I won't cry! I won't! I— Gus started to wail.

"Oh dear." Darcie grabbed a tissue and mopped her face. Gulping back a sob, she picked up her baby. "Don't cry, Gus. It'll be okay. We have each other." She held him close and pressed her cheek against his hair as she swayed back and forth. "But I hope you can forgive me if I tell you that I would like to have that bullheaded fellow downstairs, too. If he could see his way clear to becoming a family man, he could make my days as bright as a calm sea with the sun in all its glory shining on it."

She sniffed again. "You see, Gus, someday you'll grow up and live your own life, which is as it should be. But when that happens, it would be a comfort if I had a man...if I had Joe...to be my...companion."

Gus's tears slowly subsided as he snuggled against his mother. *And have him you shall, or my name isn't Angus Sean O'Banyon.*

"I love him, Gus."
I'll help you get him. Trust me, lass.

JOE THOUGHT OF FOLLOWING Darcie upstairs and trying to straighten things out between them, but he figured that could take a while, considering he was still pretty uncertain about everything himself. So he went back to work on the display.

They'd have more time to talk through their situation after they'd made it past tonight and the judging of the display. He hadn't meant to give her a speech detailing his views on marriage at this critical moment. Yet it had come tumbling out anyway. Apparently, he was a little edgy on the subject.

He could guess why. His perspective was shifting and it scared him to death. After making love to Darcie, he'd held her close and started thinking all sorts of crazy things, like whether he really wanted to move to Colorado and go into business with his cousin, and whether his single life was really as much fun as he pretended it was, and whether he might not enjoy having a little guy like Gus around on a regular basis.

Maybe he'd allowed his teenager's view of caring for triplets to color his whole view of marriage and kids. And quite possibly that view was dead wrong.

When he woke up this afternoon, more questions bombarded him. He'd always figured that having a kid would make a woman more child-oriented and less interested in passionate sex. Darcie was very child-oriented, but, despite that, she was wonderful...no, *incredible* to make love to. And she'd even been *tired* for Pete's sake.

As Joe started testing the lights on the display, he began to think back over the conversations he'd had with his buddies who were married. He'd been looking for information to back up the theories he'd concocted at sixteen, and he'd found it. Or so he'd thought.

His friends had talked about being up late with a fussy baby, about scraping up the money to add on a room to the house instead of taking a vacation to Hawaii, about toilet training and which kind of formula was really the best. But now that he thought about it, none of the guys had ever said their sex life was dull. He'd assumed it would have to be, though. Surely, with all that…

And yet, there had been nothing boring about going to bed with Darcie, and she dealt with all those same worries every day. Of course, it was only one night and they weren't married. If they were married and made love a lot, they'd probably slip into a humdrum relationship pretty quickly.

He tried to believe that. He really, really tried. But every time he thought about Darcie—her Irish brogue, her sweet body, her saucy personality—he was anything but bored. In fact, he could hardly wait until all this yard decoration business was over for the night so he and Darcie could pick up where they'd left off.

"Okay, Northwood," he lectured himself as he un-rolled another orange extension cord out to the display. "You're getting obsessed with the woman. Now stop it, or you'll find yourself hog-tied for sure."

He plugged the extension cord into the chasing lights that would form the sign running across the top of the Allied Tower Building. Darcie had lit up just like that when he'd made love to her last night, he thought. She'd…

Joe sighed and shook his head, astounded at himself. He couldn't get her out of his mind. "So what if she's great in bed?" he muttered.

"Now, honey, would that question be hypothetical?

Because if it's not, then you and I have some things to discuss.''

Joe turned to find Dolly Parton standing behind him, arms crossed over her balloon-filled chest.

14

"UH, HI THERE, GERALDINE," Joe said. "Where's your limo?"

"I couldn't have Stanley sitting here at your curb and interfering with the look of your display, so I drove myself over. I parked across from the Tannenbaum entrance and walked through the neighborhood so I could check out the other displays." She imitated Dolly Parton's giggle. "And, honey, folks are *so* friendly. I signed two autographs."

Joe shook his head. "People get thrown in the clink for impersonating celebrities, you know."

Geraldine patted his arm. "You let me worry about that. In the meantime, I need to know exactly how friendly you've been recently. Confession is good for the soul."

"My soul or yours?"

"Mine." She giggled again. "I love juicy confessions."

"This doesn't concern you, Geraldine."

"The hell it doesn't. That girl came to my house seeking protection, and I plan to see that she gets it."

"She was seeking a telephone!"

Geraldine waved a hand, making her balloons jiggle under her bright red dress. "Totally symbolic. She was seeking communication and guidance from an older, wiser woman."

Joe rolled his eyes. "Guidance of a mechanical nature, considering that her car died."

"Also symbolic. Her feminine independence was threatened and she needed someone to protect her from being dominated by a male authority figure."

"Oh, yeah, that's me all right. Your wig must be cutting off oxygen to your brain if you seriously think I'm a dominating male authority figure."

"I have adjusted my perception on that score, especially after watching you take care of little Gus. You're good with him, I'll give you that. But I still worry about that innocent, tender bud of womanhood falling into the clutches of some oversexed, undercommitted stud. That would be you, hot stuff."

"Innocent, tender bud? She's the one who showed up in *my* bed!"

"Aha! So you did the nasty after all, you bad boy! I should have followed my instincts and moved in with you when she did."

"Excuse me? You weren't invited to move in!"

"Never mind that now." Geraldine lowered her voice. "Listen, I've seen the other entries, and you and Darcie have your work cut out for you if you're going to win that money. I'm here to help."

"Bull. You're here to keep me in line."

Geraldine sighed. "That was my original intent, but unfortunately, I'm too late for that. All that's left is damage control."

DARCIE FINISHED SNAPPING Gus into his flesh-colored bodysuit and fastened on a second diaper, one that was for show only, over that. She was carrying Gus into her bedroom so she could get into her Miss Millennium outfit when Geraldine called up the stairs.

"Darcie, can I come up?"

"Sure." Darcie went to open the baby gate at the top of the stairs. "I could use some help with my costume."

"You need help with more than that, toots." Adjusting her balloons, Geraldine climbed the stairs. "I gather there's been some slap and tickle going on around here."

Gus waved his arms. *While you've been lollygagging around posing for holy pictures, I've had to take matters into my own hands.*

"Joe told you?"

"Not intentionally." Geraldine came to the top of the stairs and wrapped an arm around Darcie's shoulders. "He was in the yard mumbling to himself and I happened to overhear him."

"In the yard mumbling to himself? Is he all right?"

Geraldine smiled. "No, he's not all right. He's totally confused, and you need to make sure he stays that way until he proposes to you."

We'll get him to the church, we will. I've a mind to uncork my secret weapon.

"Ha!" Darcie said. "You think Joe Northwood will propose? He just delivered a speech on the subject of marriage and he thinks it's more boring than a pub on Sunday morning, as my da would say!"

Geraldine guided Darcie down the hallway toward her bedroom. "He might think that of marriage in general, but he doesn't think that of marriage in particular, or marriage to you in even more particular. The boy is salivating to marry you. He only has to vault over his prejudices long enough to realize it. I know you've been debating whether to wear the long gown I loaned you or the bikini, especially after what Joe said the other night. Wear the bikini. At least for the judging."

"Are you sure?"

"Absolutely, and for many reasons. For one thing, I picked up a flyer from the information booth at the entrance and learned a very interesting fact. The ratfink will be one of the judges."

"*Your* ratfink?"

"Not mine for much longer. The divorce is going along splendidly and money will flow like wine—in my direction, of course. But, in the meantime, if you want to win that contest, you need to appeal to the ratfink's weakness for feminine pulchritude. And that should also help nudge Joe toward the altar."

Nudge? That sounds a wee bit gentle. 'Tis a cattle prod I had in mind.

Geraldine reached over and tweaked Gus's nose. "And what are you up to, you little leprechaun? Something's going on in that fertile little brain of yours. I can see it in your eyes."

Been saving this trick all my life, I have. And tonight's the night.

WEARING A WHITE WIG, white bathrobe and a beard that reached to his toes, Joe stood behind the backdrop and watched the judges huddle as they discussed the display next door. Two men and a woman made up the judging team this year, apparently. The neighbors' Christmas train was cute, but Joe didn't consider it real competition.

He'd already heard from the guy with the train decoration that the biggest threat in all of Tannenbaum featured a giant Santa puzzling over his huge computer screen and a host of animated computer bugs dancing and whirling through the display. Rudolph stood beside him with a computer disk in his mouth. The entry was called A Y2K-Compliant Christmas.

Joe admitted it was clever, but nobody, not even the

computer-display folks, had Baby New Year. A live Baby New Year.

Behind him, the house was dark so it wouldn't detract from the lights on the Times Square backdrop. Darcie, Gus and Geraldine stood inside the front door waiting until Joe turned on the sound system playing "Auld Lang Syne." At least he hoped to hell they were standing there as arranged. They'd had no time for a run-through. Joe had worked on the display right up to the minute he'd raced inside to shower and throw on his costume.

Geraldine had been in Darcie's bedroom with the door closed. When he'd rapped on the door and asked if they were ready, Geraldine had given him a not-very-reassuring "almost."

Across the street, the Elderhorns' display looked abandoned. They hadn't even bothered to change the sign, so it still announced Christmas Spa, but the mess in the yard didn't look much like a resort. Music from *2001: A Space Odyssey* played, but the speakers weren't working very well and the sound kept fading and then surging back when a breeze touched the wires and helped them connect again.

A faint light glowed from the Elderhorns' upstairs bedroom. Red.

Shaking his head, Joe glanced next door. The judges were on their way. Punching the button on the sound system, he adjusted his 1999 sash and picked up his scythe. Then he stooped over like the decrepit old man Geraldine had told him to be, stepped out from behind the display, tripped over his beard and fell on his face.

"Are you all right?" the woman judge called.

Damn beard. "Heh, heh," he cackled, trying to sound ancient. "When you trip over your beard it's time to get off the stage," he said as he staggered to his feet. Then he tossed the beard over his shoulder and proceeded to make his stooped way across the red carpet as the judges chuckled.

Comedy wasn't a bad thing, he told himself. Now for the special effects. He made it to the far side of the carpet and reached for the switch that would bring the lighted ball up over the top of the display. The motor whirred and the ball rose, exactly as he'd planned, right over the Allied Tower Building.

A collective intake of breath from the judges was his reward. He gazed upward, incredibly proud of himself. If they won the prize, he could take some credit for it after all.

Then the judges gasped again. He glanced at them in surprise. That was his only special effect. Then slowly his attention turned to what had created such a reaction, and his breath caught in his throat.

Darcie stood there holding Gus, who was wearing his sash and top hat. He looked extremely cute, but one look at Darcie and Joe knew the gasp had been for her. She was wearing a tiara, silver spike heels, her Miss Millennium sash...and very little else. A few scraps of material covered the essentials.

His first thought was that she was the most beautiful woman in the entire world. His second thought was that she was practically naked, and he didn't want any other man to see her that way except him.

But he wouldn't ever have the right to request that of her unless... Joe winced as the noose tightened around his heart. Then Darcie smiled, and he knew he'd risk anything to be able to see that smile for the rest of his life.

He might have stood there with a dopey grin on his face forever if the judges hadn't started chuckling and pointing upward. Looking up, he discovered his lighted ball had become a yo-yo.

Fixing it was out of the question unless he took the whole thing apart, which he sure couldn't do in the middle of the show. Darcie stared at it in dismay, but Gus crowed in delight. The judges acted as if the whole thing had been planned, so Joe tried to look nonchalant. So much for his great special effect.

Darcie raised her eyebrows as if asking whether she should send Gus over anyway. He nodded.

She eased Gus down to the red carpet, displaying quite a bit of cleavage in the process. Joe wanted to take off his robe and throw it around her. Geraldine was responsible for this, he thought as he clenched his jaw.

Thank God the judges were focused on Gus finally. The woman judge looked totally enraptured as the baby started crawling over the red carpet toward Joe. As Gus crawled, his top hat tilted over one eye and the woman cooed like a devoted grandmother. No doubt about it, Gus had the franchise on cute.

This, at least, was going right, Joe thought with relief.

Then Gus stopped and sat down in the middle of the red carpet.

Joe glared at the baby, willing him to start moving again. The rugrat had better not louse up or he'd never get another French fry from Joe. The kid had crawled around the living room like a champ. All he had to do was get back on all fours and make it another thirty feet.

Gus glared back from under the brim of his top hat. He looked as if he'd planted himself to stay.

Joe glanced at Darcie.

She mouthed the words, *Call to him.*

Joe didn't know if Gus cared much whether Joe called

him or not, but it was worth a try. As it was, the display had gone flat. "Come on over here, Gus," he said.

Beg me, blarney breath. We're playing for all the marbles this time.

"Come on, short stuff. Crawl right on over here."

Down on your knees, then.

Getting desperate, Joe crouched down and put all he had into his plea. "Come to me, little guy. You can do it, Baby New Year. Make us proud, you little leprechaun."

'Tis more like it. Now for the grand finale. Gus leaned over and put his hands on the rug.

"That's it, Gus. Come on. Come to Joe."

Gus got his feet under him, crouching like a little bullfrog. Then slowly, painstakingly, he wobbled to his feet.

"Gus!" Darcie cried.

Don't bother me, lass. Have to concentrate, I do.

Joe stared in disbelief as Gus took one swaggering step. He looked like a little bowlegged drunk, but he put the next foot out, and the next.

"Gus, oh, Gus." Tears sparkled in Darcie's eyes and she sniffed, but she stayed where she was.

And suddenly, Joe knew what he was supposed to do. He held out his arms. "Come on, Gus," he said, his voice hoarse. "Come to Joe, little guy."

Gus gave him a grin the size of Phoenix and kept coming. When he was only two feet away, he held out his own chubby little arms. "Da-da," he said.

Joe gathered him close, his throat tight. "I think you've got something there, you little leprechaun."

THE NEXT FEW MINUTES WERE a blur for Joe as the judges crowded around, congratulating him and goo-gooing at

Gus, the man of the hour. Geraldine showed up about the time the judges moved on down the street.

"I think it's in the bag, your bouncing Times Square ball notwithstanding," she said.

"Gus won it for us," Joe said as he tried to keep his beard out of the baby's grasp. "Who would have thought he'd pick that moment to start walking?"

"He has a sense of the dramatic, which is part of his Irish heritage. Now why don't I take him for a little bit so you can go congratulate Darcie for her part?"

"Okay. Sure." Joe handed Gus over, although he was a little reluctant to let go of him. "Where is she?" He glanced around the yard.

"Inside putting on the long dress she intends to wear for the rest of the time you do this display. She'd freeze to death in that outfit night after night."

"No joke! That was positively indecent."

"But it worked."

"I say we didn't need it."

Geraldine gazed up at him. "We'll know that in a little while, won't we? Now get on in there and say your piece."

"You mean my congratulations."

"If that's all you have to say."

That wasn't all Joe had to say, but he wasn't about to let Geraldine know that. "Be right back."

"Take your time. The general public won't be let in for another thirty minutes."

Joe threw his beard over his shoulder again, picked up the hem of his white bathrobe and hurried in through the front door of the dark house. "Darcie, where are you?"

"Upstairs," she called back. "Thought I'd get changed while you and Gus soaked up the limelight."

Joe grinned as he crossed the living room. He started up the stairs and crashed into the baby gate. "Dammit!"

"Oh, sorry." Light flooded the hallway as Darcie opened her bedroom door. "I closed it in case you brought Gus into the living room."

Rubbing his banged knee, Joe opened the gate. "Geraldine has Gus. I just came in to…" He paused as Darcie appeared at the head of the stairs dressed in the sort of long white dress he'd hoped she'd wear for the competition instead of the bikini. Emotion lodged in his throat.

She looked like a bride.

"What?" she asked.

He couldn't find the words as he gazed up at her, the light from the hall surrounding her red-gold curls with a halo of light. She was everything he'd ever wanted, and now that he knew that, he was petrified that she'd refuse him.

"Joe? You look sick to your stomach. Is it the glue from your beard?"

His voice came out as a strangled croak. "It's you."

"Me? I make you sick to your stomach?"

"No! You make me…" He took a deep breath. "You make me want things I thought I didn't want. But now I do. With you. Everything."

"Joe, I think it's the glue talking. And the glue isn't making much sense, sad to say."

"It's not the glue, dammit! It's me! I love you! I want you to marry me, and now I'm afraid you won't because I told you I thought marriage was as boring as diced zucchini, and so you probably think that I would be that boring! But I won't be. I promise I won't."

He took a deep breath and kept going. "I thought staying free was the way to get somewhere, but I'm going nowhere, Darcie. I need a reason to get where I want to go. You're that reason. You and Gus. Give me a chance, Darcie." He finally ran out of steam. "Please," he whispered, gazing up at her.

She slowly descended the stairs. It seemed to take about five hours. At last she was on the step right above him, their faces level with each other. Her green eyes sparkled as she gazed at him. "That's quite a speech for such an old man. You must be Irish."

"Darcie, I don't think there's a drop of Irish blood in me. But if that's what it takes for you to love me, I'll search my whole family tree until I find a Murphy or an O'Malley or a Finnegan."

She rested her hands on his shoulders. "Doesn't much matter if you are an Irishman so long as you can think like one."

His heart started beating even faster. Maybe she would consider spending the rest of her life with him. Just maybe. "And how would that be at this moment?"

"An Irishman wouldn't be wasting his time flapping his jaws." Her saucy mouth tilted up in a smile. "An Irishman would be taking action."

"Right here on the stairs?"

"No one's here but us."

"Okay." Joe reached for the sash of his robe. "Why not? I'm certainly in the mood for it after watching you running around in that skimpy outfit, which I hope never to see you wearing in the fresh air again, but in the privacy of—"

"Wait!" Darcie grabbed his hand, laughing. "I meant you should kiss me, not get to work with that jib of yours!"

"Oh."

"We can see about that later on, though. For now, a kiss will do to seal the bargain."

"What bargain? Did you agree to a bargain? I didn't hear of any bargain."

"That's because I was never asked, just lectured to about diced zucchini."

"Oh." Joe cleared his throat. Then he cradled her beloved face in both hands, hardly daring to believe in his incredible luck. Maybe he was Irish after all. "Will you marry me, Darcie O'Banyon?"

"Yes, I will, because I love you with all my heart and soul, Joe Northwood. Would you kiss me now?"

He didn't know such happiness existed. "Yes, now. And for the rest of our days. Which will be, I promise, much more exciting than diced zucchini."

"I could have told you that."

When his lips touched hers, he half expected to hear the sound of a door closing on his other life, a life he was more than happy to leave behind. But instead, all he could hear was the joyous sound of doors opening wide as love flooded into his heart.

Epilogue

WELL NOW, THEY WON the blessed contest, which was destined to happen with me in the title role, of course. Got married, they did. Blarney breath got the license quicker than an Irishman can down a pint in a pub at closing time.

Geraldine landed a fine settlement from the ratfink and determined that she'd fancy becoming a silent partner in an interior decoration and custom cabinetry shop. Cabinet making and interior decorating go together like holly and ivy, they do. Oh, yes, and 'twas a grand Christmas. Nearly pulled down the tree, I did, bringing in the New Year.

'Twill be quite a New Year from the sound of things. Getting a wee cottage with a yard and a sandbox, we are. Maybe even a dog I can be chasing around the yard when I've nothing better to do. And I hear talk of competition coming my way in the wee babe department....

As if some red-faced interloper could ever unseat me— the great, the clever, the unforgettable and endlessly darling Angus Sean O'Banyon.

TRACY SOUTH

Frisky Business

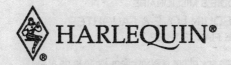

HARLEQUIN®

TORONTO • NEW YORK • LONDON
AMSTERDAM • PARIS • SYDNEY • HAMBURG
STOCKHOLM • ATHENS • TOKYO • MILAN • MADRID
PRAGUE • WARSAW • BUDAPEST • AUCKLAND

Dear Reader,

My heroes have always been...business majors?

I went through college with no clear idea of where Fraternity Row was. I was into poetry and theater, classes full of pale-faced, skinny young men who needed someone to buy them a cup of coffee. I was so convinced that my soul mate would need to be the "artsy" type that when I met my husband, my first thought was "I hope he's not a business major."

He was, but he was also a guitar player, which barely qualified him as "artsy." Ten years later, I've discovered that the heroes I create in my novels are those who share my husband's spirit and his sense of fun, those who tackle life with humor and style.

Laura Everett, the heroine of *Frisky Business*, is pretty sure she knows what's behind co-worker Kyle Sanders's smile. Thoughts of golf. Thoughts of lunch. Plans to steal the corner office from her. More golf. More lunch. But Kyle's got more going for him than a set of pearly whites and a line of glib patter. And Laura's about to find out exactly what that something is....

Tracy South

Books by Tracy South

HARLEQUIN DUETS
8—MADDIE'S MILLIONAIRE

HARLEQUIN LOVE & LAUGHTER
12—THE FIANCÉ THIEF

Don't miss any of our special offers. Write to us at the following address for information on our newest releases.

Harlequin Reader Service
U.S.: 3010 Walden Ave., P.O. Box 1325, Buffalo, NY 14269
Canadian: P.O. Box 609, Fort Erie, Ont. L2A 5X3

For my parents, Charles and Becky,
who never thought I wouldn't be a writer.

1

LAURA EVERETT HAD practiced this speech a hundred times in her bedroom mirror. But now that it was time to deliver it to her boss, she was faltering.

"Harris, I'd like to talk to you about the project I'm assigned to. I'd like to work on something a little more, um, high-profile. I mean, I know that you have some projects picked out for Kyle Sanders...." The name of her too handsome office rival stuck in her throat, and, too late, she thought she shouldn't have brought him up at all. "But I really want..."

Her portly boss stared at her. "You want what?"

I want a job that doesn't suck, she screamed inside her head. That was the way more than half of her practice speeches had ended, and she bit her lip now to keep from saying it aloud.

Chances were, though, that even if she had said it, her boss simply wouldn't have heard her. His attention was already gone, as he searched for something on the plush gray carpeting under his seat. When he raised up, he asked, "Have you seen my napkin?"

"Your what?"

"I need a napkin. Where did mine go?"

Maybe a company baby shower for his secretary wasn't the best place to get Harris alone, Laura thought, gazing at the head of the conference table where Tricia, the mama-to-be, was tackling another box of professionally wrapped loot. But Laura had to talk to Harris now. It was the only time she'd seen him all week without Kyle Sanders, Boy Wonder, hanging on his every word. Laura knew that yes-men had their attractions. This yes-man, in particular, had lots of attractions, like being tall, fit and handsome, which Laura did her best to ignore. Laura knew that what her boss liked best about Kyle was his can-do attitude and his sunny optimism. Well, of course he did. Positive people were nice. Laura *liked* positive people. But sometimes caution, not optimism, was the best reaction to a situation. Pointing that out, though, always made her look like Ms. Can't-Do to Kyle's Mr. Go-Getter.

Her thoughts were interrupted by a chorus of "Oh, how adorable!" as Tricia held up a tiny Atlanta Braves baseball cap.

Harris stopped his napkin search and glanced at Tricia, then back at Laura, staring at her intently. *Finally, he's taking me seriously.*

"Who got that cap?" he asked her. "I could keep

some around to give to clients when they say their wives are going to have another rug rat.''

"I don't know," Laura said. It was hard to decide which she knew less about, baseball or babies. "But I could find out for you."

"Nah, Tricia can do that. Tricia," he shouted. "Order up a dozen of those guys."

Tricia simply smiled at her boss. Amazing. No matter what Harris did or said, she always responded with that same sweet expression. Laura was never sure whether to nominate the secretary for sainthood or hit her up for some of whatever she was on.

"Who's it from?" Harris asked again.

"It's from me." Laura heard Kyle Sanders's smooth baritone from somewhere over her left shoulder. Well, of course it was. If the sun rose in the morning and the little birdies sang, Kyle Sanders was in on it somehow.

Go away, go away, she ordered silently. Instead, her body tensed as he took the chair next to hers, and she waited for the bump or kick he always managed around her. Boom. He jarred against her as he sprawled his legs out under the cherrywood table.

"Sorry," he said.

"No problem," she answered, forcing herself not to turn around. Not only did she not want to be distracted by him, but her chance to have Harris hear her out was slipping away. But before she could make plans to finish their talk later, Harris had angled around her to address Kyle. "Where'd you say you got that hat?"

Plan B. A girl should always assume an interest in her boss's hobbies. Years ago, that *Seventeen* magazine advice had been applied to dating, not working, but she'd had many more opportunities to use it in the corporate world than at romantic Italian dinners or in the back seats of cars. She swiveled around, ready to fake a good show of enthusiasm. But the second she looked at Kyle, she regretted it.

No one, but no one, could take up as much physical space as Kyle Sanders. It was baffling, considering he wasn't even that big. He was tall, and he was buff, but seeing him on the street, you'd never dream that he could make a whole quarter of a room his own just by the way he stood or walked or lounged. Laura knew it was a trick of perception—she supposed she practiced her own version of it with her high heels and stylish power suits.

But Kyle Sanders didn't need the props. She'd seen him look just as confident, just as powerful, on a working Sunday afternoon, wearing baggy khaki shorts and a faded University of Georgia T-shirt. Right now he had on an obviously expensive white cotton shirt with the sleeves rolled up, his royal-blue silk tie loosened and hanging slightly askew. His thick brown hair curled above the back of his shirt collar, and a wayward lock across his forehead lent added interest to a devilishly good-looking face. The outfit made his blue eyes even bluer and played up the bronze of his skin. If she didn't know that he was a regular Mr. Outdoors, she'd suspect him of sweet-talking some peroxided young thing out of her tanning bed appointment. Or talking her into letting him share it.

Danger, Will Robinson, she thought, turning back in Harris's direction as Kyle named the store where he'd gotten the hat. Among the secrets she hoped to take to her grave was the way the thought of Kyle Sanders, always and inevitably, led to the thought of…well, Kyle Sanders. Kyle Sanders in contexts that were definitely outside the boundaries of their working relationship.

She wasn't even someone who normally noticed stuff like that. Stuff like well-defined arms, bright eyes, a smile that moved from slow to dazzling in six seconds. Her previous relationships, the couple she'd had before she let her job become her life, had been based on the guy's intelligence or compatible life goals—not what he looked like in jeans. If that had made them a little dull, well, so be it. While all her girlfriends could chat about the contours of men's der-rieres as though they were talking tomatoes at the Fresh Market, she'd never even looked twice at a man's butt until she'd caught sight of Kyle's.

This physical attraction to Kyle was nothing more than a case of crossed wires. The first time she'd seen him—six months, four weeks, two days and two hours ago, not that she didn't *hate* herself for remembering that—her immediate response had been, *That man is a threat to my career.* There was something about the casual way Kyle leaned against the doorway, or the way his eyes went to the slate-gray walls of the hall, as though sizing up how his own picture would look there. True, she was a little paranoid, since she was the only female Harris had ever made a full-fledged consultant, and she had long suspected that she was about to hit some kind of special glass ceiling Harris had created just for her.

Here was where her natural pessimism proved right once again. Shortly after he had hired Kyle, Harris had started playing with the ''warring tribes'' theory of employment, the idea that employees stayed on their toes by being competitive with each other. The stakes in this competition were pretty high—the firm was large enough only for one vice president, a position Harris was going to fill, one day, with one of them. Harris Associates specialized in remaking high-tech firms, with a growing sideline in the lucrative health care industry. Some of the firm's most notable successes had been on her watch, but she was past expecting anyone to notice that. Kyle had worked for several of their competitors, while she'd stayed with the first organization who hired her out of graduate school. She'd had offers, but she was loyal, not like *Mr. Take the Company Car and Run.* Why couldn't he run out of here so that Harris didn't have to choose? This continual waiting was like always being on the wrong end of eeny-meeny-miney-mo.

Unfortunately, just as she'd realized he was a shark circling her warm and safe position in the company, she'd also realized that Kyle was the best-looking man she'd seen since she broke herself of buying *People* magazine and started buying *Fast Company* instead. Her subconscious, a little slow on the uptake and obviously way too chummy with her hormones, had taken in her anxiety and attributed it not to the threat to her career, where it belonged, but to the threat to her celibacy, where it didn't.

Her subconscious was a twit.

"You have icing on your shirt," Kyle said. He leaned in front of her, close enough for her to smell the spicy scent of his shampoo. She looked down, and as she did, he tipped her nose. A trick straight out of third grade, and not a touch that could be in any way responsible for the curiously warm feeling that coursed through her.

"I meant Harris," he said.

"Oh."

Harris glared at her. "I told you I was looking for my damn napkin."

As if by magic, Kyle, who hadn't even had any cake, produced a paper napkin. Why hadn't she given her own napkin to Harris? Then it registered that the napkin Kyle was offering *was* hers. He'd already slid her Pooh-decorated paper plate, with its untouched cake, to his seat.

"Is that my cake?" she asked as the napkin changed hands in front of her.

"You don't eat supermarket cake, do you?" His tone was deceptively innocent. "I thought you saved your calories for quality desserts."

The couple of other women in the room put down their plates of half-eaten cake. The stares they gave her could only be described as murderous. Even Tricia's lip curled a little, though she quickly went back to one of her bright smiles.

"It's not that—" Laura began.

But Tricia cut her off, saying, "Kyle, you didn't get any cake." She made as though she were going to stand up, but he waved her way.

"No, no, I'm just going to eat Laura's cake, take temptation out of her way."

With one sentence, he had managed to make an endearing little used-cake martyr of himself *and* reinforce the idea to all the women there that she was above the siren call of gooey, sticky white icing.

Brandi, the receptionist, jumped up and grabbed the knife, quickly commandeering an extra large corner piece with one and a half blue roses for Kyle. She walked over and set it in front of him.

"Eat them both," she said.

He was already polishing off Laura's piece. "Thanks, I think I will," he said.

The man had the metabolism of an army of Huns.

"You don't know what you're missing," he told Laura. Just before sticking the fork in the second piece, though, he looked around, then started to stand, very slowly, in a way Laura had learned to identify as "Kyle has no intention of really getting up, confident that someone will take care of his needs." She'd seen this move, too. As usual, someone fell for it. She kept her attention on him, telling herself she was only interested in who the sucker would be, not that she liked to watch him move and stretch and stand.

"What do you need, Kyle? Do you need some coffee?" Brandi asked. She'd been on her way back to her seat, but now she stopped, waiting.

He paused in midstand. "We don't have any milk, do we?"

"Sure, there's some in the break-room fridge."

"Great. I'll go—"

"No, I will. No trouble at all." And away Brandi flew.

Unbelievable. Yet when one of the other guys asked Brandi where something was, she wouldn't budge from her seat to help, even when it became clear that they were fully incapable of locating the heads screwed onto their scrawny shoulders. Laura had even had to rescue a few of them from the supply closet herself, after Brandi had left them stranded there. But if Kyle needed so much as a square inch of tape, she would, instantly, whip out the office supply catalog and order a jillion cases, so he would *never* be without again.

Part of it was his looks, sure, but it wasn't totally a lust thing. It was a response to the little-boy side of Kyle, some kind of instinct that said he needed protecting from the big bad world outside. Poor thing, so defenseless.

Defenseless as a king cobra.

Kyle thanked Brandi as she returned with the milk. Now, with his mouth full and Harris's attention restored to this end of the table, Laura knew she should reach some kind of closure on her muddled conversation with Harris. Instead, she found herself trying to explain to Kyle about the cake thing.

"It's not that I don't eat dessert or anything. It's just that I travel so much…"

He swallowed, nodding sympathetically. "How do you keep them in lard and sugar after they've tasted real cream?"

"No, no," she said. "But if I'm going to splurge on something, I want it to be something worthwhile."

"You have to plan for spontaneity," he said, still nodding.

The man was impossible.

"No, that's not what I'm saying at all. I'm saying I like being in control of my whims."

"But if you're in control of them, are they really whims?" His voice was agreeable, but his deep-blue eyes were intense. This was Kyle-in-for-the-kill mode, her left brain registered, but all the other parts of her mind and body were acting as though that attentive gaze belonged to her and her alone. *Snap out of it,* she told herself, but instead she kept staring at him as he said, "When is a splurge a splurge and when is it something you're calling a splurge, because you've heard you should have one every once in a while?"

"I don't—" she began, flustered, but was saved by the sound of Harris's low chuckle. She looked up to see him shaking his head.

"If you two could only work together instead of fighting with each other, I'd have a hell of a team," he said. He stood up and started to walk away. Laura was about to follow him, but then he stopped, turned around and stared at her and Kyle.

He had an odd, quizzical expression on his face. Frankly, he looked possessed. Linda Blair could be handing him an Oscar right now. She shrank back in her seat and glanced at Kyle. Of course he was trying not to betray visible alarm, but she noticed with satisfaction that the last bit of cake was going down hard.

"If you two could work together instead of fighting with each other, I'd have a hell of a team." This time Harris said it in a detached, nearly Zenlike tone, the kind people used when they wanted to tell you they had found the universe in a grain of sand and would soon be carted away for their own safety. Everyone else in the room had shifted their attention to him, and Laura saw Brandi, carrying Kyle's glass of milk, shrink back from the doorway.

Now Harris's voice held more than a hint of anger. "If you two could work together instead of fighting with each other, I'd have a hell of a team."

"You already said that," Laura and Kyle chimed. She looked at Kyle, surprised by this moment of rare accord, and felt his arm come down hard around her shoulders.

"See what a team we were just then? Right, Laura?"

"Right, Kyle." Great, she sounded like a newly minted six o'clock anchorperson. And Harris wasn't convinced, she could tell. Tricia was standing up now, making murmurs about Harris's blood pressure, but his stare was relentless, his bushy eyebrows knitted together on his forehead.

"I need to talk to both of you," Harris announced. "Tricia, I need to talk to both of them later."

This is it. Today he tells us who's the VP and who gets to be the one who takes over "in the event that the winner cannot fulfill the duties of the position." If Kyle didn't get to be vice president, he would leave the company. Would she? She would have to, for her pride. Just the thought of trying an unfamiliar environment made her stomach start to wiggle and her ears grow hot.

Hot ears. The last time she'd had hot ears was in college, when she'd found herself on a frat house couch next to her longtime crush while his girlfriend threw up in the bathroom. Surely Kyle's arm around her wasn't causing this reaction?

"I'd be glad to have a meeting with you and Laura, Harris," Kyle said. His arm around her grew nicely, but alarmingly, heavy. It could even be said that he caressed her shoulder slightly. Trying to rein in a sudden wave of lust with a stern inner lecture, Laura only half heard him say, "But I've also got some ideas I'd like to run by you. Is there a good time for that today?"

See, Laura chided herself, *there you go, getting all hot and bothered over a man whose only purpose in touching you is to render you speechless while he steals your audience with Harris.* All that fiend had to do was pat her on the shoulder, and she was ready to break her vow of abstinence.

Well, she had never actually taken a vow of abstinence—her life had just sort of worked out that way, and after a while it was easier to pretend that it had been intentional. Did an unwilling state of virtue count as much to her general good person points as a willing one would have? She was ready to start a furious internal argument with herself over this when the one tiny part of her brain that was still rational registered what Kyle Sanders had said.

I've got some ideas I want to run by you.

"No," she said, more loudly than she'd meant to, wrenching her shoulder away from Kyle and jumping up from her seat. She knew how she sounded on those rare occasions when she lost her temper—she made Cruella De Vil look like a gap-toothed Brownie scout. But she couldn't stop herself.

"No, you may not talk to him alone today," she said to Kyle. "I've been trying to arrange a meeting with Harris all afternoon."

"You were sitting right by him," Kyle said. "Why didn't you ask him?"

Because he wasn't listening to me and then you came in and made me go all hormonal. She couldn't say that. So instead she said, "You can't have my cake and eat it, too."

"I got an extra rose, so you get a meeting with Harris before I do? That's a pretty good consolation prize."

My life is one big consolation prize. But before she

could snap back something at Kyle, Harris bellowed, "Enough. I said I would see you later."

Laura sat back down. When Harris got angry like that, he looked an awful lot like Brian Keith playing Uncle Bill in *Family Affair*. She watched her sixtyish boss stomp out, red-faced, and decided she wasn't going to stop him to tell him that.

She looked back at Kyle. He was staring a little off into space, his expression guarded, and she could tell that the encounter had troubled him. Troubled, Kyle looked even better than he did when he was smiling.

She wasn't going to tell him that, either.

So THE REPORTS of his colleague's temper hadn't been exaggerated. Although she'd caught herself before she completely let go, Kyle had gotten a hint of what it must be like to be near one of those legendary Laura Everett meltdowns. According to Tricia and Brandi, once, when Harris had yanked control of a project from her at the last minute, she had thrown dishes across the break room. Foam coffee cups, actually, and then she'd started blushing and apologizing, but the word was out.

When they'd told him that story, over brownies in the office kitchen one afternoon, he'd tsk-tsked and shook his head. But secretly, it fascinated him. The first time he'd seen Laura, he'd gotten a flash impression of wildness, a dangerous glint in those incredible hazel eyes. Industry gossips had been eager to tell him that the highest-ranking management consultant at Harris Associates was a woman, but no one had ever said she was a beautiful woman. Even a standard-issue power suit couldn't hide her curves, and her sleekly professional hairdo only accentuated the classic lines of her face. When she spoke, though, he was discouraged by the controlled, modulated tone of her voice and the pure-business freeze of her smile. But hearing her today brought back his first thoughts about her, and reminded him of the attraction he'd felt that day. Officially, Kyle didn't like conflict, which might have been how he wound up dating airheads whose standard response to every question was "I don't care, Kyle. You decide." But a woman who cared enough to throw plates—that was interesting.

Don't go there, Sanders. Laura, just now walking briskly past his office, photocopied papers in one hand, cell phone in another, was not ever, ever, going to be hurling discount store china around his apartment. For one thing, she loathed him. For another, she had reason to.

He wasn't after her job, not exactly. Right now they were at the same level in the company, so if he were promoted, she wouldn't be losing her position, but gaining a vice president. Yeah, right. Like she was really going to see it that way.

It was just a bad set of circumstances, and though

he was tempted to blame Harris, he really couldn't. Oh, hell, why not blame Harris? It would serve him right if Kyle left. He had left other jobs under much better circumstances. If there was one thing he trusted, though, it was his intuition, and killer timing. Something told him that his résumé of job hopping was starting to look a little checkered. He knew he'd been lucky with his first job at another Atlanta consulting firm. They'd given him their lowest priority assignment, restructuring an Internet service provider on the verge of bankruptcy. A few months later, his first client had gone public and the owners, friendly engineering school dropouts, had made a point of letting everyone know that Kyle Sanders was the man behind the transformation. Restless, he'd followed better offers to other consulting firms, but hadn't stayed at any one place long enough to have an impact. He was starting to worry that he was playing a game of musical chairs. A game that would eventually leave him without a seat. He knew it could happen: he'd seen it happen to his father. Like Kyle, he was always gung ho on the next big thing, right before the jobs started drying up and he'd decided to use his MBA to play househusband.

And even if he were still willing to job hop, he liked it at Harris Associates. He liked Harris's bluster and Tricia's cookies and playing golf with the other guys who worked there. He liked the technology firms Harris consulted with, and he knew that their reputation was growing. He shoved aside the thought of Laura's contributions to that reputation. She was a brilliant worker, but she didn't have the temperament for leading a company. She was a bean counter, and bean counters, even deliriously attractive, sweet-smelling ones, weren't good vice president material.

"Kyle?" Tricia buzzed. She sounded sympathetic. "Harris is ready to see you."

He crossed the corridor to the executive suite, where Tricia manned a cozy reception area in front of Harris's office. There was also an extra conference room, and next to it, a smaller empty office. Harris had let it be known that this was being saved for the future vice president. Kyle usually poked his head in to remind himself where he was going to hang his Braves schedule, but today he went straight into Harris's inner sanctum. Laura was already seated across from Harris's desk, while their boss stood looking out the window at the suburban office park below.

Kyle took the leather chair next to Laura, his foot hitting her in the calf as he did so. She gave him an annoyed look, and he tried not to stammer his apologies, instead giving her a quick "sorry" grin. He'd learned early in life that he was never going to be able to sit quietly, and would always fidget and squirm, leaving the space around him looking as though he'd trailed his own personal hurricane in his wake.

He'd tried to use that as an advantage, to welcome the spotlight, make it all look like one big case of "I meant to do that." It was only when he was around Laura, not a wrinkle on her suit, not a smudge in her makeup, that he started feeling like a little kid knocking priceless knickknacks off someone's keepsake shelf.

"I suppose you're wondering why I've called you here," Kyle muttered to himself. Not to himself, obviously, because he caught a quick smile from Laura, a real one. Her eyes lit up and her face became even more beautiful. It reminded him why he sometimes poked his head in her office to share the lame jokes he'd received in the morning's E-mail. Forty-nine out of fifty times he got the preprogrammed robot grin, but on the fiftieth he hit pay dirt.

She stopped smiling, and so did he, when he caught Harris glowering at them.

He didn't know what he expected Harris to say. But it wasn't what followed.

"I've been thinking about New Horizon," Harris said as he turned away from the window and strode over to his desk, where he stood, looking down at them.

Hearing the name of one of their closest competitors turned Laura on instant corporate autopilot. Before Kyle could say anything, she blurted out, "They've managed to capture a niche in the health care consulting market, but I predict that further analysis will show a falloff in their client base.''

More glowering from Harris. Kyle tried not to betray his nervousness, consciously keeping his hands away from his tie and collar. He felt Laura shift in the seat beside him.

''What I'm about to say to you is strictly confidential,'' Harris said. ''I'm thinking of buying New Horizon.''

Kyle sneaked a look at Laura, who was blinking rapidly. ''Their markets can only add value to our product,'' she said quickly.

Smooth, Kyle thought.

''Right, Kyle?''

Right, Kyle? There was never a tape recorder around when you needed one.

''Right, Laura.'' He should let her squirm a second more, but as much as he liked playing with her, he didn't like being played by Harris. Why would their boss go ballistic on them over cake and punch and then reward them with privileged information? ''That's great news, Harris. I assume that's what you wanted to talk to us about?''

''When I'm ready to tell you what I want to talk to you about, I'll talk to you about it.''

Laura shifted noisily in her seat again. He was attuned to her every move, wasn't he? It was just that he'd never seen the Ice Princess so flustered.

Kyle didn't say anything, and although he imagined that it was an effort for her, neither did Laura. Finally Harris said, "I'm ready to talk about it." He sat down in his oversize leather desk chair. "We have two different company cultures. They believe in in-house co-operation, not in-house competition. Walt Williams, the founder of New Horizon, believes that associates are more productive when they're working with each other, not against each other."

As his seven-year-old niece would say, *Duh*. But try getting Harris to see it that way.

"So you're appointing us to the hazing committee or what?" Kyle asked. He looked at Laura, seeing if he'd drawn a smile. He hadn't. He frowned at her, which for some reason made her blush.

"I don't know how to say this any plainer," Harris started.

Try, Kyle thought. *Try*.

"Walt and his partner Bill Brewster want to step away from day-to-day operations and serve instead as salaried consultants. If we acquire New Horizon, I have room for two VPs, not one."

Laura found her voice before Kyle did. "Are you saying we'll both be promoted?"

There has to be a catch, Kyle thought.

"On one condition," Harris said.

Here came the catch.

"You two have to learn to cooperate, to work together as a team. I know you can do it, but you'll have to overcome some pretty bad habits.''

Gee, I wonder where we got them? Kyle thought. He felt Laura visibly relax beside him, but he was only getting antsier. How was he supposed to prove that he and Laura had learned to cooperate? Even if they did learn, how was he going to share his position with someone whose view of the business world was so different from his?

"Next Thursday," Harris continued, "I'm going to Bellamy Island with Walt and Bill to talk about the deal."

"We'll be on our best behavior," Laura said.

Speak for yourself, Kyle thought. The churlish, rebellious side of him didn't want to be cooperative. He wanted to slip his sneakers on and take a long run down one of the office park's side streets, or go home and let the kid next door badger him into shooting some hoops at the condo complex's basketball court. Anything but sitting here playing lapdog to Harris's demands.

But that was the attitude that made him leave job after job, and it was also the attitude that had left his father puttering around the kitchen and garden when he should have been in the prime of his working life. So he feigned patience as Harris said, "You aren't going. I've made arrangements for the two of you to go to a camp in the mountains.''

The mountains? He thought about it. Late spring in the mountains with a beautiful woman by his side. Nothing wrong with that. Except that this fantasy scenario included a beautiful woman who didn't like him very much and a boss who had ulterior motives for sending them there. That sounded less like a fantasy than a bone-chilling campfire story.

"What do you mean, camp?" Laura asked.

Kyle had been to camp when his parents went to Mexico one summer. He'd hitchhiked out of it a dozen times before figuring out a way to make the system work to his advantage. Then he'd loved it, so much so that he'd gone back the next summer to play lifeguard while less lucky souls escorted small children into the wilderness. Could he work out something similar here? Him lounging around the pool with a Corona while Laura made crafts with macaroni pieces?

"It's called Serene Dynamics." Harris picked up a brochure and squinted at it. "Walt left this for me."

"That was nice," Laura said. Kyle and Harris both stared at her. "I mean it," she said.

Harris continued reading. "It offers hands-on learning, hands-on team building."

Kyle knew what that sounded like. That sounded like...

"Is this one of those places where they make you walk across log bridges and climb up the sides of cliffs?" Laura was clearly horrified.

"And play paintball," Kyle added. She blanched.

"I don't know the specifics," Harris said. "But they've promised me they can get you two thinking as one person in less than a weekend."

"And if they can't?" Laura asked the question Kyle was afraid to ask.

"If they can't, then I'm letting you both go. You're in this together now."

2

THE AIR OUTSIDE the car was lush with the smell of blooming flowers, but Laura had her car windows rolled up tightly against it. Every curve of the road seemed to hold yet another picturesque spot, but Laura accelerated past all of them. Her trek from the suburbs of Atlanta to the mountains of north Georgia was starting to remind her of her niece's reaction to the Impressionists' show at the art museum downtown: "A boat, a mountain, a garden. Let's go, already."

Wicked Aunt Laura had dragged five year-old Haley around the gallery a little longer, dangling promises of ice cream, but now she empathized. Flowers, trees, nature. She'd seen it, thanks, and could she go home now?

Cooperate with Kyle, learn to trust Kyle, see how the two of you can work together as a team.

Okay, she got Harris's point. Now why didn't they just skip this weekend get-together and get back to work? She didn't have time for this.

But, if you don't make time for this, you'll have to

find another job, right? Ever since she'd met Kyle Sanders, her head had been filled with circular arguments like this one, stuck in her brain like some terrible TV theme song.

Hoping that Harris would change his mind if he saw her getting along with Kyle, Laura had been beyond nice to her rival all week. That had been difficult, since she needed to be friendly without giving her adolescent-brained hormones the idea that she was getting *too* friendly. Finally she'd reverted to her old sorority girl persona, practically squealing and hugging him every time she saw him, whether that had been five minutes or five hours ago. Unfortunately, the devilish smile he gave her in return reminded her that he was no sorority sister.

Think of something else, Laura told herself. Consider what work still needs to be done at the office after you've placated Harris and kissed and made up with Kyle.

An unfortunate metaphor. Try again.

She visualized her in-box back at the office, reprioritizing all the unexciting items there. There was something to be said for boring assignments, she supposed, because after a few minutes her jangled nerves had unjangled a little, and for the first time since Harris had gone off the deep end, she felt in control.

Then a familiar vintage blue Austin Healey loomed up in her rearview mirror. She saw Kyle wave and smile, gestures that gave no indication that he knew his proximity to her car's rear end was positively indecent. They could have had a shotgun wedding by now.

She wasn't going to even act like she noticed. She certainly wasn't going to speed up. Maybe she'd even decelerate a little, just to prevent herself from speeding up. Was that illegal? While she tried to remember what the Department of Motor Vehicles handbook had said to do about cute men who were deliberately tailgating you but were probably not dangerous, Kyle passed her.

On double yellow lines. To add further insult, the last thing she saw before he maneuvered around her was the car's stupid smiling bug-eyed front. It was the perfect car for Kyle, who believed that his disarming grin allowed him to do whatever he liked.

Before she even thought about it, she had her sturdy sedan on his bumper, telling herself there was no way she could pass him, she had no idea—

But she was already flying around him, sending up fervent prayers that nothing was coming from the other side. If her life were a movie starring Sandra Bullock, she would whisk back into her own lane just as an eighteen wheeler careened around the curve, and when she passed Kyle, he would give a good old "Curses, foiled again," Snidely Whiplash sneer.

Instead, the road remained deserted, and far from

cursing her, Kyle looked like he was searching around in his seat for a cassette. He barely even nodded as she passed.

If her life were a movie starring Sandra Bullock, she decided, she wouldn't be on this mountaintop.

A few minutes later, she spied a tastefully carved wooden sign with the words Serene Dynamics on it. The drive up to the cabin was straight out of the brochure. Gorgeous old hardwood trees and pink flowers poking up out of the native red dirt lined the road. As she'd expected, the cabin was much shabbier than the one in the brochure. But it was also a lot bigger than she'd expected. In fact, this one was plainly built for two.

Kyle had parked a few yards away from her and was dragging a green canvas duffel bag from his car. Either he hadn't noticed that they were sharing an address or he just flat didn't care. And why should he care? Men didn't have to scrape off makeup and shave their legs and defeat pillow head and worry about whether their butts looked big in their pajamas.

Did Kyle wear pajamas? He didn't seem like a pajama guy. He seemed a lot more like a strip-to-his-briefs guy to her. She jerked her mind away from the image of Kyle in briefs. She was just going to have to loan him her cotton robe and wear her exercise shorts under her cotton nightgown. And a bra under her nightgown, too. Heck, she should just keep her clothes on and make Kyle do the same.

Kyle? He was no longer in the small dirt driveway, and when she looked toward the cabin, she saw that he was already headed in. Not without her, he wasn't. Knowing Kyle, a two-second lead could be the difference between sleeping on a mattress or snoozing on the authentically splintered hardwood floor. With the first sprint she'd done since fifth grade field day, Laura caught up with the ambling Kyle.

Inside the cabin they were greeted by a slimly built man in a fuschia golf shirt with the Serene Dynamics logo. His name tag identified him as Rand, and his clipboard identified him as the man in charge.

"Did you two ride up together?" he asked.

"No," Laura said, as Kyle added, "We just happened to pull up at the same time."

Rand nodded knowingly. "One of you saw the other on the road and took that opportunity to pass, without regard to the safety of others?"

When he put it that way…

"I've seen it all in situations like yours," Rand said, waving the clipboard dismissively. "Put two insanely competitive clients on a twisting mountain road and it's a miracle that either of them gets here alive."

"Is that step one of the Serene Dynamics plan? To get rid of us before we get here?" Kyle asked. Laura caught the edge in his tone. He was smiling his Kyle

Sanders, Regular Guy smile, but it wasn't meeting his eyes. Clearly he didn't like being bossed around, she realized. Not by a man with a clipboard, not by a man in a logo shirt. Interesting.

"Levity will get you nowhere," Rand said. "We take our team building very seriously."

Alienating the counseler was not a good way to start their retreat.

"Rand," Laura said, "I don't want you to think this situation is more extreme than it is. For instance, I wouldn't say we're insanely competitive."

"That's not what J. Herbert Harris told me on the phone," Rand said. "Although, frankly, I don't usually see this dynamic between a man and a woman."

I don't like you, Laura thought, but then Kyle surprised her by saying, "That's because most organizations aren't secure enough to promote a woman as competent as Laura."

Did he mean that, or was this just a clever way of throwing her off track? Not so clever, if she saw right through it, but if it weren't a trick, then she'd just discarded a perfectly good compliment. So which was it?

Rand answered for her by making a little "huh" noise in his throat. Laura knew that noise. She used it herself. It meant, "I know better, but since you aren't listening to me, why waste my breath?"

Surely it didn't sound so unpleasant when she made it?

"What?" she asked Rand. "What were you going to say?"

Kyle looked at her. "What makes you think he was going to say something?" he asked her, as though Rand weren't still standing there.

"That little noise he made in his throat."

"You make that little noise in your throat, but you never say anything after it."

"Because no one ever asks me what I was going to say."

"So why were you asking him?" Kyle looked back at Rand, then toward Laura again. "Did you want to know?"

"Yes," she said. "I wanted to know. Rand?"

Rand, she noticed, seemed suddenly very pleased with himself. He shrugged delicately. "Just that we see a lot of reverse psychology here. One minute he'll be passing out compliments, the next he'll be hiding your food supply."

Food supply? The brochure hadn't said anything about a food supply. She had a multigrain fruit-filled breakfast bar in her purse, but that was it. Newly alarmed, she looked at Kyle, and saw his jaw tighten and his blue eyes grow cold. He looked like an action hero—kind of thrilling, really.

"Why don't you just tell us what we have to do?" he finally said.

Rand started reciting from the Serene Dynamics brochure, which Laura had already memorized. She tuned him out while she surveyed the cabin. Most of the square footage was devoted to one central room, paneled in knotty pine, and dominated by a scuffed card table and a lumpy couch. Angling around Kyle a little, she saw that the two bedrooms branched off one side of a short hallway. She was going to be sleeping one thin wall away from Kyle. What if she could hear him snore? What if she snored? Her niece had told her she snored, but then until last year she had also believed that small people lived inside the television set. As Rand droned on about the years of research that had gone into developing their program, Laura interrupted.

"Is there a reason Kyle and I are sharing a cabin?"

She watched as Rand mentally held his place in his memorized lecture. "In an intensive program like this one, cohabitation breaks down initial barriers."

Kyle looked at Laura, as if she could translate. She obliged. "We're getting *The Parent Trap* treatment."

"How scientific," Kyle said, grinning at her. She smiled back, a little surprised at their camaraderie.

The thrill was short-lived. "Go ahead. Bond over your resentment of me," Rand said. "That's an important first step. You'll need to be at the main lodge in fifteen minutes. We're going to have an icebreaker, followed by lunch. Then I'll tell you about the rest of your afternoon.''

He tapped his clipboard. ''As I said, I'm also going to need your pagers, cell phones and planners. Plus your car keys and wallets.''

''I don't remember you saying that,'' Kyle said.

Rand looked exasperated. ''I just did.''

''I wasn't listening. Why should I give you my stuff?''

''It was in the brochure,'' Laura said. He gave her a look that said she should know better than to assume he'd read it. ''It's to stop you from bringing the office with you.''

''And to remove the trappings of corporate power,'' Rand added.

She could have told him that was the wrong thing to say.

''I'm not the one obsessed with the trappings of corporate power,'' Kyle began, but Laura stopped him.

''It's fine, Kyle. Let's just do this.'' Under normal circumstances, she would be pleased that he was the one playing grump while she cooperated. But she didn't get any points for his behavior—if they didn't both cooperate, both of them lost out.

Kyle was obviously still skeptical. ''How do I know you aren't just someone who wandered in here off the street, pretending to work for Serene Dynamics? How do I know you aren't going to steal my car?"

If *she* had said something like that, Kyle would have teased her that she was watching too many *Scooby-Doo* reruns—how do we know the real Rand wasn't bumped over the head and stuffed in a closet somewhere? Then, of course, she would have panicked, wondering if he knew that she really did, occasionally, before she went to bed, indulge in an episode or two. She had to get rid of her cable hookup. And she had to keep reminding Kyle that they were trying to impress Rand with their eagerness to change, not alienate him.

"Kyle, do you think any self-respecting impostor would agree to put that shirt on?"

So maybe that was an example of what not to say to Rand. Still, she was rewarded by a big grin from Kyle.

"I don't need your car," Rand said. "I have one of my own."

"Let me go ahead and give you my stuff," Laura told the facilitator, staving off another tussle between the two men. At least worrying about Kyle's state of mind gave her an excuse to postpone her feelings of Acute Gadget Withdrawal.

She understood about giving up her business toys. Rand could say what he wanted about Serene Dynamics's cutting-edge personality theories, but she had seen this same scam in a dozen made-for-TV movies about cults, not to mention *An Officer and a Gentleman.* First, you took away all the symbols of someone's old identity, then you put a new identity, with new symbols, back in its place. Since she knew all that, it wasn't going to work with her.

Take my planner, she thought as she trotted back to her Toyota. *But don't think it means you've got my soul.*

"DAMN." Kyle reacted to the sting as a bush full of thorns sideswiped his knee.

"You shouldn't have worn shorts into the woods," Laura said from somewhere on the trail behind him.

"Thank you, Eddie Bauer."

"Can we stop for a second?"

"Gladly."

He didn't know why he was so surly. Well, yes, he did. First there were all these idiotic rules the retreat had, like having to give his stuff up, although he'd kept his radio and headphones safe from Rand, at least, along with a couple of candy bars. And he was already feeling weird about sharing a cabin with Laura, especially after the first thing he'd done when they'd gotten there was pipe up about how competent and smart she was. Then there was that awful ice-breaker at the lodge, where they got secret identity tags taped to their backs and he had to go around asking giggling strangers demeaning questions like "Am I a man?"

Still, he would have pretended to stay stumped longer if he'd known Rand was going to drag the early finishers into a stupid role-playing exercise where different hats represented different parts of your personality. The other participants looked delighted as hell to be decked out in Dr. Seuss headgear or velvet berets, but when Rand tried to stick a purple-feathered number on Kyle—"perfect for those who take themselves too seriously"—he'd snapped. He must have scared the counselor, because he and Laura had been given hiking gear and shoved onto one of the retreat's longer trails—before he'd had time to change into long pants. It had been a while since he'd gone hiking, but he knew better than to walk out here with his flesh exposed to every known bug and bramble in the Georgia highlands. He was just leaning over to inspect the damage already inflicted when Laura said, "I have some iodine in the first-aid kit. Would you like to put it on the scratch?"

He wanted the iodine. But just as there were women who had never been forced to open their own beer bottles, Kyle Sanders had never had to tend to one of his own injuries. He couldn't help it that women liked to take care of him—he'd popped into the hospital nursery with an aura that sent all the labor and delivery nurses flocking to his bassinet. He'd then come home to an older sister who thought he was the coolest baby doll Mattel had ever produced and a mom who treated him like the Young Sultan of Suburbia, at least until she went back to work when he was a teenager. If he put iodine on in front of Laura, he was going to look like a dolt and a klutz. He looked at her—hair pulled back in a smooth ponytail, makeup intact. Her only concession to sweat was a charming debutante's glow.

"Save it," Kyle said. "Are you ready to head on?"

She nodded, drawing a hardbound blank book out of her backpack, followed by a tattered softcover wildlife guide. "We haven't identified any plants or animals yet, although I don't think the guide Rand gave us is very comprehensive anyway. It only has three kinds of lizards identified, and I've already seen at least four."

Kyle stared at her for a second. "I'll bet when you used to baby-sit, you called Dr. Spock 'the instructions.'"

She looked up at him, her bottom lip puckered in concentration. Then she reddened and said, "Everyone does."

"Yeah, but not everyone has to consult Betty Crocker to boil eggs."

He shouldn't keep teasing her. Wasn't that what got him here in the first place? But he was rewarded when she said, "You know, it's a lot more complicated than just putting some eggs in water."

"Gotcha." He turned around to say it, but immediately bumped into her, getting close enough to see the flecks of green in her hazel eyes and smell the floral scent of her perfume. He scooted out to the edge of the narrow trail, barely avoiding another bush.

She waved the journal and the guide in front of his face. "Rand wanted us to collect information about what we see. I think it's odd that he would send us on this mission with nothing more than this outdated guide."

Kyle rubbed his hand through his hair. Was Laura deliberately obtuse or did she just play it that way? "We're not Lewis and Clark—"

"Lewis and Clark weren't naturalists. You're thinking of William Bartram."

She *wanted* him to ask who William Bartram was. So he wasn't going to.

"This stuff," he said, taking the journal and the guide out of her hands—for effect, but also because his face and other body parts were safer from her gesturing if he did—"is a prop. Rand doesn't care if we say we saw the yellow-breasted booby hatcher. We're supposed to start out talking about mushrooms and end up talking about our feelings."

She looked as terrified as he felt by that prospect. "So this whole walk is a fake?"

"If the walk were fake, I wouldn't be sweating," he said. "It's busywork. Like when you wait tables, they'll spend the whole first day showing you how the fries should be in the nine o'clock plate position, garnish on the three. After your first shift, you realize the plates never look like that."

She looked completely puzzled. Of course she'd never waited tables. She was probably like all the women he'd dated, born with a silver Cross pen gripped between her fingers. But then she said, "Mine did."

"Your what?"

"I always made my plates look like those pictures. I couldn't understand why the cooks didn't do it right the first time."

She wasn't obtuse. It was worse than that.

For the first time since he'd met her, Kyle understood how truly without guile Laura was. He'd always thought it was just a deliberate exaggeration of her personality—like the way he played up his own fun-and-games persona. But now he saw that it wasn't an exaggeration at all.

She believed in the hike, believed that if they got along, Harris would magically grant them both their coveted positions and they would live happily ever after. Kyle knew that if trekking through the woods was what it took today to keep this job, then he would trek, but if tomorrow he needed to go to a martini bar and feign interest in old jazz standards, he'd probably do that, too. Laura still thought that tangible work, the day-to-day progress reports and numbers crunching, would guarantee her a slot. She might accuse him of being all style, which he wasn't, but she was all substance. And she didn't have a clue about why that wasn't enough.

In a strange way, that made him feel responsible for her success on this trip. He wasn't sure he liked that. He needed to get along with her, but not to the point where he was dulling his own instincts.

Laura got ahead of him, and to his own dismay, he let her. *See, I'm already weakening,* he thought, watching her stop to run her palm over the bark of a tree. He wouldn't have pegged her as a toucher. He wouldn't have guessed she looked so good in jeans, either, since he'd never seen her in a pair before today. Even when they had to come into the office on weekends, when he made it a point to wear his most casual clothes, to remind everyone that he was taking his own precious time off to do the company's work, her idea of dressing down meant flats instead of heels, and a flowered skirt instead of solid one. Besides the jeans, she had on a red Polo shirt that was a twin to his dark-green one. It did a lot more for her than it did for him. Before he had a chance to think about it, he said, "You know, you should wear jeans more often."

She turned around and grinned at him. A real smile. "No, Eddie Bauer, thank *you.*"

All right, he deserved that one. He fell into step beside her again, and he noticed, as he had at the cabin, that her tennis shoes took something off her height, so that she now fit comfortably right under his arm. He bumped her again, and to cover it up, said, "So why don't you?"

Great. Now he was The Grand Fashion Inquisitor.

"I don't know." She knelt down and stared at a bright-purple mushroom on a log, then looked back up at him, her nose wrinkling. "I don't want to pretend I'm...sporty."

The idea of being somehow uncomfortable in his body, of not being able to fall back on using his muscles and his stamina as an escape from the world's chatter, was totally alien to him. When he'd looked at Laura before, he'd seen someone who wore her business garb as armor. Now he saw someone who looked at ease in her own skin, and he couldn't understand why she felt self-conscious about it. "What's wrong with being sporty?"

She stood up. Gracefully, he noted. "Nothing wrong with it. It's just not me. In gym class, when we played volleyball, I was told to never move, because I might get in the way of someone who could actually hit the ball." She started walking again, turning around to say, "You're quite the jock, though, right?"

"It sounds so ugly when you say it."

She looked honestly stricken. "I didn't mean it that way. It's just a term. Haven't you called me a nerd or a bean counter before?" Without waiting for him to tell her that *nerd* hadn't been one of his words, she said, "I thought so. I guess I should be glad that I don't have to play golf with Harris anymore since you came along."

But you don't know that my playing golf with Harris is what allows me more access to him than you have, he thought.

"I hear you have quite the swing," she continued.

He shrugged, uncomfortable with his thoughts. "I went to college on a golf scholarship, so I guess I ought to."

She stopped, and he stopped too, this time a safe distance away to keep himself from bumping into her. A leaf on the forest floor caught her eye, and he took the opportunity to stare at her as she bent down, her shirt hugging the outlines of her body, the sun playing tricks with her golden-brown hair. Even in jeans, she exuded elegance and class. So why had he told her he had a golf scholarship? She already thought he was a stupid jock, brawn instead of brains.

But when she rose and turned back to him, she said, "There is no such thing as a golf scholarship."

So she wasn't making fun of him; she was calling him a liar.

"Yes, there is. I endorsed the checks to the university." He should have guessed how she felt about sports. "Are you one of those 'no funding for college athletics' kind of alumni?"

"No. I mean, I don't watch football, but I understand that money comes in from the people who do. But who would pay you just to play golf?" As soon as she'd said it, she grinned at him, slowly, and there, again, was that glint in her hazel eyes. "Besides your boss, I mean."

He wondered, once again, whether he had seriously underestimated this woman.

3

LAURA HELD a dandelion in front of her face and concentrated. This one, finally, she was going to blow away with just one puff. One, two, three—

"Damn it. Plastic piece of crap."

Startled, she snorted sharply, sending some bits of white fluff into her nose and her mouth but mostly just leaving them on the stem. Coughing, she turned to see Kyle bashing his portable radio against the flat rock beneath him.

When they'd reached the clearing that Rand had told them was the end of the trail, Kyle had taken a radio and headphones out of his backpack and sat down on a large rock to listen to a ball game. She thought the headset was against the rules, and told Kyle so, even though he tried to bribe her with a Snickers bar, a move that would have worked better if the melting chocolate hadn't made a small spot on her shirt.

Kyle told her that they were only supposed to get rid of business things, not recreational things. But, she had reminded him, they were supposed to be working on their journal. Well, Kyle had said, if she sat her little butt down on the grass, she'd probably see lots of ants and beetles and bees and maybe, if she was lucky, a butterfly would come by and she could spend the next half hour ignoring it while she looked for its picture in her stupid book.

All she could think about was that he had referred to her butt as little.

"Is it halftime?"

Kyle stopped pounding and glared at her. "There is no halftime in baseball."

"So there's no break at all? You just run to the beer stand and pray nothing exciting happens?"

He got that superior look men often wore when talking sports with the ignorant. That was sexist of her—she'd known women who were just as disdainful of those who didn't know their way around the tennis court.

Still, no mere Junior Leaguer in a flouncy skirt and gold tennis bracelet could look as arrogant as Kyle Sanders when he tried.

"It's the seventh inning stretch," he conceded.

"So that's what this is?"

"No, it's the my-damn-batteries-gave-out stretch."

"Oh," she said. The day Harris had asked to speak with them, she'd noticed something about Kyle that she'd never had a chance to notice before. He was really cute when he was angry.

Good grief. What was her problem? What kind of

woman preferred cranky to charming? No doubt this was a sign of all kinds of deep-seated problems she was harboring. If she could figure out why she found the glaring Kyle more attractive than the smiling one, she could probably also figure out why she stayed someplace that appreciated her talents as little as Harris Associates did, when just last week she'd gotten another recruiting call from Mallory Management, followed by an invitation to lunch with the founder, Susan Mallory.

But maybe there wasn't anything wrong with thinking Kyle was cute when he was mad, she thought, watching as he stretched his arms to the sky. Maybe he was.

He seemed to notice her staring as he hugged his arms to his chest. "It's getting cooler, isn't it? Since my game's a washout, are you ready to go back?"

"Sure," she said. "Wait one second." She picked a handful of flowers and stood up.

"Are we supposed to bring back specimens?" Kyle asked.

"I was going to make these into a necklace for my niece," she said. She walked over to the rock where he was sitting. "Or try to, anyway."

He took the flowers out of her hands, their fingers brushing as he did so. She stifled the urge to jump. He was always bumping into her at the office, but at least there she had her defenses about her. Here, he was uncomfortably close.

He started weaving the flowers together deftly. "Yoda says, 'No try, only do.'"

He had his head down, studying the necklace, and she was glad he couldn't see the look of surprise on her face. "Are you a closet *Star Wars* geek?"

He gave her a lazy smile, and she shivered. It was getting chilly out here, wasn't it? If her ears weren't so hot, she'd really be cold.

"I wouldn't say I was ever exactly a geek of any kind," he said. "Not that I look that cool making you a daisy chain."

She sat down on the long rock, but as far to the opposite edge as possible. "How do you know how to do that? My niece keeps trying to teach me."

"My niece did teach me," he said. "We have to hang outside together, because if we're inside, we fight over the remote."

"We don't have that problem," Laura said primly. *Because we're both addicted to the Cartoon Network.*

"You never did this when you were a kid?" he asked her.

"Well." She leaned toward him conspiratorially, even though there wasn't another listener in sight and it wasn't a very dark secret. She leaned anyway. "I told my parents I would get hives if I were exposed to sunlight."

Finished with the necklace, Kyle up at her, his expression amused. "Laura Everett lied?"

"No, of course, not," she said. "I could make myself have hives, just by concentrating."

Was that a look of admiration or amusement on his face? He ceremoniously placed the ring of white flowers around her neck. "You, Laura, are a trip."

As though all her senses had suddenly been turned way up, Laura was ultraconscious of the feel of the nippy air across her face, the scratch of the stems across her collarbone, and the very close heartbeat of one Kyle Sanders.

What if I kissed him?

That hypothetical question jerked her right out of fairy-tale mode. She was supposed to be merely getting along with Kyle Sanders, not hurling herself at him atop a piece of granite. *If* she kissed him, and *if* he didn't fend her off, they would never be able to take their actions back. Kissing a co-worker in the coat closet at an office party was one thing, or so she had heard from Brandi, but doing it cold sober was another. That was exactly the kind of thing that the Kyle Sanders she knew, the one who was already picking carpet colors for that empty space in the executive suite, would use against her. Imagine how unstable he could make her sound to Harris. She scrambled off the rock.

"You have a niece, too? How old is yours?"

He blinked, slowly and oh so sexily. She had never

before understood what was meant by *bedroom eyes,* but the allure of his was drawing her right back to that rock. Then he shook his head and said in a normal tone, "She's seven."

"Mine is five," Laura chirped. "We'll have to get them together when we get back to Atlanta."

He gave her a bemused look, then put his radio in his backpack. "Now that you've got your jewelry, let's go. What time is it?"

She looked at her watch, a small knot of worry forming in her stomach when she realized it said eight. As in the a.m.

"I think my watch gave out a while ago," she said, twisting the plain brown leather band on her wrist.

"Oh," he said.

If she didn't know better, she would have thought he was worried. "Is that a problem?"

"Well, I had just sort of counted on you wearing one."

Like he just sort of counted on her always having an extra legal pad and an extra pen at meetings. But Kyle usually wore a watch, too, one that was expensive enough to say he could afford the best and battered enough to say he didn't care.

"Where's yours?" she asked, following him.

"I gave it up in a bet last night," he said over his shoulder as they crossed out of the clearing and back onto the wooded trail.

The darkness was odd and unexpected, like piling on multiple pairs of sunglasses. There didn't seem to be any sunlight making it through the canopy of trees. *It's okay,* she told herself. *As hard as it is for you to cede control to Kyle, he's in his element here. You can trust his judgment. Even if he is obviously some sort of compulsive gambler type person.*

"Do you often lose things in bets?" she asked as casually as she was able. A few days ago, that would be the sort of information she would have wanted to take to Harris, but now that they were in this all-for-one-one-for-all thing, she supposed she'd have to be the one to help him get treatment.

"I lost it to the kid next door, playing basketball. When I lose, he gets to wear my watch until the rematch. I used to have my watch all the time, but he's been practicing."

"Oh." Great, she was about to rat out the poster child for Big Brothers.

"How are you doing back there?" Kyle asked.

"Super," she said. Was nature normally this dark? She wanted to ask Kyle if she should worry, but she was afraid he would say yes. He must have sensed her nervousness, because the next time he spoke, his voice was loud and hearty. Kyle was normally rowdy, charming, fun, but not, she would say, hearty.

"So, why haven't you gotten your watch fixed?"

Kyle was not normally a nag, either.

"It's not really broken. Sometimes my body chemistry just screws it up."

Before she could even finish, he said, "Urban legend."

"It is not an urban legend," she said. "It's my watch. I should know."

Kyle pressed on. "It's just that I wouldn't think you'd fall for something so flaky."

Flaky? She of the cross-referenced to-do list? And since when did the original Good Time Charlie turn into the guy who made the trains run on time?

"And if it does stop whenever you wear it," he continued, clearly ignoring her silence, "Then why would you?"

"It's—" She was about to say it was the watch that went with her blue jeans, then realized that sounded…flaky. "It's not something that happens all the time, only when I—" *Get nervous,* she almost finished, *like when I'm around a cute guy.* Damn. That was the truth. "It's the watch that goes with my blue jeans."

"So you chose vanity over efficiency?"

That was rich, coming from a guy so well dressed that he knew the difference between beige and taupe.

"I thought I'd give the world a day off from my high standards," she said. "It's not always easy to believe that the universe will explode if you aren't keeping it together with your own powers of concentration.''

It was the most personal thing she'd ever said to him. And he completely ignored it. There was an odd hint of worry or annoyance—she couldn't tell which—in his tone as he said, ''You know, today might not have been the best day for you to decide you weren't holding the planet together.''

''Now you tell me. And after I let all those terrestrial fragments just spin out into the universe.''

''Not the best day for you to have unearthed a morbid sense of humor, either,'' he said. ''If you'd obsessed about the time like you always do and hounded me to go, we wouldn't be stuck out here.''

She skipped the parts where he said she was humorless, shrewish, and obsessive, and focused instead on the part where he said they were stuck.

''What do you mean?'' She meant to be sharp and firm, but her voice came out broken and wispy. She sounded like Lamb Chop. She cleared her throat and tried again, pitching her tone lower. ''Can you say some more about being stuck?''

Now she sounded like Large Marge the Phantom Truck Driver.

''When it gets completely dark, we won't be able to see the trail.''

''What do you mean we won't be able to see the trail? How dark can it get?''

Suddenly it was as though a light switch had been flicked off somewhere in the heavens. Laura had never been in this kind of dark: no streetlights or house lights to break it. There wasn't even a moon or stars. It was like being plunged to the bottom of a deep cave.

"What on earth just happened?" she asked, resisting the urge to grab Kyle's arm.

Kyle's voice came from somewhere near. "It's called night."

LAURA KICKED HIM. "Ouch. Laura, that hurt."

"Sorry," she said. "Too dark to see a thing."

"That's what I was trying to tell you. Sometimes in the mountains it gets totally dark like this. It's hard for the moonlight to make it through the trees anyway, and now the moon's covered with clouds."

"Was it cloudy?" As she spoke, a thump echoed through the woods and he felt her jump next to him.

"What was that?"

"A woodpecker," he guessed.

The relief in her voice was sweet. "Thank goodness you have experience at this."

Experience? His experience with woodpeckers was limited to having seen the eponymous Woody on television. But he did feel a little guilty about letting the ball game make him forget the time, and if his pretending to have it all under control was going to make her feel better, plus have the added bonus of making him look good, he wasn't going to argue.

"There wasn't a flashlight with my stuff," he said. "Was there one with yours?"

Her voice was small. "No."

"That's okay." What kind of idiot had packed their bags? Rand Idiot, that was who. "We're on the trail, so as long as we move slowly and don't lose it, we'll be fine. There were some clouds, but I don't think they were thunderstorm clouds."

"Oh, good."

He was on a roll. "On the radar this morning—"

"The radar?" Sweet went south very quickly. "You mean you were watching the weather on TV?"

"Is something wrong with that?"

She sounded agitated. "Kyle, I could have done that. I thought you could step outside and smell the air or something. I thought you were an experienced outdoorsperson."

"Outdoorsman, Laura. Since you're talking about me specifically, you can say 'outdoorsman' without being sexist."

"When was the last time you went camping?"

"It was... When do I have time to go camping? I work every weekend." He was conscious of how loud his voice was getting in the dark stillness.

"Work? You come in and play darts and drink Cokes from Harris's fridge."

"You could have Cokes from there, you know."

"That's not— Ow, rock."

He started to tell her to take his hand, so they wouldn't get separated, but he didn't want to risk her refusing. "Why don't you hold on to my backpack?"

She did, and as he felt her near him, his mood softened a little. She was worried. She thought that because he hadn't been in the woods in the last month or so she was going to be eaten by bears. "Laura, I went camping all the time in college. Geological time is slow. The woods haven't changed that much."

"Did you go with a bunch of people and drink a lot of beer and play guitars and eat junk food?"

"Yeah. Did you do that, too?" He tried to picture Laura with a bag of barbecued chips in one hand, and a drink in the other. He couldn't.

"Of course not," she said. He tried to decide if she sounded wistful or if the night was twisting her tone. "Are you sure you were paying attention to the woods back then?"

"Laura, this goes back to the office thing. You feel guilty if you come in on a Saturday and don't spend every second multitasking. I think it's okay to take a dart break every once in a while."

She didn't say anything and for a second he imagined that he had convinced her. Then she asked, "How is your dart game going to keep me from being eaten by bears?"

So it *was* the bear thing. "You don't have to be the best at something to do it well enough. A happy kid with a B average is better than a neurotic A kid, right?"

She didn't say anything for a while, then said, "I don't think that's a value that I can get behind at all."

"Laura."

"Well, I'm sorry, I don't. You're going to have to explain the advantages to me."

They took a few more steps along the trail. She stumbled a little, and the subsequent yank on his backpack made him feel like Howdy Doody in the hands of a nervous puppetmaster. "Here, take my hand." To his slight surprise, she did, and he felt the warmth of her hand in his. "Okay, I once knew a guitar prodigy named Stan."

"Are you making Stan up?"

"He's my best friend."

"It's just that I've never heard of a guitar prodigy. Piano prodigies, yes. Violin prodigies."

"Well, there are guitar prodigies and golf scholarships. It's a whole big world out there."

Just then the shriek of an owl was followed by the sound of a small crash in the distance. Laura screamed and practically broke his hand squeezing it. "Did you have to remind the world how much bigger it was than us?"

"Sorry," he said. *Resist the urge to tease her about bears. Try harder at seeming like a grown-up who is not trying to scare a pretty girl with a snake.* "Okay, Stan. His riffs would leave you dumbstruck. His progressions would make you cry. Women would throw themselves at him after gigs. But he couldn't talk to them because they weren't holding guitars." He paused, allowing her to imagine the bleakness of Stan's situation. "Now, there was another guy, a friend of Stan's, a passable, okay player. He enjoyed it, but when a woman started making chitchat about his guitar, he could eventually move the conversation to other things. Take that same lesson—"

"Wait, what lesson? Did I miss a lesson?"

"And apply it to the swimmer who has to get up at 3:00 a.m. to train and the guy who was also on the swim team, but who chooses to sit in the lifeguard chair getting paid to tan."

"Remind me not to drown while you're on duty."

He ignored her. "Same for the pool player who becomes obsessed with the big score to the exclusion of all else, and the guy who has every girl in the bar hanging around the table while he shoots."

He shouldn't have said *girl.*

"That guy sitting around playing James Taylor covers, that was you, right?"

"That's not relevant."

"It seems relevant to me."

"Let's say he's a composite character."

"Okay, this composite character, coincidentally

named Kyle, his point is that it's better to give up try-ing to be the best at something if it's going to get in the way of your social life.''

He started to say she'd misunderstood, his natural reflex to any argument, but then he realized that was exactly what he meant. The hell with it. He was taking a stand.

"Socialization is an important human skill."

A hungry bear would have sounded more pleasant than the cynical laughter that followed. He tried to re-group.

"Laura, all I'm saying is that balance is a valuable thing in a person's life."

"I'm glad Marie Curie didn't think that way," she said. "Or Albert Einstein. Or Vincent Van Gogh." She yanked her hand away. "And that's just the famous people. Think of the ones who aren't famous yet—the dancer in the chorus line, the aching gymnast, the artist sculpting in her studio."

He was still walking, but he realized she wasn't. "Laura? Keep moving. We don't want to lose the trail."

She acted as if she didn't hear him. "Think of the ordinary, unsung men and women who give their all every day in emergency rooms and classrooms and fac-tories and mediocre management consulting firms—"

Uh-oh.

"Where their bosses don't even try to hide their belief that excellence is a thing best pursued on a golf course by aging frat boys.''

"Aging? *Aging?*"

"I'm taking your philosophy as a spit in the eye to all things I hold dear.''

Retreat, retreat. "Laura, I'm making conversation in the middle of the woods because you're scared and I'm trying to take your mind off bears, okay? Don't go hysterical on me.''

"I've worked hard, I've sacrificed, I've postponed lots of things I wanted out of life so that I could devote one hundred percent of myself to Harris Associates. And I can't believe you think all that is nothing—nothing—compared to looking good enough to get laid regularly.''

Bears or no bears, that was going too far. "Laura,'' he warned.

"I'll find my own way back home,'' she said, trying to shove him aside on the path.

"Fine,'' he said, but as she tried to pass him on the trail, he kept getting tangled up in her hair and her backpack and just her in general. As they started to move, he felt his foot hit something on the trail, and suddenly his face was in grass and dirt, and Laura was falling, too, landing with an ''oomph'' somewhere near him. His first thought, after ''So that's the ground,'' was to wonder if Laura was okay.

He stuck his hand out, connecting with denim. Her

leg. She smacked his hand. "I'm not trying to cop a feel, Laura. I'm making sure you're okay."

"I'm fine," she said finally. "Fine."

It was his fault they'd fallen. He never should have let her get the best of him like that. There were very few things in life worth losing your temper about, and defending your ego shouldn't be one of them. "Look, I want you to know that everyone knows how hard you work and everyone appreciates it. And look where it's gotten you. A great place in the industry."

"I don't know," she said, but she sounded tired. "You've done all right for a guy who doesn't seem to have gotten a business degree for any other reason than to pick up the right kinds of women."

Ouch.

4

KYLE WAS A MAN of the nineties, with all the complications and adventures that being such a man entailed. Still, he couldn't remember the last time he had woken up with a wild-eyed gorgeous woman sitting on top of him, her hand plastered across his mouth.

"Be quiet," Laura whispered.

"What are you doing?" he said, but it came out, "Mwa, mwa, mwa mwa?"

With her free hand, she reached up and stuck an escaped lock of hair behind her ear. "I think we're in trouble," she said.

He definitely was. It was taking his brain a few seconds to process the whys and wherefores of what he was doing flat down in a bed of pine needles anyway, his clothes soaked with cold dew, but his body had all the information it needed to react. He took one short second to call himself an idiot for what he was about to do—shove her off.

Before he could get his hands up, though, she shifted her weight, and he froze, a charge volting throughout his body. He met her eyes, which were at first shocked, as he'd feared, then embarrassed, as he'd expected, and then...knowing.

And sly.

And a whole bunch of other adjectives he'd never associated with the real Laura Everett, but which seemed lifted straight from his fantasies about her.

She smiled, a slow, deep smile, and he thought he had never seen a woman so beautiful, her hair backlit by the morning light filtering through the canopy, her face kissed with pink from the sun yesterday. He reached over to take her hand off his mouth, then, without thinking, pushed his palm against hers, watching their hands twine together. When he looked back at her, he knew the erotic challenge in his eyes mirrored hers. She leaned over, the movement sending an exquisite pain through him, and he put his free hand around her neck, pulling her face down to his.

There had been one brief second in the glade yesterday when he'd thought they were about to kiss. There was no reason now to regret that they hadn't, since now he'd had the pleasure of waiting for this one. His tongue traced her full lips, and his hand slid from her soft ponytail down her back. He broke off the kiss to move his lips to her neck, and she sighed.

"Did you hear something?" bellowed a rough voice.

What the hell? Laura quickly got off Kyle, and motioned for him to be quiet. The thought of homicidal maniacs tramping through the woods ought to have had a dampening effect on his desire, but instead of finding out who was out there, he wanted to hold Laura for one more kiss.

He touched her arm, but she pointed to a thicket of kudzu forming a tent between several large trees. As the men's shouting came closer, Kyle took Laura's hand and they forced their way through the vines into the hideaway.

After they had stumbled off the path the night before, they had agreed that continuing seemed like an invitation to broken bones, and that they should sit near the edge of the trail until they could see. He'd sat there listening to Laura fidget and squirm, worrying about what awful thing was going to crawl over her, wondering if she'd throw herself on him if something did, and hoping that something would. He couldn't believe he'd ever slept, but obviously he had.

Had Laura? She didn't look tired. In the darkness of the greenery, he could still see that her eyes were bright, and she had an unfamiliar expression on her face. The necklace he had made for her was brown and dried, but she didn't seem to notice she was still wearing it. If he didn't know any better, he'd say she was having fun. But this was Laura, a woman who was never swayed from her work by any of the indulgences that were offered to them when they traveled—gourmet coffee, muffins with organic blueberries, or reservations scored at a city's trendiest restaurant. So why, in the midst of danger and very possibly backwoods war, did she look so damn happy?

Whish! Pop!

Kyle squeezed Laura's hand to reassure her, then peeked out through a small clearance in the vines. For one brief, hideous second, he thought the red stuff dripping from a nearby tree was blood. Then he realized some of it was green. Unless Mr. Spock or one of his compatriots had just been obliterated here, this wasn't a homicide.

"It's a paintball game," he whispered to Laura.

"You said there'd be paintball," she whispered, her breath a warm breeze against his ear.

He had said that, hadn't he? He was about to give himself a mental high five for his incredible trend-spotting skills when Laura whispered, "How five years ago."

"Really," he agreed.

"Markers ready," yelled someone from across the trail. Kyle peeked through again to see men garbed in protective padding and goggles walking around on the other side of the woods.

"Should we go out?" Laura whispered.

Kyle shook his head no. And say what? *Hey guys. We were just, uh, hanging out here because we mistook you for the Hatfields and McCoys. Now that we see you're just nerds with costumes and pellets of food coloring, how ya doin'?*

And who exactly were the nerds here? The ones who had eaten dinner, then spent the night in real beds with real sheets or the ones who had split a candy bar and slept on the ground?

Then again, he was willing to bet the ones who'd slept in real beds hadn't had a wake-up call nearly as exciting as his.

"I think this is a wild-goose chase," said a higher-voiced man. "The blue team went up the trail."

"I heard something," said the man with the deeper pitch.

"Who else would be out here?" his friend asked. "The two lovebirds who escaped last night?"

He hoped his face wasn't as red as Laura's was turning. Embarrassment became alarm, though, when he heard the first man say, "They're not lovebirds. You don't know Harris Associates' favorite pair of pit bulls? That guy stole an account from me in Macon last year, when he was working for Delusk. They're probably on their way to Bellamy Island to get Herb Harris the hell out of hot water."

Laura removed her hand from his and pinched him on the leg, a sign that the Laura who had been willing to make out in the woods had been replaced by Laura the ever responsible Harris Associates employee. He wondered if those two Lauras were ever the same person.

"What kind of hot water?" the other guy asked, but

his question was followed by a crash from somewhere down the trail. "There's the blue team," he said.

"You go on," said the original bellower. "I've got to take care of some business."

Kyle heard his friend traipse away, then heard what he assumed to be the paintball weapon hitting the ground. Why was he putting his paintball gun down?

Oh, *that* kind of business.

He was out of the kudzu before the guy could reach his zipper. "Wait, wait," he said.

The ruddy-faced man gaped at Kyle. Although Kyle didn't remember him from past business dealings, he did recognize him as someone who had taken an unhealthy amount of pleasure in the hat incident yesterday. A second later, he was reaching for his weapon, but Laura's sneakered foot came down on it first, and she picked it up. "It's us," she told the man. "The pit bulls."

Kyle decided that if they were ever going to trade endearments, that was not going to be one he chose for her. She looked mighty irritated. She was really cute when she was mad. He wondered if he'd get slapped if he said so.

The guy's hands had gone back to his sides, but he stared at Kyle, looking angry. "Make her give me my weapon back."

"I can't do a thing with her," Kyle said. He suspected that truer words had never been spoken.

"After you tell us why we have to go to Bellamy Island and help Harris," Laura said.

"Can't do it," the guy said.

"Then I guess you just go back covered in paint," Laura said. "How far away does he get to be before I can shoot him safely?"

"Give me that," Kyle said, grabbing it out of her hands. "Seriously," he told the man. "I heard you say I stole an account from you. I'll give you a lead on one in Forsyth in exchange for your information."

"I would have started bargaining smaller," Laura said.

"You lack compassion," the man said to Laura.

"That's why I have the gun," Kyle told him. "Come on."

"Okay." The guy shifted his weight from one leg to another and dug a small hole in the carpet of pine needles with his shoe. "New Horizon's in trouble. They want Herb Harris to buy them at what you guys think they're valued at. If they were being honest, they wouldn't be able to give the company away."

Kyle looked at Laura, who was visibly troubled. "Are you sure?" she asked. "Does everybody know this?"

"No," the guy said. "I've been dating a woman who worked there. Her paycheck bounced, and Walt and Bill gave her some bogus cover story. She heard them on the phone the next week, saying they were going to use your company to pull them out of the hole. But things have been bad there for a while. They expanded too fast, let their reputation get ahead of what they could do.''

Kyle imagined that Laura's eyes were on him when the guy said that, but he didn't want to prove himself right by looking her way. He thanked the guy and reminded him to call him for the lead at the first of next week.

''Hope you've still got a job,'' the guy said, taking his weapon from Kyle. ''Rand was really unhappy about your disappearing act, and he was going to call your boss right before he went out with another group this morning. I bet Herb Harris is really steamed.''

Laura broke into something between a power walk and a jog, heading down the trail. Kyle started running, too, the chirps and cheeps of the waking forest around him drowned out briefly by the sound of his stomach rumbling.

He caught up with her. ''No way we can eat breakfast before we find Rand, is there?''

''Kyle, this is serious,'' Laura said. She was still half walking, half jogging as she spoke. ''If this deal is bad, Harris is going to look like an idiot.''

''And there's only going to be room for one of us again,'' Kyle said.

She stopped and stared at him, her eyes wide. Looking at her, he saw that she still had a bit of twig at her forehead. He reached to brush it away and she flinched slightly. "I hadn't thought of that," she said.

She didn't have to add the unfinished part of that statement: *Obviously, you did.*

"Listen," he said. "Let's not worry about that until we talk to Harris. Maybe the guy's right and he's so ticked at us that we don't have jobs anyway."

The look on her face was a disturbingly familiar one, one she wore at the office whenever she thought he was getting away with something. "You always know how to make a woman feel better," she said, turning down the trail again.

They didn't speak again as they followed the path to a stand-alone office near the main lodge. Inside, the smell of coffee wafted through the small lobby, and although Kyle didn't drink the stuff, he watched Laura practically start to tremble at the aroma.

"Would you mind if I had a cup of coffee?" she asked the receptionist, identified by the nameplate on the desk as Andrea.

"Help yourself," the woman said. "But, who are you?"

Laura had started to drift away toward the hallway, but Kyle grabbed her arm and pulled her back. "You can have coffee in a few minutes."

"I need it now," she grumbled.

"Andrea," he said, "We're the missing campers."

"Oh, I'm not Andrea," she said.

At the same time, Laura said, "She's not Andrea."

He turned to Laura, who was wistfully looking down the hall. "How do you know?" he asked her.

"There's a picture of Andrea in the brochure," she said. "'Our smiling receptionist, Andrea.'"

He hated it that she knew things he didn't, just because she paid attention to details, and that she could spout those details even when she claimed to be brainfogged from lack of caffeine.

"I'm Stacy," the woman said. "Andrea's off. But I did hear that you two had taken off. Rand was going to call your boss, but he didn't have a chance before his accident."

"We didn't leave," Kyle said. "We got lost." So Rand hadn't called. Their jobs were safe.

"What accident?" Laura asked, and again, Kyle felt like a dolt for not asking himself. She'd been a very equal participant in that kiss this morning—why wasn't it slowing her thinking down the way it was slowing his?

"He lost his center of calm and fell off a log during a training exercise. He's sort of unconscious."

"How terrible," Laura said. "We feel so responsible."

"I don't feel responsible," Kyle said. "He's the one who didn't pack a flashlight."

"I need some coffee to deal with this guilt."

Kyle took her arm again and this time left his hand

there, conscious of the warmth of her skin next to his, trying to focus on what he had to do to get them out of there and Harris out of his bad deal.

"I'm very sorry to hear about Rand," he said. Normally if he were talking to an attractive woman, he would turn on the charm. In some weird way, though, he felt that it would be disloyal to Laura to do so. "But we left our keys and wallets with him. Do you think we could get our stuff from you?"

She started shaking her head even before he had finished speaking. "All your stuff is locked in a couple of lockers. He put your suitcases there this morning, right before, you know, the calm thing."

"But someone else has the combination," Laura said. She hadn't phrased it as a question, but Kyle was afraid he already knew the answer.

Stacy shook her head again. "No," she said. "He's the only person with it."

They were all silent for a moment.

"I can get someone to weld the lock off—" Stacy started.

"Do that," Kyle said.

"But I would have to wait for my boss to approve the charges, and he isn't due back until later this afternoon."

"What are we supposed to do? Besides pray for Rand to regain consciousness?" Kyle asked.

"I can have a driver take you back to Atlanta," Stacy said.

"Coffee," Laura said, pulling away from Kyle and walking down the hall. Once he would have assumed that he worked better when Laura wasn't around; now he felt unfocused without her, as he tried to decide what to do.

"Listen, I need to use your phone," he said. He tried Harris's cell phone and got his voice mail. Damn. He knew from a past visit to Bellamy, a semiexclusive island near Georgia's Golden Isles chain, that there was only one good hotel there. A call to the hotel revealed that Harris and his two colleagues were already playing golf.

Where was Laura? Just as he looked around for her, she came down the hallway carrying an extra-large Serene Dynamics travel mug and a plastic bag full of cookies. Inside that bag he could see another bag that held the necklace he'd made. She had washed her face and smoothed her hair, and he could see a bit of water on her shirt where once there had been a tiny chocolate stain. Even in yesterday's clothes, she looked wonderful.

"Did everything get worked out?" she asked, handing him a cookie. "I hope you don't mind," she told Stacy. "We haven't eaten since yesterday."

Kyle didn't wait for Stacy to answer. "They're all playing golf together," he told Laura, stuffing the cookie in his mouth and swallowing it before he spoke again. "That means he thinks things are going well."

She bit her lip, then turned to Stacy and said, "Why don't you order us that car to Atlanta?"

Kyle couldn't believe it. "But that's not—"

"Then we'll borrow someone else's car and we'll go see him."

"That's a waste of—"

The look she gave him was stern. "I really don't see what choice we have," she said. "Stacy, we'd really appreciate it. We'll be waiting outside."

"Outside?" Kyle asked her, but she was already out the door. She had started down a side trail near the lodge, and he followed her, still talking. "If you wanted to be outside, couldn't we have just sat on the porch? You should buy a treadmill when you get home. Exercise is clearly your thing." She hadn't said anything, and he now noticed that she had led him to a gravel lot below the lodge. A small white sign hanging from a post identified it as Staff Parking. "A parking lot? I could have found a more scenic route."

"Will you hold this?" She handed him the bag of cookies, then reached into her pocket and pulled out a key chain loaded with keys, dangling it in front of him. Where the hell had those come from? Were those her keys? When he looked in her eyes he had no doubt that on at least some level, she was enjoying herself.

"I don't need you to find a scenic route," she said. "I need you to find Rand's car. We're taking it."

WHY WAS KYLE LOOKING at her that way? She had never seen him so ruffled. Well, she had seen him irritated yesterday. And this morning, during that impromptu kiss, the unflappable Kyle Sanders had certainly seemed a little, uh, *flapped*. Her ears started burning, just thinking about it. But why did he look so horrified?

"Are you stealing Rand's car?" he demanded.

That explained the look.

Eager to clear up this misunderstanding, she said, "No, no. I got his keys from a pegboard in the office, and since we don't have our cars, I thought we could take his."

His expression had changed to one of annoyance, which looked a lot better on him. He walked over to her and grabbed for the keys, which she held behind her back. She was still a little miffed that he'd taken her weapon from her in the woods.

"He's not using it," she protested. "And if by some miracle he gets out of the hospital today and has to drive somewhere, he can take mine." She took another welcome sip of coffee. "You want a ride, I'm getting you a ride. My own problem right now is figuring out which particular Chevrolet it is."

He folded his arms across his chest. His dark-brown

hair was ruffled, his green Polo shirt was wrinkled, and there were a couple of grass stains on his shorts. Lord, he was handsome. "You don't know?"

"No, but I'm going to find out." She started with the first row, pointing the lock mechanism at a white Lumina and pushing the Unlock button. Nothing. Okay. She went down the row.

Kyle cleared his throat loudly and she looked up to see him, two rows down, arms still folded, leaning against a fuschia Cavalier. Two Serene Dynamics bumper stickers bookended the license plate, and a Serene Dynamics air freshener hung from the rearview mirror. "Oh," she said, walking toward him. "I didn't think cars came in this color."

"I think it's a custom job," Kyle said.

Laura tried the lock. "This is it," she said, hearing the click. "So you're in?" When he didn't say anything, she turned on him, exasperated. "You said I should have more whims."

His eyes were dangerously blue today, she noticed, as he walked toward her. "Grand Theft Auto is not a whim," he said. He waved the bag of cookies at her. "A whim is don't eat a healthy breakfast."

"I already didn't do that," she said. "Give me one of those." She took a cookie from him.

He swallowed a few bites of his own cookie before he spoke again. "I meant, stay out too late."

"Did that, too."

When he looked at her again, she couldn't read him, but she hoped he wasn't thinking what she was thinking. *Make out in the woods with your attractive coworker.* There was a whim. Boy, was it ever a whim. He took a step toward her, and she backed away. She had kissed him this morning thinking that there was still a place for both of them at Harris Associates. Okay, she hadn't been thinking that, exactly. She hadn't really been thinking at all. But now that she was thinking about it, she knew that although she owed it to Harris to get him out of trouble, she owed it to herself to keep her emotions out of this rivalry. No matter how good a kisser Kyle happened to be.

She had backed right into the door, and now she opened it quickly, starting to get in the front seat.

"Wait a minute," Kyle said. He still looked attractively troubled. "If I'm going, I'm driving."

One leg half in the car, she turned to him and shook her head. "No, I can't let you do that, considering that neither of us has a driver's license. If we get stopped, pretend you're my hostage."

He glared at her. "Oh, yeah, Laura, that's going to look really good. Get in the passenger seat."

Ah. It was a guy thing. Relieved that he now seemed involved in her plans, she got out and moved to the other side, handing Kyle the keys as she did so.

He slid in behind the wheel. "How do we get to Bellamy Island?"

"I'm sure Rand has a map of Georgia in here," she said, popping open the glove compartment. The car's interior was tidy and clean, but also overpowered by the sickly smell of the air freshener was making her sinuses flare. She pointed at it. "You couldn't leave that here in the parking lot, could you?"

"And add littering to my sins?" Kyle asked. "Why not?"

As he opened the door and set the air freshener down in the gravel, Laura quickly located the map.

"What made you so sure he would have a map?" Kyle asked.

"I have one," Laura said. "Don't you?"

"In case I turn off the interstate in the wrong direction and wind up in Florida? No." She watched him study the map for a minute, as she tried to identify the odd feeling she was having. If this situation weren't so serious, she would almost suspect that she was having fun.

"Okay," Kyle said finally. "It's about four hundred miles. He's got a full tank, so pray that he gets good gas mileage. How we get back, I don't know."

Laura put her mug in the cup holder. "Harris will front us some money. And if we need a little more gas before we get there, then I'm sure Rand has an emergency ten or twenty stuck in the glove compartment somewhere."

"What makes you think that?"

She looked at Kyle. "Don't you?"

"I don't even have a working glove compartment," he said, shaking his head. "Fasten your seat belt."

He got the car out of the retreat's grounds without Andrea or anyone else running out of the office to stop them. So far, so good. On the same road where she and Kyle had passed each other, she saw a limo heading for Serene Dynamics. Their car.

Kyle's arm knocked against her several times as he fiddled with the radio, until finally, flustered, she said, "Here, let me" and took over trying to find a classic rock station. Almost any topic seemed too charged for this small space, whether it was their ordeal yesterday, or the ordeal with Harris yet to come. Everything led her right back to thoughts of their rivalry which wasn't supposed to be a rivalry, and the kiss that had complicated it.

Finally, she settled on talking about their nieces, and stories about Haley and his niece Jessica carried them into the afternoon, as the landscape outside shifted from the thick mountainous regions to the flatter lands nearer the eastern coast of the state.

She was impressed by how much time he seemed to spend with Jessica, and told him so. "Well," he said. "My dad watches her after school, so if she's eating dinner there, sometimes I head there from work."

"So your dad's retired?"

Kyle looked uncomfortable. "I guess you could say

that." He seemed to struggle with wanting to say something, and she waited. "He, uh, informally retired when he was in his early forties. My mom had gone back to school and gotten a really great job, so he started cooking and cleaning and hanging out with us." He shot her a fierce glance, as if he dared her to say anything negative about it.

"I think that's great," she said, thinking of her own dad and how he had seemed to put his job ahead of her and her sister and mom, and how he had taught her to do the same. "Had he just burned out?"

"He was burned out," Kyle agreed, then said, in a lower, tougher tone. "And I guess he'd burned a lot of places out on him." As if suddenly aware that was revealing too much, he said, suddenly, "So, is your niece feeding your cat this weekend?"

Laura was baffled. "I don't have a cat."

He turned to stare at her, obviously puzzled, and she resisted the temptation to tell him to keep his eyes on the road. "I could have sworn you had a cat."

Cat ownership. Just the sort of thing you would expect from an uptight spinster such as herself. Never mind that she had kissed him with abandon or stolen him a car. It hadn't altered his opinion of her at all. "I don't even like cats," she said, which was not technically true, but he didn't have to know that.

He looked disappointed. "You don't like cats? Are you allergic to them?"

"No, I've just never had one."

"Every household should have a cat, if only to keep the dog in line."

"You don't have a dog or a cat," she said.

"No, and I don't have kids, either, but I'll have them all someday."

She looked out the window at the green grass and Queen Anne's lace springing up by the interstate, fighting the sudden vision of Kyle with two little blue-eyed mini-Kyles, a boy and a girl, flanked by a gold cocker spaniel and a fat white cat. He would be a good dad, she thought, somewhere between the slacker he considered his own dad and the workaholic who was hers. Her vision was nice, except that it wouldn't be complete without a beaming wife. A beaming, unrepressed, *whimsical* wife.

A sudden feeling of loneliness hit her in the stomach. "We should eat," she said, opening the glove compartment again and rummaging through it until she found a twenty, tucked away between the pages of the car owner's manual.

"Okay," he said, looking at her curiously. "Do you care if we stop at a place where we can get gas, too?"

Laura usually made pit stops only at fast-food chains, but that sounded stuffy, so she said it was fine. He pulled off at the next exit, and after putting five of the twenty into the car, asked her what she wanted from the deli inside.

"A slice of pizza." She headed for the ladies' room, taking one last look back to see him standing in line, more than easily the best-looking guy in the whole place.

Out of your league, Laura, out of your league, she chided herself. Sure, he had kissed her, but she was crawling on top of him at the time. More proof that he was an opportunist. What would she do with a guy that good-looking, anyway? It had been way too long since she had been kissed, and if she were honest with herself, she knew she'd never been kissed like that. She needed to have started with someone further down the dating food chain, someone more bland and boring and safe.

She fretted about all this while she washed her hands in the bathroom and inspected her hair in the mirror. A skinny young woman in a tank top was fumbling with a machine on the wall. "Damn," she said, as it spewed something out. She turned to set it on the edge of the sink next to Laura. "I got the wrong kind."

Expecting something else, Laura looked at the small wrapped package, which sported the word latex. A condom. A condom machine in the ladies'? Was this what she had missed by never using gas station bathrooms?

"He only likes ribbed," the woman explained, as Laura simply nodded, drying and redrying her hands on the paper towel she had grabbed from the dispenser.

The girl pocketed her second purchase and left, the first packet still sitting there.

Laura stood and stared at it for a while. There was no question that the next woman who walked in here would need it more than she did.

The door opened, and a small, elderly woman with a cane entered. Okay, maybe not. Laura grabbed the packet and stuffed it into her jeans pocket, smiling and nodding at the woman as she left. Hah. Who was repressed now?

5

KYLE WAS ON HIS second hot dog and Laura still hadn't returned to the car. Was it his imagination or had she acted strange about the cat thing? A cat hater. Who would have thought? He'd had this picture of her in his head, longer than he cared to remember, of her going home to a tortoise-shell cat, a spot of life in an orderly apartment. It wasn't a lonely picture—Single Woman's Only Friend, the Cat—but a tempting domestic one. But it wasn't true.

He'd never bothered to ask Laura personal questions before. He knew the dress sizes of the other women in the office, but with Laura, he had pieced together gossip and added his own imagination to make a portrait. That was a stupid way to operate, and he'd never done it with anyone else. What was so different about Laura Everett? It was almost as though he'd been afraid to build a real relationship with her. Why?

Certainly no one whose ears were as red as Laura's were could have looked less threatening. Or more adorable. "Thanks for getting the food," she said, climbing into the passenger seat. "Why are you staring at me?"

"Your ears are all red."

She grabbed at them, nearly upsetting the pizza from its place on the dashboard. "Are they? I guess the sunburn's just now showing up, huh?"

"I don't think it's sunburn," he said. He put down his hot dog and touched one ear, moving her hand as he did so. "Does that hurt?"

"No," she said, almost in a whisper.

"Does this?" He leaned over and kissed her ear. She shifted in her seat and he was suddenly kissing her mouth again, and although he had decided the kiss this morning had been a fluke, he had hoped it wasn't the first and last time to taste Laura's lips, to feel her heartbeat next to his. His tongue teased her mouth open and she responded with a small sigh that sent his body reeling. Laura, he realized, kissed like a natural born kisser who hadn't gotten a chance to practice in a while. That he alone was going to get to be the one to experience Laura's charms sent a sort of proprietary thrill through him. A caveman kind of response: mine, mine, mine.

She wrapped her arms around his neck, and he had never felt anything that was both so comforting and so exciting as the weight of those arms around him.

She was the one who broke off the kiss. Her ears were now an even brighter red. When she looked at him, her hazel eyes completely serious, he felt an ache of responsibility for how open and honest and vulnerable she was.

"Let's not talk about it," she said.

Huh? "Not talk about what?"

"Why we've been kissing," she said. She lifted her arms from him, took a sip of the shake he'd placed in her cup holder and then held it to her face for a second. "You know and I know that I like to overanalyze things, but Harris is counting on us, and I can't use my brain trying to figure out why we suddenly can't keep our hands off each other."

"Because we're attracted to each other?" Kyle ventured.

She frowned at him. "You're talking about it."

"Sorry," he said. He took a sip of his own shake, and handed Laura a pack of M&M's to open up. He steered the car back on the interstate. "If you'd like to kiss again without talking about it, let me know."

He heard the *ping-ping-ping* of dozens of M&M's hitting the car floor.

Laura was rattled. Again he felt that caveman feeling of triumph, but it was tempered somewhat by the realization that she had also rattled him. He glanced over at her. Did she even know what she'd done?

Around four o'clock she pointed out the long bridge that would take them across to the semiexclusive Bellamy Island. Seeing a pay phone in the parking lot, he pulled into the last chance gas station at the foot of the bridge.

"More M&M's?" Laura asked. After she had individually dusted off each piece of fallen candy, they'd made quick work of the bag.

"No, I need to call Brandi," he said. He rubbed the bridge of his nose. What he wouldn't give for a shower and a shave. "We're going to go into the hotel and claim that Harris asked us to come and that's it okay for our rooms to be charged to the corporate tab. It would help if Brandi called beforehand."

"So you have to sweet-talk Brandi," Laura said, nodding.

Yes, he almost said, then decided he was insulted. "I do not have to sweet-talk Brandi. I just have to ask her nicely."

"You flirt like crazy with her," Laura said. "And she flirts back."

"That's just not true. She has a very serious boyfriend. It's her nature to be lighthearted and friendly."

"There's friendly and then there's *friendly,*" Laura said.

He grinned at her. "Why, Laura, I didn't know you cared."

She busied herself refolding the map. "You're talking about it," she warned.

"Do you want to listen in on my conversation with Brandi?"

She waved him away, and he got out of the car and went over to the pay phone, trying to punch in his calling card number and watch Laura at the same time.

On the second try he shifted his body and his attention away from her, finally getting the numbers in the right sequence. The afternoon sun was hot, and he could smell the tangy ocean breeze rolling toward him.

He prayed that Tricia and Brandi wouldn't have taken advantage of Harris's absence to leave early. They hadn't. Without going into the details of the New Horizon deal, he explained to Brandi what had happened at the camp and what he and Laura needed her to do.

"Am I going to get in trouble for this or are you going to smooth it all over?" Brandi asked.

"I'm smoothing already," he said. He heard the car door open behind him and turned to see Laura getting out. He watched as she basked in the fresh sea smell, her attention distracted by a small spaniel that reached her from the end of its owner's leash. After asking if she could pet it, she bent down, the dog covering her with kisses.

"Kyle? Are you there?" Brandi asked.

"Yeah. What were you saying?"

"I was asking you if Laura was getting on your nerves."

Laura smiled at the dog's owner, who didn't, Kyle could see from here, wear a ring on his left hand. Picking up women by carrying a cute dog around—what a tired trick. Kyle had used it just last week, taking his niece and her pug to the park in his sister's neighborhood.

"No, I wouldn't say she's getting on my nerves," Kyle said. "I've got to go, though. I'll talk to you later."

"Ready?" He was at Laura's side instantly, as she traded one more pat with the dog and smiled goodbye at his owner. He practically dragged her back into the car.

"Listen," he said. "I'll deal with the desk clerk, but you have to deal with Harris. If we can't get him alone at first, make up some story about why we had to see him right now."

That jerked her attention back to him. "Why do I have to lie to Harris?"

"He trusts you more than he trusts me."

She snorted. "Right. He thinks your every word is gold."

"Is that what you think?" Oh, right, that's what he had wanted her to think, back at the office. Now he needed her to have a clear-eyed view of their strengths and weaknesses. "No, Laura, he *likes* me, but he trusts you. You have that earnestness thing going."

"But I'll be lying."

"So you'll lie earnestly," he said. The Bellamy Hotel dominated the marshy island, and they reached the grounds just a half a mile after leaving the bridge. He maneuvered Rand's car into the grounds of the complex, pulling up to the valet parking section next to the elegant main hotel building, a beautiful stucco structure dating from the turn of the century.

The look on the valet's face was priceless. And that was before Kyle emerged from the fuschia car in his tousled shirt and shorts. Laura still looked the picture of elegance from the neck up, but she was wearing jeans, and Kyle got the idea that jeans were not standard attire at the Bellamy.

Kyle slipped the valet the rest of the twenty, which wasn't much, and explained, "Rental. They were going to take an extra four hours to scrape the bumper stickers off. We said leave them, you know? We were in a hurry."

The crew-cut young man, whose name tag said Nick, didn't blink. "Your luggage?"

"Lost," Kyle said. "They're going to ship it here when they can. Can you imagine the kind of day we've had?"

"Driving around in that car, sir? No, I can't," said the valet, before getting in. Kyle noticed he had to move the seat up to reach the pedals. Hah.

"Well, that went well, didn't it?" Laura asked.

He stared at her. "Are you kidding? He didn't believe a word I said." He put his hand on the small of her back and guided her through the heavy oak doors. "I think I'll have better luck with the clerk."

"If she's a she, that is," Laura said. When he started

to respond, she raised a hand to silence him. "Just stating the facts." She pointed to a luxurious embroidered emerald sofa in a lobby dominated by a large antique chandelier and numerous small oil paintings and fragile-looking vases. "I'll be sitting here waiting on you. Wouldn't want to cramp your style."

He didn't bother with a response. It was bad enough that she suggested he flirted to get his way, since there may have been some truth to that, but for her to suggest that he couldn't flirt as effectively when she was around. Well, that was...

That was true.

The desk clerk was a soft and pretty redhead. He smiled at her, and she smiled back, but then he took a look back at Laura, who hadn't settled on the couch, but was admiring the paintings in the lobby. He couldn't do it. He delivered his cover story straight to the clerk, without overplaying the charm he usually used with the opposite sex.

And she bought it. After confirming that Brandi had called a few minutes ago with last-minute reservations, she accepted his directive that their room and meal charges be covered with Harris's corporate card. She also told him that Harris and the other men weren't back yet, but that if they wanted to have appetizers and drinks at the Sea Spray, the outdoor bar, she thought the men were going to stop there before dinner in the main dining room.

"We're in," Kyle whispered to Laura, who was studying a small still life.

"Our office needs more art, don't you think? It would make it feel more polished."

"Places that spend a lot of money on atmosphere are throwing it down the drain. Like all those fresh flowers every day at Mallory Management. Get real."

Kyle opened the door for her to the casual Sea Spray. Well, casual for the Bellamy. He saw Laura smooth her hair and look self-consciously at her jeans. He guessed that she had never been less than properly dressed for anything, and it made him feel protective of her. He directed her to a table near the door, the better to spot Harris if he showed up, and held her chair for her as she sat down.

"Order whatever you want," he said. "Harris is paying."

She grinned at him, relaxing in her wicker-backed seat. "How generous of you." She bit her lip as she studied the drink menu. "I'd like to have a margarita, but do you think it would take away from my earnest points?"

"It would take more than one margarita to take away from your earnest points," he said. "I'm going to have a beer." The waitress came, and they gave her their order, adding chips, spinach-stuffed mushrooms and a large shrimp cocktail to it.

"You've got your speech for Harris planned?" Kyle asked Laura.

"More or less."

The waitress came back with their drinks and the chips, and Kyle watched as Laura licked the salt off the rim of the glass. *Oh my, oh my.* He gulped his beer.

"So, you never told me what happened to Stan," she said.

He was still staring.

"Kyle?"

"Stan who?"

"Your best friend? The imaginary guitar prodigy who was too obsessed to have a social life? Did he ever figure out his life or is he still delusional and lonely?"

No, that would be me, obviously. Kyle ordered another beer as the waitress arrived with the mushrooms. He busied himself with them, trying to take his attention off Laura and her seductive ways with a chip. "No, actually, he, uh, met a female bass player on a gig a few years ago. They're married now."

"You left out that part of the story," she said.

"Because it didn't…"

"Didn't go with your point. Gotcha."

He dared to look up at her, expecting a teasing look, and saw that she was instead staring into the distance. He didn't expect what she said next. She put down her margarita and looked at him earnestly. "Kyle, do you really like your job?"

Like I would tell you if I didn't, he thought, but then he understood that however odd it seemed, he would tell her the truth. "I love my job," he said. "You know, I told myself I was going to stay there awhile anyway. But there's something about it—everything fits. Do you? Do you like your job?"

She doodled a circle into the condensation on her glass, then said, "Well, I've never worked anywhere else. That's not…like or dislike…it's not…"

"A value that you get behind?"

She blushed. "I did say that phrase to you last night, didn't I?"

"Yeah." He thought of something he had wanted to ask her when she was in the car with him today, talking about her niece, whom she obviously adored. "What you said about neurotic A students being better than happy B students, you didn't mean that, did you? I mean, if you were married, and had kids—"

He didn't get a chance to find out whether she was going to defend her position on maladjusted little progeny or a chance to ask himself why he wanted to know. He heard a familiar voice say, "Well, I'll be damned. If it isn't my feuding future vice presidents. What are you all doing here? And who's paying for all this?"

LAURA HAD EXPECTED Harris to be skeptical about their being here. What she hadn't expected were the waves of nervousness and mistrust coming off of his companions, a tall, heavyset blond man in his midthirties and a small, dark-haired man about ten years older. Better to face these sharks, though, than continue the personal conversation she and Kyle were having. She'd come *this* close to admitting that she disliked her job, saved only by Kyle's odd detour into her hypothetical child-rearing habits.

She looked at Kyle, who nodded at her almost imperceptibly. Show time.

"Harris," she said, standing up. "What a—" She couldn't really say what a surprise to see you here, could she, since she and Kyle were basically stalking him? She watched Kyle's blue eyes grow dark with alarm. "What a *pleasure* it is to see you."

"Is it?" he asked. She was tempted to bail and let Kyle take over, but if there was one thing that could be said about her, it was that she always met her obligations. Meeting one's obligations didn't sound as attractive as a willingness to put on some lacy underwear and seduce a man by moonlight, but too bad. She wasn't here to be attractive. She was here to keep her job.

She said to Harris, "We wanted to tell you how meaningful our stay at Serene Dynamics was. That it was the most positive experience of our lives, wasn't it, Kyle? We're just filled with new energy and new direction.''

"New dynamics," Kyle added. "Serene ones."

"And you couldn't wait until Monday morning?" Harris sounded more amused than skeptical, thank goodness.

"We had to thank you in person. Right away," Laura said, catching a small nod from Kyle again. The other two men were still not on her team, she could tell, and so she turned to the large blond one and said, "Didn't Harris tell us that you've been to the camp? That you recommended it?"

Small no, no, no shake of the head from Kyle. "Yes, we did," said the smaller man. "Glad you enjoyed it."

"Sit down, sit down," Kyle said. "Have some chips." He stood up. "I'm Kyle Sanders," he said to the blond man. "And this is Laura Everett."

"Bill Brewster," said the larger man. "And my partner, Walt Williams." Laura tried to keep them straight. Bill, big. Walt, weaselly. She wasn't nearly as good with names and faces as Kyle was. Harris pulled a few extra chairs up to their table, but instead of sitting down, Bill said, "Could you excuse us?"

Harris grabbed a chip. He looked relaxed and happy. "They go everywhere together. Like a couple of damn women."

"I don't know," Kyle said. "Laura's been short of girl talk over the stalls this trip."

Harris looked puzzled, and then said, "Oh, hell, Laura, I didn't mean you."

Because you're a robot, not a real woman, she finished.

"But if Kyle's defending your honor, that's a big step, right?"

"That's what our counselor said," Laura told him, getting a small grin from Kyle, who knew that Rand had said exactly the opposite. "The only downside is that they accidentally sent our luggage home with some other campers." She didn't care what Kyle said. She was going to explain why she wasn't properly attired.

"Pick up a couple of things at the clothing store off the lobby," Harris said. "Did you all check in?"

Laura looked at Kyle for approval before saying yes.

"Well, have your rooms billed to me," Harris said. Laura felt a twinge of guilt until he added, dryly, "If you haven't already."

"So did you get some golf in?" she asked Walt and Bill when they returned.

They nodded, then Harris said, "Kyle can rent some clubs tomorrow. I can't wait for you to see him in action."

"How about some volleyball right now?" Bill asked Kyle.

"I'm not sure that's such a good idea," Laura interrupted. "We've driven a long way on just a little sleep—"

"You're saying he's not up to it?" Bill asked.

"Of course I'm up to it," Kyle said, frowning at Laura.

Great. She had attacked his masculinity again, just like with the car this morning. Bill had thrown down the challenge and Kyle couldn't resist it, like a bunch of little boys issuing double-dog dares.

Kyle stood up, and when the waitress came over, he signed the bill. Laura speared one more shrimp as Kyle put a hand on her shoulder. "If you want to go on to your room," he said, "You don't have to feel obligated to watch."

"She wouldn't miss it for the world, would you, Laura?" Harris asked. "I'm going to play. How about you and Walt?"

They both demurred, Walt heading back to the bar, and Laura going with the rest of the group down to the beach. While they inspected the net, she walked the shoreline, turning a piece of driftwood over with her shoe, taking deep breaths of the funky sea air. She felt the stress ease out of her shoulders. Why had it been so long since she had been to the beach? Because she never took the vacation time she was allotted, that was why. A large maroon-and-orange shell, delicately whorled, tempted her, and she picked it up, turning it over to see some sort of slimy gray prehistoric creature opening and closing a hole that could have been its mouth, but may not have been.

"Eek." She put the shell down at the water's edge and looked back to make sure no one had heard her yell. Okay, that was why she didn't come to the beach more often. Dusting her hands, she moved back down to the game.

Kyle was holding a volleyball, talking to a teenager. Then he and Bill moved round to one side of the net, Harris and the boy on the other.

Laura started to sit down directly on the sand, before spying an army of red ants hurrying across. She remained standing, since all the beach's lounge chairs seemed to be occupied by older people sporting largish drinks. Who was scoring in the game didn't hold her interest for long, but watching Kyle—that was very interesting.

He had taken his shirt off, revealing a tanned and muscular chest and wiry, corded arms. She allowed herself exactly two minutes of ogling before forcing herself to look away. A couple of men around her age walked by, and she looked at them, trying to decide, objectively, whether or not she was right in thinking that Kyle was the best-looking man on the beach. Bellamy attracted an older and richer crowd than some other places, but the competition was still stiffer than it had been at the gas station. When she looked back at Kyle, satisfied that she wasn't wrong, she saw that he was watching her watch the men, an odd look on his face. Was he jealous? *In her dreams,* she thought, giving another twenty-something guy a second glance as he walked past. Nope. Still Kyle. Definitely Kyle. She turned back again in time to see Kyle hit the dust, hard, in front of Bill. Men and their games.

"Men and their games," said a voice near her ear. Walt Williams, she saw, turning and looking down. She had the feeling he enjoyed sneaking up on people. He had gotten a drink, gin or vodka and tonic, with a lime slice floating at the top of the glass. With his golf clothes and cocktail, he looked positively colonial as he surveyed the beach, as though it were his new world to claim.

"I'm sorry?" she said, pretending she hadn't understood.

"Men and their games. Isn't that what you were thinking?"

"Well, no, actually I was thinking that Harris is going to have a heart attack if he keeps huffing and puffing like that."

"You're a loyal employee. That's a good quality."

Great. She had worked her butt off for recognition in her chosen field, and her reward was being treated like a faithful old canine companion by an *Addams Family* reject.

"Kyle is also very loyal, isn't he?" Williams said. "Surprising, considering his flashy record."

"I don't know. I don't listen to gossip," Laura said, hoping he would take the hint and stop talking to her.

There was a subtext to his words, but she couldn't figure out what it was. Now would be a good time for her to get a dose of women's intuition, that magical ability to put together words and tone and body language and figure out what someone was really saying to you. She'd never had that gift.

Kyle did, though she could just imagine his reaction if she called it "women's intuition." Kyle would be able to talk to Walt Williams and figure out whether he was making small talk or trying to pump her for information. *Kyle, come on. Stop the game. I need you.*

Kyle looked over at her, as though he had heard her silent entreaty. He waved, and she tried to wave back in a way that said *Get over here* but didn't tip Walt off. She didn't succeed.

"So what brought you here today? Couldn't stand being out of the loop any longer?" Walt asked.

"I wasn't aware there was a loop I needed to be in," Laura said, which, she realized, could have probably summarized her whole career with Harris Associates.

Kyle, though—in Kyle, Harris had recognized someone who would be truly happy at his company, who would be in his element, and in the loop. She watched Kyle now, serving the ball, and thought how wonderful it would be to be as comfortable as he seemed with himself right now. There was no trace of whatever latent clumsiness kept him stepping on her toes or bumping her in the shoulder. This was a man at home in his own body.

"Do you have any thoughts on the takeover?" Walt asked.

She had waited forever for someone to ask her opinion on something, and now that she just wanted to watch Kyle, this little man wouldn't shut up. She heard Kyle whoop and knew she needed to do something drastic to get him out of his game. Maybe if she fainted. No, then she'd land facedown in a bunch of fire ants, which would no doubt provoke some kind of allergic reaction.

Allergic reaction.

"Really, you caught me at a bad time," she told Walt. "I forgot that sometimes citrus fruits make me break out. Do you think they used real lime in the margaritas?"

He drew himself up to his full height, which wasn't much. "This is the Bellamy," he said. "Of course."

"I just feel a little, oh, peculiar."

"Maybe you should go in."

Bingo, Walter. Thank you. "Oh," she said, "Kyle has my room key. Maybe I could interrupt him for a second."

"The clerk has a duplicate," Walt said. "No need to stop the game."

"Oh, I would hate to trouble the clerk. Let me just

get Kyle." *Before I have to break out in full-blown welts.*

"You don't trust me to get you safely to your room?" There was something familiar in his tone, and she tried to place it. Oh, yeah. He sounded like Boris Badenov, the spy in *The Adventures of Rocky and Bullwinkle.*

"Oh, no, it's not that. It's just that, uh, Kyle would feel really bad if I got sick and he didn't know about it. You know, since we've bonded and all." *Bonding.* That word didn't nearly do their kisses justice, did it?

She took a few steps toward the game, watching as Bill dove for a ball, barely missing Kyle. Weren't they supposed to be on the same team? She waved to Kyle, to no avail, and then heard Walt say, "Laura?" His voice had lost some of that secret agent slur, and he now sounded more worried than sinister. "You weren't lying about the margaritas. You're breaking out."

"I am?" She rubbed at her neck again, feeling a telltale bump. She started itching. "Oh, I am. Kyle," she called, taking a few more steps toward the net and waving at him.

He turned around to look at her, and his eyes bugged out—in horror or worry, she couldn't tell, but she suspected horror. Oh, she hoped she hadn't overdone it. That was all she needed—for Kyle to see her looking like a case study at a dermatologists' convention.

"Laura," he shouted, holding his hand up to stop the game.

She didn't know whether Bill saw it or not. As for Harris, he was still chugging and plugging away. He knocked a ball over the net, a ball that would have been Kyle's if he weren't looking at Laura. In the split second it took Kyle not to move, Bill had jumped for the ball.

"Watch out," she yelled.

Bill landed, with a crunch that was audible even from a distance, on Kyle's ankle.

Kyle gave Laura a look she could only describe as goofy. Then he crumpled to the sand in a heap.

6

HE DIDN'T HEAR a heavenly choir singing. He couldn't see the pearly gates. But he did hear the splash of water and the sweet strains of "A Dream is a Wish Your Heart Makes," sung by an angel who sounded remarkably like Laura would sound if she could sing. Was that Laura singing? Where was he?

He was aware that he was conscious, but that didn't rule out the possibility of being dead, especially since he seemed to remember that his last moments on earth were spent facedown in the sand with a throbbing ankle, with a hive-covered Laura hovering over him. Now he seemed to be in a soft bed, pillows piled around him, a cotton comforter at his cheek. The vicious throb in his ankle was a dull pulse. Maybe heaven was just an upgrade in circumstances, like going from coach to first class. With difficulty, he opened his eyes, only to see Laura, in a killer green sundress, pacing around a sumptuous hotel room holding a phone. Her hair, wet at the ends, was down, but she lifted it, revealing a neck free of blotches. Yep, definitely first class. He shut his eyes again before she could see that he was awake.

"Kate, I am not so desperate for a social life that I have to seduce a comatose man," Laura said into the receiver.

Talk her into it, Kate.

Laura paused, then said, "I told you he was cute when he started working at the company. Now he's cute *and* likable. But he's still a vegetable—"

Am not, Kyle thought.

"And he's still after my job."

Ah. Am so, Kyle thought sadly. Surely there was some way they could both work there with no egos lost? That one would take the vice presidency and the other wouldn't mind? Yeah, right. What if he refused the vice presidency and Laura did, too? Then Harris would lose all respect for them and probably go recruit some other hotshot.

This was too much thinking for someone whose head felt as fuzzy as his did. He understood why when Laura said, "I don't know. It's not a bad sprain, but I didn't read the directions on the over-the-counter painkillers until I had shoved three of them down his throat." She listened for a second. "One. I was supposed to give him one. And I forgot that he'd had two beers. Remember when the dog ate all the antihistamines you spilled on the kitchen floor and slept for four days?"

When she'd finished her conversation, she turned on the television and sat down on the edge of Kyle's bed.

"I had the strangest dream," Kyle said, as Laura

jumped up from the bed, her hand on her throat. "You were there, only you were covered in welts."

"Oh, thank goodness you're awake." She rushed around to his side, and bent down toward him, smelling of perfumed soap and shampoo. He noticed that she skipped telling him about the painkillers, while also skillfully avoiding the issue of the blotches. "Bill jumped on your ankle, do you remember?"

"I remember how it sounded," he said. "Like stepping on a cockroach."

She sat down on the bed, near him, looking a little queasy. "Could you not mention that sound? I'm squeamish."

He changed the subject. "What have I got on my ankle? A bandage or one of those cool plastic things?"

"One of those cool plastic things," she said, pulling the covers back from his ankle. "The hotel doctor put it on while you were out cold. He left you some crutches, too."

He tried to lean up and look, but felt dizzy and put his head back down again. Laura moved as though she were going to get up, and he said, "Could you adjust this for me?"

"Oh, of course," she said, yanking the pillow out from under his head. He felt a bounce and a wave of wooziness before she got it all arranged. Maybe encouraging Laura's Florence Nightingale side wasn't such a great idea. Unless it included sponge baths.

"Hey, am I still wearing yesterday's clothes?"

"Of course," she said, sounding a little shocked. "Did you think I was going to change them for you?"

"A man can dream," he said, and stifled a grin as she blushed. He wasn't a vain guy, but he had been unconscious for who knew how long and was desperate to make sure he wasn't drooling in front of her or something. Maybe if she got up for just a second, he could sneak a look in the mirror.

"So you charged a dress to Harris. Let me see it," he said.

"You're looking at it," she told him.

"No, I meant stand up." She did, but he was too captivated by the sight of her curvy legs and rounded chest to bother looking at himself in the mirror.

"I got you some pants and a shirt," she said, holding up a pair of khakis. Since they looked like every other pair of khakis he'd ever owned, he took a peek at the mirror. Drool-free, but at what a cost to his head. He laid back down again, moaning a little, counting on the moan to bring her to his side.

"Are you okay?"

"Yeah, just sit with me a minute," he said. She sat down next to him again, and he reached for her hand. "I hope you don't mind," he said. "It makes me feel grounded. You know, like when you have bed spins and you put one foot on the floor."

"I've never had a bed spin," she said.

Ignore that opening. Ignore that opening.

From the television he could hear the twisted vowels of Mr. and Mrs. Howell on *Gilligan's Island.* "Which episode is this?"

"The one where Mary Ann gets knocked on the head and thinks she's Ginger."

"Do you know what my favorite episode is?" Kyle asked her.

She leaned toward him, looking interested. "No, which one?"

"The one where they almost get off the island but Gilligan screws it up."

Real smile. Definite real smile. Their eyes connected, and the smile turned to something more. She was thinking about kissing him. He rose up a little, wanting to connect with Laura, but she suddenly stood up again, dropping his hand.

"Shouldn't I get some ice for your ankle?"

"If it makes you feel better. Do you like playing nursemaid?"

"Well, it's my fault your ankle's busted. But no," she admitted. "I'm not very good at this nurturing stuff." She laughed, a nervous sound. "But if you need someone to do an instant market analysis, I'm your woman."

"You are my woman," he whispered, pulling her back down beside him on the bed.

"Kyle? You're talking about it."

"Not now I'm not." He stretched his arms around her and brushed a soft kiss against her lips. Her mouth opened hesitantly against his, and the slow sweetness of her kiss was unbelievably rousing. He told himself to take it slowly, that he didn't want to scare her. But when she claimed his tongue with her own, he recognized a need in her that was as great as his own.

He pulled her down toward him, his hands tracing the pattern of the zipper along the back of her dress. He hadn't known how right she would feel in his arms, how her body would seem made for his. He reached for her still-wet hair, pulling it off her neck, moving his lips to her collarbone and up to her earlobe as she sighed.

Her mouth was buried in his hair, and he scooted a little, forgetting about his ankle, to catch sight of her breasts straining against the dress. Time to get rid of that. Retaking her warm and eager mouth, he moved her off him so that she was beside him while he worked the zipper. Once undone, he pulled it off her shoulders, aching with the want of her as he stared at her creamy breasts pushing up from black lace.

She blushed. "They didn't have plain white underwear at the clothing shop," she whispered.

"My kind of place," he said, pulling her arms free of the garment as he kissed her. Then he leaned back to admire her, saying, "You're so graceful, do you know that?"

She blushed. "No, I'm not."

"Yes, you are." It was important that she know she could trust her body, that she could trust him as well. He ran a hand along the top of her breasts, and, feeling her shake with want, moved her hand to his chest.

Her fingers etched a pattern down his chest to the beginning of his waistband, and he gasped with anticipation. He looked at her, afraid that his gasp was going to make her think he'd done something to his ankle, and saw that sly smile he'd first encountered this morning. He returned it with one of his own, and he didn't see any more hesitation in her face as he unhooked her bra, swallowing hard as he cupped one of her breasts.

He leaned over to take the nipple in his mouth, and as he did, her hand unbuttoned his shorts, reached below his waistband and closed around him. He groaned a response against the full roundness of her breast, and his hands moved up her thighs until he met more lace.

She buried her head against his chest as he moved her on top of him, the lace pressing against his own cloth barrier. He slid his hand under the lace and felt the welcoming warmth there.

"Laura." With his free hand he caressed the back of her neck. "I'd give anything to make love to you."

"Me, too," she whispered hoarsely, and he, a man used to a lot of blandishments and meaningless chatter, thought those two simple words were the sexiest he'd ever heard.

"But we don't…"

She hurried off the bed, the dress hitting the floor as she did so. He was an idiot to have put a stop to their lovemaking before it grew out of control, he thought. He'd never felt so empty and alone…and aroused…in his whole life.

But Laura wasn't leaving the room. Instead, she picked her jeans up from a chair near the door and took out a foil packet. How the hell?

She bit her kiss-swollen lip a little before her chin went up and she said firmly, "It was a whim."

"And a damn good one," he said, relieved. "Come back to bed."

KYLE HAD THE MOST beautiful body in the world. Not that she had seen all the male bodies in the world, or even a handful of them, but she just knew no one else's chest was such a combination of planes and muscles. No one else's hands were so gentle and accomplished. And for the moment, all this was hers.

He wanted her as much as she wanted him. She knew that by the throaty sounds he made as he eased the lacy underwear down her hips, and she felt a thrill of power as she watched him overtaken with desire. His mouth claimed her breast again, the roughness of his unshaven chin bestowing an extra sensuality on the sensation of his mouth and tongue moving across her nipple.

She was lying beside him now as he moved his mouth to hers, their gazes locked. She thought again that she had never seen eyes like that, like a painting, all sharp and muted blues. Then he touched her, his touch moving inside her, and she heard herself beg, "Please, Kyle, now, please."

He moved her on top of him and she had a dry-mouthed feeling that there was no way she was going to be able to do this. Then her hips came down to match his thrust and she felt him fill her. Oh, did he fill her. She rocked a little on top of him and felt him moan as she bent toward him, his hands catching her breasts, handling them with an unexpected strength that made her bolder in her own movements. She reached behind her to run her fingers up alongside his thighs, taking pleasure in the expression on his face as he watched her body arch. Then she was past thought as instinct took over. No need to worry that she didn't know how to do this. She knew. Oh, did she know.

He grabbed for the ends of her loose hair as she bent her face toward him, and he captured her mouth in a hungry kiss as she felt an unfamiliar joy fill her body. She moved her lips to his chest, tasting the sweat on his body and soaking in the feel of him beneath her as he cried out her name into the room's stillness.

Afterward, she still couldn't get enough of touching him, curling up against his chest, pushing her hands over the muscles on his arms. She might have felt self-conscious about it if it weren't clear that he couldn't get enough of her, either. He enjoyed her body, the body she'd never given a moment's thought to. He turned on his side and kissed her, then ran a gentle finger over her chin.

"I need a shave, huh?"

"Mmm." Laura pulled him down for another kiss, tasting the sweet and salt of his mouth. Would she ever get tired of kissing this man? "I bought you a razor, but I used it."

"She's already stealing my razors," he said, and she blushed at the familiarity of it. "I do kind of like the way your face looks after I've kissed you. It matches your ears."

From now on, she was going to wear her hair down whenever she was in danger of seeing Kyle. This ear thing was clearly giving her away. She poked him in the shoulder, and he said, "That pain shot down all the way to my ankle."

She ignored him, stretching her arms above her head. "Since you're an invalid and all," she said, "I wonder if we could talk the room service guy into bringing some razors when he brings dinner."

Kyle appeared to think about it. "Since the room service guy is going to get razors anyway, I wonder if we could talk him into another purchase in the personals department? With a suitable tip, of course."

He wanted more. This was encouraging. Not only

had she just had the most incredible erotic experience of her life, with the man who made her pulse pound the way no one else ever had, but now she had a chance to top it. Or should she leave? She should leave. She should take some time to figure out why and how she had slept with her biggest rival. Well, the why part, she thought, looking at his body beside hers, that was pretty clear. And she'd been celibate for a long tine, but the how part had pretty much handled itself the way nature intended. What she really wanted to know was What Did it Mean?

"I should get my room key from you and leave right after dinner," she said. "You know I can't stay all night."

He didn't say anything, only pulled her toward him for another kiss, his arms wrapped tightly around her.

She stayed.

KYLE HAD the strangest sensation that somebody was upset with him about something. And whoever it was would not stop pounding on the door. He flung an arm out to make sure Laura was still beside him. She was. As long as she wasn't the one pounding, he was happy. Obviously she wasn't so easily pleased. She bolted up out of bed, bouncing his head and his ankle, which both felt a lot worse today. Then she started shaking him.

"Laura, don't, please." He threw his hands over his eyes.

"That's Harris," she said. She pulled his hands off his face. "He's at the door."

"Kyle." *Pound, pound, pound.* "Have you seen Laura this morning?"

"Damn, damn, damn," she whispered, struggling into her dress. She'd forgotten the bra, which he dug out of the covers and handed to her from his place in the bed. She looked at it blankly, then stuffed it into a bundle with the rest of her clothes. She paced around the room with the clothes for a second before throwing them in the closet and slamming the door.

"I'm here," she called through the door. "I'm helping Kyle with his ankle."

He thought of all the things they'd done last night, none of which involved his ankle.

"That's a new one," Kyle said. He was met with a heap of new clothes in his face. Then she was dragging him out of bed.

"Go get dressed in the bathroom," she said.

"You've got five seconds before I throw you out of this hotel," Harris said from the hall. "Do the words *stolen fuschia Chevy Cavalier* mean anything to you?"

That got Kyle's attention. He let Laura push him into the bathroom.

She was back to being all-business Laura, a Laura who didn't sing in the bathtub or spend the night doing incredible things with his body. Fine. He'd get back to being Boy Wonder.

"Hey, Harris," Kyle said, after he had dressed and reentered the room. He sat down in the chair that had held Laura's clothes. "What seems to be the trouble here?"

"Rand's awake," Laura said, folding her arms across her chest. Her face was pale and tight. He didn't care if she regretted last night or not; he was never going to forget how she looked in—and out—of that dress.

"And he's pissed," Harris added.

"Me, I'm still feeling serene," Kyle said lazily. "How about you, Laura? Are you serene?"

She was giving Harris a disapproving glare. "Brian Keith would never have used the word *pissed*."

"I don't give a tinker's damn what Brian Keith would and wouldn't say," Harris roared, causing both of them to flinch. "Suppose you start by telling me why you stole the man's car and finish by telling me what you're really doing here?"

They did, alternating their telling of the story. Laura still looked worried, but Kyle got the feeling that Harris believed them, as much as he didn't want to.

"So based on the gossip of some guy pissing in the woods, you raced right over here?"

Laura nodded miserably. Kyle made his face blank.

Harris smiled ruefully, then sank down on the edge of the bed. "I had a feeling it was too good to be true."

"What do you mean?" Laura asked.

"New Horizon has been trying to bust our butts in the health care market forever. They've built their whole company on *not* being us. So I should have looked harder when they suddenly did want to be us."

Laura looked surprised. "You believe us?"

"I believe you heard what you heard. I can't say if it's true, though, can you?"

Laura was the only one still standing. She leaned against the wall, her arms still folded over her chest. "Why don't you just ask them today?"

Kyle started shaking his head even before Harris did. "I can't do it that way," Harris told her. "We got all the business stuff squared away the first few hours of this trip."

"You don't want getting cheated to interfere with your golf game?" she asked.

"That's not what he meant," Kyle said, quickly forestalling an eruption from Harris. "He hasn't signed anything yet, and isn't going to, this trip. Am I right?" Harris nodded. "That's going to happen back in Atlanta. What one of us needs to do is find out whether and why Walt and Bill are lying about how their business is going."

"Whether I'm about to buy a pig in a poke," Harris told her. She nodded, although Kyle guessed it took her a second to translate that to "whether I'm purchasing an overvalued commercial enterprise." What a contradiction of smarts and naivety she was.

Harris seemed back in fighting spirits, which Kyle recognized as a good thing, but also as a thing which would compromise how he wanted to spend the day, crawling back into bed with Laura. But that seemed highly unlikely now that she was back in her MBA-robot mode, nodding as Harris said, "We'll worry about getting that pest's car back to him later. I already told him he could take Laura's."

Harris stood up. "Laura, I'm going to bring you my planner. I've got a list of New Horizon's clients in there. You stay at the hotel and gather all the hard facts you can about New Horizon—make phone calls, go downstairs and use the Internet. Kyle and I will go golfing."

Translation: *Laura will do all the hard work and we'll go golfing.* No wonder she thought he was a slacker. It was going to take more than hitting the links to earn her respect.

"I'm the one with the sprained ankle," Kyle said. "Shouldn't I be doing this and Laura going out with you?"

"Play to your strengths," Harris said.

And his strength was BS-ing on the golf course, huh? "I can't golf."

Laura let out an exasperated sigh. "So today you can ride around on the cart looking cute," she said. "Give Walt and Bill tips on their hitting."

"It's called a swing."

"Whatever."

He wasn't going to convince Harris or Laura that he'd become a research genius overnight. He tried a different approach. "I should stay here with Laura," he said. "I know it seems like it's just a sprained ankle, but I read this news story about a girl who scraped her knee on the pavement, and bam, the next day, she was dead from a blood clot to the brain."

Harris looked impressed, until Laura ruined it by saying, "That's an old made-for-TV movie they showed on late-night when we were kids. I've seen it at least fifteen times."

"I never dreamed you watched this much TV," Kyle said. On another woman, it might not be an attractive trait, but with Laura, it brought up visions of seducing her on the couch while movie marathons played.

"There's a lot no one knows about me." She went into the bathroom and came back with a hair band, pulling her loose hair tight again.

But I know a lot more than I did yesterday, Kyle thought. *And I like what I see.* But this latest development complicated things. "Harris, if you can't acquire New Horizon, does your offer still stand? The twin vice presidencies?"

To his credit, Harris looked miserable. "If we acquired them, I could reorganize into two divisions. But staying the way we are, well, you know the old saying about too many chiefs."

"That sounds like a big no," Laura said brightly. Kyle looked at her, but her expression was blank. "I've got a ton of work to do, so why don't you guys scoot?"

Harris walked toward the door, but Kyle stayed seated. "Are you coming?" Harris asked.

"This is my room," Kyle said.

Laura's face turned bright-red. "Oh, right," she said, fleeing. Harris followed, telling Kyle to meet him in twenty minutes in the lobby. After Harris had gone, Kyle used his good leg to slide his shorts toward him. He picked them up and took out a room key.

Thirty seconds later, there was a knock on the door and Kyle hopped up to answer it. Laura stood there, still blushing, her hand outstretched.

He grinned at her, hiding the ache he felt from not holding her. "Missed me already?"

She smoothed back her hair. "I, uh, I don't—"

He handed her the key. Gone was the confident siren from last night. She stuttered her thanks, backing away from him before making a break down the hallway.

"Laura?" he called.

She turned back to him, rolling the key over and over in her hand. "Yeah?"

"You're in room 119."

"Thanks." She dove into the elevator.

He knew that it made sense for him to be the one to distract Walt and Bill with his company on the golf course. Face it, he had leisurely patter down to a science. Dividing labor among business colleagues was one thing, but their romance had changed things. He wanted to take care of her, provide for her. And although she would deny it, he'd bet that buried deep in her subconscious was a judgment about him: not good breadwinner material.

Kyle knew that he had an advantage over other guys not necessarily because he was more handsome or athletic or charming, but because he made it his business to understand women. Women loved guys who understood them, so long as you didn't understand them so much that you were nibbling chocolate with them or whirling daiquiris in the blender or crying at black-and-white movies.

One of the things he understood about women was that they were biologically programmed to look beyond a nice body and a line of talk to what really mattered—could the guy bring dinner home?

A freshly slaughtered bison beat a cute butt any day. Of course, Neanderthal Guy didn't have to worry that his mate might bring home a carcass that was bigger than his, or that she might beat him out for the vice presidency. Or maybe worse, *not* beat him out for the vice presidency and hate him the rest of her life for it.

Neanderthal Guy didn't know how good he had it, Kyle thought, limping down to the lobby to meet the other men, the New Horizon duo dressed once again in bright golf clothes. Both of them easily accepted

Harris's explanation that Laura wanted to relax on the beach.

"Sorry about your ankle," Bill said, giving Kyle a hearty slap on the back. Apparently stomping on someone made you friends for life.

Before he could accept Bill's apology, Harris had waved it away. "For a jock, Kyle can be clumsy. He's always tripping over Laura."

Kyle frowned. "I didn't think you noticed."

Harris shook his head. "How could I not notice? She's always squawking about it."

If Harris noticed everything, how was it that he had never noticed how unappreciated Laura was at his firm? And anyway, he had realized this morning that bumping into Laura had nothing to do with being a klutz. Now that he had actually held her in his arms and felt her body next to his, he didn't feel any of the hyperactive jumpiness he once felt around her. All that jolting and jostling was misdirected attraction. Of course, if she decided for some reason that she wasn't going to see him again, he guessed that he'd be right back to kicking her in the leg.

The Bellamy's golf course was a manicured dream, one that drew aficionados from as far away as Scotland and Japan. Normally he'd go crazy watching someone else play on it when he couldn't. Today, though, he was okay with offering tips and coaching from his shotgun position on the golf cart, his mind mostly on Laura.

At one point, when Walt and Bill had their backs turned to him, Kyle grabbed Harris's cell phone and tried to call Laura's room. No answer.

"Beer and oysters at the Sea Spray on me?" Bill, the clear winner of the day, was in an ebullient mood as they walked into the hotel lobby. "Harris, why don't you call Laura? And Kyle, don't even try to tell her that you could have played better than I did."

With my eyes closed, Kyle thought. Good grief. All he had to do was be in the same building with Laura and his normally laid-back self went right into thoughts of "My club is bigger than your club." Testosterone poisoning, his sister Melanie would have called it. At least Kyle knew that Laura wasn't going to be impressed by anyone's golf score. What would impress Laura? Hard work. The kind she could do just fine by herself.

"I'll call," Kyle said, maneuvering to the desk. Maybe if he talked to her before she came down he could emphasize how much he would have rather stayed at the hotel with her.

To his annoyance, Harris followed him to the desk. Loitering around the counter, flirting with the pretty desk clerk, was Nick, the valet parking guy who doubled as the bellboy who had delivered certain...personals to the room last night.

"Hey, Nick, can I use the guest access phone?"

"Be our guest," he said. He snickered. "Oh, you are our guest."

That didn't earn him much of a real smile from his target. Kyle would have to give him some of his joke-delivery pointers for the hard cases. Kyle accepted the phone, conscious of Harris behind him, but before he could dial out, Nick said, "If you're calling Ms. Everett, she's gone." He reached below the counter and brought out an oversize manila envelope. "She left this for you guys. She was down here for a couple of hours on our computer typing it." He shook his head. "That's one long goodbye."

"It's the report," Harris said, taking it from him. Kyle saw him look around for Walt and Bill, who had apparently made another one of their co-trips to the bathroom.

"What do you mean she left?" Kyle asked Nick.

"Took the purple car and drove away."

"She doesn't have any money," Kyle said, conscious that he was raising his voice. "She doesn't have any money," he repeated more softly.

"She borrowed forty bucks from me." Nick turned to Harris. "Are you her boss? She said you'd pay me back."

Harris pulled a few bills from his pocket and handed them to Nick. "Appreciate your loaning her the money," Harris said.

"Why are you thanking him?" Kyle asked. "He let her go."

"What do you mean 'Let her go'?" Harris asked. "You all weren't even supposed to be here, so I can't really say anything if she wants to cut her trip short, can I? She finished the report. What's the big deal?"

Nick blushed a little, presumably on Kyle's behalf, knowing exactly what the big deal was. Until Laura gave him permission, Kyle didn't want to tell Harris exactly how his and Laura's relationship had changed. Or even give him the condensed, sanitized version.

Not knowing what else to say, Kyle blurted out, "The big deal is that she doesn't even have her driver's license with her." That alone would have kept the Office Laura safely in the hotel, but the woman who had been revealed to him on this trip was a woman of risks, of freedom. He felt the blood rush to his face as he remembered exactly how wild she'd been last night. "She's a loose cannon."

"That's sounds like a case of pot and kettle," Harris said. He looked over at Kyle, as though he had—or was about to—put two and two together, but then Walt and Bill returned.

"Problem?" Walt asked. Kyle thought Walt looked like a man who was always looking for problems, waiting for bad news. If they had tried to deceive Harris, Kyle thought, they must have been pretty desperate.

"Laura had a family emergency, had to get back

right away,'' Harris said smoothly, as the men walked into the Sea Spray.

Kyle made an effort to appear carefree and relaxed, but he wasn't sure how well he succeeded. Not well at all, apparently, since Bill soon asked, ''What are you moping about, Kyle?''

I miss Laura, he wanted to say. His ankle would have given him a reasonable excuse, if it hadn't been Bill's fault, and if it hadn't been as deliberate as sending them to that camp so that he and Walt could schmooze Harris without his right-hand man and woman around. He wanted to know what Laura had found out about these guys. Oh hell, that wasn't it. He wanted to know if she was running from him, from what they'd had.

''Too much sun,'' Kyle said finally.

He wished there were some way he could get hold of her, hear her voice, sweet-talk her with his. It was too early for her to have gotten back to Serene Dynamics to get her cell phone. The idea of her on that mountain in the dark concerned him. What could have put her out on the highway, if not regret?

He let out a sharp sigh, and looked up to see the other men staring at him. He realized that his fists were balled on the table.

''You know, the doc said for you to take it easy,'' Harris said. ''Well, you weren't awake when he said it, but he did. Maybe you should go rest for a while.''

Kyle assumed Harris was giving him a graceful exit, but when he caught the expression on Harris' face, it said, *Get with the program or get out.* Fine. He would get with the program.

He stretched his leg out. ''Nah, I'm fine. Nothing a little listening to Bill's bragging won't cure,'' a remark that drew chuckles from Harris and Bill and a wan smile from Walt.

Nothing that a phone call from Laura right now wouldn't cure.

''Mr. Sanders? It's Ms. Everett.'' Kyle looked up to see Nick handing him a cordless phone. What was this place, Fantasy Island? He grabbed the phone.

''Where are you?'' Kyle asked.

''Um, that's complicated,'' Laura said. Just the sound of her voice enticed him. He had it bad for her. ''Did you and Harris read my report?''

''I don't care about that,'' Kyle said. ''Tell me where you are.''

''Oh, so you haven't read it. Well, I came to some decisions,'' Laura said, ''And I decided I would get back to Atlanta before I changed my mind about them, but it didn't exactly work out that way.''

Kyle had thought she was calling him from a pay phone, but the background noise didn't sound like a restaurant or gas station. He heard the clank of metal, a man's raucous laughter, and the ding of a computer starting up.

She continued. "You see, I'm…"

"You're where?"

She cleared her throat. "I seem to be in jail."

7

LAURA HAD NEVER had a speeding ticket. Laura had never had a parking ticket. Laura had never even had a *library fine*. What happened was this. She'd been about a third of the way home when she decided to go back and grab the report before Harris and Kyle had a chance to see it. Or rather not the report—they could see the report—just not the letter that she had left with it. She pulled a U-turn on the two-lane highway, feeling the screech of Rand's tires beneath her. About a mile later, she realized it was a completely stupid move. She'd made her decision—why not live with it? She turned around again, heading back to Atlanta.

But then she thought how cowardly it was not to have said goodbye to Kyle, even though she wasn't sure of the relationship between them. Just because it was the most incredible romance of her life didn't mean it was the same for him. It was unrealistic to think that she was anything more than a fling to him. Still, that was no call for her to lose her own manners, was it? She pulled Rand's car into a grassy median and headed again for the coast.

That last U-turn was the one the cop spotted. Laura had always assumed that if she were ever to encounter a real-live policeman accusing her of something, she would be a model detainee. Instead, she'd found herself arguing with him that were no signs forbidding what she'd done. Things had been further complicated by her not having her license, registration and insurance. When the cop had figured out that the owner of the car hadn't exactly given his permission for her to take it, she'd gone straight into the squad car.

The policeman, a man about her dad's age, hadn't said anything else on the way to the station. The silent type, like her dad. As if to prove that old adage about girls marrying their fathers, Laura's sister Kate had found her own man of few words, a sweet engineer who couldn't get two sentences out without effort. Laura would have said she liked that kind of guy, too, had she not recently proved herself wrong by falling for a charming, smooth type.

Fallen she had. So much so that her feelings for Kyle had resolved the internal war she'd been having for so long, the war between safety and security and the desire to try her talents somewhere else. Kyle wanted the vice presidency with Harris Associates. And in her heart, she didn't. She wanted it because her father had drilled into her the need for security, security, security. Kyle wanted it because he liked being there.

She'd spent most of the morning talking to clients

and tracking down figures for New Horizon Consulting, finding out that Walt and Bill had been up to a lot of talk and very little action. They still had a large client base, but they'd been careless with their clients' time and resources. Definitely a pig in the poke, as Harris put it. Which left her and Kyle right where they started: vying for the same position within Harris Associates.

Except that she had decided to quit. The last item in the package she'd left for Harris was her resignation letter. She imagined that Harris would be mildly sorry that she was leaving, but it would also solve a lot of his problems. It was Kyle she worried about. She had no idea what his reaction would be, or if he would even share it with her. Would he miss her? Would he be sorry to see her go? Would he take this—wrongly—as a sign that she regretted their time together? Would he take this—rightly—as a sign that she was scared of the intensity of what had happened between them, scared that he would regret it? His wild weekend with the office drudge. Except that she wasn't part of his office anymore. And whether he knew it or not, she wasn't a drudge anymore, either. She guessed she had him to thank for that.

Although the jail, a squat brick building in a yard devoid of vegetation, had looked depressingly squalid on the outside, the inside was actually light and airy. The secretary-dispatcher, a cheerful and talkative woman named Peg, had painted the walls white and resanded the oak table that dominated the room. She knew because Peg had told her all about it. When they first walked in, the policeman had mentioned the three cells in the back of the building. Laura's stomach had flip-flopped, but Peg had shot him a scolding look, and Laura was allowed to sit at the table and wait for Kyle and Harris, a stack of outdated *Time* magazines to keep her company.

She hadn't wanted to call Harris or Kyle to rescue her. Well, that wasn't true. Her immediate thought had been to call Kyle and ask him to rescue her. She might have resisted, except that her sister was incommunicado, probably on a picnic with her family. Besides, Rand was bringing Kyle's car to the police station, so Kyle would have to come to pick it up anyway. When the policeman reached Rand, he was ticked, but not ticked enough to say Laura had stolen his car, especially since he had been happily driving around all day in Kyle's "all-original Austin Healey 3000," as he kept calling it.

"I thought you were driving my car," Laura said when the policeman handed her the phone.

Rand paused. "Your windshield had an unfortunate encounter with a tree branch in the parking lot."

She sighed. "Great."

They figured out a plan. Rand would bring Kyle's car to the station. Harris would bring Kyle to the station, too, but since Harris would get there first, Laura would go ahead and go back to Atlanta with him, leaving Kyle to wait for his Austin Healey and watch over the Randmobile in Where-the-Heck, Georgia. Rand could bring Kyle's stuff with him, and Laura and Harris could swing by Serene Dynamics and pick her stuff up there, worrying about her car later.

It made sense to Laura, and it made sense to Rand. It seemed to make sense to Kyle when she explained it to him on the phone, although she wasn't sure he was really listening to her, hung up as he was on the jail thing. The policeman made it clear that it was the most complicated scheme he had ever heard, so Laura tried to draw it out on a simple flowchart, which he still didn't follow. Anyway, it didn't matter if the policeman didn't get it. It mattered that Kyle got it. And that he wasn't too upset that Rand was driving his car.

How was she supposed to know that the car would be the least of his worries? She had scanned all the entertainment, business and social sciences features in the old magazines and was reluctantly tackling articles about NATO when she saw Kyle and Harris pull up in Harris's beige luxury sedan. "That's them," she said to Peg, watching Kyle get out. He wasn't even using his crutches, hopping with a vengeance.

Harris introduced himself to Peg and the cop. "You're the last employee I'd have ever figured on bailing out of jail," Harris said to Laura. "Or maybe quitting my company has changed you already." His tone was joking, and he didn't seem upset at the news of her resignation, or that he had to help her out. She couldn't say the same for Kyle.

His tan face was paler than she'd ever seen it, and there were unhappy lines around his mouth. He braced himself on the table where she sat, her mouth suddenly very, very dry as he loomed over her. "How could you do it?"

"It was just a U-turn," she said lightly. "It's been a long time since I memorized the highway rule booklet."

"Laura." She had only heard that tone in his voice one time before: the night before last, in the woods, when she had accused him of using his intelligence and charm only in pursuit of women. "How could you quit? Do you know how this makes me look? It makes me look like some guy who got his job because a girl gave it to him, that's how it makes me look."

So that was it. Gee, for a second she thought he'd missed her! Once again she had tripped over his need to be a Manly Man. *Well, sorry.* It was one thing to let him drive because it made him feel better, but it was another to make her decisions about her future based on whether or not they made him "look bad."

"Are you two okay?"

Laura glanced up to see Harris, Peg and the policeman staring at the two of them with interest.

"We're fine," Kyle snapped.

"Is there someplace we could talk in private?" Laura asked Peg, ignoring Kyle's sputters that he said they were fine, and he meant it, and that certainly meant he didn't have to go talk about anything.

"The cell block," Peg said. "It's clear this week."

Laura stood, offering her arm to Kyle, who said, "I can walk on my own, thanks." Having a sprained ankle should have made him more clumsy, more likely to bump into her, but he held himself far away from her as she walked down the short hall to the cells. Unlike the bright and open office, this was a dismal, cheerless place, dank with the smell of mold and, she imagined, bad deeds.

"How can you quit?" He almost spit the last word out, and when she looked into his eyes, they were cold with fury. Today was one time he was *not* cuter when he was mad.

"There isn't room for both of us," she said, keeping her own voice calm. "If you read the report, you know that things are screwed up with New Horizon. Harris is not going to acquire them, not now. I'm trying to make the choice less awkward for everyone."

"That's not a fair fight," Kyle said.

Silly her. She didn't even know it was a fight. "So you'd rather go back to being rivals, just so you can say you didn't win by default? Is that important to you?" She leaned toward him as she spoke, trying to look intimidating, but it had the opposite effect. She had forgotten until now that she wasn't wearing a bra, but Kyle's eyes strayed to her chest, reminding her, and she felt her skin prickle against her dress. She crossed her arms. "I'm not competing on those terms, Kyle."

He gave her a tired sigh and gripped the outer bars of one of the cells.

"But you don't have to find somewhere else to work," he said. "Harris isn't going to make a decision today or tomorrow or even next week. Just come back and everything will be like it was before."

Of course she had already thought of that. She could go back and ride out her employment with Harris, even though she'd admitted it wasn't working. She'd gone way beyond the call of duty at the firm, so she'd earned the right to coast, doing the minimum required. But that would mean that her main interest in life would become Kyle and doing whatever it took to get him. That was her sister Kate's way of operating, not hers. When Kate had met her future husband, she had pursued him with such a vengeance that she had become the only elementary education major in the history of her college to have had a double major in computer science. Of course it had worked, and now that the romance thing was settled, she took her teaching job seriously. She had the only second graders in the county who could explain fuzzy logic.

Fuzzy logic. That was a good term for what she and Kyle were using right now.

"It can't be like it was before," she said slowly. *And if you have to ask why, if you can't figure out that this is the first chance I've taken with my life and that I can't go back to being the office good girl, then you don't understand me.*

She thought he got it. Then he straightened up and said, "All right, then. I'll be the one to look for a job."

She stared at him. "You'll what? Why you?" But then, with dread, she realized that she knew exactly what he was going to say. Don't, Kyle. *Don't do it. Don't go there. I can't stand to think that you pity me.*

He went on, oblivious to her warning glance. "Because it'll be much easier for me to find a job than it would be for you."

YOU WOULD HAVE thought he had slapped her. Those deep hazel eyes were filled with such raw pain and anger that a sharp dig went through his chest, but then the hurt in her eyes was replaced with a vacant coldness. Ice Princess Laura was back, and when he looked at her again, he saw no indication that she was anyone he knew, that they had ever melted body, soul and mind together, that she had been his partner in the most fulfilling romantic experience of his life. She spun around. He caught her on the shoulder as she started to run out of the corridor.

"Did you think I meant that as an insult?" As though he would say anything like that to hurt her, when it was precisely because he didn't want her to be hurt that he was going to make sure she got to keep her position at Harris Associates.

She put her hand on her hip. "'Gee, Laura, why don't you keep your job, because you're too lame to get another one.' Kyle, if that isn't an insult, then I don't know how to calculate mileage for an expense report."

"No, it's just that you've never dealt with headhunters and job searches and corporate recruiters. It has nothing to do with how talented you are. You don't know how to play the game."

"Great, a sports metaphor. You know how I love those." She gave him a shrewd look, and for a scary second he thought she could see right down into his soul. Could she love him if she did? Was there anything there to see? "And you know what? It has *everything* to do with how talented I am, not what a good game I talk. And that's why I'm not going to have any trouble finding *and keeping* another job." Her sandals clacked on the cement floor as she hurried ahead of him. "Are you ready?" she asked Harris, pushing out of the door before she got an answer.

"I was waiting on her," Kyle heard Harris say to Peg. Kyle went through the door after Laura.

Laura had opened the back door of the car and

yanked out the tasteful gift shop sack full of Kyle's belongings, dropping it on the pavement.

"Your jeans are in there," he said.

"Keep them."

"Your necklace from the woods," he said.

"Keep it, too."

"Your bra."

"Kyle, I'm warning you." She yanked open the passenger door on the front seat, where the report lay in its manila envelope. Kyle grabbed it out from under her before she sat down, brushing against her as he did so, feeling the shock of her skin against him. Reaching for the envelope, she said, "That's my report. Give it back."

"I'm the one stuck here. Let me keep it and read it again." He took her resignation letter from the back of the envelope. "You can have this," he said. He got depressed just touching it.

Laura twisted around in the seat and looked at him with a serious expression. "What are you going to do with the report? Not that I'm interested."

"I'm going to figure out how there's room for both of us at the top. That's a promise."

It was a good thing he knew women as well as he did, because a clueless guy would have taken the look she gave him as symptoms of a headache or indigestion. He, with his superior skills, knew it meant, "Whatever you say, you poor deluded man."

Sometimes it didn't pay to understand women.

"Kyle," she said. She reached, as though to touch his arm, then stopped. "Listen to me, because this is the last time I'm going to say it. I don't want the vice presidency anymore. Even if I could have it. Even if I could have it and you could have it, too. Do you understand that?"

"Whatever," he said, making sure she was all the way in the car before slamming the door. He passed Harris on his way back into the building and snarled a response to his boss's cheerful goodbye. He forced himself not to turn around and watch her go.

After a quick nod to Peg as he entered the station, he sat down in Laura's seat and propped his foot up on another chair. His ankle was killing him now. He probably should have asked Laura more questions about any instructions the doctor had left for him. But, then, that would have taken away from the time he and Laura got to spend doing and talking about other things, and he'd rather have this pain the rest of his life than to have given up a second of that. Probably his ankle wouldn't heal right and fifty years down the road he'd be able to predict it was going to rain just by the ache. And his kids and grandkids wouldn't believe him, and he'd yell at them...

Where was this coming from? He had never considered becoming an angry old man. There was no reason to assume that he wouldn't be a perfectly cheerful old man, since he had until this minute been a happy young one. But that was BL. Before Laura.

At his sigh, Peg said, "Your ankle or your heart?"

He looked around and saw that the policeman had gone back into his private office. This place was pretty homey for a jail, wasn't it? He wanted to thank Peg and the cop for taking such good care of Laura, but understood that if he said that, it meant that he was totally, completely, all the way gone, and that everyone—or at least everyone in Podunk, Georgia—would know it. "Nah, it's the ankle," he said, trying out one of the smiles that always worked with his mom. "No danger of a broken heart. I go through hearts like…like used printer cartridges."

"Hmmmph."

See, Peg saw right through him, to the sensitivity beneath the bluster. All women, young or old, did, except Laura. Why couldn't she? But then he noticed that Peg was shaking her head.

"You've never changed a printer cartridge in your life."

His charm was gone. Laura had probably taken it, too. But then she said, "Would you like some pecan pie?"

"Yes, please. I can get it," he said, standing up, wincing as he did.

"Get real," Peg said, bustling over to the small fridge on the far side of the room. "You might as well

get all the sympathy you can." She set the pie and a
glass of milk down beside him. "I take it that Laura
wasn't impressed with your injuries."

Kyle was already several bites into the pie, and Peg
got up and retrieved another slice, sliding it onto the
paper plate in front of him. "Thank you. Laura— Well,
I think maybe I've cried wolf to her too many times,
you know? She sees right through me."

"So a bleeding head wound wouldn't impress her.
What would?"

He didn't know. The policeman came back into the
room and handed Peg some paperwork, which she tack-
led right away. Kyle flipped through the *Time* magazines beside him. In the middle of the stack was a piece
of blank typing paper with Laura's writing on it. Had
she left him a note?

He stared at it for a while, trying to see it as some
secret message to him—something along the lines of
"Kyle, I'm crazy about you and I know you aren't
really a slacker." But to his disappointment, it looked
like some kind of flowchart. It was. Of all things, it
was a chart detailing how Rand was going to get his
car back to him. So much for secret messages. He
turned it into a paper airplane, sailing it toward the
trash can. Then the door to the inner office opened, and
the draft caught the plane, sending it into the policeman's chest as he walked by.

"Isn't your ride coming?" the policeman asked.

"Yes, sir. The details are right there on that paper."
What kind of woman drew flowcharts for fun? The
kind of woman who had spreadsheet parties, probably.
The kind of woman who looked for substance in a guy,
not just style. From having to borrow pen and paper
from her at meetings to letting her work on the weekends while he played darts in the conference room, he
had given her every reason to think he was a superficial
party boy, a good haircut over an empty head, a total
waste case. If he were Laura, would he want a deeper
relationship with him? No. They'd had amazing sex,
but he had such a reputation that she probably thought
he had that kind of sex with all kinds of women. No.
Only with her had it been like that.

He had to accept it—he had been a fling. Granted,
Laura didn't seem like the fling type, but that's what
flings were about, going against type. People had vacation flings and shipboard flings and "I'm trapped in
a hotel room with a drugged and bedridden man"
flings. But he wasn't the kind of guy she would choose
for life.

He pushed his plate away. What would it have been
like, he wondered, if he and Laura had worked as a
team from the beginning? If he had gotten to know her,
acknowledged his interest in what was behind those
eyes? If he hadn't walked into her place of business,
given her a metaphorical pat on the head, and started
sucking up to her boss?

Harris was going to regret that he took her resignation so lightly.

He rose and went over to where Peg sat. "Could I borrow a sheet of paper?"

Her eyes crinkled in surprise. "He walks." She handed him a sheet.

"I may need a couple."

Peg looked at him curiously. "You working or making more airplanes?"

"I'm working," he said. "Why does everyone think I never work? It just looks easy. That's my gift."

He took the paper and a cheap stick pen from Peg, then sat back down at the table. He had told Laura he was going to figure out how they could both keep their jobs, and he was going to do just that. Taking out the report, he gave it a quick read through. A stranger would have never guessed that it had been produced by one person in less than a day. It was error-free and perfectly formatted and filled with facts and logical analyses.

"She eats like Shaggy, she walks like Daphne, but she's got the soul of Velma," he muttered to himself. Wonderful—now she had him seeing the world through television reruns.

What the pristine report didn't have, though—what Laura didn't have—was his own gift for reading between the lines. Using Harris's contact list, she had done an incredible job of collecting confidential quotes from clients and vendors. Because she had quoted many of them verbatim, he was able to read the subtext, to see which of these guys were ticked off beyond the possibility of mending fences and which ones still held some fondness and excitement regarding the firm.

What if a better deal was still possible? He wrote down questions that he wanted to ask the people quoted in the report, as well as a master list of the pros and cons of Harris acquiring New Horizon in its current state. Peg left in the early evening, after first bringing Kyle a sack of greasy cheeseburgers from the diner next to the police station. Policeman One left, replaced by Policeman Two, who looked exactly like the first. As the sky outside turned dark and the fluorescent lights buzzed brighter, Kyle heard someone say, ''Kyle? Your car's here.''

The voice was the only clue that this was Rand. Gone was the starched-and-pressed counselor. This guy was sporting two-day stubble, a torn white T-shirt, and a look of delirium.

''Rand?'' Kyle stood, balancing his weight on his good ankle. ''What happened to you?''

''Total and complete personal transformation, that's what happened to me.'' His eyes glittering, he approached Kyle, who blinked as Rand pulled up the sleeve of his shirt. The bright Serene Dynamics logo glinted from his upper arm. ''I was angry at you,''

Rand said as Kyle edged toward the door and the parking lot. His car looked great, despite a new Serene Dynamics air freshener and despite having been driven here by a maniac with a head injury.

Rand continued, "I've never had a duo defy my orders the way you defied yours."

"Wait a minute," Kyle said. "We didn't defy any orders. You left us without a flashlight, then just assumed we had left, not that we were stuck."

Rand continued. "But then I realized that you were here to teach me a lesson about the greater gifts that can come to us when our plans go awry."

"I like my plans to stay wry, personally," Kyle said, inching toward his car and freedom.

"When I was unconscious, I had the most incredible insights into our training programs, our future, everything. And I have you and Laura to thank for that, for teaching me what it's like to let the unexpected take over our lives."

He and Laura had learned that lesson, too, hadn't they? Only it seemed to be one that Laura now regretted. Well, he was going to see that she didn't. He was going to show her that he could be the kind of person she could respect. Let Rand become less obsessive and ambitious. It was time Kyle became more so.

Rand seized his hand, shaking it vigorously. "I want you to remember this," he told Kyle. "Sometimes it takes being knocked on the head—quite literally—to shake you toward where you're meant to be.''

Kyle opened the door to his beloved car. ''I don't know,'' he said to Rand. ''A sprained ankle and a case of hives, those seem to work pretty well, too.''

8

THERE WAS A LIMIT to the amount of television you could watch. This came as a deep shock to Laura, who had assumed that there was no such thing. But when you knew all the episodes of *The Waltons*, *The Brady Bunch*, and *Little House on the Prairie* by heart, you could watch them and still have room in your head to obsess about whatever you were obsessing about. Kyle, mostly. Well, purely Kyle.

Laura had decided to take her week of leisure and do a real forget-you-slept-with-the-office-hunk blowout, full of chips and popcorn and Hershey's Kisses. She was going to neglect to spray Clean Shower on the tile walls and let the pizza boxes pile up around her.

It didn't work. She found herself obsessively bleaching countertops and scrubbing the kitchen floor by hand. Even the rerun troubles of John Boy and Elizabeth, Peter and Jan, and Laura and Mary Ingalls were not even remotely as interesting to her as the *Life of Kyle Sanders*, going on now without her.

He hadn't called. Well, why should he have called?

The last time she had talked to him, hadn't she been a little dismissive? A little dismissive? She had blown up in his face. Still, the last thing he had said to her was that he wanted to figure out a way they could still both get their promotions. Never mind that she didn't want that promotion now. It was the thought that counted, the thought that he wanted to see her again. So why hadn't she called him? Because she feared that as soon as she'd gotten in Harris's car, Kyle had been struck by a blinding light of "Hey, Kyle, if she leaves, you don't have to deal with the awkward fact that you made mad, passionate love to that woman while you were under the influence of a massive dose of painkillers."

There was also later that night, after the painkillers had worn off. And later again, when she'd felt him reach for her while the room clock blinked 4:00 a.m.

She felt her face grow hot. If she thought about them making love, her face started to tingle feverishly and her knees grew weak. Oh, sure—gripping, Emmy-winning drama couldn't hold her interest, but she could spend hours replaying Kyle touching her. Her touching Kyle. Her mouth on his chest. His hands on her breasts. She shook her head, got up and pulled open the blinds to her apartment, surveying it with a critical air. It was a little messy, but nothing like what she'd wanted to achieve. She just wasn't the kind of woman who could let herself go.

Except when she was with Kyle. She could let herself go with Kyle, let herself go beyond conscious thought, beyond propriety, beyond her to-do lists and her obligations and into pure pleasure.

She grabbed an Oreo from the Bugs Bunny cookie jar on her counter. It was a gift from Haley, and there had never actually been cookies in it before. She took one bite and tossed it out, then opened the cabinets and started searching for a can of soup. So much for being bad. She was no good at it. If you didn't count watching too much television, the only vaguely wicked thing she'd ever done in her life was have a one-night stand with Kyle Sanders.

Even then, she had a feeling that her constant thoughts of Kyle somehow went against the spirit of one-night stands altogether. Maybe for a split second she had thought she could sleep with Kyle without wishing their relationship was a real one, but it hadn't happened that way.

Was a one-night stand a one-night stand if you still held out hope that there would be a second night? And how far apart could night one be from night two for them to be separate stands altogether? If you, every three or so years when the moon was full and the month didn't have an *R* in it, made love with the sexiest, hottest man you ever met, could you eventually add all those encounters up and call it a relationship?

And what would she do between stands? She could marry someone nice and bland—not that a candidate had shown up in the past few years, but now that she had fallen hopelessly for Kyle, fate would decree that Mr. Sweet show up. And whoever he was, would he ever excite her imagination and her body the way Kyle did? No. Better just to live alone, not take advantage of Mr. Sweet. Eventually, she would get a cat. People were always trying to force cats on single women, and someday she would be too tired to refuse. And Kyle liked cats. Maybe she would need tips on cat behavior and she could give him a call.

Arrgh.

Maybe she would take a walk in one of Atlanta's parks. Being outside had made her feel better last weekend, all that fresh air.

All that fresh air and Kyle.

She had just grabbed her car keys when the phone rang. She dove for it, only to hear Brandi at the other end of the line.

"Oh, hi, Brandi," she said, trying not to let disappointment creep into her voice.

"I hate to bother you, but some of us were wondering about something. Would you like a going-away party?"

She couldn't imagine anything more excruciating. People had left Harris Associates before, but those had been guys who were starting their own businesses or bragging about their better offers. She wasn't sure a party was an appropriate response to "I just figured out that I don't like it here anymore." And where would Kyle be, when they were throwing that party? Avoiding her like crazy?

She declined as graciously as she could, inquiring about Tricia, who was on maternity leave, telling Brandi that she would come in sometime next week and turn over her files and clean out her desk.

Things would be easier for the next woman who worked at Harris Associates. Laura was sure about that. On the way back to Atlanta with Harris, she had been surprised to discover that her boss knew exactly how difficult it had been for her there, how she had gotten stuck with the grunt work, how she had been underused and unappreciated. He'd had a lot of time to think out on that golf course with Walt and Bill, apparently. He had been sorry she was resigning, but not shocked. Most surprising of all, he had told her that he knew that his firm was somewhat of a cultural dinosaur, and that the old-boy mentality he had used to run it was not going to cut it in the twenty-first century. When he'd asked her if she'd considered working for Mallory Management, she'd confessed that she had. She had expected the fresh-flowers-and-espresso diatribe that he'd given before when he talked about the upscale, woman-run company, but instead he had nodded thoughtfully and said he would write her a sterling letter of recommendation. In turn, she'd promised she would send any suitable job candidates his way. It was a good way to leave the firm, and it came during a naturally slow time, so that she had only a few loose ends to clean up.

And she was not going to consider Kyle one of those loose ends. Though she couldn't resist asking Brandi, "How's Kyle's ankle? Is he making you wait on him?"

"No, not at all," Brandi said. A note of worry entered her calm tone. "I think it's healing fine, but you should see him. He gets his own Cokes, his own sandwiches. He doesn't even call me when he needs to find a file on a project, just limps around here doing everything for himself."

Whoa, back up. "This is Kyle?"

Brandi lowered her voice to a whisper. "Laura, he gets into the office before I do, and he actually stays at his desk and works. Not only that, but he actually did his own expense report this time."

"He wasn't doing his own reports before?" *Kyle, you fiend,* thought his former interoffice rival. *Kyle, you charmer,* thought the woman who had spent the weekend in and out of bed with him.

Brandi evaded her question. "He has big circles under his eyes, Laura."

Could he be staying awake nights thinking about her the way she was staying awake thinking about him? "Has he said what he's working on?"

"Top secret," Brandi said. She changed the subject. "I heard you have a big interview tomorrow."

"Does—" She paused. She didn't want to accuse Brandi of being gossipy, but she really wanted to know the answer to this question. "Does Kyle know that I'm interviewing somewhere else?"

"Well," Brandi said. There was that unhappy tone again, such a rarity for Brandi. "Actually, he leaves the room every time your name comes up. But I'm sure he doesn't mean anything by it."

No, nothing short of wanting her to join the witness protection program for women who needed to conveniently forget that they'd slept with Kyle Sanders.

"Oh, well, could you tell him—" *Tell him I'm going to be perfectly fine without him, even if I never have a chance to feel that cherished, that sexy, again.*

"Tell him what?"

"Never mind."

"I'M HERE TO TALK to you about balance in your life."

Kyle looked up from the pages spread across his dining room table to see his mother, clad in a nononsense business suit, standing in his living room, holding a casserole dish of what smelled like his father's killer lasagna. He rubbed his eyes. Had to be a dream. And if so, as much as he enjoyed both his mother's company and his dad's lasagna, it was definitely a step down from the dreams he'd been having, dreams of Laura and their night together. Dreams of new nights together.

Then his mother walked past him on her way to the kitchen, straightening out his shirt collar as she did so. It wasn't a dream. "Why are you in my apartment?" He thought of a more important question. "How did you get into my apartment?"

She came into the dining room and sat down at the table with him. He pushed away his pages of notes on the upcoming New Horizon deal. It looked like it might happen. He'd had to sweet-talk the prickly Walt, then sweet-talk Harris, both conversations backed up with extensive documentation. It was cards-on-the-table time in a face-to-face meeting next week. Then Laura would know he was the one who had pulled the deal together, that he was indeed capable of hard work. She might come back. He was so close to that happening that he could feel it.

"Your sister gave me a key," his mother said.

"Mom. You can't just walk into my apartment." He grinned at her. He could always make his mother blush. "Mom, I could have someone here."

"Not the way you've been working, you wouldn't have someone here," she said briskly. "Your dad and sister say they haven't seen you at all in the week since you got back. Jessica misses you. They decided I should stop by on my way home from work to talk to you about balancing your work and personal life."

"Mom. Only Dad and Melanie would consider hard work for one week extreme."

She ignored the implied insult to the other members of the family. "You're limping, what happened?"

"Nothing happened." He continued walking "carefully" to the kitchen. He lifted the top of the dish, his stomach growling. His dad might be a slacker, but he was a slacker who made one heck of a lasagna. He cut into it and called, "Did you want some or are you just here to deliver a message?"

She poked her head into the kitchen, her blue eyes, just like his, dark with suspicion. "Are you waiting on yourself? Kyle?"

He didn't answer her, merely took two of his four plates out of the cabinet and loaded them with food. He carried them both back into the dining room, his mother following him with silverware and paper napkins.

"See, about balance," he said, slicing into his piece. "It's way overrated. Sometimes what a guy needs is a quest, a big pursuit, something that will make his loved ones proud." Then remembering that his own dad had abandoned the corporate world for house and home, he said, generously, "I mean, not that all women care about that. You don't, and you're great. But other women, I think they want a guy who can bring home the bacon, you know?"

She burst out laughing. Laughing. *You've sunk far*

in the world when your own mother laughs at you. If he didn't deliver on his promise to Laura, she was going to be laughing at him, too. If she wasn't already.

"Kyle, honey, I would have said that you understood women as well as anyone I know."

"Thank you," he said, blowing on the lasagna before biting into it. "I think so myself."

"But some woman has plainly thrown off your radar."

He scowled at his mother. "She has not."

She got up and went to the kitchen, then returned with colas for both of them. "Why don't you tell me about her?"

He did. In deference to his mother's tender ears, he edited his story heavily, but he went through the path of their relationship, from Laura's initial distrust of him as a job stealer, which he was, to her quitting the firm.

"And you haven't talked to her since?"

"No, because I've got to get this deal finalized, prove that she can take me seriously. You know, finish the last part of the quest."

"Does she know you're still on this quest?"

"Well, I...I don't know. I haven't talked to her."

"You haven't called her! Kyle, what must she think?"

"I can't call her yet," he argued, a sinking feeling going through his stomach. "For all she knows, I'm still the same guy she doesn't respect."

His mother closed her eyes. He knew that look, all right. That was the old "I'm shutting my eyes against your foolishness" look. "Kyle. This woman is sitting around right now wondering if you hate her, if you think whatever happened between the two of you was a mistake."

After she was gone, he sat back down with his notes. But his thoughts, as always, were on Laura. Was it possible for two people to seem so opposite and yet fit together so well? But what if they only fit together in bed and not in the rest of their lives? Was he a fling for her, or a real "renovate the old farmhouse in the outer suburbs" kind of love? Or maybe she'd always wanted to live in Midtown Atlanta, in one of those in-town neighborhoods like Inman Park or Virginia-Highlands. That was more expensive, and harder to have pets and kids there. And kids—he didn't know how many and how far apart and whether she believed in public education or whether he should start saving for private school. Actually, he had already upped his contribution to the company's 401K plan, just in case. He felt his stomach roil, then the truth hit him like the crack in his ankle.

He was a coward. He'd had girlfriends—he'd always had many, many girlfriends—but this was what it was like to be serious about somebody, to eat, sleep and breathe thinking about her. He knew that old joke about how a woman could take one look at a man on an elevator and meet, date, become engaged to, marry and divorce him before the third floor. So which one of them was sitting around worrying about their kids' orthodontics?

You'll plan your retirement together, but you're too scared to actually see her. Well, not anymore.

HOW LOW has a grown woman stooped when she's this excited about watching Josie and the Pussycats? What the heck, Laura thought, ripping open the bag of microwave popcorn and pouring it into a large salad bowl. She deserved it. Her interview with the partners at Mallory Management had seemed to go very well, and at the end of the meeting, the elegant Susan Mallory and her business partner, the brasher, older Beth Lunsford, were using phrases like *your accounts* and *when you start to work.*

There had been only one bad moment, toward the end of the lunch, when the three of them had indulged in a bit of light chat about mutual acquaintances.

"I heard Kyle Sanders was working out quite well there," Susan Mallory said. "I think it's the perfect place for him."

Laura twirled her spoon through the foam in her cappuccino. "Do you know Kyle?"

Susan nodded. "I've met him a few times, and of course he has quite the reputation in the industry."

"And with the women," Beth said.

"Beth," Susan Mallory scolded.

Laura had already figured out that Susan Mallory tried, with little success and much humor, to rein in her partner.

"Well, I'm only saying it because it's true. I'm glad I'm not thirty years younger, or I don't think I could stand it." As Susan looked on disapprovingly, Beth added, "That man could charm a nun out of her habit."

And a defenseless spinster out of her habits, Laura thought, flicking up the volume on *Josie*. Suddenly she heard a loud knock over the screeching music. Had to be her sister, who hadn't checked in with Laura at all today. She got up and gave a cursory glance through the peephole, only to see one very gorgeous man staring back.

One very familiar gorgeous man.

Hands shaking, she opened the door for the full view. What a view it was. His blue eyes were warm and alert on her, immediately bringing to mind the last time he had looked at her that intensely. The sleeves of his dress shirt were rolled up, and she wanted his strong arms wrapped around her. She held on to the door for support and looked up at him. That curl of hair was hanging on his forehead, and she resisted the urge to push it away.

He had the Bellamy Hotel gift bag in one hand and a pan of something in another. "Couldn't get your jeans over my legs," he said.

She had an involuntary vision of Kyle's tanned and muscular legs. She turned away, stepping back into the apartment.

He followed her, then strode past her to the kitchen, his shoulder brushing against her as he did. This time it didn't feel like the kind of clumsiness he used to display around her, but a quite deliberate nudge. She shut the door after him and saw that he was already rummaging through the cabinets that hung over the snack bar. Was the man ever not at ease?

"Hey, Kyle, would you like to come in?"

"Thanks, Laura, I think I will." He grinned at her, and she felt herself soften in response. He found a plate in her cabinet and started loading lasagna on it.

Why was he bringing her food? To make up for not sleeping with her? Was he here to mend fences? So they could go on with their lives and forget about each other or so they could go on with their lives and not forget about each other?

Well, gee, Laura, he's the one who came to see you. Let him talk. But she jumped right in anyway.

"Look, I feel really bad for the last couple of things I said to you at the police station," she began.

"Wait—" He came back into the living room, abandoning the lasagna to stand beside her. He didn't say anything for a second, and she could feel her heart beating all the way up to her ears, ears growing more tingly by the second. The catchy *Josie* theme was rebounding through the room while she waited for Kyle to speak.

"I've been thinking…"

Her experience with men was less than some other women in their twenties, sure, but she knew that when a man said he was thinking, it was almost never about anything good. But surely he wouldn't come over here to tell her something bad, when he was doing it so well by not calling her at all?

She had total cotton mouth. "I'm going to get a Diet Coke. Do you want one? I'll get the lasagna out of the microwave, too. Smells great."

He stopped her with a hand on her shoulder, a touch that made her want him to hold her tight.

"I was thinking we shouldn't talk about work. Add that to our list of things we don't talk about."

She blushed, remembering the first topic on that list.

She stumbled to the coffee table and took a handful of popcorn, as though somehow the little kernels would protect her from the force of Kyle's charms.

When she didn't say anything, he almost seemed to falter, but then his intensity came back. "So no work talk. Nothing about mergers or consultants or any kind of business."

"'Til when?"

He looked like he was calculating in his head. "A few days."

"What happens then?" *You have to ask? Cinderella*

turns back into the little ragamuffin, the coach turns back into a pumpkin.

He looked like he had swallowed a big secret. "Let me worry about that."

Oh, that was reassuring. He was waiting for her answer. Finally she said, "Gee, Professor, that's so crazy it just might work." She popped a kernel into her mouth.

"This *Gilligan's Island* obsession," Kyle said. He went back into the kitchen and came back with her plate of lasagna, plus two cans of Diet Coke.

"You don't think kids should be allowed to watch TV indiscriminately, do you? I mean, before they do their homework?"

"Of course not," she said. "I don't watch TV indiscriminately." Together, they looked at the TV, where Josie and Melanie and the bunch were shaking tambourines. She jumped up to turn it off.

After all that obsessing about Kyle, he was here, sitting down with her while she ate the best lasagna she had ever put in her mouth. Kyle regaled her with college stories about him and Stan and with tales of Jessica.

"Have you seen her a lot this week?"

"No," Kyle said, getting up to get more cola. "I've been working."

"Oh, really? What have you been—"

"No work talk." He moved back to sit beside her

at the table. "Remember?" he asked, smiling at her. She would have missed those blue eyes if she had never gotten the chance to look into them like this again. His hand covered hers on the table, and she moved instinctively toward him, her lips parting. His arm encircled her as she felt his mouth claim hers. The kiss was even better than she'd remembered. He moved his hand to her face, caressing her cheek.

The phone rang. "The machine," she whispered. She had the machine set to pick up after just a couple of rings, in the pathetic hope that Kyle Sanders would call.

They were still in a kiss when she heard her sister's voice on the machine.

"Baby sister, are you there? I hope you're out somewhere trying to get over the Office Romeo. Has he called you yet? How did your meeting—"

She jumped up to turn it down, hitting Kyle's ankle. Finally, she reached the volume button.

"Well." She turned around. "The Office Romeo, that's, uh, that's—"

His own face was turning a light shade of red but it wasn't a wild embarrassed red like hers. More, she would have to say, like an I'm-pleased-with-myself kind of red. Charmer. Flirt. Seducer of Women. And she was awfully crazy about him.

He grinned. "I think I know who it is."

IF THE FLOOR could have opened, he suspected she would have dropped right through it. He'd let her out of the moment gracefully, he decided. What a guy. Right. He had come over here with the idea of getting Laura to take him seriously, and the first thing he'd done when she got within six inches of him was try to make out with her. Office Romeo. He deserved that one.

"So, she called you baby sister," Kyle said, limping a little back to the table.

"Are you sure your ankle's all right?"

"Yeah, it's fine. You don't seem like a younger child."

"Don't tell me, I act like a firstborn, right?" Laura picked up her plate and stood. "We're only eleven months apart."

"Eleven months?"

Her ears turned red again. Damn, but he could know her for a lifetime and never get tired of how cute she looked when that happened. She moved to the kitchen. "I know, I know, my parents couldn't keep their hands off each other. It's not something you want to think about, though."

"Or talk about, right? So you were in different grades?"

"No, we were in the same grade. In elementary school there was only one classroom for some of the grades, so they wanted to hold me back, but my parents wouldn't let them. When we went to high school, Kate convinced everyone we were fraternal twins.''

"And you went along with it?"

She grinned a short, quick grin that set his pulse racing. "I'm awful at lying, but I'm great at sins of omission." She bit her lip. "Since Kate had Haley, though, she pulls a little older sister rank."

"That 'I brought a human being into the world and you're still carefree and single' stuff?"

She nodded. "You know that line, too?"

"I know it pretty well," he said. The thought came, surprising him with its intensity: But maybe not for long.

SHE FELT AWFUL about the office Romeo thing, especially since she wasn't the kind of woman who kissed and told. Not that she ever had much to tell. And it was just her sister, and she hadn't told her everything. She found it impossible to explain: How Kyle made her feel. After the comment, Kyle had stayed at her apartment a while longer but hadn't made another move to kiss her. That was that, then.

But the next night he was back, right after work, taking her out for hot dogs at the famous Varsity. The next night they went to an outdoor concert. True to their agreement, they didn't discuss about business, although she was dying to tell him that she had gotten the job at Mallory Management. But he was a lot more inflexible about his no-shop-talk rule than she had been about her no talking about kisses rule.

Now not only were they not talking about kissing, they weren't kissing, which was a real shame, since they did it very well. When they went to the movies she unbuttoned an extra button on her blouse and snuggled against him. He never made a move, which only made her want him more. When he sneaked an arm around her at a revival showing of *The Terminator,* it was one of the most romantic moments of her life.

"Are you satisfied that Stan's not imaginary?" Kyle said, following her into her apartment. It was Saturday night, and they'd had a blast at a bar in Little Five Points where they'd gone to see his friend Stan play. Even Laura, who didn't know a thing about guitar, could admit that if there were guitar geniuses, he was one. She'd met his wife, too.

"I'm satisfied," she said.

Kyle sounded casual as he said, "It takes a certain kind of guy, you know, to keep a close friendship up since high school. Not a fly-by-night guy."

"Are you talking about you or Stan?"

He'd been doing this for the past few days, bringing up what a sterling character he was. She'd heard how he'd helped his grandfather build a boat, helped his sister train for a track team, and made the dean's list in college. He sounded like the original Boy Scout, until she looked into his eyes and saw the smooth, carefree guy who'd seduced her so easily.

"Hey, Laura," he said, his face was so serious that she thought he must have something awful to tell her. "Listen, I want to break our rule for a second."

The no talking about kisses rule? Or the no kisses rule that seemed to have gone into effect?

"I wanted to make sure you were coming down to the office Monday. Brandi said you were."

That rule. "Yeah, I am." She put her hands on her hips. "She's not throwing me a goodbye party, is she? I told her I didn't want one."

He looked confused. "Party? No, I don't think she's throwing you a party."

"Good," she said, kicking off her shoes and resisting the urge to carry them to her closet. "I hate surprises."

Disappointment and—what was it, worry?—flitted across his face. "You really hate surprises?"

"A dozen red roses, I could handle. But mostly, I hate them."

"Even if it was a surprise that..." He cleared his throat. "That someone thought you might like."

Good lord, he'd probably gotten her a cat. She looked up at him, and he looked so sincere and troubled that without even thinking, she slipped her arms around his waist.

"Kyle, you worry too much." Who'd have believed she would have ever said that about Kyle Sanders?

His own arms reached around her, and she tipped up her chin for a kiss, a kiss full of sweet longing, the kiss of two people who were meant to be kissing each other. How had they kept from doing this all week? Why had they kept from doing this? If she had been as newly empowered as she thought she was, she would have taken a chance, dared a kiss, seen what she could do to him. It was never too late to take a chance, she thought, deepening the pressure of her mouth on his as he groaned.

He crossed her small living room in just a few steps, pulling her along with him, his hands pushing her dress to her hips as they sank down together on the couch. She fiddled with the buttons on his shirt as his tongue played along her lips.

"Laura," he said, breaking off the kiss. "I want you to know... I want..."

Whatever he wanted to say, he was too aroused to say it. She kissed his lips gently, still playing with the buttons on his shirt.

"All I want is for you to want me," she said.

He broke off the kiss and pulled away from her, a troubled expression on his face. "But I want you to want more than that."

"Okay." She pulled him back down, knowing that she would say anything to get his body next to hers again. "Okay," she said, feeling the brush of his hands on her body as he eased her dress off. "Mmm-hmmm," she murmured, as she felt the sweet weight of him on top of her. It was only much later, when they were spooned together in her bed, that she wondered what he really meant and why she was too scared to ask.

9

REALISTICALLY, this was not the most important day of his life. That would be the day he married, and then the day his children were born. This was just the day on which all those other days might hinge, the day he finally had proof to show Laura that he wasn't a total goof-off, a pretty boy. That he was more than a bed-mate. He was permanent relationship material.

He took the now familiar steps to her apartment door and knocked. He expected her to answer in one of her linen suits. Instead, she stood in front of him, her gorgeous brown hair down around her shoulders, wearing the famous green sundress. She looked beautiful.

"You're wearing that to work?"

A puzzled look passed through her hazel eyes. "I don't work there anymore, remember?" She held the door open for him and he entered. "I'm going shopping afterward, and this dress comes off more easily than anything else I own."

"Laura, you don't have to tell me how easily that dress comes off. I know." Did he ever know. It was all he could do to keep from kicking the door shut and spending half the day in bed.

"Oh, yeah," she said, red ears peeking out from beneath her hair. "Do you want a jelly doughnut?"

The thought of a jelly doughnut twisted his stomach beyond belief. "No, I don't want a jelly doughnut." He watched her as she put on a pair of sandals. "Hey, if you had kids, you wouldn't let them eat jelly doughnuts every day for breakfast, would you?"

He tried to slip these parenting questions into the conversation casually, but it never worked.

She grinned at him. "Who are you, the emissary for the stork?"

The man who wants to bear your children, he thought. *No, that wasn't right. The man who wants to father your children. The man who will fix the kids bacon and bring you all the jelly doughnuts and anything else you want, if I have to go to the moon to get it.*

Shoes on, she walked over to him and touched his shoulder. "Are you okay? You seem a little...odd."

Nothing that having you take me seriously won't cure. He looked at his watch. Bill and Walt were going to meet them there in an hour. "No," he said as casually as he could. "My ankle hurts a little." It didn't, but that was an easy and sympathetic lie.

She crossed her arms. "Kyle, you're not a hypo-

chondriac, are you? I mean, I know your ankle was
really sprained—''

How had he forgotten that Laura wasn't one who
fell for any kind of poor-me tricks? ''No, I'm not a
hypochondriac,'' he snapped. ''Are you ready?''

''Absolutely,'' she said, grabbing her purse.

He put his hand on her back and escorted her to his
car. ''You aren't the kind of person who never believes
anyone is sick, are you? If you were married and your
husband had the flu, you wouldn't begrudge him a cup
of tea, would you?''

She smiled an odd smile. ''If he wouldn't let the cat
sleep on the bed if it turned out I was allergic to it.''

She had him there.

Once they were in the car, she said, ''So, why is it
so important that I be at Harris Associates today? And
you swear it isn't a surprise going-away party.''

''I swear.''

She snapped her fingers. ''I've got it.''

''Got what?''

''I know what's going to happen. I'm going to arrive
and everyone will pretend their work has been in total
disarray since I left, and I'll feel so needed that I won't
be able to resist joining in.''

''No, actually, things are going fine since you left.''

''Oh.'' He looked at her, now staring out the window.

''I didn't mean it like that. I meant that I've been

working extra hard to pick up the slack. Besides, that sounds like a *Brady Bunch* episode. It *is* a *Brady Bunch* episode," he said, recognition dawning. "The one where they all faked crises so Alice the housekeeper would stay."

"I didn't know *you* were such a fan," she said pointedly.

They pulled into his parking spot at Harris Associates. As he led her through the front entrance, and he saw her looking around suspiciously, waiting for the surprise party that wasn't going to happen.

They got to the doorway of the inner office, and he took a moment to gather his thoughts. Laura, though, had already pushed open the door, with a quiet "Knock, knock."

He saw Walt and Bill sitting with Harris in the office. "Well, hi guys, long time, no see." She turned to Kyle with a puzzled look.

"Laura," Kyle said, nodding at his boss and the other men. "Thanks to your report and my follow-up work on it, we're acquiring New Horizon."

She looked confused. Well, of course. She had doubted him and now he had proven that her doubts were wrong. "That's great, guys. So, uh, is one of you coming onboard, then?"

"Well, no," Walt said, pulling on his red tie. "Kyle told us you were going to be the vice president of our division."

She looked at Kyle, who was shaking his head.

"You brought me here to offer me my old job back?"

"I think it's romantic," Walt said. "She gets hives for you, you get a crappy job for her."

Kyle pointed toward the door. "Out, all of you," he yelled. The three men snapped to attention and hustled out, leaving Laura staring at Kyle.

"This is your big secret? Kyle, I don't need a job. I have a job. I'm touched that you're worried about me." She sat down in one of the leather chairs. "Well, actually, I'm sort of insulted that you didn't think I could get a job on my own, that you have to rearrange the company to get me one."

His jaw tightened and his eyes grew cold. She was just going to have to control the urge to sleep with him until she found out what was behind this scheme of his.

"You think I'm a waste of a perfectly good office."

"Kyle, I never said that."

"That's what you used to think."

She forced herself not to look in his eyes. "Okay, I thought that for a while."

"I wanted to show you that I could keep my promises. That I could roll up my sleeves and do some hard work." He fidgeted with his sleeve as he said it.

She wanted to know why. She wanted to ask. She wasn't going to be too scared to do it. Kyle had taught her that she had instincts and whims, impulses that were best yielded to, even if you didn't know what was going to happen afterward.

"You did this for me?" She heard her voice, too soft in the plush room. She made it stronger as she asked, "Why?"

He stared at her in such an intimate way that she thought he must be privy to every thought she had ever had. He knelt down next to her, his arms around the chair where she sat.

"Because I love you," he said.

She kissed him then, breaking off the kiss only to say "I love you so much. But Kyle, I would have loved you even if you hadn't kept this promise. You know that?"

"I wanted to be the kind of guy you wouldn't be worried about marrying."

Was that...

"Will you?" he asked. "Marry me?"

"Not because you completed this task," she said. "Not because you crossed something off on your to-do list." She touched his face. "I'm marrying you for you."

He grinned at her, and it was that patented Kyle Sanders grin. Only now she knew how much substance there was to the man behind it. "Even though we did everything backward?"

"Even though we did everything backward."

"But when we have kids," he said, "we want them to meet and marry in the normal way."

"I don't know," Laura said. "They just might have their parents' talent for a wisely chosen whim."

Epilogue

"LOOK HOW GOOD Laura looks since she quit," Harris said. "We should all quit. Tricia? Don't you think so?"

Tricia smiled her same benign Tricia smile, made even brighter by the presence of her new baby asleep in a carrier on one of the chairs. She kept loading slices of cake onto paper plates. Laura had no idea what the etiquette was for a bridal shower at your former place of employment, and whether or not it differed from the etiquette for a bridal shower at the place where your fiancé was now a company vice president.

"Can I help?" she asked Tricia, but Brandi, coming in with the cups and punch, shooed her away.

"You're the guest," she said.

Guest. It felt…weird. But good.

"It feels weird, doesn't it?" She heard Kyle's voice over her shoulder, a welcome sound. He pulled out the chair next to her and took it, and she braced herself for the inevitable kick in the leg. It didn't come. He'd gotten surprisingly adroit since their engagement. She was going to have to ask him about that. He leaned over and kissed her, and she marveled again how strange and wonderful it was to be in this room and not have to convince herself that she was not attracted to her sexy co-worker.

And how wonderful it was to be able to see him somewhere other than this room. On her couch on weeknights, watching VH1 *Pop up video*. In the park with her on weekends. In her bed every night.

Her job was working out beautifully. She had interesting projects, great resources at her disposal and no one had ever asked her to play golf.

Kyle said they missed her gift with numbers, but Weaselly Walt had come on board and had turned out to be a whiz with numbers, sort of an idiot savant.

Speaking of savants... "Is Stan going to be able to play at the wedding?"

"Guitar in hand," Kyle said. "Your sister asked me if it was going to be a hippie wedding."

Laura smiled. "I have plenty of wedding gaffes to mention to her, thank you."

"Walt and Bill are going to give you a couple of nights free at Bellamy Island," Harris said.

Tricia and Brandi frowned. "You aren't supposed to tell."

"It's okay," Laura said. "Our nieces couldn't keep their gift a secret, either." With help from their parents, they'd had the withered daisy chain framed in a shadowbox.

"I even told Kyle what I'm getting him. A cat," she said, as everyone looked up in surprise.

"To keep the dog in line," Kyle explained.

"You don't have a dog," Harris said.

"What do you think I'm getting Laura?" Kyle asked. "Besides a little crocheted cozy for her remote control."

She kicked him.

"Ow, that was my bad ankle."

"You don't have a bad ankle. You have a formerly sprained ankle that healed just fine."

"Says you," Kyle said. "I get no sympathy from her," Kyle told Tricia and Brandi, who shook their heads in unison. They started to hand him a piece of cake, but he said, "Let Laura have the first piece."

"I didn't think you ate cake, Laura," Tricia said.

"I do now," Laura said, smiling at her future husband. "I do now."

Start celebrating Silhouette's 20th anniversary
with these 4 special titles by
New York Times bestselling authors

Fire and Rain
by Elizabeth Lowell

King of the Castle
by Heather Graham Pozzessere

State Secrets
by Linda Lael Miller

Paint Me Rainbows
by Fern Michaels

On sale in December 1999

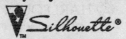

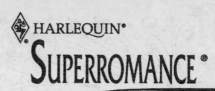

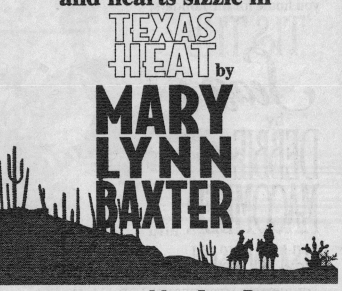
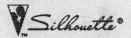